Shadows at Atlantic Point

John R. Hertzler

Shadows at Atlantic Point

Editor Antoinette M. Donley

Cover Designer Starla Huchton

Dedicated With Love to

Barbara and Jack Hertzler

and Streak

Prologue

The woman forced the key into the old lock. Three decades had passed since anyone had walked through the gates, yet she could still hear the cries of the thrill seekers—haunting echoes from yesterday. She gazed upward. The gates had once been glossy black, but time had rusted their every inch. They stretched twenty feet to their highest point, spiked rungs pointing toward the waning rays of a darkening sky. In either direction, a fence that matched the gates design and deterioration ran as far as the eye could see. Massive letters forged into the iron still announced, Atlantic Point Park.

Focus. She had to focus. An involuntary sigh of relief came when the tumblers turned. The heavy gates gave way with a slight lurch, and a soul-wrenching groan. She grunted as she pushed them open inch-by-inch. An eerie wail wafted through the night as the stiff parts grated in protest.

Northern winds alternated between a fierce howl and an unsettling whisper as snow flurries swirled. She grasped her coat in the cold, gusting air. Autumn's end was several weeks away, but heavy shadows announced winter's early arrival. There was a time when the off season had passed by in moments rather than months. For a century there had been winter preparation for the next season—always one more thing to do. Now though, the encroaching winter was like the final curtain about to descend on her life.

The trek would be long. The abandoned amusement park sprawled over eight hundred acres on a deserted parcel of land just outside Atlantic Point Island, New Jersey. The woman sighed as she began the journey, picking her way along the snow dusted paths. Her destination was at the farthest reaches of the property.

At another time, the old walks had been bordered with flowers, shrubs and decorative colored lighting. Today the paths were crumbling—overgrown to the point of being invisible, the light strings hanging in tatters and odd angles. Time was reclaiming the ancient park. Even using a high-powered flashlight, the walkways seemed to disappear into nothingness.

She aimed the flashlight ahead, the beam cutting a slice out of the darkness. Sadness consumed her—deterioration was evident at every turn. The diffused beam settled upon one of the old booths where most of the paint had peeled from the weathered exterior.

Faded letters still read *Tickets*. Just ahead the old picnic pavilion sagged—the caving roof crushing the warped tables it had once sheltered. She forced herself to take a deep breath as she gathered her courage to edge past the morbid scenery.

Progress was slow. Snow clung to leaves and debris making what remained of the pathways slippery. After tonight it would never be necessary for her to return here again. She had created many memories here a lifetime ago… but not like this. Deserted rides in varying states of decay lurked in the shadows, hiding as if ashamed of their appearance. Horses, zebras, and elephants stood on the carousel, waiting in silence for their next riders as the tarnished brass ring she had once grabbed dangled from above. High in the distance, the tall, wooden roller coaster groaned as it made a ghostly stretch toward a starless sky, waiting for screams that could no longer be heard. A lump formed in her throat—each sight reflected her past.

Craunch. The woman gave a stifled yell as a million shards of glass protested under her feet. She looked up at the moving picture theater where broken windows had showered to the ground. The v-shaped marquis still proclaimed *Now Playing*. Letters that had once spelled out the theater's current show had long been removed. Try as she might, she could not remember what had been playing when the projector beamed its final reel.

She was deep inside the park when a startling sound broke the unearthly silence. In fright, the woman jerked around as the flashlight went flying. An instantaneous feeling of panic swept over her. It would be impossible for anyone to climb over the high piercing rungs of the fence. Had she secured the front gates? Pausing to remember, she recalled that she had indeed closed and relocked them. Her feet made a few more resistant steps as the outline of a low black building emerged from the night.

Moonlight illuminated the jagged roofline of the haunted house. BANG—the wooden entrance door swung open and then slammed repeatedly into its crooked frame. It was as though the haunted house were gasping its last breath. A chill raced up her spine. She could not stop the involuntary shudders that followed.

Now in the dark, she began to tremble. Reaching around the ground for the flashlight, her shaking hands felt snow, and at last, the cylinder. Palpable relief came as the bright beam broke through the night. She forced herself onward, rounding a bend in the trail. The dance hall was still visible as the final light from the moon waned behind dark clouds. She brushed a tear from her eye. Their first date had been there. Empty windows stared back blindly from the old hall—a monument to a time gone by, an era forever past. If only the clock could be turned backwards.

Despite careful steps, she slipped over and over on the snow dusted ground. Desperate grasps at the bare, hanging overgrowth prevented an outright fall. At last, a large, three-story building loomed into view. Atlantic Point Corporation had been etched into the concrete apron between the first and second floors of the amusement park's massive offices. Her destination was in sight.

Fright and a sudden gust of wind took her breath away. A chill, through to her bones, wrapped around her as she gazed into the night. The offices conveyed a feeling of grandeur and presence—no expense had been spared. It was their final project. A small fortune spent to create a lasting tribute to an end that had come far too soon. There had been no choice. Weeks later the entire amusement park had been shuttered for eternity.

All these years the empty building had concealed the events of a night long ago. Smoked glass windows mirrored her stare, yet revealed nothing. Tears began welling in her eyes as she realized she would have to face yesterday one final time. She shivered again as she took in the frightening surroundings. Bare tree branches swayed in the wind, whispering eerily in the dark night, reminding her of what she had done. With tremendous effort she forced herself toward the entrance.

She grasped the doorknob. Still locked as tight as the fortress it had been designed to be. Holding the flashlight and juggling the key ring was next to impossible. At last, she located the single key that would unlock a long-forgotten past. The door opened with a piercing screech. Her heart raced. She moved through the silent foyer and up the grand staircase, glancing around as if a specter from yesterday would appear at any moment. Each stair groaned in protest as she ascended into her dark past.

Chapter One

Monica Scott shielded her eyes against the late afternoon sun, bright even with her sunglasses. Gazing upward at the gleaming mirrored skyscraper, thinking it appeared to be a shimmering oasis in the hot New York City desert. It was hard to believe that it could be so hot in June. Monica supposed it had something to do with the lack of natural green space. Concrete permeated every inch of the city, as did the continuous noise, hustle, and bustle. Random horns from irritated drivers sounded with regularity in the background.

As she stood there, someone banged into her, almost knocking her over. The person hurried by without as much as a word of apology. Rudeness was something else she would never get used to. Monica resided most of the year in Palm Beach, Florida but she was a regular visitor to New York City. It wasn't that she didn't like the city; rather there were parts of it to which she preferred not to be exposed to. Glancing at her watch, she realized that she didn't have much time until her appointment with Horace Goldsmith.

A continuous stream of people flowed through the massive skyscraper's two revolving doors. Monica stepped into a short line of people and was whisked into the building. The cool air brought calming relief, from the heat and from her nervousness.

The lobby extended up through the first three floors. Sheets of marble covered three walls; the other was covered with a soothing waterfall. The floor was also covered in marble, littered with groups of plushy furnished seating areas and giant, overflowing pots of natural plants. The

1

rear wall housed a bank of elevators. Horace Goldsmith's offices were on the top floor.

Monica ducked into the restroom to freshen herself. Having come directly from the airport, the heat and lengthy limousine ride had taken their toll on her appearance. Glancing into the mirror, Monica used deft strokes to touch up her makeup, then brushed her long, blond hair. At twenty-nine years of age, Monica was as beautiful as she had ever been. Although she was of average height, she had done some amateur modeling in her younger days. Now her business concerns kept her very busy.

Monica was attired in black dress slacks, flats, and a champagne colored blouse. She had dressed for both comfort and appearance. Despite her longtime friendship with her attorney Horace Goldsmith, she still wanted to look professional. The meeting would be difficult enough without uncomfortable clothing adding to her anxiety.

Exiting the restrooms and heading for the elevators, she chose the one on the left, and found herself alone inside. She pressed the button for the top floor. Monica took a deep breath as the elevator rocketed skyward. Though it felt as if she were moving at the speed of light, the ascent seemed to take forever. At last, a small electronic voice indicated "floor seventy-five."

Monica stepped into a small reception area. Across from the elevators were two large frosted glass doors, with slim, vertical handles running their length. "Horace Goldsmith, Esquire and Associates" was spelled out in gold, block lettering. Monica reached for the heavy door and pulled hard.

Just inside sat Marie Morris, Horace's long-time office manager. Across the room was another secretary whom Monica didn't know. Marie was a plump, but otherwise spry woman who was about sixty years old. Horace had once told Monica that Marie's main job was to put clients at ease, but Monica suspected that Marie was the real reason Horace's busy office ran an efficient operation. In any case, she did both jobs well.

"Monica," exclaimed Marie, "How wonderful to see you! It's been so long!"

"Yes, it has Marie, too long. I'm glad you're still running things for Horace. What would he ever do without you?"

"Well," chuckled Marie, "one of these days he's going to have to find out. Monica darling, how are you? The news was terrible and so unexpected. You have been in my thoughts and prayers many times."

Monica sighed, "Yes, it was, but the family business had to continue. I couldn't stop to grieve."

"I knew you were a very determined person from the first time your mother brought you here, when you were just a little girl." Before Monica could respond, the door to Horace Goldsmith's office opened and Horace appeared, greeting Monica with a fond embrace. Despite his seventy-two years, Horace was as strong and vibrant as ever.

"Monica dear, I never thought we would be meeting for such an occasion. I still can't believe what has happened."

"Neither can I, Horace, but knowing that I have you to take care of things has meant the world to me. I couldn't have gotten through without your help and support."

Horace patted Monica's hand, "Let's go inside my dear. Marie, please don't allow me to be disturbed. I want Monica to have my undivided attention."

"Don't you worry, Horace," Marie smiled, "no one's gotten past me yet!"

Inside the conference room was a large mahogany table. Expansive tinted glass covered the top half of the east wall, looking out over the bustling city. A second wall had a set of double doors that led into Horace's personal office. On the last wall was a mahogany sideboard that matched the conference table. An expensive silver coffee set was placed on an elegant tray in methodical fashion. Monica could smell the brewed coffee and was relieved when Horace offered her a cup.

"Cream?" Horace inquired.

"Yes, I still use cream; my taste never seems to change when it comes to my coffee habit."

"No reason that it should," Horace said without thought. "How are things progressing with the hotels?"

"Everything is fine. Each day I learn a little more about the corporate operations and it seems to be getting easier for me. I had no idea how many responsibilities my mother had."

"Your mother was an excellent businesswoman, Monica. After your father disappeared, she took over everything. Her hotels have done very well through the years. Your mother has left you a very wealthy young lady. Today I'm going to provide a general review of the estate and your financial position, and then we can answer any questions and concerns you may have."

Monica drew a deep breath, exhaled slowly and waited for Horace to begin.

"Your mother's final will and testament leaves virtually everything to you." Horace began, "This includes the New York penthouse, your home in Palm Beach, and the beach house in New Jersey. Included are the entire contents of the homes as well as her personal accounts and securities. In addition, your mother has left you as the major shareholder of the five Caprice Hotels."

Monica looked confused. "I expected to be Mother's main beneficiary, and I'm glad to hear this officially, but when you phoned me to set up our meeting you said that there was something unusual with the estate that you needed to explain."

"And so there is Monica," Horace replied. "You'll have to be patient while this old man winds to the point."

"I'm sorry, I don't mean to be impatient," Monica answered, as she nervously folded her nervous hands into her lap.

Horace continued. "There are several bequests to long term employees and a $500,000 trust for Jeanette, your mother's long-time housekeeper. There are also several modest bequests to her favorite charities."

Monica moved forward to the edge of her chair. It seemed to be taking Horace forever to get to the important matter to which he had alluded when he requested the meeting. For several minutes, Horace droned on, but in time he came to the part that Monica had been waiting to hear.

"Your mother also left you a business you didn't know she owned."

"What business could Mother have had that I wouldn't know about?"

"Well," Horace said, "it's not a business any longer. Although it was once a very thriving entity, it's no longer in operation."

"All of Mother's hotels have always been very successful." Monica replied.

"Not everything was successful Monica. The business which I'm referring to is Atlantic Point Park."

Monica stared incredulously at Horace. "What in the world is Atlantic Point Park?"

Horace responded with even tenor, "Atlantic Point Park is the amusement park where your family's business first started."

Still confused, Monica insisted that Horace tell her the entire story.

Horace continued, "Atlantic Point Park is somewhat of a mystery, even to me. It was started in the late 1800's; no one seems to know quite when. It's located on a sprawling parcel of land just outside a nearly deserted beach town in east central New Jersey, not far from the old beach house. From historical accounts, it started as a place for the local fishermen to sell their daily catch. Then a restaurant was started. As time passed, more restaurants, rides, a movie theater, a dance hall and other facilities were added. Over many years, it became a full-fledged and very successful amusement park.

It was because of your family's success in the amusement industry that your father decided to enter the hotel business. In the 1960's, your father recognized that there was a need for visitors from afar to have a place to stay, so he built the first Caprice Hotel to accommodate them. Although it was set up as a separate operation, the hotel was added to serve the needs of travelers coming to the amusement park. It was not until later that the hotel end of the business became the main concern."

Monica stared at Horace, a puzzled look on her face. "Why wouldn't Mother have shared this information with me, Horace? Why would she keep her owning a closed down amusement park a secret?"

"That is a question I can't answer Monica," Horace replied, "but I will tell you what I do know of the business's demise. I've been taking care of your family's legal business for many years. In the mid 1970's, the park began to encounter financial difficulties. Newer facilities began opening in many areas of the country, and with the automobile people were no longer limited in their ability to get from one place to another.

It was the start of a decade-long decline. During that time that your father decided to expand the hotel side of the business and several more hotels were added to your family's portfolio. His timing in the expansion was impeccable. He was very astute in knowing what to do, at least in most respects."

"I'm sorry that I never knew him, Horace." Monica commented, "As you know, he disappeared before I was born."

"I remember that event all too well," Horace stated with a note of sadness in his voice. "In the spring of 1983, there was an accident. The wooden roller coaster was being tested before the season started. The track had been checked for defects, as had all the mechanical parts of the roller coaster. The final check involved taking it through its paces before it received final approval to open for the season.

There was one employee in the roller coaster and a second employee in the operator's booth. As the roller coaster rattled up the first hill, all seemed to be normal. The cars crested the top of the hill and then derailed from the tracks. They went into a free fall and smashed into the ground killing the lone rider. Your father made a huge settlement to the family of the man who was killed; it never even went to court. Your father told me that as the proprietor, he would take care of the man's family.

Even after a thorough investigation, no one could explain how or why the roller coaster had derailed. The publicity was terrible. Although the company's safety record had been near perfect until that point, the accident caused a steep decline in revenues during the following summer. Your father refused to give up, despite recommendations from his business advisors, including me. He insisted that Atlantic Point Park could be made viable again."

"He sounds as determined as I can be," Monica observed. "Perhaps my unsalable drive comes from him."

"I wouldn't doubt it. I see a lot of him in you."

"Tell me the rest, Horace, all of it…"

"Atlantic Point Park reopened again in 1984, but financially, things were no better. The park had garnered a reputation for being unsafe. The crowds had been declining long before the accident, but the perception was that no one was going there because of the accident. At the end of the season, I recommended that your father close the facility, and as always, he refused. Then in May of 1985, he went on the business trip from which he was never seen or heard from again. Your mother was forced to take over the operation of Atlantic Point Park as well as the hotel operations."

"I had no idea Mother had taken control under such difficult conditions. I knew that she had run the hotels after my father disappeared, but she never even mentioned an amusement park."

"She had a great deal to learn at first. My office provided her with a good deal of assistance. I even sent one of my junior associates to work with her for some time."

"When did Atlantic Point close down for the last time?"

"Everything was ready for the 1985 season when your father disappeared. Your mother decided to open as planned. We recommended that she cut her losses and discontinue operations before another losing year went by. She refused. I believe she intended to continue indefinitely, as she started a large construction project right after taking over."

"That's surprising, Mother was always so careful with her investments. Why would she start a construction project when you had recommended closing the park down?"

"I never knew. By the end of the 1985 season, the losses from Atlantic Point's operations were staggering. If it hadn't been for the success of the hotels, your family would have gone into bankruptcy. As it was, your mother closed the park in the nick of time."

Monica had turned white. "This entire story is beyond belief. It's as though you were telling me about someone I have never known."

"Sad my dear, but unfortunately, very true. I suspect that since Atlantic Point Park is where your family's businesses started, both your parents were reluctant to give up on it. Also, your mother wanted to believe that your father would return. She wouldn't give up hope. Closing the park and meant giving up her last hope. She was expecting you at the time and it was her first year as the sole decision maker for the two businesses. Her judgment may not have been what you knew it to be in later years."

Monica sat back trying to absorb all that had been revealed while Horace continued.

"During that last year, your mother completed the construction project she had started after your father's disappearance. It was a large office building set far back into the park. The building has a very grand stature and she was in a great hurry to see it finished. I told her that she

9

should never sink so much money into Atlantic Point. She always responded that keeping the park going was something she had to do.

By the end of the 1985 season, her overall financial position had become so precarious that I made a personal visit to see her at the new office building, which was only partially completed inside at that time. I told her if she didn't cease operations that she would be ruined. She never gave me a definite answer, but she had the facility's manager lay off all of the winter maintenance staff and Atlantic Point Park never reopened the following year or ever again."

"Why has she kept it a secret all this time?" Monica pondered.

"I just don't know. For years I've recommended that she sell the deserted property. She's had several good offers. The township has also pressured her to sell the property for redevelopment purposes. She said it was not for sale and never commented any further. She also instructed me never to mention Atlantic Point Park in your presence."

"I can't believe this. Are there any other businesses that have been kept secret from me?"

"No, the hotels and the amusement park are the only businesses that your family has ever been involved with to my knowledge."

"When did you last visit there Horace?"

"I haven't been there since I made that special trip to warn your mother about her precarious financial position in the autumn of 1985."

"I guess I'm going to have to reopen the beach house and take a look at Atlantic Point Park."

"You should consider selling the property Monica." Horace recommended. "There's no reason for you to continue paying taxes on an abandoned amusement park."

"Not until I understand why Mother refused to sell it. Then I'll decide what to do. I want to see what it is she was holding onto before I make any decisions."

"Monica, I don't know what conditions you will find after all these years. Please be careful if you decide to venture there. When you're ready to sell it, I can recommend a commercial broker and help you with the legal aspects. I expect to have your mother's estate settled within the next twelve months, provided there are no unexpected contests to the will."

"As always Horace, I appreciate your help *and* your advice. I'll let you know what I decide to do."

"Monica, there's something else. Last November, one week before she died, your mother phoned me. She seemed distraught and wanted to check that her will was in order. It would be unusual for her to ask such a question, as she already knew the will was fine. She had made the original will after your father was declared dead and we updated it once each year as her circumstances changed. I told her that everything was in legal order and she thanked me for all I had done for her through the years. I asked her if she needed my help in any way, but she assured me that everything was fine. Still, I felt as if something wasn't right. It was as though your mother knew she was going to die."

Chapter Two

Disoriented, Monica exited Horace's office in a daze. After the unexpected revelation about Atlantic Point Park and the discussion about her mother's final phone call, Horace had continued with a few remaining points. Monica could not have repeated anything he said if her entire fortune depended upon it. She was in shock. Why had her mother kept this from her? Horace had Marie phone a limousine company to pick her up outside the building. On the way out Monica gave Marie and Horace a hug as she said goodbye. She had to suppress tears as she made a quick exit.

The heat hit her like a tidal wave. Shadows were falling as day turned to night. New York always came alive at nightfall, but on this particular evening Monica didn't even notice. She was trying to absorb all that Horace had told her about the mysterious amusement park. The fact that her mother had kept the park a complete secret weighed heavily on her mind—it made no sense.

Moments later, a large black stretch limousine glided to the curb. Lighted coach lamps adorned the sides. The driver's door opened and a uniformed, male chauffer with black hair, about 30 years of age, climbed out of the car. "Monica Scott?" he inquired.

"Yes?" Monica questioned.

"We were sent to pick you up."

Monica, always polite, gave a quick thank you to the driver and climbed in after he opened the rear door for her. Marie had provided the address of her New York penthouse and the car whisked into the darkening New York cityscape.

Cold air blasted from the vents, isolating her from the scorching outside world. Traffic appeared to be heavy, but of course, when wasn't the traffic heavy in New York? Monica rested on the large rear seat and allowed the cold air to wash over her. For several moments she attempted to block all thoughts from her mind, but they keep breaking through in a mixed-up jumble.

Twenty minutes later, the car slowed, then pulled into the driveway of the Colonnade, the condominium complex where Monica's penthouse was located. Monica attempted to pay the driver for the trip, but he stated that the charges had been taken care of. Horace looking out for her yet again. Monica provided the driver with a generous tip and asked if he would be available to provide her with transportation services while she was in New York. He handed her his card, then waited until she had safely entered the lobby of the condominium building.

Monica was still in another world. George, the senior doorman, startled her with a hello as she entered the building. He was semi-retired and he liked to chat. Tonight was no exception. Monica was in no mood to stand and talk, but she didn't want to offend him. He commented how much he missed seeing her mother, and then realizing how distracted she was, he brought the conversation to a smooth ending as he pressed the button to call for the elevator.

Grateful for his sensitivity, Monica thanked him and said she looked forward to a long talk the next time she saw him. George reminded her about her luggage. The building manager had placed it in the secured storage closet off the vestibule of her penthouse. Monica had forgotten all about it. She was glad it had arrived—one less thing to worry about. George offered to go up and carry it into the condo for her, but Monica declined, stating that she had packed very little for this trip.

A soft ding announced the arrival of the elevator. George reached inside and pressed the button to send the elevator to the top floor. The doors slid closed. Monica inserted her security key and then lifted off toward the top of the building. She fumbled for her key card as the elevator alighted.

Monica opened the door, then disarmed the security system before finally retrieving her luggage. Normal actions in a world that was no longer normal. With the security system reset, Monica sank into the huge white sofa, kicked off her shoes, and fell into a light sleep.

She awakened with a pounding headache, wondering how long she had slept. The modern glass clock above the television indicated that it was almost nine o'clock. Four hours. Monica stretched and tried to shake off the negative effects that the unexpected nap had added to her day. She wanted to call Maxwell Williams, the president of her hotel group, but decided to wait until after she had refreshed in the oversized whirlpool tub within her ensuite.

Monica entered the bathroom and flipped on the lights. Relaxing or functional? The bathroom had multiple levels of illumination. Soft, ambient lighting provided for stress free baths. There were several brighter levels that were more suitable for makeup and dressing. Monica dimmed the lights in an effort to relax.

Next, she flipped on the water taps. Water streamed from the dual taps and was as hot as she could stand. She undressed and then stepped gingerly down the two small steps into the swirling water and bubbles. It was almost too hot, but the reward would be relaxation for the first time since she had arrived in New York.

The tension lifted in measures. After a long soak, she stepped out of the tub, dried herself on a thick white towel and wrapped herself in a terry bath robe. She headed out to the kitchen and opened a bottle of Chardonnay that had been chilling in the freshly stocked refrigerator. After a few sips of the wine, she felt the last of the day's tension evaporate. Monica planned to call Maxwell and then turn into bed. An early night, how unusual for her she realized. Monica gazed out over the balcony at the bustling city. In a past life she would have been part of the night set. Not tonight. Total exhaustion had taken control.

Monica dialed Maxwell's number and listened with heightened anticipation as the phone began to ring. Maxwell had never married. He lived alone in a large house with his loyal housekeeper, Evelyn Smith, a formal servant from a bygone era. Evelyn's recognition of Monica's voice stemmed from the many years that Maxwell had been part of her extended family. Although he was not actually a blood relation, Maxwell was the only father that Monica had ever known. He had been close to her mother for as many years as Monica was alive and she was eager to discuss the day's events with him.

"Good evening Monica," Evelyn greeted her with stiff formality.

"Good evening, Mrs. Smith." Although Monica had known Evelyn Smith for as many years as she had known Maxwell, she had never felt comfortable calling the older woman Evelyn, as Maxwell and her mother had always done.

"Let me get Maxwell for you."

"Thank you Mrs. Smith," Monica stated with a gentle smile in her voice.

"Here he is Monica."

Maxwell came onto the line. "Well hello Monica, how is New York?"

He sounded like his usual self, but Monica detected something tentative. Did he already know what she was about to say? "So far it's been very revealing Maxwell." Monica replied with a steady voice. "Horace had some very surprising news."

"Good news I hope? Maxwell queried.

"I have some assets that I didn't know about."

"Are you talking about Atlantic Point Park?"

Monica was shocked. "You knew about this and you never told me?"

"Monica, please don't be upset with me. I knew the day would come that you would find out, but your mother had forbidden me to ever discuss the park with you. The decision to keep Atlantic Point a secret from you was not mine."

Monica was still not satisfied. "It's been seven months since Mother's death Maxwell. I think you should have told me, but I didn't call

16

you to start a fight. I just wanted to check on the hotels and to let you know about what I thought would be a revelation."

"The hotels are all fine. I reviewed the daily financial reports in detail this morning, and although cash flow is a little tight with two new properties under development, there's nothing to worry about. Construction is progressing on target and I expect to hear from Drake any day now on the renovations to the Virginia Beach property. Take care of your business and do not worry. We'll talk about the old amusement park when you return to Florida. Oh, and Monica, just one more thing…"

"Yes? Monica queried.

"This is very important. Don't sell Atlantic Point Park or make any decisions about it until we've had time to talk face to face."

Monica was suddenly wide-awake. The tension that had permeated the evening returned with full force. "Maxwell, what is it that you're not telling me? Monica demanded.

"There are no more secrets to tell you. When you return to Florida, we'll spend some time together and I'll answer your questions to the best of my ability with what knowledge I have. However, this is not something to discuss on the phone."

Monica agreed to hold off with her questions until she returned to Palm Beach. After a few more words the conversation ended and she hung up, still frustrated.

The thought of sleep had disappeared. Without realizing it, she began to pace. She opened the television guide and not seeing anything that interested her she flipped through a hundred channels before she located an old black and white movie that piqued her interest. She watched the movie for a while, but eventually gave up, still too distracted to concentrate. Once again, she began to pace through the condominium.

The entire unit was decorated in contemporary décor with light colors that created an airy feel throughout. It was one of Monica's favorite places and she had considered moving the hotel's corporate offices to New York so she could live here permanently. Yet doing so would disrupt the lives of the company's many loyal employees and she was determined not to have that happen. She also liked the warm winters that Palm Beach offered.

In addition to the oversized living room, the condominium included a separated formal dining room, which could easily accommodate ten people, as well as a large kitchen with a cooking island and breakfast nook. Monica had a large bedroom suite and there were two other suites, one of which had been her mothers. Each had its own bathroom and seating area. There was even a fully equipped office with the latest equipment so Monica could conduct hotel business from New York, saving rental costs on separate office space when she was in town for an extended stay.

One of the benefits of living in this particular building was the high level of amenities. Prior to her arrival, building services had cleaned the entire condominium and had restocked the refrigerator with a list of Monica's preferred foods, all of which had been e-mailed to them by her assistant Francine Crowley.

Monica realized that she hadn't eaten since she was on the plane earlier in the day. Perhaps she would feel better if she had a bite to eat. She assembled some fresh whole grain bread, crisp lettuce, and a tomato into a sandwich, then added some pretzels on the side and a fresh orange.

After she was finished eating, she stacked the few dishes into the dishwasher and headed for the bathroom. While brushing her teeth she considered taking a sleeping pill, but decided against it. Monica didn't believe in taking medication unless it was necessary, and she had already consumed some wine. She headed back to her bedroom and pulled down the comforter on the king-sized bed. The sheets were clean and fresh, cool to her touch. She heard the central air-conditioning kick on as she climbed in and pulled the comforter up. Except for the air-conditioning, the condominium seemed unnervingly quiet.

Monica and her mother had shared many happy times in New York—shopping, touring, seeing Broadway shows. A feeling of sadness seized her and tears welled in her eyes. With her mother gone, she had a lot more responsibilities, and she had lot of questions. All of a sudden she felt very alone. At last sleep overtook her and she fell into a restless slumber.

In the dream Monica was a child and she was at Atlantic Point Park. Everything was shiny and new. An earlier storm had left small droplets of rain on every surface that were drying as the afternoon sun broke through the clouds. Smiling people walked along curved sidewalks lined with bright flowers, some holding hands, others were pushing strollers. The path reached a wide, round circle. In the center was a clown. "Balloons for all the children," he yelled, as he handed Monica a bright red balloon. She giggled when the clown smiled at her. The path continued. A familiar man appeared.

It was her missing father. He smiled down at her, but as hard as she tried, she could not see his face.

He and Monica continued along the path. Vendors were everywhere selling peanuts, popcorn, ice cream, shakes and cotton candy—anything you could think of that tasted good. Her father told her she could have anything she wanted to eat. After all, this was her very own amusement park. Monica wanted cotton candy. A heavyset lady was working the stand and she smiled as she swirled the strands and placed the cotton candy into Monica's small hand.

Monica spotted the carousel and started to squeal. Even as her father placed her on a large wooden horse, she still could not see his face. The carousel started going around. With one arm he held onto Monica and with the other arm he held onto the shiny brass ring that hung from the top of the carousel. Around and around they went. When it stopped, her father took her to the next ride.

This attraction had little boats that were floating in water no more than a few inches deep. Dark clouds began gathering overhead. Monica climbed into a blue boat and she waved each time she went around. She had never been happier.

Once again they neared the circle with the clown, but this time the clown was not smiling, and Monica pulled back. The clown grabbed her arm and tied the entire bunch of balloons around her wrist. "No, no," Monica screamed. She didn't want them. Monica became more and more scared as shadows descended and the sun hid behind the darkening skies. Thunder rumbled and lightening shot through the sky. She tried to let go of the balloons, but they were tied too tightly. Frantically, she looked for her father, but he too had disappeared.

All at once the balloons began to lift Monica off the ground. She floated higher and higher until she was near the top of the roller coaster. The cars were about to go over the crest of the old wooden coaster. At the last second, she grabbed onto a car and pulled herself inside. As if by magic, the balloons released into the sky. Monica was now inside the roller coaster and all alone. She knew the roller coaster was a scary ride, but at least she would reach the ground when the ride came to a stop. All at once, the roller coaster plummeted over the top of the hill and started down the other side. The tracks gave way and the un-tethered cars hurtled toward the cement pavement below.

Monica screamed. The sound of her own voice awakened her abruptly. Daylight was streaming into the windows of her suite. She sat up in bed still shaking from the nightmare and chilled to the bone. She could not stop a shivering as the air-conditioning blasted from the vents. The nightmare seemed to be a warning of what would come next.

Chapter Three

Maxwell Williams stared off into space. Monica's phone call the night before had disturbed him. Yet, it was not an unexpected call. He knew that sooner or later Lydia Scott's estate would have to be settled, and he knew that Monica would find out about Atlantic Point Park. Maxwell had always believed that it would be long after he was gone. He had already celebrated his 70th birthday. Lydia had been his junior by about 10 years. In his wildest dreams, he never would have believed that he would outlive her. It just served as a reminder that life could be cut unexpectedly short.

Maxwell pondered the horrific events of the past seven months. It all started last November with a newspaper article and a call to Lydia from the president of the township council for Atlantic Point Island. For years, the town had been pressuring Lydia to do something with the defunct amusement park. Always professional and charming despite her cunning business skills, Lydia had agreed to meet with the mayor and the council to discuss redevelopment. The city wanted to return Atlantic Point Island to the days when it had been a prominent and profitable vacation destination—and that depended on what happened to Atlantic Point Park.

For 30 years, Lydia had always been adamant that she would not do anything with the closed down amusement park. At the time, Maxwell had no doubt that the township's latest overtures would produce the same result from Lydia that they always had—nothing. Still, Lydia had agreed to the meeting. It had not turned out well. For the first time the discussions about Atlantic Point Park had turned nasty. The mayor and the township committee accused her of ruining the town by refusing to sell the deserted park.

There was little Lydia could say since she knew that the land she owned would have to figure prominently into any efforts to return travelers to the nearby beach town. Still, she was unwilling to sell them her land, no matter what she had to do. Lydia promised, as she had many times before, to have studies done on the economic viability of various uses for the old amusement park. In the past when Lydia made such promises, the studies were never completed or always showed that the costs to re-open or remove Atlantic Point Park were too exorbitant, just as she made sure that they would. Her standard response was an offer to increase her tax burden to assist the town. Until now, Lydia's tactics had placated the many township committees that hounded her through the years. This time was different.

The mayor and the council threatened that to use their "right of eminent domain" to seize the land from her, provided she remained unwilling to sell. Of course, a land confiscation would be very expensive and Lydia knew the township could not raise funds from the tax base on the faded resort town. She would drag out any such legal maneuvers for years in the courts, but Lydia also realized it would just be a matter of time.

Late in the evening, on the same day as the township meeting, Lydia had phoned Maxwell while speeding toward Atlantic Point Island in her black Jaguar coupe. She was hysterical and Maxwell had encouraged her to hang up and phone him when she reached the beach house and had calmed down. Lydia agreed between sobs, but she never reached the house. The speeding Jag lost control on Atlantic Point Bridge, an icy span that joined the mainland where the park was located and the beach area of Atlantic Point Island. The car smashed through the guardrail. The autopsy report showed that Lydia died in an instant when the car smashed into the rocks and muddy water below the bridge.

Maxwell remembered when the phone call came into the corporate office from the New Jersey state police. They had requested Monica by her full name. Maxwell had intercepted the call and identified himself as Lydia's business partner. The police informed him of Lydia's untimely death and Maxwell had been devastated—he would be the one that had to tell Monica.

Monica had been inconsolable. She had always been very close to her mother. Maxwell too found that it was difficult to go on without Lydia. The three of them had been like a family, ever since Monica's father disappeared in 1985. Maxwell and Monica spent many hours together grieving together over the loss of Lydia. In the end, they both realized that they owed it to their loyal staff and to Lydia's memory to pull together and continue the hotel company's operations. Still, there had not been enough time to grieve.

After the funeral, Monica and Maxwell assumed temporary legal control of the hotel corporation, pending final settlement of the estate. Monica assumed the CEO position that her mother once held. Maxwell had taken Monica's suggestion that he assume the title of President, although his duties changed very little from the position he had held as Director of Operations under Lydia.

Through the years, Monica had worked in just about every area of hotel operations and Maxwell had gone about the task of orienting her to the responsibilities that her mother had handled. Monica did quite well. She learned about the corporate end of the business and her experiences in operations prepared her to assume the CEO position. The thought brought a fleeting smile to Maxwell, interrupting his grim thoughts. He realized just how very proud he was of Monica. Her looks mirrored the Lydia he remembered from his youth.

Now she knew about Atlantic Point Park. Explanations would be expected and he had to think which explanation he would give her. Monica was bright and she was sure to see through any lies. She had her mother's cunning insight and she had her missing father's sharp intellect.

Maxwell headed to the bathroom. The lights seemed to be too bright. A migraine headache coming on—just what he needed. He turned the cold water tap and let the water flow for a moment, then half-filled a glass, and downed a pill for the migraine. He allowed the cold water to continue running while he turned on the hot tap to wash his face. The old man staring back at him from the mirror was not the same one that gazed back at him just seven months ago before all this had happened. He seemed to have added more wrinkles than he could count and his hair had turned stark white. Penetrating blue eyes stared back at him. Maxwell knew that like all the other tough situations during his life, he would get through this mess somehow.

Maxwell exited the bathroom and considered leaving the office for the day, but the thought of any early departure was fleeting. There was just too much work to do and Monica would be back any day now. He reached for the first file, but his mind kept drifting off.

It was 1968. Maxwell had just joined what was then Atlantic Point Corporation, working in a variety of jobs at Atlantic Point Park. He was just weeks from his college graduation and was looking for experience in the entertainment field. Maxwell loved the amusement park and the excitement that working there provided—it was a natural fit. Every year, Monica's father travelled to Europe to bring back new and exciting rides. Maxwell had learned just about every job that there was. It was an exciting time in his young life and one that he never realized would end in tragedy.

In time, he became good friends with the Scott family that owned and managed the park, especially the Scott's son Ronald. Ronald was the same age as Maxwell and the two became close friends. Despite the friendship, they were always in respectful competition. Ten years later, Ronald had married Lydia who also worked at the park. Maxwell was the best man at their wedding. It seemed like another lifetime.

Ronald was brilliant. When he decided to open a hotel on the island in 1970, he asked Maxwell to become general manager of the new establishment. Maxwell, who had continued with the company, jumped at the opportunity to head up the new enterprise. Maxwell was so successful that the company decided to open several more hotels: Palm Beach, Virginia Beach and others. In retrospect, it was quite lucky that they had branched out. It was just fifteen years later that Ronald had disappeared and Atlantic Point Park had closed down forever.

Lydia continued to use the Atlantic Point Corporation name for several years after the park was shuttered, even though the hotels were a separate division. After much coaxing, Maxwell had persuaded her to change the company name to "Caprice Hotels Corporation." Caprice was the name that Ronald had given to the first hotel. That first hotel on Atlantic Point Island was now closed, but the other five hotels were doing well, and two more were under development. Lydia had been as pleased as Maxwell at their continuing success, even without the park.

When his office phone beeped, Maxwell thudded back to reality. It was his executive assistant, Janice Laneer. "Yes, Janice," Maxwell responded.

"Drake Donovan is on line one."

"Thank you, I'll be with him in a moment."

Maxwell pondered what Drake wanted as he pressed the button to retrieve the call. "Drake, how are you?"

"I'm great Maxwell. But you're not going to be great when you hear the news."

"It couldn't get any worse than the day I've been having," Maxwell commented, "but you might as well tell me what it is."

"We're going to need a larger budget to complete renovations at the Virginia Beach hotel," Drake announced, "The project has met a major snag."

"I'm not even going to get into this with you on the phone," Maxwell stated, his voice raised. "Monica will be returning in the next few days. I suggest you come to headquarters and we'll both discuss it with you in person. Money is tight right now and until Lydia's estate is settled, we don't have lot of options."

Drake responded coldly, "I'll be in town for the next executive staff meeting. Get out your checkbook."

"Goodbye Drake," Maxwell answered with finality as he slammed down the phone. Drake had a way of getting under Maxwell's skin. He was in charge of new hotel development, renovations to existing properties and Monica's latest endeavors to make the hotels environmentally friendly. Drake did well with all his responsibilities and even Maxwell had to admit that Drake was largely responsible for the high-quality ratings and four-star status the properties maintained with the ratings agencies and social media web sites.

Drake had an attractive girl waiting for him in every one of the hotels. He was just tall enough to be considered above average with chiseled, good looks, and that dark edge that women always seemed to swoon over. And Drake was not humble in his realization of that fact. His smug attitude didn't help matters either. Perhaps Maxwell was just jealous that women were no longer swooning over him.

Monica and Drake had become quite close during the years that she had worked at the various hotel sites. Rumors had reached Maxwell that Monica had been one of Drake's conquests, but neither Monica nor Drake had ever confirmed the rumors, and Maxwell preferred not to know. In any case, he would have to see the jerk to resolve their current crisis. Just one more thing to worry about. Maybe it was time to consider retirement. Maxwell had the means to retire, but he refused to accept the thought of sitting home and doing nothing after all these years, he could not accept irrelevancy.

The phone beeped again. Maxwell didn't answer it. Instead he hit the voicemail override button and leaned back in his executive chair. His administrative assistant knocked on the door.

"Come in Janice," Maxwell groaned as he held his head. "What can it be now?"

"It's unusual for you not to answer your phone Maxwell. I just wanted to be sure that you were all right. You're not looking well today."

"I'll be all right," Maxwell responded. "I've just developed a migraine."

"Well the call you didn't take was from Monica. She's spending another day or two in New York and she wanted to let you know when she would be returning. She said to have you call her when I located you."

"Will do. Just hold all my calls for now. I'm going to get lunch and see if I feel any better. If this headache gets worse, I'm going to make it an early day no matter how much work you pile on my desk."

"I don't have any more work to pile on your desk," Janice commented with a sly smile, "but if you're inviting me to lunch, I accept."

Monica hung up the phone after trying to reach Maxwell. She was frustrated that he had not been in, but she decided to put Maxwell and all her concerns out of her mind. A nice walk through the city and a light lunch would be her distraction. Monica didn't know if the uneasy feeling in her stomach had more to do with hunger or the lingering effects from her nightmare.

The nightmare was not rooted in any reality, but it had left her shaken just the same. Monica had never even been to Atlantic Point Park, nor had she ever met her father. It was funny how the subconscious could just fill in the blanks, even if it wasn't the truth. As she exited the condo, she armed the security system and locked the door behind her.

Monica pressed the button to call the elevator and it arrived a second later. The elevator made several stops to pick up passengers on the way down. Monica greeted every one of them with a smile or a hello, but even after living here off and on for many years, she still didn't know anyone by name.

The elevator reached the lobby and all the passengers disembarked. Monica headed for the main doors. They glided open as she approached. The day was cooler than yesterday, and the air felt wonderful. Even though she was in a crowded city, the feeling of being outside was still better than being cooped up in the condominium.

Monica headed north. There was a little café that had a delicious "fresh breads" menu and the world's best coffee. Monica began to feel better as she walked the five blocks to the restaurant. The June sun was making her feel warm and comfortable and she had dressed in light summer clothes, anticipating another hot New York City day.

Monica spotted the sign for the restaurant, The City Croissant. She entered the little café and found a seat along the left wall in a cozy booth. A waitress appeared with a menu and a steaming carafe of coffee. "Would you like a cup?" the waitress asked. Monica accepted, as she reached for the menu. She savored the aroma before she took a long sip. What to do next. A plan began to form in her mind. Monica was startled when the waitress reappeared and she had to tell her that she hadn't decided on her order yet.

Diverting her thoughts, she decided to have a croissant with some natural spreads and a cup of vegetable soup. When the waitress returned, Monica gave her the order as she reached into her handbag for her phone. She glanced at the favorites list for the number of her best friend, Trisha Marshall, who managed a small art gallery. Trish answered on the first ring.

"International Art Gallery, Trisha speaking."

"Surprise, surprise, I'm in New York," Monica exclaimed into the phone.

"And just who might this be?" Trisha pretended ignorance.

"Your favorite customer and friend."

"What brings you back to our fine city, Monica?"

"I'm here on business, but I was hoping you had time for an evening out tonight."

"Well, as you know, my calendar is always booked," Trish joked, "but I do believe I can squeeze you in for just one evening. What time would you like to meet?"

Monica paused for a moment as she gathered her thoughts, "I'll have the limo company pick me up at seven and I'll pick you up at seven thirty."

"Sounds good to me," Trish sounded excited.

"We'll do dinner at a fantastic restaurant and then we'll go to a great club and stay out late. I need your advice about something and then I want to forget all about my problems and hear all about your problems."

"Why Monica, I never have any problems. I live a very dull life as you are well aware!"

Monica chuckled. Trish had the most active social calendar of anyone that Monica had ever met. She was taller and thinner than Monica and her skin was fair and flawless. Her sleek black hair was long and straight and she had an exotic look that was perfect for working in the art world. Monica knew as soon as she hung up that Trish would be calling someone to cancel whatever it was that she had planned for tonight. Monica was grateful to have a friend that was always available at a moment's notice.

Monica clicked on the link of a chic Italian restaurant that they both loved. After making an online reservation for eight o'clock, she put the phone away. The waitress returned with her lunch. Monica accepted a second cup of coffee and leaned back. For the first time since Horace had told her about her unexpected inheritance she felt like her old self. There was something about familiarity and routine that could restore the feeling of personal control that unexpected events took away.

Monica finished the meal, paid her check at the register, then exited the cafe. She noticed that some new shops had opened nearby and she nosed through them in a half-hearted attempt to shop and pass some time. After a while she grew bored and started walking back toward the condominium. George was on duty again and she duly completed the overdue conversation she had promised him the night before. Minutes later, she headed for the elevator.

When she reached the penthouse, she noticed that the red light was blinking on the answering system. She pressed the retrieval button. It was Maxwell returning her call. She paused, then decided she would not call him back just yet. This last night in New York was going to be fun, no matter what. Anything that might disrupt her evening with Trish was not what she needed right now. Monica hit delete and headed for the bedroom. Since she planned to be up very late tonight, a nap might just help, especially after her lack of restful sleep the night before. In moments, Monica fell into a deep and dreamless slumber.

Chapter Four

Monica awoke about five o'clock feeling very refreshed from the nap. She glanced over at the phone and was pleased to see that the message light was not flashing. All was set. Monica rolled over onto her back and stretched out. Try as she might to think other thoughts, questions about Atlantic Point Park were continuing to dominate her consciousness. Maybe Trish could put things into perspective.

Monica reached for her handbag, which was lying on the nightstand. She searched inside for her wallet and extracted the business card that the limousine driver had given her when he dropped her off yesterday. In seconds, she dialed the number and reserved a limousine for the evening.

Stretching as she walked into her dressing room, Monica selected a short black skirt and a sheer gray blouse for her night on the town. She wanted to look alive for a change. A pair of black platform heels would complete the effect. Next, she went into the bathroom and started the water running in the shower. Water pulsated out of the three showerheads on the walls of the oversized shower. Monica stepped into the spray and the steaming hot water massaged her body. The effect was one of both invigoration and relaxation. It was 30 minutes later when she finally picked up the sponge and organic body wash to finish up.

After drying off, Monica put on a plush, monogrammed bathrobe. She put her hair up in a towel and walked out to the kitchen. The wine bottle that she had opened the night before was still half full. It wouldn't be for long. She poured herself a glass and headed back to the bathroom. After applying her makeup, she dried and styled her hair. For the final touch, she selected a chunky silver necklace and matching bracelet along with a set of long diamond earrings. Monica paused by the triple full-length mirrors and checked that she was ready to go. It was almost seven and the limousine would be here any minute.

Monica went over to her office and slid open the wall panel that concealed the electronic safe. She punched in her code and the green light appeared. The heavy door swung free. Inside were several stacks of emergency cash along with other important documents. Monica pulled out her entertainment credit card, then closed the safe and hit the re-lock button, pausing to be sure the red "secured" light re-appeared as the lock clicked into place. When it did, she replaced the panel and headed for the living room. Just as she was about to sit down, the house phone rang. In eagerness she grabbed for the handset. It was the doorman letting her know that the limousine had arrived.

Monica reached the lobby in record time. She couldn't wait to see Trish after such a long absence. The driver smiled as he opened the door for her. It was the same chauffer who had picked her up at Horace's office. Monica returned the smile with a quick "good evening."

As she got into the limo, the driver said, "I'm glad to see that you decided to use our services again Ms Scott."

"I'm glad you gave me your card, but if you're going to keep driving me around, you'll have to call me Monica, and you're going to have to tell me your name."

"My name is James," the driver answered, still smiling.

The door closed and James went around to the other side. After he got in, Monica gave him the address to Trish's apartment. Trish was as eager as Monica to start the evening. As soon as the limo pulled into the apartment's driveway, Trish appeared from the lobby and headed for the limo. James got out and opened the rear passenger door for her. Trish got in beside Monica and gave her a hug. James turned around and asked Monica where they were headed.

"We're going to the Naples Cove restaurant."

As the limousine pulled out onto the street, the two old friends started chatting. "Monica, it's been six months since I've seen you." Trish inquired, "How are things going for you since I returned to New York?" Trish had spent a month with Monica in Palm Beach after Lydia Scott's death. During the time since, they had not had more than a few brief phone calls as Monica had been overwhelmed with her new responsibilities.

"I've been doing all right Trish. There's a tremendous amount to learn. Mother always handled all the corporate level work, so it's still very new to me. I enjoyed the days when working in the hotel's decorating department meant seeing you for art purchases and more parties than I can remember."

Trish gave a slight chuckle, fondly remembering their good times.

"Running the hotels is something quite different. We sure did some great projects together Trish."

"Yes, we surely did." Trish had met Monica and Lydia on one of their whirlwind shopping trips to New York. Lydia Scott had purchased a large oceanic print from the International Art Gallery and had it shipped back to her home in Palm Beach. Monica had enlisted Trish thereafter to provide original art and paintings for all the hotels' lobbies in the Caprice chain. They had developed a close friendship along the way.

"Is Maxwell still helping you?"

"Oh, he's still as much a part of the company as ever."

"Do you think that he's going to retire soon?"

"I hope not. He's getting up in years, but I don't think he would like to stay home all day."

"Well, he always seems to be right there for you I must say."

"Trish, there's something I need to talk to you about." Monica became serious and her tone had darkened.

"Monica, you know you can discuss anything with me, what's bothering you? Trish sounded alarmed.

"Nothing with me personally Trish, it's news that I received yesterday from Horace Goldsmith, our family attorney." Trish remained silent while she gazed intently waiting for Monica's reply. Finally she continued, "I'm in New York to settle mother's estate. Along with the hotels and the Palm Beach house, I found out she also left me a large, closed down amusement park in New Jersey. What bothers me is that she never told me anything about it. I didn't even know it existed!"

"An amusement park? What an unusual inheritance. It doesn't seem as though you should be upset though Monica. Maybe because it was closed down, your mother didn't even think to discuss it with you."

"That's not the case. She directed Horace Goldsmith never to discuss the park in front of me or to let me know anything about it. I just feel that something isn't right. Mother and I were always so close. We never kept anything from one another. There's more to this than meets the eye and I'm going to find out what's behind keeping this a secret from me for thirty years."

"A closed down amusement park?" Trish pondered in a perplexed tone.

"It's huge. Horace said it covers 800 acres. It was where our family business started. It should have been something that we would have been proud of, not something to keep hidden for decades."

"Now that you put it that way, it does sound as though there's more to the story. What are you going to do with it?"

"I don't know. Before I do anything, I need to find out the reason for the secrecy." For a moment they both became introspective and before the conversation could resume, they were pulling up to the entrance of the restaurant.

"They always have the best food and atmosphere," Trish exclaimed as the restaurant came into view, "You know I love this place!"

"It's one of my favorite places too," Monica replied, still pondering the secrets that her mother had kept from her.

The limousine pulled into the red-bricked driveway, passing small trees covered with white lights that lined both sides. Expensive cars had been valeted on the right side of the driveway, and a larger parking lot was located beyond the cars. James continued to edge the limousine toward the front of the restaurant. It was a large building, at least three stories tall, and had been added onto many times through the years. The various facades were lit up with white spotlights adding a graceful touch to the historic architecture.

In front, two more limousines were unloading well-dressed passengers. James paused, then pulled forward as the other cars moved away. The limo stopped and Monica and Trish waited for James to come around and open the door. Monica told him they would be there for at least two hours and would phone him about 30 minutes before they were ready to leave.

Monica and Trish headed for the entrance. Inside, the maître d' greeted them with a formal "good evening ladies." Monica gave him the reservation information and he led them up a curved stairway to one of the dining rooms on the second level. Candled wall sconces and white table candles provided the only lighting. Several high-quality antique oil paintings were highlighted with small accent lights. The room had four tables and there was only one other party in the dining room.

The table was set with beautiful crystal, silver, and a crisp, white, doubled tablecloth. They sat across from each other, both glad to be together for the first time in many months. As fast as the maître d' disappeared, the wine sommelier appeared to present them with the restaurant's extensive wine list. Monica handed the list to Trish.

"You're the wine connoisseur Trish. You do the honors."

It was true. Trish often held open house events at the art gallery. In addition to the art exhibitions, one of the highlights of the events was enjoying the fabulous selection of food and wines that Trish personally selected for each event. Trish studied the wine menu and selected a 20-year-old cabernet sauvignon that was imported from Chili.

When the sommelier returned, Trish provided him with their wine selection and after a brief wait, he returned with their selection. Trish sampled the obligatory taste, then informed him the wine was indeed satisfactory. He half-filled both of their goblets with the dark red liquid and then vanished silently.

As he finished pouring, Monica proposed a toast. Both of them raised their glasses, and Monica said, "to the best of friendships, the best of futures, and the answer to my mystery." The glasses clinked together and both women took a long sip.

"Monica," Trish began, "I've been thinking. You may be on to something. There must be more to this story about the amusement park. Why would your mother have kept it for thirty years after it had been closed? She could have sold it at some point during that time."

"I agree Trish. I'm going to find out what's going on."

Just then the server appeared with dinner menus. After handing the elegant white menus to Monica and Trish he proceeded to review the restaurant's specials de jour. Both became quiet as they began perusing the selections. After debating the entrees, they placed the menus on the table and resumed their conversation.

"So Maxwell knew about the park and didn't tell you?" Trish queried.

"He did know all along. I want to find out as much as I can from him when I get back to Palm Beach. It's not like Maxwell to keep anything from me. Horace Goldsmith, I could understand. He's bound by attorney-client confidentiality, but Maxwell's not. If he couldn't tell me about this before Mother died, then he should have told me about it soon afterward."

"Does the park have a name?"

"It's named after the town it's located in, Atlantic Point."

"I've never heard of it."

"We have a beach house near there," Monica replied. "Mother never used it much. I remember being there once when I was very young and Horace says that it's in the will, so I guess we still own it."

The server reappeared to take their orders. Monica and Trish both ordered their appetizers as well as their entrées so they could continue talking uninterrupted.

"Are you thinking of re-opening the park Monica?"

"I'm not thinking that far ahead. I have to find out what's there and why the park has been kept a secret for so long."

"This could be interesting!" exclaimed Trish.

A short time later, their server reappeared with their appetizers and the conversation about Atlantic Point Park concluded as they enjoyed the wine and cuisine.

After dinner Monica and Trish relaxed sipping coffee with Irish cream. The conversation turned away from business and toward personal issues in each of their lives. Monica had always hoped Trish would leave the art gallery and join her at Caprice Hotels. Trish had always responded that she would never leave New York City. She loved running the art gallery and her busy social life took up the rest of her time. Monica would have to settle for assistance in decorating the hotels from time to time, no more.

After refilling their coffees, the server proffered their check. Monica insisted on settling the dinner check and while she did, she handed her cell phone to Trish so she could have James pick them up in the limo.

A short time later, the maître d' appeared to let them know that James had arrived. Soon they were back inside the black limo and Trish was giving James directions to New York's newest nightclub. As the car pulled out of the Naples Cove driveway, Trish gave Monica a rundown on the club. Monica sat back and listened while Trish continued with a look of excitement on her face.

Monica could not put the recent events out of her mind. James dropped them at the club after a quick drive through the night. He told them to phone him when they were ready to leave. The nightclub was spectacular. It had originally operated as a movie theater in the 1950s, the original art deco style having been restored and enhanced. Many of the theatre's original design features remained, including the ticket booth, popcorn stand, and original movie posters.

Inside the actual theater, the sloped floor had been partially leveled into multi-tiered sections. Some of the sections had intimate seating areas and some were conversation bars. At the front, music videos and light spectaculars appeared on high definition screens where movies had once been projected. A dance floor had been created below the screens. The atmosphere was electric. Trish stopped at the closest bar, picked up two drinks, and handed one to Monica. Monica congratulated Trish for selecting this venue to wind up their evening. After a brief search, they located a vacant table. The music was too loud for extensive conversation, so they both sipped their drinks and enjoyed the energized atmosphere and music. Later they met a group of young professional men and spent a good portion of the evening on the dance floor.

The night passed into the next day. Realizing that she had a busy day planned, Monica went over to grab Trish before the next dance started. Trish swayed and said, "Hey, I was just getting started!"

"No you weren't," Monica shouted over the din. "I have to fly home tomorrow. We've got to get going."

"Ok, ok," Trish yelled over the music which had started playing again, "You phone James while I run to the ladies' room. I'll meet you in the lobby."

Monica headed for the lobby and Trish headed for the ladies' room. Moments later she reappeared, looking ready for more partying. They both paused to admire the original framed movie posters that adorned the walls of the lobby. Before they had time to look at all of them, a text announced James' arrival.

James dropped Trish off first. Alone in the limousine, Monica's thoughts returned to Atlantic Point Park. At the condominium, there were several old photograph albums. She had seen them many years ago, but she wondered if looking at them now might yield a clue to a past that until yesterday she had not known about. She was wide-awake as the limo pulled into the driveway of The Colonnade.

After reaching her condominium, Monica took a quick bath and padded into the office that she had shared with her mother. There was an imported glass hutch with several doors in the lower half. Inside the doors were the old photograph albums. Monica placed the large old albums onto the desk and then looked at the faded photos they contained.

The photos were black and white, with some in faded Polaroid instant color prints. There were many pictures of her father and mother at various events through their lives. Monica recognized the pictures of her father. He had disappeared at a young age, so to Monica he was eternally young. She also recognized the young pictures of her dazzling mother. How stunning Lydia had been, even to the end.

Monica gazed intently at the pictures. She was now able to recognize an amusement park in many of the backgrounds. The amusement park setting was dominant throughout the albums. It had to be Atlantic Point Park. When she reached the last album, Monica pulled out several of the pictures and looked at the dates stamped on the back. The last pictures were dated April 1985, the month before her father disappeared. There was one sheet of stationary placed in the rear of the album. Monica recognized her mother's elaborate handwriting on the faded, old letter. The brief note said, "Ronald, I'm so very sorry."

Monica was shaken. What could her mother have meant by writing that and placing it at the end of the last photo album? After looking at it one more time, Monica placed the note back in the album and replaced all the albums back into the hutch.

Chapter Five

The squeal of tires meeting pavement announced the plane's arrival at the Palm Beach airport. It was after five o'clock. Earlier that morning, Monica had prepared the condominium for her departure. Guest services had overstocked the refrigerator, as usual, so Monica gave the excess perishables to George when he came to bring her luggage down to the limousine. She turned on the dishwasher, wrote a list of what cleaning and laundry needed to be done and asked George to contact the resident services department for her. He promised he would take care of it.

The same limousine company that had taken care of Monica's transportation needs during her time in New York had driven her to the airport about an hour before her scheduled departure. James had not been available, and a middle aged, female chauffer was the driver of the day. George stowed her luggage in the huge trunk of the car, gave her a wave goodbye and closed the door. The trip to the airport was as uneventful as the flight to Palm Beach.

Monica disembarked from the plane and after picking up her two bags, headed for the terminal exit. Earlier during the flight she had phoned her executive assistant, Francine Crowley, to request that one of the hotel courtesy cars pick her up at the airport, provided none of the hotel guests had reserved them for the same time. With Monica, her guests took priority over her own needs. She was not above riding in a taxi or getting a rental car if her guests required the hotel's transportation. The driver spotted Monica before she spotted him.

"Good afternoon, Monica. How was your flight?" Monica had always insisted that the staff call her by her first name, just as they had with her mother.

"Just fine Harry. I'm glad to be home."

"The car is over here," Harry indicated with a gentle gesture, "Is that all of your luggage?"

"It sure is, I was in New York for three days and you know I don't like to over pack."

Harry was an older gentleman with snow-white hair. He had the classic look of a beloved grandfather. Harry had been employed with the hotel company for years and had picked up Monica at the airport on many occasions. They headed to the car, and while Harry took care of the luggage, Monica opened the passenger door and climbed into the front seat. Harry climbed into the driver's side.

"How is everything at the hotel Harry?" Monica asked as she started up a conversation. Despite the steps she took to have the staff treat her in the same relaxed fashion that they would treat anyone, she sometimes felt that they were uncomfortable chatting with the hotel owner.

"Everything is just fine."

Harry skillfully negotiated the car through traffic toward the airport exit. He began talking about some of the general goings-on at the hotel, mentioning that the lawn sprinkler system was broken and that a recent board-game-player's convention had checked out and seemed to be happy with their stay.

"I won't be going to the hotel today Harry." It was already past the time that the corporate office staff would have left. The Caprice Hotel, Palm Beach was the company's flagship property and the corporate office was also located there.

"Just take me home so I can unpack and change into something more comfortable. Tomorrow is soon enough to start into the piles of work that I'm sure are stacked on my desk."

"Yes, ma'am," Harry replied.

Harry drove to the entrance of the luxury development where the home that Monica had shared with Lydia was located. He paused at the gated entrance until the guard recognized the Caprice Hotel's logo on the side of the limousine and waved them through. Palm trees lined all the streets in the development, perfectly interspersed with tall, frosted glass street lamps concealing bright LED lights. Sprinklers were watering the enormous lawns that fronted the homes. Moments later Harry pulled into Monica's driveway. As they proceeded, a large multi-roofed house with an elegant white façade appeared.

As she exited the limousine, Monica noticed that the heat and humidity were even worse than on her first day in New York. Because of the climate, summer months were Florida's off-season, and the Palm Beach hotel was not busy at this time of year. The opposite was true of the company's northern hotels. Monica reached into her purse and extracted the keys to the house. Harry retrieved the luggage and they headed for the front door.

As soon as they were inside, Midnight, Monica's black Labrador retriever bounded at them, full of energy and glad that Monica was home. Star and Swirl, the twin kittens that Monica had found abandoned in the back yard, were not far behind. Cold air from the central air-conditioning was a welcome relief from the Florida heat as Monica disarmed the red-blinking alarm system. Jeanette, the live-in housekeeper, was not home. Harry asked Monica where she would like the luggage and she told him to just leave it in the foyer.

Even though he was one of her employees, Monica gave Harry a tip and thanked him for picking her up at the airport. The day was still bright and light filtered down through the vestibule's skylight. The house always had a lonely feeling since Lydia died and Monica liked to let as much light as possible in. It was a vain attempt to provide a measure of cheer to the empty house and what was now her very lonely life.

Leaving her luggage in the foyer, Monica went up the steps and through the hallway to her bedroom suite. She had never moved into her Mother's larger suite, even after all these months, preferring not to touch or disturb any of Lydia's things. She changed into a more comfortable shirt and yoga pants, dumping her business attire into the hamper until it could be dry cleaned.

Monica had never gone into her mother's suite since the day she learned of her death. Jeanette had been instructed not to go into the rooms even to clean; the door was kept closed at all times.

The thought of having to go through all her Mother's personal effects, many with attached memories, seemed overwhelming to Monica.

She had considered telling Jeanette to box up the entire room, but now she was glad that she had not done so.

Just then she heard a sound coming from the rear of the house and realized that Jeanette was returning from whatever errands she had been taking care of.

Monica ran down the steps and gave Jeanette a warm hug.

"I have returned!" Monica exclaimed. Jeanette was from Honduras. She still spoke with a slight accent and slightly broken English. Monica loved her as the family member that she had become. Jeanette had come to Florida as a young girl and was hired by Lydia to run the Scott household after Lydia moved to Florida in late 1985. She had been with the family since before Monica was born. Even after all these years, Jeanette still sent money home to her family in on a regular basis and visited them whenever she could get away.

"Oh, Miss Monica, I did not realize that you were coming home today. I have not planned dinner for you, and I made plans to go to a movie with a friend tonight."

"You go and have a good time Jeanette, I have plans of my own this evening."

"There is a large bowl of homemade soup in the refrigerator and some freshly baked bread. Let me heat some soup for you."

"No need to make me dinner," Monica stated with faux firmness. "Go and have a good time. I've been telling you for years to get out more."

"Are you sure you do not want me to heat the soup for you?"

"Jeanette, even *I* can heat soup," Monica said with a smile.

Jeanette headed for her own apartment, which was located behind the main house. She gave Monica another hug before she disappeared through the door.

Monica did not know if Jeanette had fed the dog and cats. Although well fed, the dog was always hungry and would not have turned down a second meal had Monica provided it. The cats however could be quite finicky. Monica opened the kitchen door and called out to Jeanette who was walking toward her apartment, "Have you fed the kids yet?"

"Yes, I feed all of them Miss Monica, it is you who I do not feed," Jeanette answered back as she paused in her walk across the lawn to her private apartment.

Monica gave Midnight a natural treat to keep her busy and Star and Swirl were treated to some organic catnip. She had a difficult project to accomplish and she didn't want to be disturbed. It was getting darker inside the house and shadows began to fall with the diminishing sunlight. Monica headed back up the staircase, but at the top she turned in the opposite direction from her own suite and instead headed toward the suite of rooms that had been her mother's.

Monica stopped at the door. Her heart was pounding. She took a deep breath and reached for the doorknob. The room was dark inside. Before Jeanette had closed up the suite, Monica had instructed her to close the drapes. Monica reached for the light switch. The lights on both sides of the bed came on, illuminating the room with soft light. Monica gazed around the elegant room.

A thick layer of white dust coated everything. The room otherwise appeared to be in the same neat order that her mother left it in when she went to New Jersey last November.

Monica had always known about the closed down Caprice Hotel and the beach house on Atlantic Point Island. Until now, she had never considered why her mother had gone to New Jersey last November. When the township council called her mother, Monica presumed it had something to do with the beach house or the old hotel. Lydia had not elaborated. Now Monica knew that Atlantic Point Park was the real reason for Lydia's fateful trip. At the time Monica had been too upset to question the details provided to Maxwell by the New Jersey State Police. Now Monica wanted to know everything.

Lydia's bedroom suite was spacious. It consisted of a large, amply furnished sleeping area, a sitting area with a widescreen television, a large bathroom with a whirlpool tub, dressing room and a separated office space. The dressing room was lined with sliding glass doors that housed Lydia's massive collection of fine clothing and shoes. As she walked through the dressing area, the characteristic scent of Lydia's perfume wafted through the stale air. Monica could not suppress a sob as she realized that her mother would never be with her again.

Monica continued toward the double doors leading to the office area. She paused, trying to gather her courage. After a moment, she opened the doors simultaneously and flipped on the light. The office contained a desk, a smaller television, and a large double closet. Monica had always wondered why her mother kept her personal office up here. Lydia regularly went over her affairs at the large desk with coffee and breakfast before starting her day. Jeanette had duly carried her breakfast up every morning but Sunday. Sunday was when Lydia and Monica used to take time to enjoy long champagne brunches as they shared their personal lives together.

Monica did not open any of the drapes, as if she did not want anyone to know that she had come into the office. She did turn on all the lights, hoping they could ward off the intrusive feelings she had about being in her mother's private world. Even with all the lights on, the gloom was pervasive.

The desk was without any envelopes, bills or documents that had always been present when her mother used the office. Monica had Jeanette bring the office paperwork to her when she closed up the suite in November. Monica's life might never be the same, but the utility companies still wanted to be paid. She had dutifully gone through all the paperwork. Responsibility for running the household was something else that was now left to her care.

Monica took another deep breath and began opening the drawers in the desk, one by one. There were paperclips, rubber bands, and any other number of typical items that you would expect to find inside a working desk. The items were not what she was looking for. Absent mindedly, she brushed the dust off the front of the silent computer screen.

Monica opened the double closet doors and looked into the shallow space. Neat boxes filled with paperwork, all sorted by year, were placed on two large shelving units. At least if Monica ever needed to find anything related to running the household it would be very easy to locate.

Monica gazed around the office. The wall behind the desk was covered with a bookcase that held the hundreds of hardback novels that Lydia had read. On the other side of the room was the flat panel television mounted to the wall with an old combination DVD and VRC player that still sat on a credenza below the TV. Lydia had never learned to stream her entertainment. Monica did not expect to find anything when she opened the entertainment center, but she did so anyway. The only items she found were Lydia's collection of movies. The room did have one window, and under the window was a row of dead plants. The plants reminded Monica yet again that she needed to clean out the entire suite.

Monica returned to the closet. Several of the boxes with the dated paperwork had been over stacked and were poised to fall. Monica began to push them back into place. As she did so, the entire shelving unit seemed to move. Where the two units joined in the center, there was an uneven gap where the one shelving unit had pulled away from the wall.

Monica applied slight pressure to pull the shelves out farther. She did not want the unit to tip over. She was surprised when it began to pull smoothly away from the wall. The shallow shelving units were actually hinged doors, behind which stood two large filing cabinets. Monica was shocked. She had not known the closet had a hidden compartment even though the front closet doors had been open many times when she had gone into the office to see her mother.

Monica attempted to open the filing cabinets. They were both locked. They seemed to be quite old and the metal housing was very heavy. Now she needed to find the key. She reached around the floor, and then she took another more careful look through the desk. Nothing. She pondered what her mother might have done with the keys.

A sudden thought came to her. The New Jersey state police returned all the personal effects that they recovered from Lydia's smashed Jaguar. They had placed them in a sealed box, which Maxwell had returned to her unopened. Monica told Jeanette to put the box in the bedroom, as she did not want to see the morbid reminder of her mother's death. Even after the memorial service was long past, she had not wanted to look at the box. Now Monica raced back into the sleeping area. The box with the state police seal was sitting just inside the bedroom door where Jeanette had placed it. She had not noticed it when she first came in.

Monica used her fingernail to break the taped seal on the carton. Inside were her mother's handbag, wallet and personal key set. The items were covered with dried mud and the scent of mold. Monica shuddered, as she thought of her mother inside the smashed Jaguar, semi-submerged in the cold, muddy water under the bridge. The police obviously did not take time to clean such items before they returned them to the family.

Monica grabbed for the key set and raced back into the office. Her mother had a great number of keys. Monica looked at each one trying to locate a small key that would open a filing cabinet. After several tries, she located a small, sturdy key that appeared to be very old. After brushing off the caked mud, she slid the key into the locks of the files. It fit both filing cabinets and the locks turned with surprising ease.

Each of the two cabinets had four drawers. One by one Monica opened the drawers of the filing cabinet on her left. There were personal letters and cards from her mother's many friends organized by year from 1985 until the time of her death. The first such cards were Christmas cards from 1985 and congratulations at the time of Monica's birth. Year by year they chronicled the events that had been time markers in her mother's life. Monica noticed there were no personal letters or cards from before the time her mother moved to Florida, just before Monica was born.

Monica opened the filing cabinet on her right. This cabinet contained newspapers that all pertained to the closing of Atlantic Point Park and the disappearance of her father. These were also organized by year from 1985 until the time of Lydia's death. In the early years there were a substantial number of newspapers, but as the years went by, there were fewer and fewer as the search had been concluded. One notable exception was the file containing documents from May of 2015. It had been the thirtieth anniversary of her father's disappearance, just before the final season of Atlantic Point Park's operation. *The Atlantic Point News Herald* had marked the event with extensive articles on the history of the amusement park and about her father's still unsolved disappearance. Monica intended to read every one of the articles.

Minutes later she had reached the last drawer. As Monica opened the drawer, she heard a rattling sound. The only item in the drawer was a large manila envelope that covered the entire bottom of the drawer. She picked up the envelope and heard more rattling. The envelope had once been taped shut with packing tape, which was now brittle and yellowed with age. It gave way to gentle pressure. Monica wanted to be sure that she did not damage whatever was inside. She peered into the envelope. It was just what she had been hoping to find. Inside was a circular metal key ring about seven inches in diameter, with a multitude of keys on it. She looked the ring over and found a metal tag with punched engraving on it. The tag said, "AP Master Two—Do Not Duplicate." The keys were the second master set to Atlantic Point Park. Where was the first set?

Monica wanted to visit the old amusement park without anyone knowing about it. She did not want to arouse questions from Horace or Maxwell by asking them for keys to the park, nor did she want to explain her intent. She had considered hiring a local locksmith to help her get into the park, but to do so would have aroused gossip all over the small town of Atlantic Point Island. Now she could accomplish her visit without anyone's knowledge.

Monica placed the Atlantic Point key set back into the old envelope and replaced the envelope into the filing cabinet, which she relocked. After concealing the filing cabinets with the false shelves, she latched them back into place. Then she turned off all the lights and exited the suite, taking her mother's personal keys with her.

Chapter Six

Janice Laneer had been Maxwell William's executive assistant for the better part of 30 years. She still didn't know how she had lasted at Caprice Hotels for so long. Just the thought of the time she had wasted made her furious. She punched the keys on her computer in anger as her thoughts overcame her.

Janice had been 29 years old when she gave her first husband Roger Laneer his walking papers. The thought of Roger made her even angrier. He had been such a loser. Janice had hopes and dreams back then. Roger had no hopes, no dreams and no ambitions. What she had ever seen in him she couldn't remember.

Well, she could at least chalk that up to an error of youth, but she couldn't chalk up the last 30 years to any error. Staying here had been sheer stupidity, although not from a financial standpoint. Maxwell and Lydia had paid her well. Janice had invested each payday and her investments had performed better than she could have ever imagined. Janice's investment money coupled with the money she had raked out of Roger in the divorce left her in a position of financial comfort, but comfort was not what she wanted. What she wanted, what she had always wanted, was Maxwell Williams.

After her divorce from Roger, Janice had gone looking for a job. She saw an ad in a local newspaper for a position as a secretary, as her current position had once been called. Janice though, had gone looking for more than work. She knew that most secretaries worked for male executives. The executives who had secretaries had important positions with often-promising futures ahead of them. More than one executive had been known to marry his secretary and Janice intended to be that secretary. She didn't need to find out if the executive was married. That information would not be important to achieving her goals, or so she had thought.

Janice had dressed with strategic vision for that interview, a combination of professionalism and understated seductiveness. Janice was not above using her looks to achieve her goals. Even back then her hair had its natural red highlights. Because of her fair skin, she had always avoided the sun and even now she had very few wrinkles. Maxwell had taken one look at her and hired her on the spot without even looking at her credentials. She started working for him, and on him, that first day, and every day after that for the last 30 years.

Along the way, something had gone wrong with her plan, and Janice knew exactly what that something was. It was that bitch Lydia Scott. It had been obvious early on to Janice that Maxwell and Lydia had had an affair at some point in time. A woman like Janice just knew these things. Over time, Maxwell admitted to her that he and Lydia had been together even before Ronald Scott disappeared.

Janice had convinced Maxwell to go for drinks one night after a long and tiring day at the office. Maxwell made the unexpected confession about Lydia after one too many drinks. Janice had taken advantage of the situation and had continued prying hoping to get a better assessment of what her future chances with Maxwell might be. Maxwell insisted that he had never again been with Lydia after the brief affair had broken off back in New

Jersey. Janice knew better. While Maxwell wasn't sleeping with Lydia in bed, he was sleeping with her in his every waking breath.

In the early years, Janice had been patient; figuring that time would pass and Maxwell's attention would turn away from the always aloof Lydia and toward Janice. Then one day Janice realized she was really in love with Maxwell Williams. Her growing love for the man had kept her there long after she had intended to give up her plan and move on.

One by one the years went by. Nothing. Then, just about the time Janice realized that Maxwell would never belong to her, she got a surprise. Maxwell invited her to his house one night after the two had gone for drinks after work. As Janice had always dreamed, they had indeed spent the night together. With her hopes renewed, Janice continued working for Maxwell, but their night of passion was never repeated, and Janice had turned into a bitter, angry woman who was looking for revenge for her wasted life.

How she had remained civil and cordial to Lydia Scott, she never knew. If Lydia had suspected how Janice had felt about Maxwell, she would have gotten rid of her at the earliest opportunity. It didn't matter that Lydia didn't want Maxwell, just so no one else had him either. Every day Janice hid her feelings and greeted Lydia with a smile that was killing her inside. Lydia strolled around the hotel and the offices like the queen bee. Everyone thought Lydia was a wonderful mother, a wonderful businesswoman and a wonderful boss. Everyone except Janice Laneer. To Janice she was nothing but a conniving, conceited bitch, just like her daughter Monica.

When the news came last November that Lydia was dead, Janice had felt the renewed spirit of hope flow through her. At long last, Lydia was gone and Janice had allowed herself to hope yet again that her retirement years would be spent with the man she had always loved.

Once again, her hopes were dashed when Maxwell had been unable to stop grieving over Lydia. Janice had been forced to realize that dead or alive, Maxwell would never stop loving Lydia Scott.

Janice punched the print button on the keyboard and then the save button. The updated costs on the renovations to the Virginia Beach hotel had been left on her desk with a note from Drake Donovan asking her to type them up for the Friday morning staff meeting. Now Drake was the kind of man that Janice could go for. Maybe it was time to have a drink with Mr. Donovan…

As she reached for the finished report, she heard Monica come into the office and say, "Why good morning Janice, I'm back from New York."

Janice put on her best smile and said, "Good morning Monica, it's so good to see you."

Francine Crowley pulled into the parking lot of the hotel. She pushed back her salt and pepper hair, which was cut in an efficient bob. She was running late and she still had a number of things to collect before the executive staff meeting started at nine o'clock. She also had to meet with Monica before the meeting to review the presentations that would be made to the management staff.

Francine hated when she didn't have enough time, but she had developed car trouble and had to go back into her house to wake her husband so he could try to get the thing going. Francine was petite and she couldn't have lifted the hood on the large car if she had tried. After some tinkering, her husband got the car started and Francine was on her way, twenty minutes late.

Francine knew Monica would not be upset with her. Monica was even easier to work for than Lydia, whom Francine had loved. Francine had been hired into the corporate office just one week before Janice Laneer, when Lydia Scott had moved the company headquarters of the Caprice Hotel chain to Florida from New Jersey.

Francine was working in the Palm Beach hotel at the front desk back then. Lydia had recognized and complimented her efficient nature and the warm manner in which she treated the hotel's guests. Just days later she had asked Francine to assist her in setting up the corporate office as the multitude of boxes had begun to roll in from New Jersey. Francine had taken the task as a great challenge and had stayed in the corporate offices after the project was completed. Francine held a trusted position with Lydia and now she held that same position with Monica. She was very proud of the confidence which was placed in her by her current and former bosses.

Francine shared a large open office area with Janice Laneer. Beyond Francine's desk was Monica's office and beyond Janice's desk was Maxwell's office. It was necessary to share the administrative office with Maxwell's assistant. Maxwell and Lydia had run the company together and the files and duties were shared equally with the two executive assistants.

Had Francine not respected Lydia so much she would have never stayed on the job working beside Janice Laneer. She had never trusted Janice from the first day that she met her. It was nothing you could put your finger on, something that just comes from a good ability to read people, and Francine was good at reading people. Over time Francine had become a casual friend with Janice and they occasionally lunched together. Still Francine could not think of a single time that they had done anything together like shopping or going to a movie. The kind of things that two people sharing an office for thirty years might do.

Francine bustled into the office. Monica's door was open and the light was on. Francine called out a cheery, "Welcome back, Monica," toward the open door, and without waiting for an answer, she hustled to her desk to gather her paperwork. Janice was not in the office although her computer was on. She had probably gone for coffee and Francine hoped she would bring her a cup.

Francine finished gathering the paperwork, just as Janice, returning with two cups of coffee said, "Good morning Francine, I thought you might appreciate a cup of coffee since you're running late today."

Francine thanked Janice as she reached for the coffee, and without another word, headed into Monica's office.

Drake Donovan sat in the main hotel dining room eating an oversized plate of eggs, pancakes and home fries. He was also enjoying a large glass of fresh orange juice and a cup of coffee, which he continued to refill with the small pot left by the waitress. He had just flown in from Virginia Beach the night before, as Maxwell had requested, so he could meet with Monica about the cost overruns on the current renovation project.

Drake took another bite of the pancakes. He gave no thought to running up huge food and liquor bills at the various Caprice Hotels that he was forever living in. Drake figured if he could go from hotel to hotel renovating, remodeling, and repairing, he was owed all the food and drink he wanted.

Living in different hotels your whole life had some advantages, but it could get tiring too. Drake had been doing it for 12 years now. When he couldn't stand it anymore, he would move on to another type of work. It occurred to him that the time to leave could be coming soon. Lydia had always paid him well, and he had repaid her in more ways than one. Now with Maxwell exercising more control, his future didn't look as bright.

Maxwell had been angry when Drake phoned him about the cost overruns on the Virginia Beach hotel's renovation project. Drake enjoyed pissing off Maxwell. The pompous old man had never done anything for Drake accept to provide ongoing criticism about every project that Drake ever worked on. It was never good enough, always too expensive and was never completed on time, at least according to Maxwell.

Never mind that Drake had told Maxwell 10 years ago when he had done previous renovations on the Virginia Beach property that the old heating and air-conditioning systems needed to be replaced. Maxwell had made the decision not to replace them back then and had neglected to include it in the current round of renovations. Now the system was on its last legs and Drake wasn't about to take the blame for cost overruns related to replacing it.

Last night Drake had gone into the corporate office and placed a list of the current costs and the revised projected costs on Janice Laneer's desk. Janice was cool. She still looked great for someone who was all but sixty years old. Even now, she would still wear a short, tight skirt—and look good doing it. Drake figured if she looked that great now, she must have been a knockout when she was his age. She always flirted with him when he was in town and he had no doubt that with Janice he could get anything he wanted. Drake could appreciate that in a woman.

Drake always wore a work shirt and jeans to the construction projects, but today he was dressed in a polo shirt and black dress slacks. He refused to wear a tie, even when he had to go to one of the corporate staff meetings. Of course Maxwell had commented on that many times too, which made his decision to wear the open neck polo shirt that much easier. Still, he didn't want to look like a bum. Monica would be at the meeting and she was always dressed like a million bucks or perhaps several million was more like it. Drake would be glad to see her.

Brad Roberts was the Director of Asset Management for Caprice Hotels. It was his job to research, recommend and finalize the appropriate methods to finance the company's operations. Brad was responsible to refinance existing obligations, fund the ongoing renovation projects and work with investors to develop the new properties. He was also responsible for all the accounting functions in the various hotels and at the corporate office.

Brad had been with Caprice for about 10 years. After he graduated from Florida State University with a master's degree in asset management, he had taken a position as the assistant to the former asset manager. When his boss retired, Brad had been promoted into the job. For someone who was just 30 years of age, Brad held a position of great responsibility. He ran a tight ship and was well respected. He was responsible for seeing that the Caprice chain achieved good profit margins on a regular basis.

Brad took pride in his appearance. He wasn't tall, just average, but he looked like a surfer who had just come in from a California beach. He kept his short blond hair combed back and worked out every day at a local fitness center. Despite his good looks, or perhaps because of them, he still had not married.

He had done a lot of dating right through graduate school, and even as he fell into the working world, but his desire to remain unattached had overridden his desire to settle down. For Brad there was only one person who could have even made him consider settling down. That person was Monica Scott.

Monica and Brad had been dating off and on for several years. Brad had already been well established in his current position when he first dated Monica, so it had never been assumed by the staff that his promotion was related to his relationship. In fact, back when Brad was promoted, he and Monica had barely known each other. Most of his dealings had been with Lydia and Maxwell.

Of course Brad had known Monica by sight and well enough to say hello, but she had seldom been in the main offices as her position had taken her out into the other hotels. Brad always found Monica to be very attractive and charming on the few occasions they had spoken, but it was not until a couple of years ago at the annual executive Christmas party that Brad had taken an opportunity to get to know her.

He could still see her standing in the Crystal Ballroom at the Palm Beach hotel. Monica was wearing a dark blue gown and holding a flute of champagne and she had looked fantastic. Seldom did Brad find it difficult to approach an attractive member of the opposite sex, but this time, it took all of his courage. He grabbed a glass of champagne from a passing server and edged over to where Monica was chatting with a group of people. Brad joined the conversation, skillfully reducing the conversation to topics that he thought Monica would be interested in. The rest of the group circulated off to other parts of the ballroom until Brad and Monica were left alone.

Monica was a great conversationalist, and Brad was infatuated. They discovered that they had many interests in common and enough differences to spark an interest in each other. Brad was as surprised as Monica when he asked her for a date, and she accepted on the spot.

They had dated off and on for a long time. Somehow they never seemed to be able to get serious. Some stupid argument, a work obligation or their fiercely guarded independence seemed to get in the way. Still when Brad was with Monica, he was happiest and when they were not seeing each other, he was miserable.

The make-up and break-up routine had gone on for a long time. During the last break up, Brad found out that Monica had slept with that nail-pounding jerk, Drake Donovan. Brad knew he had no right to be upset.

He and Monica were not seeing each other at the time, and she had every right to sleep with anyone she wanted to. Still his hurt ran deep. Brad had restricted his conversations with Monica to business only thereafter. During that time, Brad avoided her as much as he could, preferring instead to deal with Maxwell Williams or with Lydia.

Then came Lydia's unexpected death. Brad knew how close Monica had been to Lydia and he had phoned her to offer his sincere condolences. Monica had been glad to hear from him and Brad had given her a hug at the funeral. During the seven months since, he and Monica had been friendly enough to one another, but any further relationship seemed to be stalled. Monica had been busy with new responsibilities and there had been more for Brad to do with Lydia gone from the company. Brad knew this was not the time to press Monica for anything and he respected that she needed time to put her life in order.

Brad glanced at his watch. In just a few minutes the Friday morning staff meeting would start. This was one meeting that Brad was not looking forward to. Drake Donovan was in town and Brad despised seeing him. Drake was the kind of asshole that enjoyed seeing someone pissed off. Brad wasn't about to let Drake know just how angry he was inside about Drake's past moves on Monica. He would remain professional.

Brad reached toward the corner of the desk where he had placed seven files, one for each of the five Caprice Hotels, and one each for the two hotels that were under development. The files contained the latest financial reports on the individual properties. Brad also maintained a file for the closed down Caprice Hotel, Atlantic Point, in New Jersey. The file included the ongoing tax payments for the defunct property. Brad never brought that file to the meetings, but he wanted to ask Monica if they could unload the property as Lydia had been paying taxes on it for many years. Lydia had kept the closed down hotel against his ongoing recommendations to sell it.

There was also one other question he had for Monica. A second tax assessment had made its way to his desk. This was one that he had never seen before. It was addressed to Atlantic Point Corporation. Brad knew from old office files that Atlantic Point Corporation was what the company had been called before the name was changed to Caprice. What he didn't understand was why the assessment was for a parcel of property in New Jersey that was not at the same address as the closed down hotel. The assessment, including late penalties was considerable, and Brad figured it must be an error. Still it would have to be addressed and Brad would discuss it with Monica after the staff meeting.

Chapter Seven

Monica smiled warmly as her executive staff assembled for the meeting. Many of them stopped at the buffet table, which had been filled with coffee, tea, juices and breakfast rolls by the banquet department about fifteen minutes before the start of the meeting.

Each executive was responsible to manage one aspect of the operations in all of the Caprice Hotels. For example, the corporate executive for food and beverage oversaw the food and beverage operations in each of the five hotels, the chief engineer oversaw the engineering functions in all the properties and so on. Monica's assistant, Francine, attended the meetings, as did Maxwell's assistant Janice Laneer. Today, both were in attendance to take notes for their respective bosses.

Monica glanced around the table and saw that Drake Donovan was present. Drake was considered a member of the executive staff, but because he worked on location at the various hotels, he seldom attended the meetings. Something must be up for him to be here, Monica realized. She felt "out of the loop" even though she had been away from the office for only three days. Hopefully this meeting would cure that.

Monica glanced at her watch, five minutes until nine. She always started the meetings on time, never early, never late. As she looked up she saw Brad Roberts coming through the entrance door. Brad walked over to the buffet table, grabbed a cup of coffee and a bottle of juice and headed for one of two open seats at the conference table. Monica suppressed a smile as she noticed he selected the seat farthest from Drake Donovan.

Monica was not hungry, but she decided to get a cup of coffee before she started the meeting. She hadn't eaten any of the soup and bread that Jeanette had left for her last night. After going into her mother's suite and finding the hidden filing cabinets, she was overwhelmed by emotion. Along with the plane ride from New York, discovering the mysterious files had left her exhausted. After the evening's conclusion, Monica had tumbled into bed and then had awakened at six o'clock in the morning. Jeanette had prepared a huge breakfast for herself and Monica, which they shared together. Monica had eaten more of Jeanette's breakfast than she had intended. Now all she wanted was the aromatic coffee.

As Monica sat down, she started the meeting by greeting the staff with a pleasant "Good morning. I wanted to thank everyone for taking care of all the operations while I was in New York. I met with our legal counsel, Horace Goldsmith, and the estate is nearing final settlement. I am very pleased to announce that there will be no changes in our operations, staffing or in our growth and development plans. As some of you know, we had several competitors interested in buying the company after my mother's accident. The company is not for sale. Caprice Hotels has always been a family operation and it will continue to be so."

There was an audible sigh of relief around the table. Monica had presumed that the estate would be left to her intact, but until she had absolute confirmation of that, as well as knowledge from Horace about her overall financial position, she had not wanted to promise the staff that the company would not be sold. Now she could offer them the appropriate reassurances and it was a relief to be able to do so.

Monica turned the meeting over to Maxwell who reviewed all current issues affecting the hotel company. Following in turn, each manager gave a brief presentation of their specific department and areas of concern. Monica asked pertinent questions as the managers gave their reports. Maxwell too asked the executives many pointed questions. Brad followed up with a financial report on each hotel and asked the managers to use caution in their business spending as the company was diverting a substantial portion of its cash flow toward the two new hotels that were under development. Drake Donovan, who was not often present at the meetings, gave a final report on the renovations to the Virginia Beach property. Drake made no mention of the problems with cost overruns. He would discuss that after the meeting with Monica, Maxwell and Brad.

As she prepared to conclude the meeting Monica asked, "Does anyone have anything further to bring up?"

Maxwell responded, "We need to discuss some issues regarding the renovations at the Virginia Beach property, which is why I requested that Drake attend today's meeting." There was no hint of the anger that he had directed toward Drake when they had spoken the day before. "It will be necessary for Brad, and of course Drake, to stay for the discussion."

Monica prepared to end the meeting. "I would like to let everyone know that I will be going on vacation for the next two weeks. The past few months have been very intense and I have some personal matters to attend to. I have trust and confidence in each of you, and of course Maxwell will be available should you need his assistance. Francine can reach me at the house or on my cell phone. The meeting is adjourned, thank you all for attending today."

The executive staff filed out of the room. Only Monica, Maxwell, Drake and Brad remained. Monica suspected that Brad knew about her affair with Drake, but if he did, he had always remained quiet about it. He had an ever calm, ever cool demeanor. She respected that about Brad. He always seemed to be in absolute control of everything that came into his orbit, especially when it came to business. Monica was also finding she missed his company.

"Well Drake," Maxwell began, "Would you like to tell Monica the bad news or should I?"

"It's nothing you were not already aware of Maxwell," Drake replied. "You have known that the heating and cooling system at Virginia needed to be replaced for the last ten years. Here are copies of the memos that I sent you back then, and again when we did the budget for the current renovations. That you neglected to provide approval to replace the system is a decision which you need to accept responsibility for."

"Now just a minute," Maxwell exclaimed as his face quickly reddened. "We're not here to place blame, Mr. Donovan; we are here to achieve a solution."

Monica smiled inwardly. Drake had Maxwell on that one she thought. Maxwell and Drake had been going on like this for years. They just couldn't stand each other and nothing was going to ever change that.

"Well considering how you responded when I phoned you, I thought that you must have been looking to blame someone, Maxwell."

"Let's stop right there gentleman," Monica stated firmly. "This is not achieving a solution. Drake, how much money is it going to take to replace the old system?"

"Nearly an extra $500,000," Drake answered. "The old systems are beyond repair, they need removed and the new systems will require additional electrical wiring in every room."

"Brad, how is our financial picture related to satisfying this unexpected expense?" Monica asked.

"As you know, our liquidity is not great right now with the new hotels going up. Our credit remains excellent and we always have the multi-million-dollar line of credit with BankStar, but the interest rates on the credit line are not particularly favorable. I would prefer not to use it."

Monica continued with her questions in an attempt to reach the best possible solution. "Drake is the system absolutely shot?"

"It's been shot for years and beyond repair. It is currently operable at about fifty percent capacity. I think it will take us through the summer if it doesn't get too hot, and maybe even a mild winter, but you're talking about a project that will take a long time to complete under ideal circumstances. There's no way that you can start next season without a complete replacement."

"Drake, please start getting bids on the replacement system. When you are done, email the three best bids to me, Maxwell and Brad," Monica requested of him. "Brad, would you look into long term financing while

Drake is getting the bids. Let's use the credit line as a last resort. Maxwell, are you in agreement with this plan?"

"It sounds like the best solution we can achieve under the circumstances," Maxwell grumbled as he attempted to regain his composure.

"Let's conclude this part of the meeting," Monica stated with relief.

Brad and Drake left the room while Maxwell remained seated, as did Monica. When the door to the conference room had been closed, Monica bored into Maxwell's eyes and asked him pointedly, "Don't you have something to tell me?"

Maxwell had known this meeting was coming ever since Monica had learned about Atlantic Point Park on her visit to see Horace Goldsmith. For the past three days, he had long debated just how much he should say and just how he should say it.

"Monica, I'll tell you all that I know. Atlantic Point Park is a part of the past. It's been closed now for over thirty years. I seldom think of it, and for reasons of her own, your mother decided not to ever mention it too you. She requested that I not mention it to you, and I respected her enough to do as she asked. Why are you so upset about this?"

"I don't know Maxwell. It's just that Mother never kept anything from me and I suddenly feel as if there is a piece of her I never knew. I can't ask her why she kept this from me and I just have a lot of unanswered questions. Horace said that Mother would never sell the park and she wouldn't even discuss it with him. There has to be a reason why she would keep a closed down amusement park for thirty years."

"Monica, I don't have the answers you're looking for. I worked at the park until the first Caprice Hotel was developed and I was seldom there after that. I was busy working on the new hotel venture. I hope you can respect my achievements in that area. We've been very successful in the hospitality business."

"Of course I do Maxwell; Horace told me how close Mother had been to declaring bankruptcy."

"She was very close to bankruptcy Monica. If it weren't for the hotels, we would all have been left with absolutely nothing. Atlantic Point Park was worthless, maybe Lydia just wanted to forget all about it."

"She could have forgotten about it if she had sold it or abandoned it to the township. Instead she kept it—for thirty years, no less!"

"You know Monica," Maxwell lowered his voice, "Perhaps she felt that it was her last connection to your father."

"Oh Maxwell, I just don't know. I guess that's the most logical answer, but I need to know more."

For just a moment, Monica thought she saw a look of panic flicker across Maxwell's face. Then it was gone just as quickly as it had appeared. Perhaps it was just her imagination or the stress of the conversation. She had taken notice how much Maxwell had aged in the past few months. Actually, she was worried about him and it wasn't her intent to add to his worries.

"Monica, I am the only person anywhere in the company who knows about Atlantic Point Park. Let's put our heads together and decide what we should do. I think it's important to keep this to ourselves, as your mother wished."

"Maxwell, you have always been like the father that I never knew. I was upset that you didn't confide in me about the park and that I had to hear it from Horace Goldsmith. I feel better now, but I want you to always be up front with me. I don't want to run this company without you, and I need to be able to continue the trust that we have always had."

"Monica, you can always trust me," Maxwell said soothingly. "Take your vacation and by the time you get back, I'll have things figured out. Where are you going by the way?"

Monica remained firm in her decision not to tell Maxwell about her plans to visit Atlantic Point Island and the park. "I'm not sure Maxwell, I think that I'll just pick a destination on the map and drive there. Maybe I'll even ask Trisha Marshall to join me from New York."

Maxwell's only reply was a look of worry.

When Monica returned to her office Francine was there and Janice had gone to lunch. She asked Francine to go down to the hotel kitchen when Janice returned and have the chef make a light salad for her. Jeanette's breakfast was wearing off.

As Monica walked by, Francine commented, "You have a visitor in your office."

Monica didn't even bother to ask her who it was, she already knew. Sitting inside her office with his feet propped up on the desk was Drake Donovan.

"Greetings Monica," Drake grinned.

"Get your feet off my desk you bum," Monica retorted. As hard as she tried, she couldn't conceal a smile from her lips. "Is this what we pay you all that money for?"

"I'm worth every penny and you know it."

"No I don't know it," Monica answered even though she did know Drake was worth all he was paid and more. He had saved the company hundreds of thousands of dollars over many years.

"Where are you vacationing?" Drake asked as he removed his feet from Monica's desk.

"I haven't decided yet."

"You know I'm always available for a vacation Monica."

"Well Drake, you just announced that you had a major project to accomplish in Virginia. I wouldn't want to do anything that would cause a delay for you, so I guess I'll just have to vacation alone this time."

"I just thought I would offer Monica," Drake seldom let down his cocky demeanor. "Since you obviously can't spare me, I'll be on my way back to Virginia. I packed up my stuff while you were in the conference room and I really just stopped in to say good bye."

"Drake, I may need your help with something in the near future. Have a good flight back to Virginia and give me a call in two weeks."

Drake picked up on Monica's serious tone. He responded by getting serious himself, "You know I'm always here if you need me." He pecked her on the cheek and was on his way out of the office in a flash. Moments later the phone buzzed.

Francine's voice came over the speaker when Monica hit the button, "Monica, Brad is on line one, do you want to take the call?"

"Yes Francine, put it through."

"Monica, I have an unusual tax assessment that comes due very soon."

"What kind of tax assessment Brad?"

"I'm really not sure, I don't recognize the address, but the assessment office in New Jersey insists it belongs to one of our companies. There's something else. It came in the name of the old company, Atlantic Point Corporation.

"Are you sure it's not for the closed down hotel or the beach house?"

"Absolutely, it's near the old hotel, but the address is not the same."

Monica drew a deep breath. "Brad, take the tax assessment home with you, don't leave it in the office. I don't want to discuss it here at work. I have plans tomorrow and Sunday, but perhaps you could come over to the house for dinner on Monday night. I want to discuss something with you, and I think I have the answer to your tax mystery, or at least part of the answer."

"Sure Monica. I'll see you about seven on Monday night." Brad was so surprised that he just hung up the phone, never even saying goodbye.

Maxwell Williams left the office immediately after his morning meeting with Monica. He told Janice where to reach him if he was needed, although Janice knew never to call Maxwell when he was at the country club. She was very good at covering for him.

Maxwell had no intention of playing golf today, although he enjoyed the game on a regular basis. Today all he wanted was a few stiff drinks and a place to sort out his thoughts. He had the sense not to drink and drive, so he had his housekeeper, Evelyn Smith, drive him out to the club in his outdated Lincoln Town Car. Maxwell told her she would need to pick him up later, much later.

The events that transpired thirty years ago were beginning to unravel. He could feel it in his bones. Monica didn't seem willing to forget about Atlantic Point Park. That was something that really worried Maxwell, worried him in the way that would not let go. Maxwell knew he had to do some very fast thinking. The problem was that there was no easy solution and a wrong move could spiral yesterday's secrets out of control.

Monica went through all the paperwork that had accumulated on her desk in her three-day absence, then went through scores of emails. Finally she looked over the daily updates to the Facebook page and the various property reviews on TripAdvisor. She knew even more paperwork and emails would be right there waiting for her after the two-week vacation. Francine had offered to stay late and help, explaining that she had come in late from early morning car trouble. Monica told her that there was no need to make up the time, but she would appreciate some help with the paperwork. Francine was such a worrier and Monica knew she would be upset if she didn't make up every minute.

As they completed the paperwork, Monica asked Francine to close the door. Francine did as she was asked, then she sat down across from Monica. Monica came around the desk and sat down beside her.

"Francine, you know that we have a closed down hotel in New Jersey and a beach house, but I need to know if you were aware of any other property that the company or my mother owned in New Jersey."

"No Monica. I did know about the hotel, and the old beach house, but I have no knowledge of any other property up north, beside the other hotels of course."

"Well, apparently we own an 800-acre amusement park that has been closed for over thirty years. I'm going there during my vacation, but I don't want you to tell anyone."

Francine looked surprised enough to fall off her seat. "Why I never... I have taken care of your mother's business here for thirty years and I had no idea she owned an amusement park. I even unpacked the records as they came in from New Jersey all those years ago." Francine's voice trailed off.

"Well I didn't even know about it," Monica replied, "but I intend to find out everything that I can. I just needed to know if you had any information that could help me. I'll see you in two weeks."

Chapter Eight

Jeanette peered into the suite of rooms that had been Miss Lydia's. She heard noise upstairs when she returned home from her Saturday morning grocery shopping. Realizing that Miss Monica was now awake, Jeanette had gone up to see if Monica wanted a hot breakfast or just coffee and juice. As Jeanette neared the stairway, she realized that the noise was coming from the side of the house where Miss Lydia's rooms were located. Monica had forbidden her to go into the suite after Miss Lydia died, and Jeanette had obeyed, even though she had been sorely tempted to go into the rooms and follow her strict cleaning regimen. Miss Lydia had always insisted that everything be clean and orderly. When Miss Lydia was alive, Jeanette had cleaned the rooms twice each week. After all these years it was hard for her to know the rooms must be getting increasingly dusty.

Miss Monica was inside the suite. The drapes had finally been opened and sunlight was pouring in through the open windows as the fresh smell of the ocean drifted through the suite. There were boxes stacked everywhere and Monica was reaching into a large bucket of soapy water. She had her hair tied up in a bandana and she had on jeans and an old t-shirt.

"Miss Monica, whatever are you doing? Why do you not have me help you?"

"Good morning Jeanette, feel free to grab a cleaning rag, I won't protest."

"I have some cold items to put away from the store and I wondered if you wanted breakfast."

"No thank you. Just some coffee would be great. Why don't you bring up a fresh pot and two cups after you put away the groceries? I could use a coffee break and some company."

"I will be back with the coffee Miss Monica and then I will help you do whatever you are doing." Jeanette disappeared down the hallway.

Monica had decided to use the first day of her vacation to tackle the job of going through her mother's suite before she made the trip up the coast to Atlantic Point Park. When she had awakened around nine o'clock, she immediately donned old clothes and set about the enormous and emotional task of sorting and boxing a lifetime of her mother's possessions. By the end of the day Monica intended to have everything sorted and ready to be removed.

When Monica went to work on Friday, she had taken the pick-up truck that was kept at the estate for the gardener's weekly use. On her way home she stopped at a local discount store to obtain a hoard of used boxes to pack up her mother's personal stuff. While at the store she had also picked up some address labels, tissue paper, and packing tape for items that she intended to ship.

Monica left work Friday night with everything well caught up and a feeling of freedom, knowing that she actually would be away from her hotel ownership responsibilities for two glorious weeks. It was her first vacation in over a year. And what a year it had been, she reflected.

When Monica entered her mother's suite, she started on the massive closets that were packed with clothing and shoes. She folded item after item into the boxes, placing the hangers off to the side. Next, she carefully began wrapping the collection of shoes in tissue paper. She could have left them in their protective boxes, but they would have taken up too much space. As she closed the now empty closet doors, she heard Jeanette returning with the coffee.

"That coffee smells good Jeanette." The strong coffee aroma had already begun rejuvenating her.

"I brought you some orange juice too."

"Great, I could use some more energy."

"Miss Monica, what has come over you?"

"It's time to clean out Mother's things, Jeanette. I should have done this long ago, but I just didn't have the courage. I'm going to clean out the entire suite and then have it completely remodeled."

Jeanette looked surprised. She asked Monica what she was going to do with all of Miss Lydia's things.

"Well for one thing, I've boxed up all the shoes and clothing. The boxes are sealed, labeled and ready to be shipped. I thought that perhaps we could send them to your family in Central America, you're always commenting how they're in need of those things."

"Oh Miss Monica, you are always very good to me and to my family, just as Miss Lydia was. I am sure they will appreciate all that you send them."

"I have a man who deals in used goods coming on Monday to remove all of the furniture. Do you need anything for your apartment?"

"I need nothing. Your mother remodeled my apartment and bought me new furniture for it just two years ago, do you forget?"

"Yes, I guess I did, but if there's anything you want, feel free to take it over there."

Jeanette selected a small decorative footstool and placed it out into the hallway. Through shared memories and a mixture of tears and laughter Monica and Jeanette went through the rest of the items, Jeanette taking some things, Monica moving items to her suite of rooms and the rest of the room's contents being packed up for Jeanette's family or for local charities.

In the office area, Monica shredded the entire household records, except those for the last seven years. She might be organized like her mother was, but Monica was not a pack rat like Lydia. Lydia had saved the household records for the entire thirty years that she and Monica had lived in the house. Jeanette took some of the movies and books that had been Lydia's, as many were titles that Monica was not interested in.

The packing was nearly completed. Both Monica and Jeanette set about cleaning the thick white dust that had settled all over the rooms. When they were finished, they cleaned and waxed the furniture in preparation for the salvage man's scheduled visit on Monday. Two large trash cans were filled with discarded items and the dead plants. Monica and Jeanette started laughing as they struggled together to move the trashcans downstairs. They were clearly much heavier than they had been when they had been brought upstairs empty.

After dragging the trash cans to the outside enclosure, they returned to the suite. Jeanette began cleaning and Monica went over to Lydia's large jewelry collection. Monica knew the jewelry was insured for many thousands of dollars, but it was not the monetary value that she was interested in. The jewelry collection had been Lydia's pride and joy. She had taught Monica how to select fine jewelry from an early age. Monica had a considerable collection of her own, and she intended to combine her mother's collection with her own jewelry into one.

"Jeanette, come over and look at this." Monica was standing in front of the jewelry boxes. Jeanette walked over from where she was cleaning. "I want you to pick out some pieces that you would like to keep and that you can remember Mother wearing. Keep the items and wear them whenever you want, don't just put them away."

Jeanette had tears in her eyes as she picked out two necklaces, two rings and a broach. Seconds later Monica was wiping her eyes too. She left the suite as Jeanette began vacuuming the carpeting.

Later on Jeanette had gone out for the evening and Monica was left alone without plans. She made reservations to take Jeanette to brunch the following morning as a special thank you for her help in cleaning out the suite, and it would be a good time to share the news she had received from Horace Goldsmith about Jeanette's inheritance. Monica began remembering all the brunches that she had shared with her mother for more years than she could remember.

Freshly showered after her day of cleaning, Monica paused on her way to the kitchen to look at the oceanic print that was the focal point of the living room. It was the print that her mother had purchased in New York on their first visit to Trisha Marshall's gallery all those years ago—a lifetime ago. Once in the kitchen, Monica opened a bottle of Asti Spumante and poured herself a glass. The chilled sparkling wine was refreshing and it was a good choice to celebrate the day's accomplishments. Monica glanced at the bottle. It was one of the selections that Trish had served at an open house that Monica attended at the New York gallery. Monica liked the wine so much that she added it to her personal collection.

When Jeanette was cleaning out the suite earlier, Monica had closed the secret doors that concealed the old filing cabinets in her mother's office. She intended to go through all the files over the next couple of days, but Jeanette did not need to know.

Returning first to the living room, she placed her glass on a crystal coaster beside one of the sofas and headed up to her mother's office. When she entered the suite, it had a clean, fresh feel to it that was missing when she first entered it two days ago. It now looked like someone was moving in or out with all the boxes piled around. The room had a nice scent from the natural cleaners. Monica was glad that the difficult task was nearly finished.

She went into the office and headed to the shallow closet. The seven years of household records were sitting on the shelves where she had left them. The closet looked empty compared to this morning. Monica ran her fingers along the edge of the shelves and found the latch that allowed the units to swing freely, exposing the hidden filing cabinets.

The old cabinets looked unwilling to give up whatever secrets they held. Monica pulled her mother's key ring out of her pocket and opened the right-hand filing cabinet with the newspaper articles about Atlantic Point Park and her father's disappearance. She pulled the files with the earliest dates, 1985 through 1990, and took them down to the living room.

As she reached the living room, she turned on the lamps at the corners of the three U-shaped sofas. Shadows were announcing the arrival of dusk and a creepy feeling was settling over Monica. When she opened the files, she would learn about a chapter of her family history—a chapter that she had scant knowledge of less than a week ago. Why had her mother kept that chapter a secret from her all these years...?

She picked up her wine glass and took a long, slow sip as she opened the first file dated 1985. The headlines made bold statements:

Atlantic Point Proprietor Ronald Scott Missing

No Clues in Mysterious Disappearance

Prominent Park Owner Still Missing on European Trip

The headlines were from May of that year. They told the ongoing story of her father's disappearance. Apparently the event had garnered major attention from the local *Atlantic Point News Herald*. The story was front-page news for fourteen days straight before other news began to take precedent. Even after that it was a regular feature or second page story. The newspapers were yellowed, but in otherwise excellent condition. Monica carefully read each of the articles, but eventually focused on the last article of the original series, which provided a summary of the disappearance. The headline on that last article read:

Where is Ronald Scott?

After two weeks no new leads have surfaced in the mysterious disappearance of prominent Atlantic Point business owner Ronald Scott. Mr. Scott and his wife Lydia Scott own the famous Atlantic Point Amusement Park, as well as the Caprice Hotel, Atlantic Point, and several other hotels. Scott was reported missing by his wife after failing to return from a business trip to Germany. Lydia Scott told police that her husband had gone on the scheduled trip to visit a company that manufactures amusement rides.

Ronald Scott's Cadillac Eldorado had been found locked and abandoned at the Trenton Mercer Airport with no signs of foul play. A records search provided by Pan American Airlines at the request of the police confirmed that a ticket had been purchased in the name of Ronald Scott for a round trip to Germany, but that the ticket had never been used. Ronald Scott's luggage was found in the trunk of the Cadillac apparently fully packed and untouched. The keys to the abandoned car have not been located.

Police have questioned numerous employees from both the amusement park and the Scott's local hotel, without receiving a single successful lead. Lydia Scott was questioned extensively as she had been the last person to see her husband alive. She collapsed after questioning and had been taken to the Atlantic Point Infirmary; she was released the same day under the care of her personal physician.

Police were concerned that Lydia Scott had not heard from her husband at any time during the week that he had supposedly been in Germany. Lydia Scott indicated that, it was not unusual for Ronald to become so engrossed in his business related travels that she often did not hear from him until his return. When he did not return at the scheduled time, she had become worried and immediately notified the local police department. Police stressed that they have no suspects and that their intense questioning of Lydia Scott was routine in the case of a missing person. The regional FBI office has been notified.

The Scott family has owned Atlantic Point Park for many years. The park has been in operation since the late 1800s. Ronald Scott's father, Arthur Scott, now deceased, purchased the park during the Great Depression of the early 1930s. Until recent years, the park has been the cornerstone of Atlantic Point's tourist trade. During the past decade attendance at the business has declined. In a past interview with the Atlantic Point Herald News, Ronald Scott refused to provide actual attendance numbers.

In the 1970s the Scott family diversified into the hotel business and constructed the successful Caprice Hotel, Atlantic Point. The Scott family now owns several other hotels in resort locations.

Two years ago, in 1983, the park was the center of a local tragedy when an unsolved mishap caused the cars to derail during a pre-season test run of the park's ancient wooden roller coaster. A single park employee riding in the coaster was killed instantly when the cars derailed after cresting the first hill.

The case never made it to court. The Scott family settled the damages for an undisclosed amount. After that time, the park garnered a questionable reputation for safety and a massive public relations and marketing effort mounted by Atlantic Point Corporation had reportedly not improved attendance. Park officials, requesting anonymity, indicated that the park has been on the verge of financial collapse for several years. Ronald Scott has repeatedly denied to the press that the park was in any imminent financial danger and insisted that it remained a top tourist destination and cornerstone to the town of Atlantic Point Island.

Lydia Scott declined comment and referred all questions to her legal counsel, Horace Goldsmith of New York City. The hotel's general manager Maxwell Williams also declined our requests for an interview. Police are requesting that anyone with a lead contact them immediately.

Monica sat back and reached for her wine glass. It was so unreal to be reading about the events that were the sad history of her family. The articles continued sporadically until well into the summer of 1985. The police would receive a tip or lead that always resulted in absolutely nothing. Several more rounds of police questioning of Lydia had led nowhere and Horace Goldsmith had finally refused to allow any further questioning.

Always in the articles Monica's mother had refused comment, as did Maxwell. Monica found it unsettling. Knowing her mother as she had, she would have presumed that Lydia would have used their considerable resources to locate her father.

Monica suddenly stifled a scream. She had been so engrossed in the newspaper articles that she had not been aware of anything else. Midnight, her Labrador retriever had come up behind the sofa and licked her hand, which was hanging loosely over the back. When she realized what the wet feeling on her hand was, Monica began to laugh. Midnight came around to the front of the sofa and jumped up at Monica at which point the sleeping cats scampered off in different directions. Midnight began to "bull in" with her head. Monica knew that the dog frequently demanded her undivided attention, although they both loved the kittens too. She gently rubbed the big black dog's ears, gazing into her chocolate brown eyes. Midnight responded with a fast-paced wagging of her tail, and a continuing press for more attention.

Monica had a very uneasy feeling, most likely from reading the old newspaper articles. She got up and gently pushed Midnight's front paws back off her lap. Having the retriever there made her feel better, and so would turning on the alarm system. The temperature had been cooler than usual for a late June day in Florida and Monica had shut off the air-conditioning system so that she could air out the house, particularly her mother's suite. Now though, she would feel more secure if the house was secured and the air-conditioner and alarm system were turned back on.

As she went to each window, closing and locking each sash, the uneasy feeling continued. Monica knew the fears were only in her mind. Had anyone been in or near the house Midnight would have been barking loudly. Sometimes the dog was so defensive that when unfamiliar guests were present, Monica felt compelled to explain Midnight's aggressive behavior. The downstairs windows were finally all closed. She went upstairs and closed all the upstairs windows. In the dark of night, even with the lights turned on, the uncomfortable feeling that she had previously experienced upon entering her mother's suite returned. As quickly as she could, she closed the windows and exited the suite.

Once downstairs again, Monica armed the security system and turned on the air-conditioning. She went into the kitchen and refilled her wine glass, then resettled onto the sofa to read the remaining files from 1986 through 1990.

The May of 1986 article had announced that Atlantic Point Park would remain permanently closed and there was an extensive replay of her father's disappearance the previous year. Every year since, the newspaper had done a single article about the closed down park and her father's still unsolved disappearance. The only variation was the 1990 article marking the fifth anniversary of Ronald Scott's disappearance with one new addition: *"...he was now presumed to be dead."*

Chapter Nine

Janice Laneer awakened to an absolutely stunning Sunday morning. She paused at the mirror to admire her figure as she pulled a long robe over her negligee. She headed out to the kitchen and turned on the coffee maker, which had been readied the night before.

Janice knew Maxwell was drinking way too much ever since he left the office early on Friday. She must have fielded a dozen phone calls for him after he told her he was going to the country club. Janice told Monica he had left the office with a migraine. Then Maxwell had phoned her late Saturday night, displaying the obvious effects that too much alcohol produced. He must have continued drinking right into the next day. It seemed to be a bad pattern. She had taken the opportunity to invite Maxwell to come for dinner on Sunday night and he had accepted.

Janice intended to make her special marinara sauce. After she finished breakfast, she would prepare the fresh ingredients so they could simmer through the day. Tonight would be the last time that she would ever try to get Maxwell to start a new life with her. Janice wasn't even sure why she was still interested, but it had been the pursuit of a lifetime and it was worth one last attempt.

Janice pulled a skillet from the cabinet. She often went to brunch on Sunday when one of her male friends stayed over, but this morning she was alone and she was looking forward to a relaxing day at the condo's pool, followed later by her dinner with Maxwell. An omelet would have to do.

She cracked two eggs into a bowl and then chopped some fresh green peppers and grated some Parmesan cheese. As the omelet began to cook, Janice poured herself a glass of orange juice, opened a bottle of champagne and added a splash to the glass. By the time the omelet was done, all traces of her preparation efforts were cleaned up and the kitchen was returned to spotless condition.

The omelet slipped gently out of the non-stick pan onto a crystal plate. Janice put the dirty pan immediately into the dishwasher, and using a tray, carried the omelet, coffee and mimosa out to the main balcony overlooking the pool. She glanced around the kitchen to make sure that all was in order. You could never have too much attention to detail.

It was warm on the balcony, but it felt relaxing. She took a sip of the mimosa and a bite of the omelet. The kitchen wasn't all that Janice was getting in order. Between incoming calls for Maxwell on Friday, she had managed to call her shady financial manager and had him move the majority of her holdings, now worth about $3 million to an overseas account. Then she phoned a real estate agent to put her condominium on the market. Selling the condominium should net her another million or more. Things would move rapidly now. She had to have everything in order and be ready for her final performance when the time came.

Monica looked across the table at Jeanette. They were dining at the *Americana*. The restaurant had a busy brunch that always included some sort of live entertainment that moved from table to table. The mood was festive inside the airy restaurant and Jeanette looked beautiful. Monica always wondered why she had never taken up her mother's offer to attend business school, after which she would have been able to work at a professional job in the hotel company, but Jeanette had preferred the simple life that was entailed in running the Scott household. Today she was in a red dress and she had worn the broach Monica had given her from Lydia's collection.

They each got food from the various buffet stations and they became quiet as they began to eat. Monica wanted to tell Jeanette about the trust fund that Lydia had left for her in the will. Monica was not surprised when Horace told her that Lydia had left a sizeable trust for Jeanette. Jeanette would be the one that was surprised. She never expected to be given anything. How pleased she would be with the unexpected inheritance.

Monica and Jeanette made several more trips to the food stations and had several more glasses of the free-flowing champagne. The ever-observant service staff was constantly topping off their glasses. Now over coffee, Monica prepared herself to surprise Jeanette with the exciting news.

"Jeanette, I have some very good news for you!"

"Oh Monica, before you say anything, I want to thank you for this delicious

brunch, which I have enjoyed very much."

"Well, I have even better news than that. Mother has left a trust fund for you. Horace told me last week when I went to New York.

Jeanette looked perplexed but remained quiet.

"The trust is for $500,000."

Jeanette gasped.

"Horace explained that Mother set up the fund so the money would provide an ongoing income for you if you let it remain intact. Of course, the decision of what you do with it is entirely up to you."

Jeanette was overwhelmed with emotion and began to cry softy. Several people from surrounding tables looked at them to see if everything was all right. When Jeanette wiped the tears from her eyes and began to smile, their stares disappeared.

Monica squeezed Jeanette's arm, then hugged her.

Jeanette seemed unable to say anything, but finally said "Many years ago I came here with nothing to start a new life in America. Your mother gave me my first job. Back then I barely spoke any English. Your mother always treated me with respect. Never did she make me feel like an outsider or just a housemaid. Never though did I expect this from her. I am so very grateful to her and to you Monica. I always loved Lydia, she became my American family, and I feel the same way about you too."

"Just think Jeanette, you don't have to work anymore and you can go anywhere. The thought of your leaving makes me very sad, because you are my family too. Will you promise to visit me often?"

Jeanette looked surprised. "Monica I am not leaving. I have no intention of quitting my responsibilities to you. I intend to visit my family, perhaps for a while, but I will never move back there. This is my home now."

Monica looked visibly relieved. The thought of Jeanette leaving left another empty spot inside her. Monica began to laugh. "I'm glad you've decided to stay. I was afraid I would have to carry all those boxes down from mother's suite by myself."

They both began to laugh. "I will help you Monica, even though I am now very rich."

They walked out of the restaurant into the beautiful Florida day.

Maxwell Williams was trying to decide whether he should open a bottle of champagne this early on a Sunday. He was beginning to feel that he might have a problem with the amount of alcohol he was consuming. He didn't need that with all his other problems. Maxwell decided to wait until he was at Janice's that evening. Janice was a phenomenal cook. He knew that she would have the perfect entrée with the perfect wine. Through the years he had dinner and drinks with Janice many times.

Maxwell always knew that Janice was in love with him, even after he had turned her away on more occasions than he could count. There was that one time that he had let his guard down and they had been together, but that was long ago and he had made it clear to her that it would never happen again. Maxwell liked having her around; she was always there for him at the office, when he needed someone to talk with or when he was lonely. He supposed that he was as much to blame as Janice for her ongoing pursuit of him. The only problem was that he was not in love with her.

Maxwell always loved Lydia. He had from the day that Ronald Scott introduced her to him back when they all worked at Atlantic Point Park. Lydia though, had loved Ronald. That was until all the financial problems started. The park was losing money and Ronald and Lydia, by then married, began fighting for the first time. She wanted to get rid of the park and move to a warm southern state.

With the success of the hotels, which Maxwell ran, they could afford to go anywhere. Ronald was adamant that he would not give up on the park, which was the family's legacy. As the financial picture worsened, so did their fighting. Then unexpectedly, Lydia turned to Maxwell.

She had stopped over at the hotel one evening, explaining that she needed a friend to confide in. They went to a local bar and sat for hours gazing out toward the ocean. Lydia poured out her problems and her unhappiness to Maxwell. Then Lydia had left all alone. Maxwell had gone home to his apartment. How surprised and pleased he was when she appeared at the apartment just a few minutes later and then spent the night together. Lydia explained that Ronald was on one of his numerous trips and she was tired of being lonely. Maxwell was infatuated. Now that he had her, he would do anything to keep her. Their affair had gone on for a long time—until Ronald found out about it.

With Jeanette safely tucked away in her apartment, Monica decided to read the rest of the files that she had not finished the night before. She went up to her mother's suite. By now the feeling of uneasiness that had accompanied her when going into the suite had disappeared. In just one more day all the boxes would be gone. She headed back to the office and opened the false shelves. She had not locked the filing cabinet last night when she put away the earliest files. Monica pulled the files from years

1991 through 2005. The files from these years were not nearly as full as the first five years. She lugged them down to the living room.

Lydia had apparently had the *Atlantic Point Herald News* mailed to her at a Palm Beach post office box for all the years since she had moved to Florida. Each newspaper had a small white mailing sticker attached to the upper right side. Only those newspapers with articles about the park or her father had been saved in the files. Monica wondered if the papers had been piling up there for the past seven months or if the subscription had lapsed. Her mother's death had made news in Atlantic Point, particularly since it had occurred there and added to the mystery of Ronald's disappearance. Monica made a mental note to find out about the status of the subscription and the post office box.

In 1991 the paper had published the first news about an offer to sell the park:

New Jersey Developer Makes $5 Million Offer for Atlantic Point Park

Once again, Lydia Scott had been unavailable for comment and a spokesperson from Horace Goldsmith, Esquire and Associates, had declined the offer without explanation.

Sporadically through the years there were articles about various parties that were interested in reopening the park or redeveloping the land. Several articles were quite critical of Lydia Scott and her failure to sell or redevelop the property.

In 1995 there were extensive articles marking the 10th anniversary of the park's closure and of her father's disappearance. In 2005 the 20th year anniversary of the mystery was highlighted. Monica shivered as she wondered what had ever happened to her father. She had always blindly accepted her mother's standard explanation that he disappeared on a business trip. Through the years, Lydia had told Monica that she had used every means at her considerable disposal to locate Monica's father. The articles seemed to contradict Lydia's standard explanations. Not once had Monica read about any public effort on her mother's part to locate her missing father.

Monica trudged back up the stairs with the files. She had more questions than answers. Carefully she replaced the files in their appropriate order. She gathered the last ten years of files from 2006 to the present. Funny, these files seemed heavier than the files covering the past fifteen years.

When Monica reached the living room, the reason for the added weight became obvious. Articles in 2015 not only marked the 30th year anniversary, but also took time to present the mystery to a whole new generation of readers over a daily series of articles. In 2006, and thereafter, there were also regular articles on the Atlantic Point township council's efforts to press Lydia to sell or redevelop the park. Through Horace Goldsmith, she had continued to decline to sell the property without comment. As the township pressed harder, she agreed to do studies on re-opening the park. Each time the feasibility studies showed the park would not be profitable, and she had declined to reopen it.

Monica considered that Atlantic Point must be very isolated, as the stories had never reached her in Florida. Of course, a closed down amusement park and a 30-year-old disappearance wasn't national news after so much time.

Finally, the last article made Monica pause to take a breath. The article was dated November 1, 2015, just weeks before her mother's death:

Atlantic Point Township Council Threatens to Confiscate Atlantic Point Park for Town Redevelopment Project

The article explained how the council, using their right of eminent domain could confiscate the park to enhance efforts to redevelop the town. The mayor had observed that for years, the park's owner Atlantic Point Corporation had refused to work with the township to sell or re-open the park. The mayor commented that Atlantic Point Park was blight on the town and the reason for the town's "has been" status.

For the first time, Atlantic Point Corporation's owner, Lydia Scott, had agreed to address the township council's concerns regarding the park in person. Horace Goldsmith, the firm's legal council had commented that Lydia would work with the council to provide a resolution, but that any attempt to confiscate the park through eminent domain would prove very costly to a township that did not have a lot of money. Horace had reiterated that it was his hope that legal actions could be avoided.

Maxwell knocked gently on Janice's front door and then he tried the knob. She had left it unlocked for him.

"Come in, come in," Janice called cheerily from the balcony.

"I bring you flowers, lovely lady."

"Why thank you kind sir. I have made us a feast to remember, but first let's go out on the balcony and enjoy some chilled martinis."

Maxwell followed Janice through the living room and through the sliding glass doors to the balcony overlooking the pool. He thought that tonight, Janice looked fantastic. She had on a short summer dress that left one shoulder bare. The dress tied at her waist with a matching fabric belt. As usual, it was just enough to be seductive. Her dark red tinted hair flowed down around her shoulders and she had on wedged sandals.

A wave of sadness passed over Maxwell as he realized that perhaps he and Janice could have had a good life together, but his past still haunted him. It was as much his dark past as his undying love for Lydia.

The two of them sipped the martinis and Janice began to broach the subject of what was bothering Maxwell lately. She expressed concern that his health appeared to be declining and asked what she could do to help him.

"The pressures of the past year have been very great. First with Lydia's death and then trying to keep the hotels going, all while trying to train Monica. It's just been too much. I guess I'm not as young as I used to be."

"Maxwell, you are still young. Age is in the mind. It affects the body when you allow it to, and you *have* been allowing it to. Have you considered leaving Caprice, maybe starting something new, seeing the world, lying on a beach?"

"I've devoted my life to that company Janice, it's hard to just give it up."

"There comes a time for change Maxwell. I've known you and worked with you for 30 years. The time for a change has arrived."

"If you only knew Janice, if you only knew."

But Janice did know. She was a master at collecting bits and pieces of information, and then taking the pieces and putting them together like a puzzle. She had collected information from Maxwell for 30 years. He always had too much to drink, and when he did, he let pieces of information slip. Janice had collected those pieces one by one. She knew about Maxwell's early affair with Ronald Scott's wife, she knew about Atlantic Point Park, and she had even pieced together that Maxwell and Lydia had something to do with Ronald Scott's disappearance. On the disappearance though, she didn't have all the information. But she had enough.

"Let's go into the dining room and we'll enjoy the feast that I have prepared for us."

First, Janice served a salad with organic mixed greens and her wine selection was a soft merlot. Imported spinach pasta covered with a slow simmered marinara sauce peppered with mushrooms and seasonings that she made from scratch followed the salads. Dessert was chocolate mousse and a rich, dark Columbian coffee.

Finally they adjourned to the living room for after dinner drinks. The lighting was low and romantic, as was the setting. Candles burned gently and a light vanilla scent accented the air. When they were comfortably seated just inches apart, Janice put her hand on Maxwell's knee and asked Maxwell the question that would decide her future plans.

"Maxwell, I want you to leave Caprice and join me in a new life, a life as a couple, sharing every day and every night. Waking up together. Seeing all that the world has to offer. It's not too late."

She held her breath as she waited for his reply. She had asked this question to him more times and in more ways than she could remember. This would be the final time.

"You know I can't do that Janice; I can't just give up on all that I have worked for at Caprice. I've spent a lifetime building that company. I know I should give it up and retire, but I can't bring myself to do it. I love the hotel business and I will never get this opportunity again at my age."

Janice held in the tears. She wouldn't let him see her cry. She had never let him see her cry. Maybe she should have. Tomorrow would be her last day at Caprice Hotels after more than 30 years. Thirty years wasted waiting for Maxwell Williams. She would start a new life, but first she would get all that she was due for the years she wasted as life had passed her by.

Maxwell left shortly thereafter, gently closing the front door behind him and leaving Janice alone as he always did. Janice walked to the balcony with her drink and gazed down many floors to the deserted pool, primping her hair as the breeze pushed it away from her line of vision. She stood, looking seductive as she glimpsed Maxwell leaving the complex. Janice had tears in her eyes. She hurled the wine glass over the balcony and watched as it shattered on the cement below. Yes, it was time to start anew, but she had one last thing to take care of.

Chapter Ten

Brad Roberts pressed the weights even harder. Sweat poured off him as his workout was nearing the two-hour point. Soon, it would soon be time to finish up with a run on the treadmill after which he would head home to get ready for his dinner with Monica.

Brad had worked at the hotel offices through Saturday so that he could take off Monday. That was one thing he really liked about working at Caprice —nobody bothered you as long as you did your job and did it well. Monica and Maxwell never complained about someone taking a weekday off, and Lydia had been the same way. A wave of sadness washed over Brad as his thoughts turned to Lydia. She had been Brad's employer for a long time, given him the promotion to his executive role and she had provided him with a very large paycheck. Maxwell had gone along with the promotion as well. It was a lot of money and responsibility for someone as young as Brad.

In retrospect, it was probably the thing that saved the company from being taken over after Lydia died. Brad doubled the company's profitability and later improved it even further, not that it had done badly before his arrival—it was just that he had done even better. Then, when the unexpected happened, the company was well prepared to continue financially until the dust settled. All too many companies fail after a founding owner dies, but Caprice Hotels Corporation had been able to continue.

Another thing that he liked about working at Caprice was that as he and Monica had gone through their "make-up and break-up" routine, it had never impacted his job. Lydia, Maxwell and even Monica had treated him the same as they always did, although admittedly he had avoided Monica after he found out about her affair with Drake Donovan.

Brad put the weights back on the rack and then headed over to the treadmill. Setting it for a brisk pace, he began to jog, setting his thoughts on tonight. Brad decided that he would stop and get Monica a bouquet of flowers on his way home. There was a little store in a strip shopping center he would pass along the way. Brad edged up the speed on the treadmill and wondered what in the world was going on with Monica.

Maxwell Williams was still worried. You could feel the tension in the air around the office. Janice was showing her typically self-assured personality, yet he felt that something about her had changed and he couldn't quite put his finger on just what. He had turned down her attempts at romance on many occasions, so it couldn't be that. Today, she just seemed even more aloof and smug than ever before.

Francine Crowley was doubly busy with Monica being on vacation and Maxwell knew that he would have to give her a hand sooner or later. Other than that, nothing seemed to be amiss, still he couldn't shake the feeling that everything in his world was about to change.

Maxwell decided that he would get Monica to turn Atlantic Point Park into a mixed-use resort with shopping, condominiums and entertainment complex; maybe even rebuild the first hotel. This would satisfy the township since there was no way that he could allow the ancient amusement park to be sold. It might even turn out to be profitable. He would propose that they use the oversized office building for a museum about the park and its history—just so they didn't tear it down. A wave of nausea swept over Maxwell at the thought of returning to Atlantic Point. He thought the ordeal was finally over when he and Lydia moved to Florida, but now it was starting again after all these years.

Maxwell had to find out what Monica was up to. Not only did Monica look like her mother, she acted like her too. This meant that she was probably going to be nosing around Atlantic Point Park sooner or later. Maxwell had never been given a set of keys to the Atlantic Point office building. Lydia had taken up the job of overseeing the packing of files and the moving of their offices to Florida. Lydia was detail oriented, but who knew what she might have left behind all those years ago.

Maxwell would have to find a way into that building. The problem was that Lydia had built it like a fortress. He couldn't break in even if he had an army. He should have gone through the box that the New Jersey police had given to him. He suspected that Lydia might have gone to the park on her fateful trip to New Jersey, but he had no way to know for sure. Maxwell was too shaken at the time to think about such things and he knew it would look suspicious if the police packing seal had been broken on the box when he returned it to Monica.

Maxwell was startled back to the present when Francine poked her head into his office to tell him that when Monica phoned in earlier that morning and stated that she would not be leaving for vacation until the next day. Good. That would give him time.

Glancing at his cell phone for the number, Maxwell dialed the caller from his desk phone. The number was for a private investigator he had used when one of the hotels was having some unexplained thefts.

The phone was picked up on the third ring, Spaulding Investigations.

"This is Maxwell Williams calling for Randall Spaulding."

"One moment please, I'll see if he's available." The phone clicked onto hold.

Dead silence. Apparently Spaulding Investigations did not believe in providing music while you waited to see if they were available.

"Randall Spaulding here Mr. Williams, what can I do for you?"

"I need you to keep an eye on someone for me."

"Not a problem. I'll need a name, address and a picture. I presume this is a confidential surveillance, will you need any photographic evidence?"

"None whatsoever, I just want to know where the person goes for the next two weeks."

"Will do."

Maxwell scanned the information to Randall Spaulding with Monica's name, address and a recent photograph of her. As he studied the picture, he reflected again how much she looked like a younger version of Lydia.

Jeanette chopped vegetables while Monica pulled out the soup pot and spices. They were preparing a rich, thick, vegetarian soup for Monica's dinner with Brad tonight. He was such a particular eater. Healthy, healthy, healthy. The soup would be followed with wild caught salmon, flame grilled outside and served with wild rice and asparagus, sans hollandaise sauce. Brad would not eat anything that contained fat. Dessert would be fresh fruit served in oversized, wide champagne glasses with a dollop of fat free whipped topping. At least Brad would drink red wine, which he considered to be healthy, or maybe an imported beer.

Monica was excited as she set about helping Jeanette prepare the dinner. Tomorrow she would be leaving for Atlantic Point. Maybe she could convince Brad to come with her. Monica had made up her mind to drive the long distance to Atlantic Point Island, New Jersey. She planned on taking her new Mustang since it had a convertible top. The high-powered Mustang was her one concession to fun, outweighing her ongoing environmental concerns. The car was purchased mainly for weekend use, and the thought of being on the open road with no time constraints or preset plans was exhilarating.

Maybe she should hire someone to assist Maxwell in running the hotels and she could just travel forever. What a thought, but she just couldn't do that. Her mother had raised her to be too responsible for a life of leisure. Still, the thought was nice.

Just then the doorbell rang, startling her back to reality. Jeanette went to answer it and called back to Monica that a driver from the shipping company had arrived for the boxes. After hustling Star and Swirl into

Monica's suite, Jeanette put Midnight out in the fenced-in part of the yard to keep her from scaring off the driver. She was barking and growling, and her hair was standing up. It was all Jeanette could do to get her into the secured yard.

There were a considerable number of boxes and the man began to move them out to his delivery truck. Monica and Jeanette had stacked them on the floor in the living room. Before he was finished, the representative from the charity to which Monica was donating all the other items arrived and Monica showed him up to the suite. Since she was donating the items, she figured the rep could carry them downstairs. Monica and Jeanette were already drained from carrying down the boxes that were being shipped to Central America.

Just one hour later, with tonight's meal readied for cooking, the doorbell rang yet again. The used furniture dealer arrived along with two burly movers. The movers hovered outside by their truck while Monica and the dealer went up and settled on a price for the bedroom and office furniture in her mother's suite. The man offered her $500 and Monica accepted the man's check for payment. She figured they would turn around and sell the bedroom set for several thousand dollars, but she just wanted it to be gone. An hour later, the movers were finished.

Monica and Jeanette looked around the now empty suite. They couldn't help but feel sadness and emptiness. Jeanette commented, "Lydia was a wonderful person Monica. I miss her every day."

Without a single word, Monica answered Jeanette with a hug. With tears in her eyes, she turned to go down the hallway to her own suite. Thank goodness Jeanette was here to help her through this terrible ordeal. Pushing her sadness aside, Monica prepared to Brad's arrival.

Janice waited until Francine and Maxwell had left for the day. She would type her letter of resignation when everyone was gone. Brief and to the point. They didn't deserve more. Earlier, Janice had the housekeeping department from the adjoining hotel bring her two decent sized boxes. She had been removing her personal items for weeks and no one had noticed. Of course, she had left enough behind so that no one should have noticed, which is why she needed the boxes now to gather what remained.

She began typing:

Dear Maxwell Williams:

I am concluding my employment with Caprice Hotels Corporation effective today. My final paycheck should include all accrued vacation, per company policy. Additionally, my pension account should be settled and transferred to Metro Investments, L.P. I have filled out the required authorization, which is attached. I will no longer be in the area and do not wish to be contacted for any reason in the future. Please direct any future correspondence to my legal counsel, Vance Richards, Esquire.

Sincerely,
Janice Laneer

One paragraph to sum up more than 30 years of employment. They didn't even deserve that! Janice looked around the office that she had spent so many years working in, yet she did not feel even an ounce of sadness as she prepared to depart. She would not have to spend one more miserable day here. The weight of the world was lifting off her shoulders, and very soon, she would start a whole new life. Just one more thing to take care of—a fitting finale for all she had endured.

Janice phoned the front desk and had the staff send up a bellman to carry the two filled boxes to her car. Janice wasn't about to carry them down herself. She ran the envelope sealer over the edge of the envelope to wet the glue. Her long, red fingernail glided smoothly over the flap, sealing the envelope—and her plans for revenge.

Janice placed the resignation on Maxwell's desk, then closed and locked his office door as she always did. Every bit of work on her desk was filed. She had left nothing unfinished. All that was visible was a blotter style calendar, a telephone and a flat screen computer. On the calendar, on today's date, she wrote, "Janice's last day." With a smirk, she turned off the light, her red hair swirled as she turned and exited the offices for the last time, never looking behind her for even a moment.

Brad rang the doorbell at five minutes to seven. He had no trouble getting past the gated entrance to the development. Monica must have tipped off the guard ahead of time that he would be coming.

Jeanette and Midnight answered the door together. Jeanette greeted him with a big smile and a "Good evening Mr. Brad." Midnight greeted him by wagging her thick black tail and pushing her nose against his hand. It was obvious that the dog was friendly to those she liked. The twin kittens appeared from behind the sofa minutes later, curiously peeking around the furniture to see who the guest was.

"Miss Monica will be down in a moment; may I get you something to drink?"

"Good evening to you Jeanette. I think I'll wait for Monica. How have you been? I haven't seen you for such a long time."

"I am fine Mr. Brad, you must come over more often, even if you are not speaking to Miss Monica."

Brad could not suppress an unexpected laugh at Jeanette's blunt recommendation. Perhaps he would have to try Jeanette's advice the next time he and Monica were avoiding each other.

Jeanette turned and headed out to the kitchen, telling Brad to get comfortable as she left the room. Brad went over and sat down on the sectional sofa. Midnight followed him, settling herself on the thick carpet under the oceanic painting. Brad was still holding the flower arrangement he had picked up for Monica.

Monica called down from upstairs, "Hi Brad, be down in a minute. Have Jeanette get you a drink or help yourself."

Brad went over to the wet freezer and grabbed a frosted beer glass and selected an imported beer from the bar's well stocked selection. He took the liberty to pour a glass of the chilling white wine that he knew was Monica's, and he greeted her with it as she came into the living room.

Both Monica and Brad had dressed in casual attire for the evening as this was not their first date and neither of them had anything to prove to each other. Either they would re-establish their relationship or they wouldn't—time would tell.

Brad gave Monica the flowers. She was surprised by the unexpected gift and kissed him on the cheek. After placing them in water and sitting them on the center of the dining room table, they settled onto the sofa. They shared some small talk and Monica started into the story about her unexpected inheritance and the mystery surrounding Atlantic Point Park. With Brad, she wouldn't hold back any details. It felt good to be able to trust someone at this point, and Monica did trust Brad.

Brad listened intently as he always did. He would get all the facts and make an assessment before he drew any conclusions or made even one comment. After Monica finished with the incredible story, he sat back on the sofa and took a long drink of his beer. He replied with one word, "Unbelievable!"

Monica looked at him, waiting for more. Brad asked her several questions about the park, and in the direct manner in which he addressed all business problems, he came right to the point, "What do you think Lydia and Maxwell are hiding up there."

"I don't know, but I'm going to find out."

"I guess that answers the question of what this unexplained tax assessment is for."

"I think that Mother used to pay all the Atlantic Point Park taxes out of her personal accounts here at the house. I found a hidden closet full of old newspaper articles on the park as well as a bunch of household records. I'll bet if we look through the records, we'll find tax payments on the park."

"I wonder how the tax assessment got forwarded to me at the hotel offices."

Monica thought for a moment, and then remembered the post office box. "Mother maintained a private post office box here in Palm Beach. I found out from some mailing labels on the old newspapers stored in the files. My guess is that when the annual fee was not paid on the box, the tax office forwarded the returned assessment to her corporate address. Since Mother isn't at the hotel anymore all financial documents are sent to your office and the other mail comes to me."

Brad picked up the tax assessment, which he had placed on the glass coffee table in the center of the sofas. He handed it to Monica and she looked at it without delay. Just as she suspected, the tax bill now had penalties and interest for non-payment. "Brad, look how much this tax assessment is for!"

Brad had already looked at the assessment and knew. Lydia had been paying $250,000 each year in taxes on the closed down Atlantic Point Park. "Unbelievable."

Jeanette came into the room and announced that the first course of the dinner was ready to be served. Brad and Monica headed out to the dining room. Jeanette served the courses in an efficient manner, but never hurriedly. Brad ate hungrily, obviously pleased at the meal selection, but all Monica did was pick at her food.

"Monica, how long has the park been in your family?"

"It's been in our family since the 1930s. My grandfather purchased it. It's been closed since the end of 1985, the same year my father disappeared. Mother operated it one last summer, then moved here."

"So your mother has been paying roughly $250,000 of taxes on a closed down amusement park for 30 years?"

"It would seem so, Brad."

"Did she ever try to sell it?"

"There were many offers, one was listed in the newspapers for $5 million, but Mother turned it down."

"Lydia continued to pay all that tax money when she had ongoing offers to sell the park. It just doesn't make any sense."

"Not to me either. That's why I'm going there tomorrow to see for myself what is in that old park. I want you to go with me."

"What about the hotels?"

"You have an assistant, and in a way, this is company business. I just don't want Maxwell or anyone else except Jeanette to know about our trip."

"You don't want Maxwell to know? He's the president of the company."

"There's something he's not telling me Brad. Maxwell kept this a secret, along with my mother. He told me not to sell the park until he talked to me."

The conversation was interrupted as Jeanette served steaming coffee from a sterling silver decanter. After she left the room, Monica and Brad continued to discuss Atlantic Point Park. They made plans to leave early the next day for the long drive up the coast. Brad would meet Monica at the house around eight in the morning for one of Jeanette's oversized breakfasts and they would leave around nine.

Before he left, Monica took Brad upstairs to show him the hidden storage closet. Brad looked at the old household records, which were still stacked on the shelves where Monica had left them. He located Lydia's annual tax payments on the park, confirming their theory. Glancing at his chronograph, Brad realized that he better get going so he could get ready for their unexpected trip the next day. He paused just long enough at the front door to kiss Monica good night.

Chapter Eleven

Monica started the Mustang and the engine roared to life, then settled into a deep throated rumble. Glancing over her shoulder, she backed the car out of the oversized garage. Monica and her mother each had two personal vehicles and the garage was large enough to accommodate all of them, plus a truck for grounds maintenance. There was one empty slot where Lydia's Jaguar had always been parked. The absence of the car was a grim reminder of why Monica was going to Atlantic Point Island.

Brad pulled his dark blue Honda into the now empty spot that the Mustang had occupied. He jumped out of the car and joined Monica in the convertible. Monica paused until the automatic garage door locked back into place, then drove the car up the driveway and parked close to the house. They both climbed out and headed inside to enjoy one of Jeanette's breakfasts before setting off on their trip.

Jeanette had outdone herself as usual, and for once Brad ate some of the foods that he always deprived himself of. Jeanette had prepared omelets with melted cheese, hash browned potatoes, and mounds of pancakes with butter. The fresh smell of coffee permeated the room and there was a pitcher of freshly squeezed orange juice. The buffet appeared to have enough food to feed a convention at one of the hotels.

Jeanette was insistent that they enjoy multiple heaping plates of her cuisine. "I want that you both have a good breakfast for the start of your trip. Mr. Brad, you can eat this food since you are on vacation this week."

"Jeanette, I wouldn't think of skipping your breakfast even if it means twenty more hours in the gym, but you're right; I'm on vacation and I'm going to enjoy myself."

"Monica, you put more food on your plate! You have not been eating well. You think that I do not notice, but I always do."

"I just have a lot on my mind," Monica rolled her eyes toward Jeanette as she headed back over to the buffet table and added more food to her plate. By the time she sat back down, Brad was getting ready for seconds.

The kittens were busy chasing each other through the dining room and living room in a mad dash of youthful excitement. Midnight strolled into the kitchen in search of handouts and she found that Brad and Monica were willing participants in her quest for treats.

"Midnight, you stop looking for more food," Jeanette exclaimed! "I gave you a big breakfast already."

Midnight just looked at Jeanette with her big brown eyes and wagged her tail. She was not about to give up in her efforts to get some more table scraps.

Monica leaned over and gave her dog a hug. "I'm going to miss you. You be a good girl for Jeanette while I'm gone." Second later the kittens appeared and each received a goodbye hug from Monica, as they wriggled back to their chasing game.

Brad passed Midnight a half slice of unbuttered bread before Jeanette shooed her out the back door exclaiming that the dog was going to get too fat from the handouts. Monica and Brad laughed as they got up from the table and began to help Jeanette clean up.

"You two just leave this here and start your vacation. I have plenty of time to clean up, and nothing more to do while you are away."

"Jeanette, I am going to help clean up, a few more minutes won't make any difference to our vacation," Monica responded.

"You both go now and have a nice time and come back happy together. I will be waiting for a postcard from wherever you are visiting."

Monica felt a guilty pang about not yet telling Jeanette where she and Brad were going and why. "Jeanette, mother left some unfinished business in New Jersey. We're going there to take care of it. I didn't want you to worry, but I think that you should know this is not a vacation."

"Monica, I had a feeling that sooner or later you would be going to New Jersey. You take care of yourself and Mr. Brad too. Miss Lydia died in New Jersey. Where you are going is a bad place. I know."

Monica felt a chill run up her spine. Brad just stood beside her with a perplexed look on his face. "Jeanette, is there something more that you know about mother's last trip to New Jersey?"

"I know nothing Monica or I would tell you. But I do know that the place where Miss Lydia died is a bad place. Last November, I went into Miss Lydia's suite before she made her last trip there. She was in the office. Miss Lydia had many newspaper articles spread all over the desk and she was crying. I asked her what is wrong. Miss Lydia said that she had to go to New Jersey and that she did not want to go there.

120

I tell her, "Do not go," but she said that she had to. I did not look what the newspaper articles say, but they were very old and yellow. I gave Miss Lydia her tea and she sent me on my way. Very bad feelings came over me, and then Miss Lydia died after going to that place. Monica, you and Mr. Brad must be very careful."

After a quick glance toward Brad, Monica put her arms around Jeanette and told her she had nothing to worry about. Monica promised they would both be careful. Brad gave Jeanette a hug too. By this time Midnight, Star and Swirl had found their way back into the kitchen and Monica gave then each another goodbye hug. Midnight went over and put her paw on Brad's leg. He bent down and gave the dog a strong embrace while he told her to take care of Jeanette.

Monica and Brad picked up their luggage and headed out the door. Monica pressed the "trunk open" button on her key fob and the trunk popped up. Brad arranged the suitcases in the small trunk and pushed the lid shut. He headed for the driver's side, but Monica said that she wanted to drive so he went around to the passenger door. It was going to be a hot day, but Monica lowered the convertible top anyway, commenting that she wanted to enjoy the fresh air. They waved goodbye to Jeanette who was standing in the driveway holding Midnight on a leash so she wouldn't chase the car, as she was previously known to do.

Monica pulled onto the boulevard and headed toward the guardhouse. She waved to the guard as the car passed through the security checkpoint. Monica stopped at the entrance to the main street and then pulled out into the light traffic. She had looked up general driving directions on the internet after Brad left last night. They would need to head west for a while until they reached Interstate 95 north. They would stay on 95 north until they reached New Jersey. Monica flipped on the Mustang's GPS and as the screen began to glow. They engine rumbled powerfully as they started their adventure.

The warm air and Brad's company relaxed Monica. Brad was commenting about the great weather and looking forward to spending time on a northern beach that just might have a boardwalk. Monica and Brad were both so distracted that neither one of them noticed the two non-descript vehicles that merged into the traffic behind them as they exited Monica's development.

Maxwell Williams came into the office around nine o'clock. Janice was not at her desk and Francine Crowley was busy with a stack of files, the phone pressed to her ear and several more lines blinking. Where the heck was Janice? As Maxwell walked past Janice's desk, he noticed that it was empty except for the desk calendar and the telephone. As Maxwell looked around the office, he noticed that all of Janice's personal items were gone as well. A bad feeling settled over him as he unlocked his office and headed for the desk. There was a letter propped up against his phone.

Maxwell had a feeling this was not going to be a good day. He opened the letter that Janice had left the night before. After reading it, he sighed and sat back in the oversized office chair. Could anything else go wrong in his life? First Lydia's death, then Monica's finding out about Atlantic Point Park, now Janice's resignation. Well that was one thing that he could fix. He would offer her any amount of money to get her to return. Janice liked money and Maxwell needed her to stay on as his assistant. He had always confided in her, but he also had a feeling that she knew a lot more than she let on.

Whenever they had gone out drinking, it was Maxwell who inevitably had too many drinks while Janice limited herself to one or two. In all the years that Maxwell had known Janice, he had never seen her lose the cool and aloof demeanor that she presented to the world. Maxwell on the other hand had spilled out his secrets to her one by one after too many drinks.

As he dialed Janice's number it began to dawn on him this time something was different. Janice had never even threatened to quit before, let alone packed up her things. The phone connected but did not ring. Instead the sound that he was dreading reached his ear, *"This number is no longer in service."*

In a near panic, Maxwell ran into the outer office. Francine had the phones under control. She asked him if Janice had resigned. Maxwell said that he didn't know but that he intended to find out. What he wasn't aware of was that Francine had already tried Janice's number after she observed the notation Janice left on the desk calendar. Francine received the same phone message that Maxwell received just minutes before when she tried Janice's line. Francine knew Janice was gone forever.

Maxwell raced out of the building to his car and then sped over to Janice's condominium. He hurried to the elevator and was huffing and puffing by the time he reached it. So much for the days when he could run a marathon. Maxwell was reminded once again that he was not the man he used to be. Carrying around a dreadful secret tended to age you.

What was taking the elevator so long? Maxwell considered running up the stairs but realized that he might not make it. Sweat was pouring off him. His heart felt like it would pound out of his chest. Was this what a heart attack felt like?

The elevator doors slid open. He punched the number for Janice's floor and the elevator doors slid closed again. He was alone as he rode up. When the doors re-opened, he was at Janice's floor. He walked down the corridor as fast as he could. Maxwell spotted Janice's door. Somehow the numbers on the door seemed to blur in and out of focus as he reached first for the buzzer and then began to pound with his fist. No one from the nearby condominiums came out into the corridor despite the loud commotion.

No one answered. Maxwell's hand was shaking as he pulled his key out and opened the door. Janice had given him the house key for emergencies many years ago. The door swung open. Maxwell's mouth dropped open as he gazed around the living room. It had been emptied to the bare walls and was as spotlessly clean as new construction. He walked from room to room and found more of the same. As he approached the kitchen, he decided to open the cabinets, as if finding something there would somehow prove that Janice was still around. Maxwell was only able to open one cabinet door before the pain in his chest became too great and he slumped to the floor gasping for breath.

Francine Crowley had had enough. Monica taking a deserved vacation was one thing, but now Brad was gone, Janice had resigned, and Maxwell had just run out of the office in a panic. Too bad Janice hadn't left years ago was the thought that came to Francine's mind. Janice might have been efficient, but Francine never trusted her. Now she was gone. Francine had a bad feeling about the sudden disappearing act. Janice had access to vast amounts of confidential information. She could harm Caprice Hotels if she went to a competitor. Maybe she had just decided to retire. But if she had retired, why not give the company notice? Francine just shook her head. She had enough to do without trying to figure out what Janice Laneer was up to.

Just then the front desk brought up the mail that would need to be distributed into the individual department heads. The mail was packed in a large white postal box. Francine began to sort the mail and found that the simple task relaxed her. She was extra busy with everyone gone from the office, but it was more than hard work causing the tension she felt. The unspoken feeling of apprehension was greater than at any other time in all the years that she had worked in Caprice's corporate office. Francine was going to have a long talk with Monica when she returned from vacation. As Francine neared the bottom of the mail pile, she noticed two unusual letters.

What caught her attention was that they were identical in every aspect, but they were not commercial advertisements and they did not have a cancelled postage stamp. The envelopes were a dark charcoal color that made it difficult to read the addressee. Neither envelope had a return address. There was just one difference between the two envelopes: one was addressed to Monica Scott and one was addressed to Maxwell Williams. It was not unusual to receive individual letters from guests expressing concerns as well as compliments, nor was it unusual to receive identical advertisements addressed to different staff members. What was unusual was receiving identical personalized letters with no return address or cancelled postage. Francine took the letters and placed them on top of Maxwell and Monica's desks.

Randall Spaulding was a good investigator. His office was as respected as a private investigator's could be. He was licensed and he made it a policy to cooperate with local police departments when requested. Randall reported illegal activity when he came across it and for these reasons the local police left him alone. It also helped that he had retired from police duty.

Upon reaching the age of 40, Randall figured if he wanted to have a wealthy retirement at a reasonable age, he better do something that would be more profitable than law enforcement. Private investigations were quite profitable. At four hundred and fifty dollars per hour, twenty-four hours per day, for fourteen days, this operation alone would provide him with a massive fee. With most clients he required a retainer, but Maxwell Williams had used him before and he always paid promptly. Randall had waived the retainer. Of course, he had ways to collect from clients who refused to pay up.

This looked like an easy case. A simple tail and report. Randall rented two cars. He and one of his associates would keep in touch while they followed Monica Scott and her friend to wherever it was they were going. Neither car would follow the suspects too closely. They would interchange positions so it never seemed that the same car was following.

After the subjects stopped for dinner or settled into a hotel for the night, Randall and his associate would return the cars into the local office of the rental car company and get two new cars. In the five years he had been doing this, Randall had never lost a subject, nor had he been detected. Sometimes he or his associate would even eat in the same restaurant as the subject while the other waited outside. Constant surveillance achieved the results desired by his clients. Randall was good. He was already deciding how to invest the money he would receive for this assignment.

After reaching Interstate 95 north, Monica limited the Mustang's speed to around 75 miles per hour. She set the cruise control and the miles ticked by. It would take about three days of traveling to reach Atlantic Point, New Jersey. They could have reached it sooner, but Monica wanted to limit their daily travel time so there would be some elements of a vacation. She and Brad talked about a lot of subjects, but Drake Donovan was not one of them. Monica figured that if she and Brad ever wanted to get back together, they would have to discuss what had happened at some point in time. Now was not that time. Monica had too much to worry about already with the mystery surrounding Atlantic Point Park.

Brad and Monica discussed what she knew of the park's history and of her mother's move to Florida in 1985. They also discussed the disappearance of Monica's father and whether the closing of the park had anything to do with his disappearance. After a period of silence, Brad brought up the one subject that Monica had been evading. What would Monica do if her mother or Maxwell turned out to be involved in the disappearance of her father and the closing of Atlantic Point Park?

"Brad, whatever comes out of this, I want my mother's name and reputation to remain intact. Mother kept a secret from me, but she was the person who raised me, who provided me with a good life, and who was my best friend. I can't let anything harm her now that she's not here to defend herself." Monica was near tears. "I don't know what I'll do if Maxwell is involved, he was always like a father to me."

Rather than risk an accident, Brad suggested that they pull over for some refreshments and a break from the road. Monica wiped her eyes and agreed. When the next exit sign came up, she flicked the sequential turn signals on and pulled off. There were several restaurants located there. Monica breathed in the heavy, humid air and began to pull herself together. Brad waited while she put the top up on the car, closed the windows and locked the doors. Then they headed into the restaurant.

They chose a casual restaurant that had a large outdoor deck with umbrellas and an outdoor bar overlooking a man-made lake with scattered ducks. They were seated and a server came by with menus. Monica settled on a chilled tuna platter with lettuce and tomato, while Brad ordered a black bean burger, with lettuce and tomato and a cup of vegetable broth. They both ordered iced tea with lemon.

"You're on vacation Brad; I thought you were going to eat something different than your usual healthy foods."

"I can't seem to help myself," Brad grinned.

They both sipped the unsweetened iced teas and gazed out over the lake. The food was good and Monica felt better. Brad grabbed the check when it arrived over Monica's protestations. Monica waited at the table while Brad went to settle the check. As she gazed out at the lake, she noticed the gathering of storm clouds. So typical of Florida. One moment picture perfect weather and the next moment darkened skies and a thunderstorm.

Brad returned and Monica asked him to drive. He replied that he would be glad to, but that they better keep the top up. They climbed into the Mustang as the first raindrops started pelting the car. They were not far from the interstate and in moments they were merging back onto 95 north. The rain was coming down hard and Brad reflected that they should have stayed put at the restaurant until the storm cleared up.

Lightening split the sky in front of them, appearing to touch the ground and creating an eerie scene of light and shadows that lasted for only a second and then flickered out. They were so focused on the storm in front of them that they never noticed the two cars that continued traveling behind them, carefully watching their every move.

Chapter Twelve

Trisha Marshall was pleased. Up until this morning, sales had been below normal for the month at the International Art Gallery. Today had been an exception to the recent slow pace. Trish sold several expensive pieces in the morning, several more in the afternoon and her last client of the day appeared ready to decide on a purchase.

Trish was about to close the gallery for the day when a well-dressed woman had stepped inside. The owner had a strict policy that if anyone came into the gallery before closing, the gallery would remain open until the client had concluded their browsing or better yet, had made a purchase. Trish believed that some clients ended up making a purchase because they felt obligated to do so after she had remained open on their behalf.

Trish didn't care as long as she made the sale and her commission. She earned a very comfortable living from the sale of art through the exclusive gallery. The woman who arrived late had asked to be shown to the gallery's exclusive section of prints and originals by artist Rachael Robinson. Rachael Robinson specialized in paintings that depicted contemporary ocean scenes from destinations all over the world.

Trish asked the woman whether she would like to see works by any other artists, but the woman seemed to be only interested in the Rachael Robinson collection. The woman did not want any assistance and indicated that she would like to browse without interruption. That was just fine with Trish. There were a number of things she had to do after the gallery closed each day and she could complete them while the woman browsed. It was now six o'clock, and one hour past the regular closing time, when the woman came to the front of the store and requested Trish's assistance in making her purchase.

The woman had selected an original that was priced at just over $9,000. The painting depicted a rising sun on a tropical island. The artist had captured the lush tropical feel of the locale, and Trish believed it was one of Rachael Robinson's best efforts.

Trish asked the woman if she wanted the large piece shipped or if she would be picking it up at a later time. The woman appeared to be alone and hauling the large painting out of the gallery would be out of the question.

The woman provided an address for a moving and storage company. Trish explained that the gallery's price included shipping, handling and insurance until the piece reached the designated destination as part of the purchase agreement. She recommended that the woman arrange insurance from the time of delivery.

As the transaction proceeded, Trish asked the woman how she would like to make payment on the sale and was shocked to learn that she would pay in cash. Trish wrote up the bill of sale, noting that with sales tax, the purchase did not quite total $10,000. That was important because $10,000 was the threshold amount that would require her to fill out the governmental notification form for a large cash purchase.

The woman pulled the cash out of a black designer shopping bag. Pulling nearly $10,000 in loose bills from a handbag would have been awkward for most patrons, but the woman had the cash neatly banded as though it had just come from the bank. She removed the entire amount from her bag in one smooth movement and handed the stacks of packed bills to Trisha. Counting the smaller bills took some time, and while the woman made no indication of any impatience, Trish had the distinct feeling that the unusual customer was most definitely in a hurry.

During most transactions, Trish made conversation with the gallery's clients. She was adept at finding something in common with almost anyone. It was in this way that she developed repeat sales, and her clients often became personal acquaintances. With this particular client there was no unnecessary conversation. The woman was cool and reserved, without being rude, yet she never said a single word more than she needed to during the entire transaction.

The sale of this particular painting reminded Trish of the time she had sold a similar Rachael Robinson painting to Lydia and Monica Scott. Trish made a mental note to give Monica a call as she realized that they had not spoken since Monica was last in New York to visit her attorney. Trish wondered what additional information Monica had since obtained about her unusual inheritance.

With a final flourish, Trish tagged the painting with a "sold" sign until the item could be shipped out, simultaneously thanking the woman as she placed the sign. As Trish said goodbye, she unlocked the now closed store so that the woman could leave. The woman never said a word, even as she alighted from the store. She just primped her dark red hair as she exited the shop and disappeared down the busy New York City sidewalk.

Janice Laneer was thrilled. She had always loved the large portrait that hung as the focal point in Lydia Scott's Palm Beach home, even if she had never liked Lydia. Janice had been invited to Lydia's house on many occasions, along with the rest of the executive staff. She had been genuine when she complimented Lydia on the beautiful painting. In her condescending way, Lydia had told Janice that the piece was an *original* by Rachael Robinson and that it had come from a gallery in New York.

Janice had suspected that the piece came from the gallery where Monica made ongoing purchases of art for the hotels, but Janice had never asked. Since she was in New York, a visit to the gallery would confirm if the International Art Gallery had been the place where Lydia made the long-ago purchase. As usual, her deduction was right. The International Art Gallery had proven to be the exclusive New York dealer for Rachel Robinson's works. The piece that Janice purchased today eclipsed the painting that had been Lydia's. Rachel Robinson had improved with time. The selected painting would look fantastic in Janice's new Cayman Islands condominium.

Janice headed uptown toward her luxury hotel. She could afford the painting—and more—even if she was no longer working at Caprice Hotels. The income from her investments allowed her to live in opulent style, and with the money that she would collect from her next endeavor, she would have even greater income in the future. Janice had selected a painting that would not total over $10,000 in total purchase price. She didn't want anything to be traced back to her.

New York was a great place to spend some time. Close enough to New Jersey so she could reach Atlantic Point when the time was right. Far enough away so that she didn't have to spend time waiting in a small, run-down, former resort town. Deserted localities were not Janice's style.

It was a warm day, but Janice didn't mind. Her thoughts were on other issues. If there was ever a time in her life that she could not afford to make a mistake, that time was now. A single error could cost her everything. Janice ran over the plan again and again as she walked toward the hotel, enjoying the warm sun. No, she had not made any errors.

Janice walked into the hotel lobby through the gold sliding doors. They whisked open as she approached, and she headed over to the hotel's lobby bar once inside. Janice would have a drink, then go to her suite and get ready for dinner at eight o'clock. The man she met in the hotel's bar last night had invited her to dinner this evening. She figured that she might as well accept the offer. She needed male company since her days with Maxwell were over. For a brief moment a feeling of sadness flicked over her. This date would not lead to any permanent relationship—Janice did not intend to stay in town that long, but some male company would be nice.

Janice did not stay in the bar for more than one drink. She wanted to have enough time to get ready for her evening out, and as always, she wanted to look her best, date or no date. Janice glanced at the mirrors that were placed to make the lobby bar appear larger than it really was. As she continued to gaze into the mirror, she decided that she had time for a second drink. The image that was reflected back at her already looked great. Janice signaled the bartender to refill her glass.

By the time Maxwell returned to the hotel, his breathing had returned to normal. How long he had been passed out on the floor of Janice's condominium, he didn't know. Maxwell realized that he might have had a heart attack, but at this point, he didn't care. The events in his world were continuing to spiral out of control. If he could just get things back under his grasp, he would see a doctor, improve his health and maybe even retire. Now that Lydia was gone, he found his interest in running Caprice to be waning with each passing day.

Francine Crowley was not in the office when he got back. Maxwell glanced at his watch, as he tried to get oriented. It was well past five o'clock. Maxwell had left the office in the morning to visit Janice at her now empty condominium. Now it was evening. He must have been passed out for the entire day. The thought that he was lying unconscious on the floor for so much time left him shaken. He really should see a doctor.

Maxwell reviewed all the things that were wrong in his life: Monica was probably on her way to Atlantic Point Park under the watchful gaze of Randall Spaulding and Janice had resigned and then disappeared without a trace. What that meant, he was not yet sure of, but it couldn't be good. Worst of all was that the secret he and Lydia kept for more than thirty years could be revealed. That secret could ruin everything Maxwell had achieved in his life. A vision of his ruined reputation, along with the loss of his money, his job and even his freedom passed through his mind. Maxwell could never let that happen. He would make it all come out right; after all, he had made it come out right for more than thirty years now. Maxwell had once been the master of his own universe. He wondered if he ever would be again.

Maxwell considered going home to rest, but there was an ominous looking envelope on the top of his mail pile. The envelope piqued his interest and he could not resist reaching for the letter opener to slit it open.

The envelope had no return address. It was a personal letter, maybe a guest complaint. The administrative assistants always threw out the junk mail before it ever reached him. Inside was a single sheet of dark gray paper that matched the envelope.

Maxwell caught his breath as he read the brief note that was printed on the folded letter:

You and Lydia Scott were responsible for the disappearance of Ronald Scott more than thirty years ago. Even with Lydia gone, you are not the only one who knows the truth. If you would like to make sure that the information remains confidential, the price of that consideration will be one million dollars. The payment of the indicated amount will guarantee the continued confidentiality of the information. Failure to provide full payment will result in the simultaneous release of the information to the authorities and to the news services.

The payment is to be made in used bills in denominations of $100s and $50s. The payment is to be packed into the smallest sized suitcases that will accommodate the bills. The suitcases are to be dark in color and not conspicuous. A failure on your part to follow every direction explicitly will negate the agreement and the information will be released without a *second opportunity to secure the confidentiality that you would like to maintain.*

In the next few days you will receive a second letter with further instructions as to how the payment is to be delivered. No other contact will be made with you.

As shaken as he was, Maxwell realized that the blackmail letter was well written. Whoever had written it had information that Maxwell thought had been buried thirty years ago. Maxwell reached for his phone. He dialed the number for his broker. Maxwell's broker often stayed on duty well past normal business hours to accept calls from his wealthier clients, included among them Maxwell Williams. After about two rings, Jim Abbott came on the line.

"Jim, it's Maxwell Williams. I need to liquidate some stocks very quickly."

"Maxwell, the market was down at closing again today, so don't sell any more than you have to.

"It's not an option right now. I've decided to invest in a business venture and I need to have a check for one million dollars as soon as possible."

"I hope this venture is worth it Maxwell, you're going to take a bath on anything that you sell right now. Can you hold out for a few weeks?"

"I can't do it Jim. I need the money in the next couple of days. I just can't wait."

"I'll sell over the next three days and try to salvage what I can for you Maxwell. If you reconsider, you know where to reach me."

"Don't worry, I won't reconsider. This is one opportunity that I can't pass up."

Next Maxwell dialed Francine Crowley's home phone number. She answered after the first ring.

"Francine, it's Maxwell. I need to ask you a question that can't wait until the morning."

"Maxwell what is it. Is there something wrong? I knew something had to be wrong when you didn't return from Janice's this morning. What happened over there?"

"I can't explain right now. I need to know if you have any idea where the gray envelope came from that you placed on my desk."

"It was in with the regular mail. There's an identical one for Monica on her desk. What's going on Maxwell?"

"Nothing Francine, the letter contained some important business information that Monica and I have been waiting for. There's nothing to worry about. You said that you left the other envelope on Monica's desk?"

"Yes, yes I did," Francine was getting flustered.

"Well don't say anything to her Francine; I'll take care of it so she can enjoy her vacation."

Before Francine could say another word, Maxwell hung up the phone without even a goodbye. So unlike him, Francine mussed as she headed out to her kitchen to finish preparing dinner. Once again Francine realized that she needed to have a long talk with Monica when she returned from her vacation.

Maxwell hurried into Monica's office. There was an identical envelope. Maxwell grabbed for it. He didn't even bother with the letter opener; instead, he fumbled to open it with his fingers.

Like the letter that Maxwell had received, Monica's letter was well worded, professional and direct. There were no wasted sentences. Both letters were alike, except that the first sentence in Monica's had been replaced with:

"Your mother was responsible for the disappearance of your father."

The second sentence had been eliminated. Monica was being blackmailed for an additional one million dollars to keep Lydia's reputation intact. Maxwell phoned his broker a second time to increase his sale of shares to two million dollars. The broker went through his warnings a second time and Maxwell listened with thinning patience. His chest began tightening again.

As soon as the phone call was over, he went to his well-stocked liquor cabinet and poured himself a strong drink. It was going to be a long week. He hoped he would live through it.

Chapter Thirteen

The storm passed as quickly as it started. After the brilliant display of lightening, Brad and Monica joined a large number of other travelers at a rest stop where they could wait out the storm. When the rain stopped, they both went over to a row of vending machines for some refreshments. Monica decided to get a cup of coffee and a small bag of chocolate candy. She knew that vending coffee was not very tasty, but she wanted a cup to perk her up any way. Monica was pleasantly surprised when she sipped the coffee and found it to be very hot and quite good. Brad decided on a cup of black coffee, but he declined Monica's offer of candy.

Monica smiled and reminded Brad yet again that he was on vacation and he could have candy if he wanted to. Brad just stood there with one eyebrow raised and Monica couldn't suppress a chuckle. She was surprised when Brad put his arm around her and walked her back to the car. His touch reminded her how just much she missed being with him.

All around the parking lot rainwater was turning into steam as the hot pavement evaporated the puddles of the summer storm. Brad started the car, put the top down and merged back onto the highway. He accelerated up to highway speeds and the miles ticked by one by one. It was going to be a long drive to New Jersey.

It was getting dark when they reached the border between Florida and Georgia. Along the way they stopped several times for fuel and refreshments and took turns driving. As the long day continued Monica found herself drifting off to sleep when Brad took his turn driving. She awoke just in time to see the signs welcoming them to Georgia.

"Hi sleepy head," Brad greeted Monica as she began to stir.

"Why did you let me sleep so long?" Monica yawned as she woke up.

"Because you looked like you needed a rest."

Night had fallen and although the air had cooled, it was still thick from the high levels of humidity.

Monica looked up at the approaching night sky and a momentary feeling of contentment settled over her. Some of the stress she had been under during the past couple of weeks began to fade and in her heart she knew whatever she found at Atlantic Point Park could be dealt with.

As Monica began to stretch in the car, Brad asked her if she was ready for a pit stop.

"Whenever you can pull over."

"There were several billboards advertising a large convenience store, restaurant and refueling station at the next exit. Let's stop there. Afterward we can decide how far we want to drive tonight."

"Sounds good to me."

As signs to the exit appeared, Brad drove the Mustang off the highway and into the well-lit convenience center. Monica headed toward the ladies' room as Brad began to refuel the car.

When Monica walked toward the store, Brad couldn't help but notice that driving with the top down had given her golden hair a windswept look. It reminded him of the many days that they had spent by the ocean together. As he watched her disappear into the store, memories of the good times that they had shared crowded through his mind. Brad's thoughts were disrupted when the gas pump made a loud click to announce that the tank was filled. Brad pulled the hose out of the cap-less gas tank, waited for the receipt and then headed into the restroom before he and Monica would return to the road.

As Brad exited the restroom, he found Monica waiting for him just outside the restroom in the convenience store area.

"Would you mind if we went over to the café and had a bite to eat?" Monica asked. They hadn't had anything to eat since their impromptu stop before the storm.

"Not at all. I'm hungry too and I'd like to take a look at a map that shows a larger geographical area."

They were greeted at the door by a heavyset hostess who gave them a classic southern "howdy" as she walked them to a booth along the front of the convenience center's café. They were able to see out to the gas pumps and Brad realized that the Mustang had been left parked at the pumps. He excused himself to go out and move the car into a regular parking space.

As Brad neared the car, he noticed that a middle-aged man seemed to be looking inside the car and then back toward the front of the convenience store—almost as if he were going to take something and were trying to do so before the owner returned.

The man did not see Brad coming because Brad had used the exit that led directly from the café into the parking lot and came up the far side.

As he approached the car, the man became startled when Brad asked him what he was looking for.

The man apologized and commented how much he liked the convertible before returning to the adjoining gas pump to fill his own car. Brad glanced over at the man's car. It was a plain sedan, the kind that was typically issued by a rental car company.

Brad didn't confront the man any further. A quick glance into the Mustang revealed that nothing inside the car had been touched. He didn't buy the man's story about "liking the convertible." Something about the man and the car seemed familiar, but they were many miles from home and he could not associate any specific recognition to either the person or the car.

Brad opened the door to the Mustang and the engine roared to life. As he pulled away from the gas island, he took one last glance at the stranger and found the man was watching him as he pulled away.

The incident left him uneasy. For the past couple of days Brad had been analyzing the events surrounding Monica's inheritance. He was sure that Lydia had to be hiding a secret to have made the enormous tax payments on Atlantic Point Park for thirty years. Keeping the park a secret from Monica also seemed to support his theory.

There was something familiar about the strange man and there was no doubt that his look inside the car was not innocent. Was Maxwell in on it? Was he having them followed, and if so, why? Brad was glad Monica had invited him on the trip. At least he could try to protect her if the need arose.

As Brad neared the front of the store, he spotted an empty parking space right along the cafe in sight of their booth. He took time to put the top up and lock both doors. As Brad walked back to the booth, the waitress was just returning to the table with their drinks. They placed their food order and she disappeared into the kitchen.

Brad shared his story with Monica about the unusual man. Her first thought was to say that it was probably his imagination, but she stopped herself. Brad was not one to overreact. In the past his instincts had proven to be right over and over again. Later when Monica had gotten to know him better, she had come to respect his ability to accurately predict the outcome of situations. Monica would not doubt him now, especially with all the strange things that were going on in her life.

"What do you think he was looking for?" she replied.

"I don't know. You had your handbag with you and everything else was locked in the trunk. It was strange."

"It gives me a creepy feeling Brad. There are so many unusual things going on that a week ago I would have never believed could happen. I don't need any more strange events."

"There was definitely something familiar about him Monica. I never forget a face. I know that I've seen him somewhere before."

"What did he look like?"

"Middle aged, white, jet black hair, medium height, trim build."

"That describes a lot of people. Was there anything unusual about him?"

"Nothing else, but the more I think about it, the more that I know it's not the first time I've seen that guy."

Randall Spaulding could have kicked himself. He had never considered that Monica's companion would go into the convenience center and then exit moments later through the restaurant. Randall had been trying to see if anything had been left out in the car so he would have a better idea where he would be following Monica to. There were no tour brochures and the days of a road atlas being left open on the seat were gone with the advent of GPS systems. In error, Randall had been watching the convenience store door and not the café entrance. Now he had been spotted and it was obvious that the guy Monica was traveling with had not bought Randall's story about an innocent look at a nice car. Randall got back into the rental sedan and started the engine. The basic rental sedan reminded him of the days when he had been in law enforcement. As he pulled across the parking lot, he picked up his cell phone and contacted his assistant, Dan Tilton, who was parked in the other rental car near the on ramp.

"Dan, I've been spotted."

"Are our plans changing?" Dan's response was brief.

"I'm going to stay behind and you're going to have to take over on your own. I'll give you a fifteen-minute head start. Stay with them and let's hope that they soon stop at a place where we can get new rental cars. The guy she's traveling with is observant and I think that he's on to me."

"Will do." Dan broke the connection.

Randall always counted on a double check. He liked two guys to follow the person under surveillance. With Dan following Monica solo, it would be impossible to continue the operation if she got too far out of sight. Monica could turn off at any time, and the job would be over.

Randall wondered if Maxwell Williams might have an idea where they were going. Randall considered touching base with Maxwell, but to do so now meant that he would have to explain his reason for the call. Randall didn't want to risk losing Maxwell's confidence, so he decided to wait. He would have to count on Dan's skills to keep the investigation going at this point. There was no other choice. As Randall mulled over the situation, he observed Monica and her companion exiting the restaurant. Randall watched as they got into the Mustang, while he remained out of sight behind some tractor trailers.

The guy with Monica took a long look around the parking lot before he got into the car. That action left Randall with no doubt that the guy suspected he was being tailed. Randall continued watching as Dan followed them out of the parking lot, allowing two other cars to go before him. That was the usual procedure —don't follow too closely—but with only Dan following them, Randall wished he had gotten closer. Losing them could happen in the blink of an eye. It was not a position that Randall liked to be in, but he had no one to blame but himself.

Monica asked Brad if he would like her to drive. The nap and the food had left her awake and refreshed. By now it was dark outside. Brad had bought an east coast map in the convenience store and recommended that they try to make it to Savannah, so they would be near the South Carolina line when they set off in the morning.

"Sounds good to me."

Brad agreed to let Monica drive. Despite the late hour, he was wide awake. He wanted to see if anyone was following them. Over and over he tried to remember where he had seen the man who was looking into the car. With Monica driving Brad could watch the cars that were on the road around them.

As the miles went by, the town of Brunswick, Georgia came and went. There were no other large towns before Savannah. Monica kept the Mustang at a steady seventy-five miles per hour. The traffic was light, and they made good time.

Brad continued to keep a look out for any cars that seemed to stay near them. He didn't notice anything out of the ordinary. Several cars seemed to be following them, but they always turned off or passed by and were not seen again. It was an unnerving ride. Brad began to question whether he was overreacting. As the first signs for Savannah appeared, he relaxed for the first time since they had been at the refueling station.

Prior to reaching the heart of the city, they decided to exit and find a suburban hotel to stay at for the night. Monica pulled off the highway and they made a right-hand turn since the road had a barrier island blocking turns to the left. Several large hotels and smaller motels lined the exit and they turned into an upscale hotel named The Harrington.

The hotel was mid-sized, and as always, Monica compared the hotel to her own. Brad laughed out loud when she whispered to him that it was not as good as a Caprice Hotel.

Brad grabbed a luggage cart and Monica headed to the front desk to register. He unloaded the trunk and then waited by the elevator. Brad was disappointed when Monica handed him a key to his own room. As always, he was careful not to let his disappointment show. Brad figured if they were meant to get together it would happen. Besides, he consoled himself, it had been a very long day, they were both tired, and he could use some sleep. And there was always tomorrow...

The elevator doors slid open and Brad was startled out of his thoughts.

"Our rooms are side by side," Monica observed as she spotted their room numbers along the plush corridor.

"Monica, I want to check your room. After you're inside I want you to double lock the doors and keep the window locked. The episode at the re-fueling station left me with an uneasy feeling. I didn't spot anyone following us but I want you to be careful."

Monica was about to say something to minimize Brad's concerns, but she reminded herself again that his instincts were almost always correct, and she could see that he was taking her personal security very seriously.

"Yes, sir!" she responded with a smile.

"Don't be a wise ass," Brad grinned, "There's something strange going on with this whole ordeal. I'd rather play it safe."

Brad looked around the room, behind the shower curtain and then double-checked the windows finding that they were permanently sealed. After he was satisfied, Brad brought in Monica's luggage, gave her a quick kiss goodnight and disappeared into his own room after Monica locked her door.

Monica was surprised, although she figured she shouldn't be. She had known all along that Brad cared for her, but she was touched that he was worried over her personal safety. The kiss had been a pleasant surprise and she was left with a warm feeling as she crawled into the king-sized bed and fell asleep. Maybe things would work out with Brad once and for all. Spending tomorrow with him was Monica's last thought before she drifted into a deep sleep.

Randall Spaulding drove to the nearby Savannah airport car rental as soon as Dan had confirmed that the subjects were checked into a hotel for the night. Randall would get a new car, then return to the hotel so that Dan could do the same. If they were lucky, one of them would get some sleep. At least they could resume the double tail procedure with the new cars. Randall turned into the rental car section of the lot and realized that this case was not going to be as easy as he had expected.

Morning came at nine o'clock for Monica. She had not asked for a wakeup call, figuring that Brad would wake her up when he was ready. Instead she awakened on her own. Monica got out of bed and walked over to the bathroom. There was a note under her room door:

I've gone down to the hotel gym, it's 8:30 now. I'm going to work out for an hour and then get ready to pack up. Let's meet at 10:00 for breakfast...Brad

So like him she thought. Even on vacation Brad would not stop his daily workout sessions. Monica needed coffee so she phoned down to the hotel restaurant and requested that they bring up a pot from room service. In a matter of minutes the coffee was delivered. Monica hesitated before opening the door. Brad's words from last night came back to her. Calming her nerves, Monica opened the door and tipped the waiter after he placed the coffee tray on the table. She poured the steaming coffee into one of the cups. It took Monica longer than Brad to get ready in the morning, so she headed for the bathroom with the coffee in hand.

Ten o'clock came all too soon. Brad knocked on Monica's door and suggested they pack the car and check out before they went down to the restaurant. Brad's comment that hotel rooms could be searched gave Monica an uncomfortable feeling. The thought of a stranger going through her personal items left her feeling very vulnerable. She agreed with Brad's advice.

After enjoying a light continental breakfast, they were back on the road again. Soon after, signs for South Carolina appeared. Many hours later they were crossing into North Carolina. The miles seemed to go on forever and Monica began to think it might have been better to fly. Still, she was enjoying Brad's company and the two of them talked almost nonstop up as they headed up the coast.

They made it a practice to stop and refuel every time the gas gauge went below the halfway mark. The regular stops kept them refreshed and provided them a chance to take turns with the driving. Brad kept a close watch for anyone following them, but he was not able to spot any cars that seemed to be hovering nearby.

It was well past dark when they reached the Virginia line.

"All right, I need a good dinner," Brad announced.

"I could use a good meal too, but at this time of the night, it looks like a diner or a travel plaza."

"I saw a sign for a place called, Mom's Diner at the next exit. It said that the cooking was guaranteed to be homemade."

"Which means it's probably awful," Monica countered.

"Well let's try it, I'm starving."

They pulled off at the exit, and a large garish sign indicated the way to the diner. The diner's exterior matched the tacky signage and faced directly onto the main road. It would have been hard to miss. The place was geared toward travelers and it appeared to be clean and well kept.

"Maybe it will be OK," Monica commented nonchalantly.

They exited the car and Brad locked the doors. The top was already up. The air was much cooler than the night before, almost chilly. The restaurant's exterior was not as well lighted as she would have liked, and Monica shivered as she got out of the car.

They walked up the sidewalk to the restaurant. As they passed a row of newspaper boxes with day old papers inside and two ancient pay phones, Monica murmured, "I hope Mom's food won't be from yesterday." Brad just laughed. Inside, he asked the hostess to sit them in the front of the restaurant by the windows that were on the side of the building opposite from the pay phones.

"You're being very particular about where we're sitting tonight," Monica observed.

"I have an idea."

"After we get our drinks I'm going to ask the waitress for directions to the men's room."

"It's right over there," Monica told him.

"I know that."

"I'm still going to ask for directions. You ask for directions to the lady's room as soon as I am gone. Leave our drinks and a couple of personal items on the table."

"Brad, what are you up to?"

"There's a wall that covers the front of the restrooms to separate them from the restaurant."

"I see that."

"After you use the restrooms wait for me behind the wall."

"You'll be out before I am."

"Then I'll wait for you."

Moments later Brad asked the waitress for directions to the restrooms and headed back that way. A few seconds later, Monica did the same. As planned, they met behind the wall.

Things seemed to be going better today observed Randall Spaulding with relief. He was sure that neither he nor Dan had been spotted today. The subjects had probably written off the incident from last night by now. Just to be safe, Randall had also paid extra money to get vehicles that did not scream rental car all over them. Dan had gone across the street to get some fast food for the two of them while Randall kept an eye on the subjects who had just gotten up to go to the restrooms.

Randall was wearing a hat pulled low over his face and he had mildly disguised his look with glasses. Unless Monica's companion looked directly at him, he would never recognize Randall with the changed look. Randall did not intend to let that happen. One failure could happen to anyone. Two would mean that he was slipping.

Concealed behind the restroom divider, Brad explained his plan to Monica: "We're going to go toward the front of the restaurant, but from the opposite side that we walked back on. If we're being followed, it would be likely that the person will be looking across the restaurant from the pay phone area toward our table. Expecting us to return the same way we came from."

In an instant, Monica realized what Brad was planning. A sick feeling settled into her stomach. Her legs felt like rubber as they walked up the other side of the restaurant. They would be able to see anyone who would be looking the opposite way toward their table from the outside windows. There was only one man with a hat who was holding a newspaper and standing near the pay phones. He turned slightly and his profile became illuminated from the shadows. Monica squeezed Brad's hand. The man matched the generic description that Brad had given of the stranger who had been looking in their car last night. Monica looked at Brad, and he gave a slight nod.

Brad whispered, "He's the man who was looking into the Mustang last night, and that's not all. I remember where I've seen him. He was at the rest stop that we used during the rainstorm. I also remember the car he was driving last night. It was parked outside the gates back at Palm Beach when we left yesterday. Monica, we're being followed."

Chapter Fourteen

Panic seized Monica. She looked over at Brad for directions. He squeezed her hand. A momentary feeling of dizziness swept over her and she swayed against him. He supported her and she regained her balance a second later.

"Turn around and head back to the restrooms," he whispered. "Don't say a word."

Monica did as Brad instructed, despite the feeling of weakness that had spread to her legs. When they reached the wall that concealed the restroom doors, they both paused to catch their breath.

Brad spoke first, "I'm going back to the table before you Monica, and we're going to pretend that nothing is out of the ordinary."

"Brad, I want to leave here right now."

"We can't. We have to act as though everything is all right until I can figure out a way to lose him. We're safe inside the restaurant. We'll wait until there are other people leaving to walk back to the car."

Monica nodded in reluctant understanding. Brad headed for the table. It seemed like forever until Monica counted to one hundred and then started back to the table. Brad had picked up the menu and was looking at it as though nothing were wrong. He smiled as she sat down and they engaged in a conversation that was forced. Neither of them commented about being followed, and they ordered just as soon as the waitress appeared.

When the food arrived, Monica found that she had no appetite, and Brad was no longer hungry either. Both of them ate a small portion of their meals. When the waitress returned a short time later to check their progress, they both indicated that they were finished eating. So much food was left that she asked if they wanted a takeout box and Brad replied that they were traveling so they couldn't take the extra food with them.

Brad ordered another iced tea so they would have a reason to sit there until a larger group of people exited the restaurant. He didn't want to walk out alone. He also paid the bill right away so he and Monica could leave without delay when the right time came. Monica ordered another drink also, but she didn't know if she would be able to swallow. A knot had settled into her stomach and she felt nauseous.

A short time passed before a group of two families lined up at the cashier station. Brad made an indication that it was time for their exit. Monica grabbed her handbag and they headed for the door. She felt like running, but Brad was walking and had grabbed her hand so she would not charge ahead of him. Monica's legs still felt like rubber.

As they walked toward the Mustang, Monica shivered again. The air was much colder than last night, although the shiver could just have been from fear. It seemed to take forever to reach the car. As they passed the pay phones, they both noticed that there was no one there any longer. The exterior of the diner seemed darker than ever. Whoever had been watching them had disappeared into the night.

Brad hit the remote start button and the Mustang flashed its lights in recognition of the command as the engine turned over. Brad opened

Monica's door then headed over to get into the driver's side. He locked the doors as soon as they were inside.

Once inside, they discussed their options and decided to head back to I-95 and proceed north. Brad turned left out of the diner's driveway. No one appeared to be following them. They turned onto the entrance ramp and merged into traffic.

"Brad, what do you think we should do?"

"We're going to behave as if we had never seen him and think how we can lose him. Do you have any ideas?"

"I'm too panicked to think," Monica replied.

"They've followed us for hundreds of miles. It's no coincidence."

"Who do you think they are? Who would have sent them?"

"I think it has to be Maxwell. Besides your attorney, Trisha, Jeanette and me, no one else knows about the amusement park part of your inheritance. I've always respected your mother, but I'm convinced that she was hiding something at Atlantic Point Park. The only other person who could know about events that happened thirty years ago would be Maxwell."

"How are we going to lose whoever is following us?"

"Let's just drive for a while and see if we can spot anyone. The traffic is heavy enough that I don't think we're in any danger."

Randall Spaulding and Dan Tilton headed back onto 95 north, keeping the rental vehicles a safe distance behind the subjects. Randall congratulated himself that they had been able to continue the operation undetected despite the incident the night before at the convenience center. It just went to show how stupid people were. Randall was sure that neither of the subjects had any clue they were still being followed. If they were lucky, the subjects would get a hotel room soon. It was Randall's turn to sleep and he couldn't wait until that moment.

Thoughts fired through Brad's mind. He realized that there had to be more than one person following them. The risk of losing a person under surveillance for hundreds of miles would be too great if only one person did the tailing. He also realized that it made it twice as hard to lose the tail. As Brad pondered the best way to make their escape, he wondered just how safe he and Monica were. He also realized that Monica, in particular, could be in danger. The thought left an icy feeling down his spine.

Monica sat in silence. She felt as if she had lost control of her world. Why would anyone be following her? It had to have something to do with the amusement park. She asked herself over and over again, "Who could be behind it?" The only answer she kept coming up with was Maxwell Williams. Monica resisted the thought that Maxwell would have hired the people that were tailing her and Brad. She had known Maxwell too long, spent too many good times with him, and he had been a father to her. It just couldn't be him, yet try as she might, Monica could not come up with anyone else who would care that she had inherited Atlantic Point Park and whatever secrets were concealed there.

Brad appeared to be as calm as ever, but Monica could tell that he was thinking of a way out of their predicament. The sooner, the better, were her thoughts on the matter. The element of danger seemed to hover over the car as they headed into the deepening night.

In a moment, Brad came to a decision. "We're going to need to spend the night somewhere in a hotel soon Monica."

"You mean with someone watching us all night long?"

"I'm afraid so. There's no way we can lose them with the traffic being so light this evening."

"Couldn't we go to the police?" Monica suggested with a note of panic.

"What would we be able to tell them? We'll pull off at a busy exit and stay at a larger hotel. When you register, get a suite so I can stay near you—or two connecting rooms."

Monica remained silent, wishing that she felt safe and in control. Safe and in control were two feelings that used to be second nature in her life.

Brad spotted an exit that had many convenience centers and lodging accommodations. The largest and busiest hotel at the exit was the Callaway Inn and Conference Center. Brad pulled under the well-lit entrance, joining about four other cars that were parked there to register. He felt safe, or as safe as you could feel when you were being watched.

Brad got out of the car and ran around to the other side. Monica was just sitting there staring ahead and she glanced up when he opened the door. He was relieved when she at least smiled at him.

"Sorry, I was just in a daze."

"Thinking about me…?

"Just glad that you're with me, Brad."

They headed for the registration desk and requested a room on a higher floor. A young woman in a typical hotel uniform skirt and vest registered them without incident, giving them directions to their suite before they left the desk. They grabbed a luggage cart, unloaded the car and headed through the atrium lobby to the elevator bank that stood at the rear. For once Monica didn't make comments about the quality of the hotel. Her silence worried Brad.

When they reached the suite, he unloaded their luggage and Monica just flopped down on one of the stuffed chairs, staring straight ahead and hugging a pillow.

"I've got to move the car Monica. Lock the door and don't answer it until I come back under any circumstances."

Monica came out of her dazed state and replied with a smile, "You forget that I run a hotel company. I know all about security."

"Well just be sure to remember your own safety rules until I get back!"

Brad headed for the door, waited until he heard the door lock behind him and went down to the lobby to park the convertible. Luck was with him. A parking spot opened near the main entrance and he pulled into it. There was a security guard near the door and Brad asked him to please watch the car. The man said he would do what he could, and Brad slipped him a one hundred dollar tip to make sure that their car was watched all night.

The man's wide-eyed response and nod indicated that he would keep the car safe. Brad turned and headed back to the suite.

Dan Tilton had worked with Randall Spaulding several times. Randall was as cheap as anyone he had ever worked for. Dan knew that there was big money in private investigations, but he had never been able to get his own firm started up. Instead, he kept working as Randall Spaulding's sidekick; taking whatever jobs Randall tossed his way—always for minimal compensation.

Randall had already left for the airport car rental agency as soon as the subjects had turned into the Callaway Inn. Dan could not wait to go to the restroom. He was not supposed to do anything until Randall returned, but for what he was getting paid, he wasn't going to wait. By the time Dan came out of the restroom, Brad had parked the car near the entrance and was going back into the hotel. What Dan missed was Brad's payment to the security guard. Having missed the financial exchange, Dan was unable to tell his boss that the subjects still suspected they were being tailed.

Just then Randall returned. He barked orders for Dan to high tail it to the airport and change his rental car. It was Randall's turn to sleep tonight and he expected to get every minute of it that he could.

Morning crept out of the long night. Brad had volunteered to sleep on the pull-out sofa in the living room and Monica had been too tired and stressed to argue over who got the bed. In the morning, Brad skipped his usual workout and was just answering the door for room service, when Monica woke up.

As he returned with their morning coffee, Monica was getting out of bed.

"You brought me coffee?"

"I thought you might need some to wake up. If you spent the night like I did, you probably didn't get to sleep for a while."

"No, I didn't," Monica replied as she reached for the mug of steaming liquid. Her mind began to stir as the coffee started to wake her up. "Do you mind if I use the bathroom first since I take longer?"

"Not at all. I have my own bathroom over here."

"I guess you would since we got a suite. I didn't even look around last night."

"Well, I did, you can never be too careful when you're being followed."

"Don't remind me," Monica muttered as she headed for her bathroom and Brad headed for his.

About an hour later, Monica was ready to leave, taking her traditional thirty minutes longer than Brad to get ready. He was relaxing on the now folded up sofa bed reading a morning newspaper that had been delivered with the coffee. It galled Monica that he could appear so relaxed under their present circumstances. For a moment her spirits lifted.

"Have you figured out a plan to get us out if this mess Brad?"

"I'm working on it."

"Care to share what you've come up with?"

"I don't have an easy solution. There has to be more than one person following us."

"I kind of thought that too."

"I think we're going to just have to wait for the right opportunity and seize it."

"You'll keep me posted?"

"Don't worry, you'll be right there beside me!"

"That's what I was afraid of."

The two of them took the elevator to the lobby. Before leaving the room, they used the electronic check out feature in the flat panel television so they could head directly to the car without delay. Brad hit send and received a receipt in his inbox a moment later. In seconds the car was loaded and they pulled out of the hotel with Brad driving.

The traffic was heavier this morning and for once Brad was pleased to see scores of cars on the road. It wasn't often that heavy traffic made you happy; of course it wasn't often that you were being tailed up the east coast. Monica and Brad continued heading north on route 95 through Virginia. As the miles ticked away, they passed the Phillip Morris plant and Monica commented how glad she was that the Caprice Hotels chain had converted to all non-smoking facilities. She reminded Brad how much damage smokers used to do to the guest rooms.

"Not to mention to their health," Brad countered.

Suddenly, Brad grasped her arm.

"What is it?"

"We may have a chance to escape, make sure your seatbelt is on."

"My seatbelt is always on. What do you have planned?"

"Just hold on and be ready. I'm glad this thing has an eight cylinder engine."

Monica was about to say more, but thought better of it.

To try to keep her mind off of whatever Brad was about to do she looked out the window. The traffic was heavier and there were a lot more trucks as 95 cut northward through Richmond. Monica looked at the navigation screen and realized they were heading toward the Washington, D.C. metropolitan area. Traffic would just continue to get heavier as they headed north. Perhaps when they reached D.C. Brad would lose the tail.

Brad suddenly pulled into the left lane as they continued traveling at a high rate of speed. He passed an 18-wheeler. There was another 18-wheeler ahead on the right, and a third coming up behind them. The convertible top was up on the Mustang, but the windows were down. The trucks were noisy and Monica realized how little protection a car would offer in a collision with one of the three large trucks. The thought was not comforting.

"Hold on Monica." All at once, Brad swerved between the two trucks that were in the right lane. The truck behind them pulled up and prevented them from returning to the left lane. For the moment, the three large trucks surrounded them. One instant after pulling into the right lane Brad darted off the nearest exit ramp, heading into the heart of Richmond. The car held the road, but the tires squealed in protest as they negotiated the fast exit from the highway. Monica could feel the car start to slide sideways and she held on to the door and the center armrest with her eyes squeezed shut. Suddenly the electronic stability assist kicked in and the car stabilized.

As soon as they reached the bottom of the ramp, Brad made several arbitrary turns through the city, gunning the engine as they rounded each corner. The three trucks had successfully hid them from whoever was tailing them. By the time their pursuers realized it, they would have gone past the exit that Brad and Monica used to make their escape. There was no quick turnaround for their pursuers and Brad, Monica and the Mustang quickly disappeared into the bustling city.

Brad continued making turns, going in every direction and in no direction. At last, he pulled into a city parking garage and drove all the way to the top. Brad backed into a parking spot so that they could see if anyone else came up into the far reaches of the garage. No one did.

"Do you think we lost them, Brad?"

"I think we lost them."

"What do we do now?"

"I want to leave the car parked up here for a while. By the time they realize that they've lost us, they'll have to double back and search the city. I don't think that they'll drive through every parking garage. They'll probably head back to watch 95 north, thinking that we'll eventually pass by."

"So what are we going to do?"

"Let's go see the city and have some breakfast. We didn't eat at the hotel and I'm hungry. Today is not a day to think about healthy eating," Brad said with a nervous grin.

The two of them walked to the nearby elevator. Their relief was palpable, but not yet complete. After a short walk from the parking garage, they did find an eatery in the downtown area and enjoyed a hearty breakfast. They decided to spend some time in the bustling metropolis and requested ideas on sightseeing from their waitress. She was all too glad to keep talking and gave them enough recommendations to spend a month touring Richmond.

"Do you think that it's safe to walk around?" Monica questioned Brad.

"I think it's safe to walk around, but let's keep our eyes open."

Several minutes had passed by and Randall could not see the Mustang anywhere. Still, he was not yet alarmed, after all that was why you used two operatives in a long-distance surveillance operation. He picked up his cell phone and pressed the preset number to reach Dan Tilton.

"Do you have them in your sight?"

"Negative."

Alarm seized Randall. He put the rental sedan into high gear. Randall always regretted that rental cars always came with the cheapest engines rather than the high-performance upgrades that were available to individual buyers. He accelerated past many cars and trucks for several miles, but the subjects were not to be seen. He slammed his fist against the steering wheel and then phoned Dan again.

"Pull off at the next exit. At the bottom, turn right and pull into the first restaurant or convenience store that you see." He hung up before he even heard Dan's reply. A short time later, with his temper back under control, Randall strode toward the restaurant with Dan Tilton in tow. Randall realized that by losing the subjects in the heart of a large city, it was a sure sign that the job was over. First though, he wanted to make sure that every possibility had been checked.

Randall questioned Dan about every event that had transpired since last night when he had taken his turn sleeping. Dan did not offer Randall the information that he had left them out of his sight while he went to use the restroom.

There was nothing that Randall or Dan could do. Neither of them even knew which exit that Monica had used to escape. Several exits had been passed before Randall even realized that the subjects were no longer on the interstate. His first failed operation. Randall tried to think of a way to locate Monica and her companion, but it was obvious that they knew they were being followed and had waited until the right time to elude them. Richmond was huge. Randall was sure that they would have made elusive maneuvers once they pulled into the city. He smiled a bitter smile. Monica and her companion were better than he realized. Randall couldn't help but respect that.

Through the rest of the day, Randall drove all though Richmond, but there was no sight of the Mustang, Monica or her companion. Dan had been sent back to watch Interstate 95 north in case the subjects had made the mistake of returning to their original route.

Randall picked up his cell phone to call Maxwell Williams. He used a number that Maxwell had provided him so that he did not have to go through the hotel switchboard. Randall had his own cell phone number blocked so that whomever he called could not observe his personal number, which he needed to keep free for communication with his partner during operations.

Maxwell picked up on the second ring. "This is Maxwell."

"Randall Spaulding here."

This was the call that Maxwell had been waiting for.

"Where are they?"

"I don't know.'

"What do you mean, you don't know?" Maxwell's voice was raised, and his tone was angry.

"She's with a guy. He's sharp. He spotted me at a convenience center and put two and two together." Randall was not about to make excuses for the failure.

"Where did you lose them?"

"They headed into Richmond."

"I hope you don't think that you're getting paid for this Spaulding."

Maxwell clicked the hang up button before Randall could respond. He should have gotten a description of Monica's traveling companion, but he already knew it had to be Brad Roberts. How convenient that Brad had gone on a sudden vacation at the same time as Monica. Richmond was well on the way to Atlantic Point Island. Maxwell would have to go to there and take care of things himself, just as he had always done.

Chapter Fifteen

Maxwell slumped back in his chair after the phone call with Spaulding. He had been feeling a little better over the past couple of days, but now the pain in his chest was back. He paused to consider that Monica might not be going to Atlantic Point, yet he couldn't think of a single reason she would be in Richmond at the present time. Maxwell had been hoping that Monica was on a real vacation. Upon her return to Palm Beach he intended to present her with the plans he had been working on to rehabilitate Atlantic Point Park. Maxwell's plans would preserve the Atlantic Point office building. Now though, other plans would have to be made, and there was no time to waste.

Maxwell had to find a way into the office building that would not arouse suspicion. To get in would either require demolition equipment or the key that Lydia had always denied him having. Lydia had told him thirty years ago that no one was getting in without her say so. It had been so stupid of him not to go through the box that the New Jersey police had forwarded to him after her death. Maxwell regretted once again that he had not done so. Well, so much for regrets.

Then there was the problem with the blackmailer. Jim Abbott had come through with the two million-dollar funding that Maxwell needed to satisfy the blackmailer's request, one million for his payment and one million for Monica's payment. Maxwell had been trying to figure out the identity of the blackmailer. If his suspicions about who the blackmailer was turned out to be right, there could be more payments required in the future. Maxwell had to get out of this entire mess and soon. If only he could just turn the clock back thirty years.

Maxwell was startled when his temporary assistant knocked and then opened the door to his office. She was attractive, but she was not Janice. Maxwell found that he missed Janice's efficiency and company more and more. The assistant handed him the day's mail. Included in the mail pile were two anonymous gray letters, this time with cancelled postage on each of them. Maxwell knew it was from the blackmailer. He fumbled as he hurried to open them, his heart racing. The contents were brief:

You have had adequate time to prepare the payment necessary to satisfy the request that was made of you. You will deliver the payment to the designated location inside the abandoned Atlantic Point Park. Don't you think that's an appropriate place for the delivery?

The letter went on to identify the day and time and was very specific how the delivery was to be made. Maxwell was shocked. It was unbelievable that the blackmailer would require the payment to be transferred at Atlantic Point Park, outside the ancient Haunted House attraction, no less.

A few seconds later, his new assistant interrupted him again.

"Did you need anything before I leave Mr. Williams?"

"Yes, just one more thing. Get me on a flight to Trenton, New Jersey and have a luxury rental car ready for me when I arrive."

170

Shadows were cloaking Richmond, as a chilly night descended on the city. Neither Brad nor Monica observed anyone watching them throughout the day. They shopped, toured and had a leisurely dinner in a quaint part of the nearby historic district.

Carrying their shopping bags, they were more relaxed than they had been in two days. At last they made their way back to the parking garage where the Mustang was hidden. The entire top floor of the parking garage was deserted, and Monica began to feel uneasy once again. The garage was several stories high. As they walked through the empty parking spaces, she could see through the safety rails to the street far below. Monica thought just how easy it would be for someone to throw them over the rails. It left her feeling dizzy and she was glad when they reached the car.

Brad unlocked the car with the key fob and opened the passenger door for Monica. Before he allowed her to get in, he grabbed the new map from the glove box. When they were both seated in the car, he began to study the road layout for a strategic exit from the city.

"Are you changing our travel plans?" Monica inquired.

"I want to find a different way to get to Atlantic Point Island. I think I found some back roads that will get us there without adding much more travel time."

Brad started the Mustang and they went around and down through the garage as they headed for the exit. Richmond traffic was light in the dusk of the early evening. Brad entered their new directions into the GPS, then followed a series of back roads, completely avoiding route 95. They would go out of their way, taking a route closer to the seaboard. By using the Chesapeake Bay Bridge-Tunnel, they would reach Cape Charles, Virginia and then head north again toward Delaware, and finally east to New Jersey.

The evening was cool and the smell of salt water permeated the air when they reached the first section of the Bay Bridge-Tunnel, which connected Virginia Beach to Cape Charles in southern Maryland through a long series of bridges and under water tunnels. They reached Cape Charles without incident, relaxing as each mile separated them from their pursuers. Several hours later they were briefly forced back onto route 95 to connect with the Delaware Memorial Bridge which would take them across the Delaware River and into New Jersey. Was the person tailing them still lying in wait somewhere along the expressway? They breathed a sigh of relief when signs appeared indicating that the twin-spanned bridge was just ahead.

After paying the toll, Brad merged smoothly onto the giant bridge, and a feeling of excitement replaced all Monica's worrisome thoughts. The two east-west bridges were a marvel of technology. They arched high into the air with the lights of Philadelphia visible to the north, Wilmington to the south and New Jersey glittering across to the east. The Mustang climbed higher and higher reaching the center of the eastbound bridge. Both bridges were several lanes wide, with red and green indicator lights to guide vehicles into the lanes that were open to thru traffic.

Just as soon as they reached the top, the bridges began their descent into The Garden State of New Jersey. The roads became very flat with scrub brush and sandy gravel bordering their shoulders. Brad headed north on route 295, finally pulling off at a quaint, garden court motel. As usual, Monica did the registration and handed Brad the key to his room. Tomorrow, they would reach their final destination, Atlantic Point Island.

Exhausted, both Monica and Brad fell into a deep sleep. They slept late into the next morning. Brad awoke at ten o'clock and went out for a morning jog. Monica slept until eleven. When she saw the alarm clock, she knew she had to get moving. Check-out was at noon and that only left her one hour to get showered and packed. She staggered to the bathroom. By the time she was finished with her shower, Brad was knocking at the door asking when she would be ready.

"A cup of coffee could speed things up Brad."

"Open the door and you might get some," he laughed.

When she opened the door, Brad was standing there with coffee. He was sweaty from working out.

"You'd better go get a shower, we have to check out soon."

"I'll see you in a couple of minutes." With that, Brad was off toward his own room. Monica gazed after him, admiring the view and hoping yet again they would soon be more than just friends.

A short time later they were packed and checked out of the motel. Monica told Brad that she wanted to drive. She put the top down on the Mustang and the warm summer air surrounded them. It was going to be a gorgeous day and the thought of reaching Atlantic Point Island filled them both with excitement. An upbeat conversation soon started, each of them firing ideas back and forth about the park, its history and what the future held.

Maybe inheriting the park would be a changing point in Monica's life. She sure could use a new focal point after the events of the past year. In a few short months it would be the first anniversary of her mother's fateful car accident. Monica unexpectedly realized that in order to get onto Atlantic Point Island they would have to drive over the very bridge where her mother had been killed. She shuddered as the realization sank in.

The GPS directed Monica onto route 73, then route 70, and finally route 72. There were long sections of desolate road as they headed closer and closer to the coast. The roads were bordered with sandy gravel and tall trees as far as the eye could see. Seagulls appeared with increasing regularity. Their cawing seemed to be an ominous warning to stay away. Route 72 eventually angled to the south and passed by the Garden State Parkway and route 9, both of which ran in the opposite direction.

As they crossed over the Intracoastal Waterway, the roadway continuously alternated from bridges to islands. Eventually, they reached the Atlantic Point Bridge. Monica was suddenly filled with a feeling of dread knowing her mother had died here. She grasped the wheel tightly as she was forced onto the bridge and finally onto the barrier island for which the bridge had been named. Brad glanced nervously toward her wishing he had been driving. Signs indicated that, Ship Bottom was to the south and Atlantic Point Island was to the north. Monica turned the car northward, heading in the direction where her unexpected inheritance was leading them. Brad reached over and gently squeezed her arm. He knew that right now, nothing could take away her pain and words were better left unsaid.

Monica could smell the fresh ocean air as the seagulls cawed, announcing their uninvited arrival onto the island. The town was now a faded resort location, a caricature of days gone by. As they drove along the old roads, there were no large hotels, shopping plazas or restaurants that had any of the typical chain names. Instead, small cottages, abandoned summer homes and anonymous eateries dotted the landscape. The bright summer sun was quite warm now, but a cool breeze from the ocean allowed them to keep the car's top lowered.

As they drove, Monica remained very quiet. Brad respected her need for silence, as they both pondered what lay ahead. In a few minute's time, they were in the center of Atlantic Point Island.

Monica didn't know if the beach house she'd inherited was habitable. She wanted to stay there, if possible, but Horace had neglected to tell her what condition the house was in at the reading of Lydia's will. All Monica had was an address, some clean sets of sheets that she had packed, and the keys that had been found in the hidden filing cabinet. She also had the keys that were returned to her from the New Jersey State Police.

So far, there were no signs of Atlantic Point Park, and no signs of the first Caprice Hotel. Monica decided to pull into a small commercial area that was near the center of town so they could get directions, as the GPS did not recognize the address of the old beach house.

There were several small stores, a few restaurants, a 20-room motel and an old clapboard restaurant that caught Monica's eye. The restaurant was called, Belle Brandt's Bar & Grille. It wasn't so much the restaurant that caught her attention as the name of the place. Monica knew the name "Belle Brandt," she just couldn't remember where from.

After parking the car and putting a quarter into the ancient parking meter, they walked into a small general store that seemed to have a bit of everything. An older gentleman with skin weathered from many years in the sun greeted them with a cheerful hello.

"Good afternoon, I was wondering if you might be able to help us with some directions?" Monica asked with a dazzling smile.

"I've lived here my entire life folks, I'd better be able to tell you where just about everything is."

"Great!" Monica replied, "The address is 408 Ocean Boulevard. It's an old beach house that…"

Before Monica could answer, the man cut her off.

"I know where that is." His reply was curt. "That's the old Scott house. Now what would you be going there for?"

Not wanting to tell the man their real reason for being in town, Monica commented that she and Brad were interested in buying the place. After giving them stilted directions, the man indicated that he had to get busy. They could feel his eyes bore into them until they exited the store. Monica shivered, despite the bright summer sun.

"That was strange," Brad commented.

"No kidding. What do you think that was all about?"

"I don't know, but maybe we should keep our identity a secret while we're in town."

They followed the man's directions, which turned out to be accurate and easy to follow, despite his cold mannerism. In a short time they were pulling up to a large beachfront house that faced the ocean. The beach house was 1960s vintage in exterior design and condition. It was overgrown and paint was peeling from its many facades, windows dark with age and dirt stared back blindly.

"Do you want to stay here or at the little motel?" Monica asked Brad.

"Let's stay here Monica, I'm game. We can come and go as we please without anyone knowing, provided the house is still habitable."

"I think that Mother stayed here last November, so I'm guessing that it can't be too bad."

"Not if Lydia stayed here."

They walked along the broken sidewalk and up the rickety wooden steps to the front door. All the glass appeared to be intact except for some small windows near the roof line. Monica fumbled with the key set that had been her mother's. Before the trip, she had rinsed the dried mud off the entire key set, but she still felt uncomfortable handling the keys that were found in the smashed Jaguar. She located the door key and the door creaked open.

The inside was not as bad as she had expected, but the furnishings were definitely from the 1960s and 1970s. A large record player with an eight-track tape deck sat just inside the oversized living room. Monica was reminded of the low budget "surf" movies that were so popular in that era. It was obvious that the layers of dust did not extend back for thirty years. Most likely Lydia had the house cleaned in anticipation of her visit last November. They were both surprised to find that the water and the electric were still turned on.

"Rural municipalities are slow at turning off unpaid utilities."

"Maybe Mother paid them in advance and the house wasn't used much."

After unpacking they took a quick tour of their new home. The corner convenience store provided the tools needed to give two of the bathrooms and two of the bedrooms a good cleaning. Afterward they decided to shower and go into town for dinner. Monica wanted to go to Belle Brandt's place. The name intrigued her, and Brad liked the idea too. They might get some useful information from a local hangout.

It was seven o'clock when they reached the restaurant. It was still light outside, but evening was on its way. Outside the clapboard siding gave the place a rundown look, but the inside was another story. It was alive with music, people and activity.

The crowd was older and the live music catered to the tastes of a bygone era, but Monica found the upbeat atmosphere interesting and she was energized by the big band sound. The tables and the bar stools were filled. The rear section of the restaurant was glass and faced out toward the ocean, providing an endless display of ocean, waves and sand.

Near the end of the bar were two empty stools which Monica and Brad grabbed. Atlantic Point seemed so deserted that it was hard to believe the restaurant could be so full. On the very last barstool sat an older woman. She was tall and thin with an air of sophistication and elegance. Her hair was streaked with lines of silver and she was poised with one hand resting on her left hip. She smiled at Brad and Monica and reached across to shake their hands.

"Welcome to my restaurant. I'm Belle Brandt."

After introducing themselves as Brad and Monica, they ordered drinks and began a conversation with the proprietor. She was all too eager to talk. Brad and Monica found her tales interesting. As a youngster, Belle had been a child film star in the 1950s. She made a lot of money in her day until her career ended as she reached adulthood. Three husbands later, she had settled in Atlantic Point and opened the restaurant in 1975.

Monica realized how she knew Belle's name. She had taken a film history class at college and they had studied early, colorized movies. "Why did you open the restaurant here?" Monica inquired.

"I had many fond memories of this place from when I was a child. There was a great amusement park here. I spent many happy times there. That was one of the benefits of making a lot of money as a kid." Belle's voice was deep and gravely as she spoke of times past.

Brad seized the opportunity to get directions to the park.

"You kids thinking of going out there? That place has been closed for thirty years. Not much to see anymore."

"We'll have to see how much time we have," Brad answered without commitment.

As the night wore on, Monica found herself caught up in the self-contained world of Belle Brandt's establishment. Everyone seemed to know the proprietor. A continuous throng of people stopped to say hello, and every one of them was introduced to Monica and Brad. There was a singer from New York City, a sophisticated older gentleman who was flirting with Belle, and an assortment of local townspeople. Some were actual vacationers whom had known Belle for many years. Monica enjoyed meeting the parade of interesting guests and even Brad engaged in the conversations.

The only time Monica felt uncomfortable was when Belle's handy man stopped by. Monica and Brad were introduced to the man who went by the name of "Old Joe." He did not offer to shake either Brad or Monica's hand. Old Joe barely grumbled two words but continued to gaze at Monica with an icy stare. He made her feel very uncomfortable.

When he shuffled off with his broom, Belle apologized to Monica for Old Joe's rude behavior. "He's been with me for ten years, but half the time he's out of it. I feel sorry for him, so I keep him around. I guess I just have a soft heart."

The rest of the night went by in a blur. Dinner consisted of Belle's freshly broiled seafood platter, delicious and filling. Late in the evening Belle informed Brad and Monica that she was closing for the night. They both expressed their thanks for a great time and promised they would return. As Monica turned to leave, she noticed Old Joe standing in the shadows of the darkened service corridor that led to the kitchen. He stared at her without flinching, even after he realized that Monica had observed him. Monica reached for Brad's hand, but she could not suppress the chill that ran up her spine.

Chapter Sixteen

Maxwell poured himself another drink. Tomorrow he would take a flight to Trenton and then drive the rest of the way to Atlantic Point Island. The thought of being at the Trenton-Mercer Airport unnerved Maxwell. The airport was where Ronald Scott's Cadillac Eldorado had been found abandoned all those years ago. Maxwell never wanted to see the place again.

Several calls to Monica had been futile. She wasn't answering her cell phone or responding to the many text messages Maxwell had sent. He had tried to get information out of Francine Crowley, Monica's assistant, but she was not divulging anything to Maxwell. Francine hadn't said two words to Maxwell since the day he had gone charging out of the office in a vain attempt to locate Janice. Francine had always been loyal to Lydia and now Monica, but as of late, she was very cold toward Maxwell. Apparently no one wanted anything to do with him. His new assistant had not returned to work after the first week and the temporary agency indicated that she had accepted another assignment.

Maxwell thought back to that final night at Janice's condominium. He finally realized that something about Janice was different that night. Maxwell should have accepted Janice's offer to leave and start a new life with whatever time he had left. The constant pain in his chest reminded him that time might be running out.

Maxwell was deep into his thoughts when Evelyn, his housekeeper, appeared to say that dinner was ready. How many dinners had Evelyn prepared for him over so many years? Maxwell did not feel like eating, but he didn't have the heart to tell Evelyn he would not eat a meal that she had spent the better part of the day preparing for him.

Evelyn opened a bottle of dark burgundy wine. She poured a glass for Maxwell and one for herself. For the remainder of the evening, Maxwell forced all thoughts of the problems he was facing out of his mind. A second bottle of burgundy followed the first, then, Maxwell and Evelyn adjourned to the main living room to relax following dinner. They talked for several hours about the great times they had shared over the years. Evelyn had taken care of Maxwell's household for longer than he could remember. He wondered just how much longer he would be around to enjoy her company.

A cool ocean breeze floated into the living room. It was very comforting. Before he knew it, Maxwell had fallen asleep on the oversized sofa. Evelyn covered him with a quilt before she retired to her quarters. Several hours later Maxwell awakened and realized he was still lying on the sofa. Morning would be here before he knew it. He turned to go back to sleep but a sudden vision forced him wide-awake. With the greatest clarity, he could see Ronald Scott's Cadillac parked in the shadows of the deserted lot beside the airport. Maxwell sat straight up. He would not get any more sleep tonight.

Brad awakened early. The old beach house did not have working air conditioning, so he and Monica had pried open some windows in their respective bedrooms. The cool ocean air was refreshing and tainted with mist, but the bright sunlight had come streaming through the open windows at 6:00 a.m. Brad decided to make the most of it and headed out onto the beach for an early morning run.

Before leaving Brad scribbled a note for Monica, left it on the old, patterned Formica table in the kitchen and then headed for the beach. He ran to the north on the hard-packed sand. It was obvious that Atlantic Point was no longer a tourist destination. The beaches were littered with debris, some from the ocean, some from inconsiderate people who dropped their trash. The beachfront was not speckled with the usual assortment of condominiums or homes that were found at more popular destinations. Run down beach cottages that looked like they were built in the middle part of the last century dotted the shoreline. Many of them appeared to be uninhabitable.

Farther along the way was a collapsing boardwalk. Large holes gaped where the boards were missing. The small shops that once lined the boardwalk were long since closed, their faded signs still proclaiming sales from days gone by. Most were boarded up or had smashed out windows that had once displayed worthless beach trinkets to susceptible tourists.

The beach had no life guard stations anywhere. If people swam here, they were on their own. Brad was sweating as he continued running along the water. He passed two teenagers flying a massive kite and ran around them so he would not interfere with their line. A rocky pier jutted out into the water and Brad slowed down momentarily. He eventually scurried over the rocks and continued jogging. Suddenly he stopped again, but it was not because of any more obstacles.

To his left, sitting along the boardwalk was a long, two-story structure, elbowing off both sides at western angles. It was boarded up like most every other building in the area, but it was not the dilapidated appearance that caught his attention. It was the building's sign suspended from two massive, rusted iron supports that made him stare. The unlighted letters were almost all broken out. But the name was still visible, despite the toll the rough northern seaside winters had taken on the fixture. Caprice Hotel, Atlantic Point, 1500 Beach Place. Brad noted the address. It was the same address that was on the unpaid tax notice.

Brad continued staring in awe at the sprawling old complex—the company's very first hospitality venture. A swarm of eager seagulls began cawing and he was startled back to his surroundings.

Brad walked over toward the old hotel. The front doors were boarded up and so were the adjacent windows over what must have been the main lobby. The strong smell of rotting wood wafted out from the building, almost as if it were warning him to stay away. Brad pulled on the doors. They moved but did not open. He pulled harder and the door on the right gave way with a splintering sound. The rotted wood had not taken much effort to break free from the old lock.

Inside, Brad strained to see. After a momentary adjustment to the darkness from the bright sunlight outside, Brad was surprised how much light filtered in from the cracks between the boards over the windows. The lobby continued through the building toward what was once the main entrance on the street side of the hotel.

The registration desk sat to the right inside the door. The desk was just large enough that one or two people could work behind it, not like the massive, marbled desks at the newer hotels. A mail rack was attached to the wall behind the desk. Brad thought just how much had changed. Five or more people could work behind the mahogany and granite desk at the Caprice Hotel in Palm Beach and there was even a self-service terminal available. For security reasons mail racks could no longer be used because mail sitting in the rack revealed which rooms were occupied to potential hotel room thieves.

Debris covered much of the floor. Small movements indicated that the hotel's current guest list was restricted to birds and mice. Brad edged around the lobby. A side corridor led back to a group of offices. Tarnished name plaques were still on the three office doors: Ronald Scott, President; Lydia Scott, Vice President; Maxwell Williams, General Manager. Despite having the amusement park, Ronald and Lydia had maintained offices at the hotel along with Maxwell. How long ago that had been, Brad realized.

He pushed open the three office doors one by one. The offices still contained dilapidated desks and chairs with dark foam stuffing bursting out. The smell of must was almost overwhelming. Ronald Scott's office was the largest. Maxwell's had been the second largest despite his rank back then as number three. Lydia's office was farther down the corridor. Brad peered into it. It was much the same as the other two. Just as he was about to leave, he spotted a white lace handkerchief. Everything in the office was dark, gray and rotting, so the white handkerchief was clearly out of place. The

185

handkerchief had fallen onto the edge of the desk but was protected from leaks by the desk's hutch.

Brad reached over and picked up the handkerchief. The delicate stitching told him that it belonged to a woman. It seemed somehow familiar to him. He brought the handkerchief to his nose and the fragrance was unforgettable. Lydia had been here sometime in the recent past. The handkerchief had not been left behind thirty years ago. Somehow Lydia had gotten inside the hotel more recently. Brad felt sure she must have visited last November when she had come to Atlantic Point to address the commissioners. The thought of Lydia inside the deserted hotel office on a cold and dark November night made Brad shudder, despite the warming day. He folded the handkerchief and placed it inside his pocket, jammed the broken door shut and headed back outside. He turned and ran at full speed in the direction of the beach house.

Monica awakened to find that Brad was not there. She knew even before she read the note that he was out for a run on the beach. There was no food or coffee in the dusty old kitchen. Monica decided to walk the short distance to the little convenience store where they had purchased the cleaning supplies yesterday. Monica didn't bother to lock the house because she wouldn't be gone very long.

The air was fresh and the smell of the ocean perked her up. She was also excited that today, she and Brad would see Atlantic Point Park. Monica slipped on a pair of sandals. Sand seemed to cover everything in a fine layer, just as it did in Palm Beach, but this town was so different. Everything in Palm Beach was manicured. Nothing in Atlantic Point Island was even trimmed. It was sad to think that it had once been a prominent vacation spot until the amusement park closed, turning the entire area into a near ghost town.

A little bell jingled as Monica opened the door to the convenience store, which was named Fanny's. A small self-service coffee area held a single pot of fresh brewed coffee. Monica put two of the cold creamers into a cup and poured the coffee into the creamer. She headed for the cash register. Monica was shocked when the middle-aged clerk asked her for just one dollar even for the large coffee. Monica felt so guilty getting such a large cup of coffee for such a small price that she asked the woman if the price was correct.

"Sure is," she replied with a warm smile.

When Monica got back to the beach house, she found Brad there. She had not thought to get Brad a cup of coffee and he pretended that he was offended. They both had a good laugh, but Monica detected that something was wrong.

Brad told her of his adventure in the old Caprice Hotel. Monica listened in rapt silence. Then Brad told her about finding a handkerchief in Lydia's former office. Monica still didn't yet understand the significance of Brad's find. With care and respect, he pulled the handkerchief out of his pocket. Monica recognized the style that she had seen her Mother carry for all their years together. Slowly she raised the handkerchief to her nose. Lydia's scent was still present. Monica breathed in the fragrance that had been her mother's and tears began to stream down her face.

The engine in the Mustang started and Brad pressed the button to lower the top, after which the bright afternoon sunlight lightened the mood in the car. He glanced at Monica as the rays of the sun glinted off her long blonde hair. Brad's desire for her was stronger than ever, especially now when she seemed so vulnerable. Vulnerability was something that had never appeared in Monica's character before. Brad wanted to hold her and comfort her, but Monica seemed unable to absorb anything except the tumultuous events that had overtaken her existence.

Monica had a good cry after Brad handed her the handkerchief that had been Lydia's. He had dried her tears and then asked her if she would like to postpone their exploration of the park. Monica had been adamant that she would not put off her first visit to the park. They had stopped at the corner grocery store, grabbed some sandwiches and then stocked a picnic cooler with ice, drinks and snacks. It would be a long day of exploration and they wanted to be prepared.

The trip to the park would take them back to the mainland. The directions that Brad had obtained from Belle Brandt led them over the Atlantic Point Bridge and back onto route 72, the same route that they had entered the island on. After passing the small housing community of Bayside, Belle had told them to drive for one mile and they would see a narrow road on their right. Belle had commented that the last time she had driven past there it was overgrown and it would be easy to miss.

Brad accelerated over the last bridge and the warm day seemed to mask the eerie feeling that had crept over both of them ever since Brad had stumbled onto his find in the old hotel. The main road seemed empty considering it should be the height of the tourist season. No one was behind them and there was only an occasional car that passed going in the opposite direction. The lack of cars was a comforting feeling to Brad and Monica after being tailed for hundreds of miles up the coast.

Brad slowed the car and they scanned the right side of the road for the park's entrance. Soon they spotted a narrow, rutted lane that was only wide enough for one vehicle to pass through. Brad turned the car onto the lane. The macadam had turned into potholes and sand. The Mustang rocked hard as the wheels dipped into the holes and shrubs brushed the car. Brad slowed down even further afraid the car would break an axle.

Creeping along at five miles per hour, they progressed down the old entryway. The trees and overgrowth were heavy. The temperature, while still warm, had dropped about 10 degrees. Trees blocked out much of the sunlight and cast shadows over the rutted lane, adding to the uneasiness that they both felt.

After driving several hundred feet, the lane widened into an overgrown parking lot that appeared to cover several acres. Bottles and smashed glass from a bygone era littered the empty lot. Several plastic soda bottles were lying around indicating that the area had also been littered in more recent times. Monica supposed the area was a great hangout for teens as it was secluded and had a history that would attract those who were not faint of heart.

As they drove across the lot, an iron fence appeared that ran along the east-west perimeter of the parking lot. It had once been black but was now covered in rust barnacles and dirt. Using the fence as their guide, they continued until they came upon two massive gates that were at least thirty feet high. The words, Atlantic Point Park dominated the massive entry gates. Monica gazed in awe at the park's grand entrance and even Brad seemed taken aback. The grounds behind the gates appeared to stretch on forever through the overgrowth. Monica could not suppress a shiver as she peered into her past.

Chapter Seventeen

Brad stopped the car and they both climbed out. Monica reached into the back seat and pulled out the fragile envelope with the brittle yellowed tape. Inside was the key set that she had found in the hidden closet back at the Palm Beach house. The massive key ring must have contained one hundred keys or more. The faded key tag indicated that the ring of keys was the second master set to Atlantic Point Park. What had happened to the first set?

"Atlantic Point Master Two," Brad mussed as he took the key set from Monica. He gazed at the massive gates. Brad had to stretch up to shoulder height to reach the keyhole that was set into the gates, wondering if the rusted lock would even open.

"Brad it might take us all day to find which key even opens the gates."

"I don't think so. I would suspect that the entrance key would be located to the left or to the right of the "AP" Master Two tag so it could be easily located each year.

Brad started with the key on the left. It was way too small to open the gates. The key on the right was larger and it appeared that it might fit. Brad eased the key into the lock. After a spray of WD-40, it went in with less difficulty than he had imagined. Now all he needed to do was to turn the tumblers without breaking off the key. The lock seemed reluctant to turn and Brad was careful not to apply too much pressure. The fence was too high for anyone to get over and it would take a locksmith to get in if the key broke off.

The key began to move to the right. Brad could feel the locking mechanism release and suddenly the massive gates edged forward about one half inch. Additional pressure moved the gates farther. Brad was glad he was strong; the gates weighed a ton and they groaned with a spine-chilling screech as they pushed apart. Brad told Monica to pull the Mustang into the park and they would lock the car in with them while they spent the day exploring. Monica started the car and pulled in through the opening. Driving through the gates was a grim reminder to Monica that whatever events had transpired here had caused her mother's death and maybe even the death of her father.

There was just enough paved space inside the park to pull the Mustang through before the overgrowth became impassable. Monica pulled in just far enough so that Brad could close the gates. By the time he was finished closing them he had begun to perspire. Brad paused to catch his breath then went over and had Monica put the top up on the car. They both grabbed some bottled water out of the cooler before they locked the Mustang.

"Where do you want to go first Monica?"

"I don't know. Let's just follow the easiest trail to start out with. This place looks like jungle land."

The path appeared to wind through the park in a giant loop that contained many side trails. Everywhere were rides and buildings in varying states of deterioration. Some were no longer identifiable. Multiple ticket booths lined the paths every so many yards. Peeling paint, smashed glass, overgrown gardens and massive decay were the park's main features. Monica was overcome by a feeling of sadness and she felt tears well in her eyes. She glanced away from Brad. Monica had already been crying once today and she didn't want Brad to see her in tears yet again.

They passed a picnic pavilion, now collapsed to the ground. As they walked along the path Monica had an eerie feeling that she had been at the park some time in her past. She remembered back to the night in New York when she had the nightmare about being in the park with her faceless father. Had it been a dream, or had she actually been in the park as a child? The thought gave her a chill that ran the length of her spine.

The merry-go-round appeared. It too seemed familiar to Monica, but then every park had a merry-go-round. They came into a wide circle that had many overgrown gardens. The feeling of familiarity persisted. There were spaces that had been for food vendors all around the circle. The carts of the vendors were nowhere in sight, but faded signs indicated that they had once held a position in the courtyard. Monica recalled getting cotton candy here in her dream.

"Brad, do you think that my mother might have brought me here at one time?"

"What would make you think that?"

"I had a dream when I was in New York, right after I learned that I had inherited the park, at least I thought it was a dream. I feel like I recognize this place. Everything looks so familiar."

They continued along the path. What had been a child's boat ride appeared next. The canvas roofs of the boats were in shreds and dank water filled the bottom of the boat canal. Monica exclaimed, "Brad I know I was here before. I was on that little boat ride."

"Lydia must have brought you here at some time Monica. The park was closed by the time you were born, but in the early years, some of the rides may have still been operable. Perhaps she returned here with you when you were a young child.

As they continued along the path the park's old wooden roller coaster came into close view, towering high over the park. Many of the support beams were lying around the bottom of the roller coaster. The eerie groaning sound left them both worried that the roller coaster could collapse at any moment. In Monica's dream, she had fallen out of the ride. As she gazed upward, she was reminded that a man had indeed plummeted to his death from the top of the roller coaster. It plagued her that she could not separate her nightmare from what seemed to be repressed memories.

Overhead, dark clouds were gathering. Despite the pending storm, they continued walking. An old movie house was the next building to appear along the path. Brad and Monica walked up to the door. Brad reminded Monica that there was a good chance that many of the buildings were no longer safe. Brad opened the unlocked door and the two stepped inside, adjusting their eyes to the dim.

The lobby was small and appeared to be decorated in typical 1980s theater motif. There were no movie posters anywhere, just emptied frames, but a large old popcorn machine sat in the middle of the former snack bar. A nest of mice had settled into the popcorn machine. Monica stifled a scream at the sight of the mice, hoping they would not exit their home. Monica and Brad proceeded through the dark lobby to the auditorium.

The single auditorium was much larger than the modern theaters that have become standard fare today. Monica was surprised by the size of the old place. A small amount of light permeated through several holes in the roof and the ever-leaking water had left behind a damp, musty smell. The theater's seats were still in place, but the curtains that had once concealed the massive screen were hanging in tattered pieces. Thunder rumbled in the distance.

"This place is creepy Brad, let's get out of here."

"I'll race you to the door."

They ran at full speed to the entrance door, which had somehow closed behind them. Brad tried to open the door but for all his strength it would not budge. Being locked in the dark theater gave him a momentary feeling of panic before his usual logical thoughts overcame the panic of being locked in the old movie house.

"Open the door Brad."

"I can't, it's stuck or it's locked."

"It can't be locked, it was unlocked when we arrived."

"We'll then it's stuck." Brad tried again but the door would not budge.

"Let me try Brad." Monica walked past Brad to the door. She reached down to the handle and turned it with ease. The door popped opened and a darkening sky appeared.

"How'd you do that Monica?"

"You forget, it's my amusement park," Monica laughed.

When they reached the outside, Brad pretended to be indignant that he could not open the door.

"It just takes a special touch," Monica replied.

As they walked on through the park, they encountered thick growth and a growing storm overhead. The path had all but disappeared, leaving the placement of the deteriorating rides to guide them through the park.

"Do you want to turn back yet Monica? I think we're going to be soaked when this storm starts."

"Not yet Brad. Horace told me that there had been one final project before the park closed. My mother built a large office building, despite knowing the park was nearing its final days of operation. I want to find it. I think it may hold the answers to the events that have transpired."

As they continued, the next amusement to appear was a low black building with faded red letters that proclaimed, "Haunted House."

"Wow, that's a creepy building," Brad commented.

"It sure is."

As they approached the haunted house, they were both more cautious after their experience at the movie theater. The old haunted house was the last place they would want to get locked inside. Brad examined the main entrance. The wooden door was so crooked that there was no way it could slam closed. It was painted black like the rest of the building. The entire structure was made of rotting wood and Brad again urged caution. Rain began blowing onto the porch prompting them to go inside the ancient attraction. They tested each floorboard for sturdiness as they progressed forward.

Various displays that were made to frighten long ago guests had taken on a surreal appearance as they aged and disintegrated. They were even more frightening today than they had been when the haunted house had operated as part of the park. The roof of the haunted house had more leaks in it than the roof of the movie theater. Lightning flashed through the roof's holes, adding to the creepy effect.

"Monica, I think we should get out of here. This place isn't safe."

"Wait. Look at that display."

The faded white sign indicated they were in, "Dracula's Lair."

"What about it?"

"Brad look again. What's missing from the display?"

Brad peered at the old display. Then it dawned on him. The Dracula display had one notable feature missing. Oblong marks on the floor indicated where there should have been a coffin but instead was just empty space. A second later, thunder rumbled and lightening flashed through yet another hole in the roof. Brad shivered, grabbed Monica and they headed for the door.

It was a massive relief when they reached the outside. It was getting later in the day and the storm was casting deep shadows over the amusement park.

"Brad, why would that display be missing its coffin?"

"I don't know Monica. It appears when they closed the park, they left everything as it was on the last day of operation, almost as if they intended to reopen at some time. I have no idea why anyone would have taken time to remove the coffin from the haunted house."

Monica stifled a chill. Thoughts were running through her mind at a mile a minute. She forced all of them to the side. She would have to sort it all out later at her own pace. Brad's analytical nature had taken over. He was pondering the missing coffin and he had become very quiet.

"Are you ready to go back to town?"

"No, let's wait out the storm here on the porch of the haunted house. I still want to see the office building. We're almost to the end of the property—it has to be here some place."

Ten minutes later the storm abated and they continued through the darkening park. They had to be careful. The overgrowth was now soaking wet and slippery. Both Monica and Brad were concentrating on not falling when a large three-story building loomed above them, imposing its will that they pass no farther.

"That's it Monica, Atlantic Point Corporation's main offices."

Monica gazed at the building. It was larger and grander than she had imagined. Sidewalks broke through the overgrowth and eased their approach to the huge office building. The structure appeared untouched by time, unlike the rest of the park. There was no broken glass and no unlocked doors. Smoked glass windows concealed whatever secrets the building held. Both Monica and Brad were amazed at the good condition of the building. Heavy overgrowth was still evident, but the office building appeared to be entirely intact.

Monica had stuck the AP Master Two key ring in her oversized bag, and now she reached for it. For the next hour, both she and Brad tried all the keys on the entire master set without success. Neither of them found a single key that would fit into the main entrance door. At one point, Brad tried to force the entry door open, but the door wouldn't budge. Impending darkness made it harder and harder to see.

"I think that we're going to have to come back tomorrow with a locksmith," Brad observed.

"Brad, I don't think the key is here."

"We don't know that Monica. Maybe we inserted it the wrong way."

"I don't think it's here Brad. For some reason, the key to this door is not on the master key ring."

Just then Monica had an idea. "I know where the key is Brad!"

"Where?"

"It's on the other key ring. The ring that Mother had with her when she went off the bridge."

"Give it here then."

"I can't. I took the key to the beach house off Mother's ring and added it to my own ring. The rest of the set is back at the beach house."

Brad gave the door one final hard shove in frustration. It did not budge or even shake, providing an impenetrable barrier to whatever was hidden on the other side.

"We'll have to come back tomorrow. This door is not going to move without that key."

Just then the storm let go again in full force soaking them to the skin.

Janice gazed into the mirror as she applied her makeup. She was getting tired of New York. The smog, the noise and the crowds were wearing on her. After so long it all became a part of you, or you got out— Janice intended to get out. The sooner the better. Just a little more time.

Janice had mailed the second round of envelopes a few days ago and it wouldn't be long until her plan was complete. Then she would be on her way to the Cayman Islands to start her new life. Janice thought that after working at Caprice for more than thirty years, she would miss something about the place. She didn't. Not for a single minute did Janice miss the oppressive environment that she had spent so many years working in. Never again would she be told what to do by that spoiled brat Monica Scott or her dead mother.

Janice had been all over New York. Broadway, shopping, expensive dinners, even a classic speak easy. She went alone or she went with a male companion, as long as he paid. It was flattering to her that she could still turn so many heads.

Janice was pleased when Vance Richards, her attorney, had sent a text message the previous day. Her condominium in Palm Beach sold for more than she expected, netting her another $1.4 million dollars. Money was coming at her from all directions. What an awful problem she chuckled to herself. The rest of her holdings were being readied for transfer to the Caymans. The biggest difficulty had been figuring out how to move the huge amount of cash that her latest endeavor would yield. Two million dollars was a lot of bills. With the drug smuggling problems, persons carrying huge amounts of cash were immediately suspect at any airport.

For Janice, it wasn't a problem; her partner in the venture was a licensed pilot. With his help, they would fly the money to the islands in a private plane using an interim destination on their flight plan. Janice would follow whatever proper procedures were necessary to get the private plane out of U.S. jurisdiction. After that it didn't matter because the officials in the Cayman Islands would not give her any difficulty. Janice had already made the payoffs necessary to insure an easy and unquestioned entry into paradise.

One last glance in the mirror told her she was ready for another night on the town. Janice phoned down to the concierge. "This is Ms Laneer, have the hotel limousine ready to take me to The Uptown Club at 7:30. Don't be late." Janice hung up without another word. She strolled over to the plush, dark gray sofa that dominated her hotel suite. Janice picked up her cell, careful to not scratch the new paint on her fingernails. She pressed the screen and the call was placed.

After four rings, which was three too many for Janice, the phone was answered.

"Hello."

"Are you on your way?"

"I'm at the airport now."

"I've made dinner reservations for us at The Uptown Club."

"I'll be there."

Janice tapped the cell phone off, picked up a glamour magazine and prepared to pass the next hour until she took the limo over to the restaurant.

The limousine arrived at the hotel right at 7:30. Janice stood at the curb until the door was opened for her. She glided into the limousine. A stocked bar was placed along the side and Janice decided to enjoy a split of champagne while she relaxed for the ride to the restaurant. The champagne was good but not quite the quality she was used to. For once, Janice had too much on her mind to complain. Yet again, she reviewed all the details of her plan. Nothing could go wrong or she could be riding in the back of a police cruiser instead of the back of a limousine. Janice shuddered as the thought fleeted through her mind.

Traffic was light, at least by New York standards. The limousine driver deftly wove through the night-lighted city and Janice began to feel more relaxed as she drank the champagne. She was too good to get caught. It would never happen. In short order the exquisite restaurant came into view. The driver pulled the limousine to the curb. He all but ran around to open Janice's door. She alighted from the limousine, pausing to hand the driver a tip.

A doorman opened the restaurant's heavy door as Janice approached. He nodded but she did not acknowledge him. The maître d' recognized her from a recent visit. Janice was a very attractive woman. The maître d' deftly weaved to the table that Janice requested when she made the reservations.

She had asked for this table because it was in a location that was not prominent and yet she could watch the door for her guest's arrival. A sommelier appeared and she ordered a bottle of very expensive champagne. Janice wanted to celebrate tonight and now she had the money to do it. Soon she would have even more money.

A server appeared to take an appetizer order and Janice explained that she would be having a guest join her in a tone that made it clear she was not to be disturbed until further notice. She glanced at her diamond-studded watch. He had better not be late. So far he wasn't.

A flurry of movement drew her eye to the reception area inside the front door. Her guest had arrived. He looked very suave, dressed in a sleek, black Italian suit with a matching tie. If she hadn't seen it with her own eyes, she would have never believed it.

The maître d' led the man over to her table. The suit made him look taller and thinner than his usual stance. As he approached the table Janice rose to greet him. He placed his hands on her hips while he kissed her hard on the lips. The man assisted Janice back to her chair and commented how beautiful she looked.

"Why Drake, what took you so long to notice?"

Chapter Eighteen

Monica and Brad retreated to the park's entrance as the storm continued dumping cold, wet rain on them. The going was not easy. The park was in near complete darkness and everywhere they stepped was slippery. Heavy clouds hid the moon, and several times they had to pause and catch their breath. Atlantic Point Park was even creepier at night than it had been in the daytime.

Monica shuddered as she thought of her mother making a visit to the park on a cold November night less than a year ago. The weather then must have been bone chilling with the relentless winds from the nearby ocean. Alone in the park and for what reason.

Even more unnerving was the discovery of the missing coffin at the Dracula display. Was her missing father buried in it somewhere in the park? Was her mother's death connected to a secret that she had hidden for more than thirty years? What part did Maxwell play in the secret? He had to know something to have had them tailed for hundreds of miles. Maxwell had admitted knowing that Lydia kept the park a secret from Monica. What else did he know?

"We're almost there." Brad's comment startled Monica out of her thoughts.

"We're drenched Brad."

"Do you have any cleaning towels in the trunk?"

"There's a couple in the trunk from the last time it was washed."

"A couple is all we need."

Brad opened the trunk and grabbed two of the towels. He placed them on the car seats and Monica jumped into the car as the downpour continued. Brad went to the gates, unlocked them and then struggled to pull them open. Monica was in the driver's seat and backed the car out of the park. After re-locking the gates, Brad jumped in the car beside her. The dry relief was comforting for both of them.

Monica drove through the dark, potholes rocking the car in a continuous splash dance. She did not want to get stuck in the abandoned parking lot in the dark. After what seemed like an eternity, they reached the main road and headed back to town.

"Where do you want to go for dinner Monica?"

"Let's go to Belle Brandt's place. It's open late and I like the atmosphere. Maybe we can get some more information before we go back to the park tomorrow."

In a few minutes Monica had driven over the bridges and back up the coast to Atlantic Point Island. The beach house came into sight a few minutes later.

"Brad I have to make some phone calls after I change out of these wet clothes. Let's leave in an hour."

Monica placed the first call to Francine Crowley, her administrative assistant. The sound of Francine's voice was a welcome familiarity.

"Francine it's Monica."

"Monica, how's your vacation?"

"It's anything but a vacation."

"I know, but I was hoping you were having some fun. Did you find the park?"

"Yes, but something happened along the way. We were tailed for hundreds of miles."

"You're kidding."

"No, I wish I were. I think Maxwell is behind it."

"Somehow that doesn't surprise me. I've never trusted him or that Janice Laneer."

"I never realized you felt that way about them."

"I kept my feelings well-hidden Monica, but not anymore. When you return, we need to have a long talk about the way things are going around here. By the way, have you heard the news about Janice?"

"What news?"

"She left with no notice. Cleaned out her desk one evening after we had all left for the day, cleaned out her condominium and left town. No one knows where she is or why she left. Even Maxwell doesn't seem to know where she is. He was gone an entire day looking for her!"

"That is a surprise. Janice was there forever. So much has happened, it seems like I've been gone a long time and yet it's only been a few days."

"I was surprised Janice left after all these years, but don't you worry. I have everything under control."

"Is there any other news?"

"Some mail is missing from your desk. I placed several personal envelopes on your blotter. I never open your personal mail, but I know what

I put in your office. An unstamped envelope disappeared. I think Maxwell took it."

"Do you think they were related to hotel business?"

"No, I open the official mail. This was unusual. No stamp, no return address and no company name. Maxwell received an identical mailing himself."

"Francine, has Maxwell been coming into the office."

"Why yes he has."

"I'll be back soon to tell you all about the park. Call me if you need me and lock my personal mail in your desk until I get back."

"You be careful Monica. You're all we have left to keep the company together."

The next call was to Jeanette. She had been worried and was relieved to hear from Monica. Jeanette reassured her that Midnight, Star and Swirl were doing fine as was the homestead. Monica heard Midnight barking from somewhere inside the house and she felt pangs of homesickness. The clothing they had shipped to Honduras had arrived intact and Jeanette thanked Monica, yet again, for the donation. After quick goodbyes, they hung up. The next number Monica phoned was Drake Donovan's. Drake answered after several rings.

"Drake, it's Monica."

"Greetings, where are you?"

"I'm in a town in New Jersey called Atlantic Point Island."

"Atlantic Point Island?"

"Yes. Are you caught up enough at the Virginia property to make a visit here?"

"I think I can manage that. What's up?"

"I have a couple of renovation projects I'd like you to take a look at."

"Not a problem. Are you buying a hotel up there?"

"No, I've inherited a house and some property. They both need a lot of fix up. Here's the address Drake. Call me when you're on your way." Monica would wait until he arrived to tell him about the shuttered amusement park.

As she was talking to Drake, Brad walked into the room. Monica glanced up and saw the angry, hurt look on his face at the mention of Drake's name. After she disconnected with Drake, she made a feeble explanation to Brad about wanting Drake to renovate the beach house and have a look at the park.

Brad said little in response. He just remained composed and then went to change out of his wet clothes while Monica made her final call. Maxwell answered on the first ring.

"Monica, how are you?" The sound of Maxwell's voice made Monica very uneasy.

"I'm fine Maxwell. I just called to check on the hotels. Is everything all right?"

"You bet darling. You have nothing to worry about. I have everything under control *as always*."

A wave of disgust washed over Monica. She debated confronting Maxwell about everything that was happening but decided against it. One thousand miles on a telephone call was not the way to confront her suspicions, especially if Maxwell was as good a liar as Monica now believed that he was. It could also be dangerous. Monica wanted Maxwell to believe he still had her trust. After a brief rundown on the status of each of the five hotels, Maxwell asked her where she was vacationing.

"We're touring all over Maxwell. Listen, I must run. See you when I get back. Hugs and kisses."

Monica hung up. She felt like slamming the phone onto the floor. Maxwell's apparent betrayal after all these years was very hard for her to accept.

Brad walked back into the room. He told her he was walking up to Fanny's store while she got ready for dinner. He didn't say a word about Drake. It galled Monica that he could be so controlled. She wished he'd just let his feelings out and even yell at her if it helped, but there was no such thing as yelling with Brad Roberts. Monica headed to the bathroom.

It was already late when Monica and Brad found their way to a table facing out onto the ocean at the rear of Belle Brandt's restaurant. A number of tables had patrons, but the crowd was not as heavy as it had been on their last visit. Monica wondered where the people came from with the town being so deserted. After thinking about it, she realized there were still several townspeople, a few old-time vacationers and very few places to go.

Both of them ordered appetizers and drinks. Conversation between Brad and Monica remained strained. They should have had a lot to talk about after their long day in the park. Brad must still be upset about the call to Drake.

A short time later the server reappeared with their appetizers and took their dinner orders. Belle Brandt made her entrance into the restaurant a short while later. She recognized Brad and Monica and strolled over to their table, drink in hand.

"Good evening my friends," she raised her glass to them.

Belle's appearance seemed to put Brad and Monica at ease. They both liked her.

"I just stopped by to say hello. I try to never disturb my guests with my stories until they've eaten. It's bad for business," Belle chuckled in her gravelly voice. "When you're finished with dinner, you're welcome to join me at the bar for a drink."

"We'll be over to see you in little while Belle. We'd love to talk with you," Monica answered.

After dinner Brad and Monica walked over to the end of the bar where Belle was sitting. Monica steered the conversation to Atlantic Point Park and the disappearance of the park's owner. She told Belle she had heard stories around town about the unsolved disappearance of the park's proprietor. Monica wanted information but she didn't want to reveal too much about herself to Belle just yet.

"I knew the people that owned the park, as they were regular patrons here. It's a small town and not much gets by me, even back then when we had a busy tourist trade. They never did find the man that disappeared and his wife closed the park and moved away. Closing the park ruined the town."

Belle did not provide Monica and Brad with any more information. Perhaps if she knew why they were asking she could have been more helpful and direct. Monica resolved to tell Belle the truth as soon as she felt she could. She had met the woman on just two occasions, and yet she felt as if she had known her for many years. Perhaps it was Belle's gutsy zest for life that she was attracted to.

Both Brad and Monica were tired from their long day of exploring and decided to leave after one more drink with Belle. Saying goodnight, they headed out the front door into the parking lot. The lot was dark and empty. Brad had parked the Mustang off to the right side of the building. As they neared the car, Monica glanced out toward the ocean and past the restaurant. Her eyes locked upon a man standing in the shadows of the building staring at her and as she spotted him, he slipped behind the restaurant. Monica shuddered as she stifled a scream. When Brad asked her what was wrong she replied, "A man was staring at me. Then he slipped behind the building. It was the same man that was staring at me the last time we were here."

Morning came too soon. Brad and Monica decided to stop at one of the few small eateries that dotted the landscape on the way to the route 72 bridge. They refilled the cooler with ice and refreshments from the store and headed out. A quick breakfast re-charged them and then they were on their way to the park. Clouds blocked the sun today and the temperature had cooled way down. Monica was always amazed that a beach town could change weather so drastically in such a short time.

Monica brought both the Atlantic Point master key set and her mother's personal keys this time. After securing the car inside the park they set off in the opposite direction from yesterday's tour. Brad suggested that they could follow the path from the opposite direction to see the other side of the park, presuming they could approach the office building from the other direction. Going in the new direction, they did not find any rides. There were three closed down restaurants on the first part of the trail but the next buildings to come into site were old service buildings. Many of them were collapsing. The larger buildings had garage style doors. Several of the doors were in semi-opened positions.

Neither Brad nor Monica went inside any of the service buildings. They appeared to hold endless amounts of rusted equipment that had not been used for 30 years. Monica commented that it must have taken an army of staff to maintain and operate the huge park and Brad responded that the payroll must have been enormous. They both chuckled and plodded onward. The overgrowth was thick throughout, and at times it was tricky to keep moving. Brad estimated that they were halfway to the office building.

Monica scratched at the many bug bites she had received yesterday. She wished she had taken time to get some natural repellant as she knew today would produce more of the same. Brad was not as bitten up as Monica was. He claimed the bugs didn't like him. They were three fourths of the way to the office building when they spotted another service building sitting farther back into the woods.

There was something about the building that drew Monica's attention. It was the one building where someone had taken time to board the windows over. All the other buildings had broken windows, open doors or some of both. This building appeared to be completely secured. Monica and Brad diverted off the main path and headed toward the old structure. Brad scouted around the outside for a way to get in. Everything was tightly locked.

Monica pulled out the Atlantic Point master key set. After about twenty tries, they located the key to the main garage door at the front of the building. The key turned in the rusty lock after much prodding from Brad. But, even after the lock turned, the garage door would not open. Brad pulled and pulled on it, but the door was rusted in place.

"Can't anything be easy around here?" he grumbled.

"Let me help you Brad."

Monica grabbed the handle on the left and Brad held onto the handle on the right. On the count of three they yanked, and the door opened about one inch. They inched it up until they were able to bend over and walk under it. It was very dark inside with the windows boarded up. Brad had brought a large, LED flashlight in anticipation of their tour of the office building.

He clicked it on and the dark walls illuminated from the shadows. The garage was empty except for a large covered object that was toward the far rear of the garage. Brad waived the flashlight at the object. It was covered in a heavy gage industrial canvas that appeared to be un-torn.

"Monica, I think there's a car under there."

"It sure looks like it."

They grasped the end of the cloth and pulled it up over the top toward the front of the car. Long dried puddles indicated the car had leaked out its fluids out many years ago.

Monica was not knowledgeable about makes of cars and she had no knowledge of antique autos, so she looked over the old black coupe for a nameplate. "Why would someone leave a single car stored in here?" she wondered aloud.

Brad returned to the back of the car and read the nameplate that was fixed on the rear. "It's a Cadillac Eldorado."

Monica let out a gasp.

"What's the matter Monica?"

"Brad. My father drove a Cadillac Eldorado. It was mentioned in the old newspaper articles I found. The car was abandoned at the Trenton-Mercer County Airport after he disappeared, with the luggage still in the trunk."

The car appeared to be in good condition despite the fact that it had sat untouched in the garage for many years. Brad opened the hood and looked at the engine. A mouse skittered across the ground as the activity disrupted his solitude. The keys were still in the ignition. Brad used them to open the trunk. The trunk was empty except for some accumulated dirt and a deflated spare tire.

The discovery of the car left Monica stunned. One by one the pieces of information that had been given to her by Horace Goldsmith and the old newspaper articles were forming a grim puzzle.

Monica walked out of the garage with Brad in tow. The fresh outdoor air was a relief from the dank, dusty smell of the old garage.

"Monica, don't get yourself upset. That car could belong to anyone. I'm sure Lydia would have sold your father's car when he didn't return."

"Why Brad? She held onto everything else."

"I guess you're right."

"Well there's no way of knowing now."

They started toward the main path when Monica had an idea. "Come on Brad, I want to go back to the garage and check something."

Brad followed.

Monica ducked down and headed through the partially open garage door. Brad switched on the flashlight and Monica went over to the passenger side of the car. She opened the door, which they had left unlocked and reached for the glove box. She asked Brad to pass her the flashlight. The bright beam overwhelmed the small, dark glove box. Inside was a faded automobile manual for the Eldorado, several yellowed maps and a small folder. Monica pulled out the folder and aimed the flashlight beam. She pulled out several documents. All of them had the name Randall Scott printed on them with expiration dates in 1985 and thereafter.

Monica now knew for sure the car had been her father's. He had disappeared from this very car at a deserted airport parking lot in 1985, or so the newspaper accounts had concluded. Monica suspected something even worse.

Chapter Nineteen

Drake rolled over. He squinted as the bright sunlight streamed through the double windows. Janice was seated at the dressing table.

"Monica's already in Atlantic Point Janice."

"Why didn't you tell me last night?"

"You were asleep when I came up from the lobby bar."

"I hope she brought her half of the payoff money with her."

"If Monica is there for the payoff, she didn't sound too upset. She just asked me to renovate a beach house that she inherited."

"That figures. Monica would have to renovate whatever house she lived in up to her high standards. Don't worry Drake; she'll have the payoff money. That spoiled brat would pay anything to keep Lydia's *good* name intact."

"I never thought she was spoiled Janice."

"You wouldn't because you were too busy assessing her other attributes."

Drake began to laugh. Janice came over and ran her hand down his bare back.

"Time to get dressed darlin'. We're leaving New York soon and I want to enjoy our last day around the town. We won't be back here for a long time, maybe not ever."

Drake got up and headed for the bathroom. He would have liked to have stayed in bed a while longer, especially if Janice were there with him, but there was no sense arguing with her. Janice always won.

Maxwell drove over to the UPS shipping station. It would be impossible to get two million dollars past the X-ray machine at the airport without questions being asked—questions that he couldn't afford to answer. Jim Abbott had the stock sale proceeds sent to Maxwell's bank, where the cash was dispensed after the lengthy reports the government required had been filled out. The branch manager had done everything he could to convince Maxwell to use a safer method of cash movement, even though Maxwell had not disclosed the real purpose of his actions. A few days prior he had purchased multiple versions of the board game Monopoly. When the cash arrived, he had opened each game box and replaced the play money with the two million dollars that the blackmailer had requested. Then he shrink-wrapped them with an old machine that was kept in a long-forgotten storeroom in the hotel. The last step was to place the games into two large cardboard boxes and then seal them with strips of reinforced packing tape. He would ship the money to the UPS station in Atlantic Point and pick it up when he arrived in New Jersey. On the shipping label, under contents, he wrote "board games."

Maxwell couldn't help but laugh at the irony. In a lifetime, he couldn't have imagined that the games he played thirty years ago would lead to this moment. He could only hope the money got to New Jersey safely, as there was no way to insure it.

After shipping the money, he headed back to the office. He wanted to clear a few things from his desk before he left for Atlantic Point. On the way back, he found his hands were shaking to the point that he could barely control the car. Maxwell pulled to the side of the road to regain his composure before he could continue.

A few minutes later he calmed down and was able to drive to the hotel without any further delays. He pulled up to the main entrance. Harry was on duty at the front door.

"Park my car," he barked at the elderly limousine driver.

"Yes sir, Mr. Williams.

Maxwell steamed through the lobby, and speaking to no one, he headed for the corridor that led to the executive office elevator. He punched the button and the door opened. Seconds later he was walking into the executive offices. Francine was there. Janice's desk was still empty. It was apparent that no one whom he interviewed wanted to work for him. The company's human resources department claimed they were still working on finding "just the right person." It was one more reminder of how miserable his life had become.

"Good morning Francine."

"Good morning."

Francine wouldn't even glance up at him. If it weren't for Lydia and Monica, he would have fired her. It took all his ebbing control to tolerate Francine's growing arrogance toward him. It occurred to Maxwell once again that she had never shown much respect to him, although he had to admit she had never been insubordinate.

"I have a few things to do before I leave for a business trip."

"You're leaving with Monica and Brad out of the office?"

Francine's condescending tone galled him.

"It can't be avoided. We have problems at the construction site of one of the new hotels."

"Where's Drake Donavan? I haven't heard anything about construction problems."

"Well why would you? You're just a secretary." Maxwell slammed the door to his office shut before he could hear Francine's curt reply. With luck she would be at lunch or out of the office when he came back.

Alone in his office, Maxwell unlocked the top desk drawer where the blackmail letters had been placed. Four gray letters with matching envelopes, two to him and two to Monica. It was about time that Maxwell involved Monica in the reality of what they were facing. He had funded all the money to satisfy the blackmailer, but he needed to gain Monica's trust once again. Telling her just enough to make her think he was protecting her and Lydia without spilling the whole story, might get Monica to come around to his way of thinking. Maybe everything could still be saved. The thought of pulling it all off and getting away with it a second time invigorated him. Maxwell placed the envelopes inside his coat jacket.

Before leaving, Maxwell made a few business calls then phoned the hotel's general manager to let him know he would have to oversee the corporate office for the next few days. With his work finished, Maxwell phoned the bell station and told Harry to have his car ready so he could leave right away. As he exited the executive suite, Maxwell found to his pleasant surprise, that Francine was nowhere in sight. Breathing a sigh of relief, he headed through the empty reception area where she was usually perched.

Maxwell went down the elevator and hurried across the polished marble lobby. His car was waiting when he arrived at the front door. Without a word to Harry, he climbed into the open Lincoln Town Car and slammed the door shut. The tires squealed as he sped through the parking lot. Several times he used the horn to alert parking cars or pedestrians of his rapid approach. Maxwell reached home in record time.

Evelyn had prepared lunch for him and had his luggage set packed and waiting by the front door. Maxwell was grateful for her thoughtfulness and he found that despite the circumstances, he was hungry. It was almost four in the afternoon when Evelyn drove him to the airport. There was no valet in sight, so Maxwell struggled with the luggage and hauled it over to the reservation desk for his flight, including the empty bags he would eventually use to deliver the blackmail money. He handed over the bags then walked to the first-class lounge to wait for his flight. All he could think of was that it would soon be over one way or the other. He had a strong feeling he knew who the blackmailer was. One payment was all she would ever receive. Maxwell would see to that.

Belle Brandt arrived at the establishment that bore her name late in the afternoon. Even after all these years, she still took an active role in the management of the bar and restaurant. Most of the restaurants had folded when Atlantic Point Park had closed thirty years ago. Atlantic Point Park.

Now what made her think of that? It was that young couple that had been in the past couple of nights. Twice they had asked her about the old park; the first time for directions, and the second time about the missing owner, Ronald Scott. She hadn't thought about the Scotts for years. Ronald Scott had been a charmer; good looking and a gentleman.

Lydia had looks to kill. Belle could still see her sitting at the bar night after night with that other guy. He was some manager who worked for the Scott's hotel. Rumors had swirled all over town that Lydia was having an affair with him. They had sure spent enough time in the bar together, but Belle couldn't have cared less—business was business. It wasn't long after that Ronald disappeared. Belle would never forget when she heard the news about his disappearance. She had almost passed out in shock. Belle had suspected Lydia's involvement from the start. There had been a horrendous argument that took place between Lydia and her male friend one night soon after the disappearance. They had gotten so loud that the bartender told them to quiet down just moments before Belle had been ready to throw them out of the bar. They never came back again after that evening.

Belle looked around the restaurant. She wanted to direct the staff to get some extra cleaning done. The place could get shabby in the blink of an eye if you didn't keep after every detail. She started making a list for each employee. Next Belle headed outside the rear exit at the right side of the building. It looked like another storm was brewing. Belle glanced around to see what needed attention. There was plenty of trash to pick up. The dishwashers were too darn careless when they emptied the trashcans. Debris was spilled everywhere. Belle was about to turn and go back inside when she spotted an old brown wallet lying on the ground. She carried it inside with her as she swept back her wind-blown hair. Belle opened the wallet to see if it contained any identification. There was no identification inside the wallet, just three one-dollar bills and some pictures.

Belle flicked through the pictures. Perhaps she would recognize someone and could still get the wallet back to its rightful owner. The pictures were all very old. Many were creased in several spots. Belle didn't recognize any of the pictures. When she reached the last picture, Belle drew in a sharp breath. The picture was as familiar as yesterday. It was a picture of a very young Lydia Scott. Being careful not to rip it, Belle pulled the picture out of the wallet. The picture was inscribed on the back: *"All my love always, Lydia 1978."* The ink had faded, and it was blurred, but the words were still legible.

Something else nagged at her about the picture. She couldn't put her finger on it, but it would come to her. Just then, the kitchen staff, two of the bartenders and Old Joe arrived. Belle divvied out the jobs that needed to be done and headed back to her office.

After about an hour of paperwork, Belle went out to the bar for a breather. She sat down and asked the bartender for a glass of ice water. No drinks for her until after three. Belle was deep in thought when picked up her water. She realized what it was that was nagging her about the old picture. It reminded her of that young woman, Monica, who had been asking about the amusement park. Belle hurried back to the office to take a second look at the picture. As she sat down, she was stunned to realize the wallet and the picture were both gone.

After finding the documents identifying the Eldorado as her father's, Monica was shaken. Brad closed up the car and covered it, while she huddled near the corner. As they headed for the garage door, rain was beginning to whip through gusts of wind. The start of yet another storm. Monica was all too glad when Brad asked her if she would like to leave the park for the day.

Brad lowered the rusted garage door and locked the handle. They began to trudge back toward the park entrance. The air continued to swirl, picking up pieces of leaves and debris that had settled over the park for thirty years. From somewhere within the park a low moaning sound could be heard through the gusts of wind. Monica could not stifle the chill that ran up her spine. When Brad asked, "Do you hear that?" She glanced upward and before she could answer, she caught sight of movement high over the trees.

"Brad, look over there."

Hundreds of yards away, the top of the roller coaster could be seen above the trees. The top was swaying back and forth in the gathering storm, providing yet another warning that they should not be there. Monica and Brad stood mesmerized as the moaning sound continued eerily through the park, growing louder with each passing second.

The roller coaster made a horrible final groan and began to topple over. The coaster was many stories tall and it fell sideways in one giant piece. A moment of eerie silence followed before the structure thundered to the ground and splintered into thousands of pieces. The brittle old timbers snapped like wooden matchsticks. The metal tracks twisted and turned before becoming a deformed accent to the massive pile of twigs that had been the skeletal frame of the roller coaster. Moments seemed an eternity until the noise of the crashing coaster subsided entirely, replaced with deathly silence.

Brad had grabbed Monica and pulled her away, covering her head. They were far enough away that they were not in danger from the falling debris, but the event was unnerving to them both. They rushed through the gathering storm to the area where the roller coaster had stood just minutes before. As they got closer, snapped wooden beams and twisted metal tracks littered the path, making it impassable.

"Brad, thank goodness we went in the opposite direction today. If we hadn't found the garage and the Eldorado, we could have been killed."

"I'm glad we went the other way too, Monica. I can't believe the old thing collapsed like that."

"It was pretty creaky the last time we were here, but I never would have believed it would come down all at once."

Monica and Brad headed for the main entrance. It was a welcome relief when the rusted entrance gates came into sight.

Maxwell's plane arrived right on time. His temporary assistant had made him first class reservations before bailing out, and there was no one in the seat beside him. He was glad for the privacy. The last thing he needed was to make small talk with some chatty passenger. Maxwell's mind was full and he wanted to be left alone. The trip took about three hours. During most of those hours Maxwell passed the time consuming strong drinks. Then the plane reached the Trenton-Mercer County Airport. Maxwell dreaded what was coming next. He had not been at the airport since the night he had deserted Ronald Scott's Eldorado in the parking lot with the luggage Lydia had packed in the trunk.

Short clips of black and white memories flicked through his mind. Maxwell tried to shut them out, but they just kept coming. There was no reason the memories should be so strong after all this time. The airport layout had been changed many times in thirty years. He didn't recognize anything. If he didn't know better, he would have believed that he had ever been there before.

Feelings of guilt began to permeate the memories. Somewhere inside he was sorry for what he had done all those years ago. But he had done all of it for Lydia. Had his long-ago mistakes cost Lydia her own life last year? Somehow, Maxwell knew that indeed it had, yet it was still not something that he could admit, even to himself.

Maxwell went to the auto rental desk and picked up the premium car that had been rented on his behalf. It was a new Cadillac sedan. The coincidence unnerved him. He asked for another car, but none were available. Shaken, he went to pick up his luggage. He stowed the luggage in the trunk. The trunk was large enough to stow all the Monopoly games he had shipped from Palm Beach. Tomorrow he would stop at the UPS shipping station and pick up the game packages.

The car started on the first try. Maxwell was breathing hard as he pulled out of the rental parking area. The airport was about three times larger than it had been all those years ago. Morbid curiosity—or was it guilt—made him attempt to orient himself to the place where he had parked Ronald's Eldorado back in 1985. After much searching, he noticed something that he could identify with. The location of the main control tower had not changed, and it still jutted above the other buildings. He could remember focusing on the control tower that horrible night thirty years ago to keep his mind off what he had been doing.

Maxwell had deserted Ronald's car in a darkened parking lot that was to the back of the tower. Like a magnet, he drove toward the rear lot. He rounded a corner and the lot came into view. It had been repaved and the lighting was much improved, just as it had been all over the airport. That night in 1985 had seemed intolerably dark, or had it just been the circumstances? Maxwell had abandoned Ronald's Cadillac at the rear of the lot, as far away as possible. That had been a mistake; the police suspected that the car was planted there. Why would Ronald have parked in a seldom-used rear lot, as far from the terminal as possible on a slow night at the airport? And why would he have left his luggage in the trunk? Maxwell and Lydia had not been thinking coherently at the time. How could they after what had happened?

Maxwell drove to the spot where he had deserted the Eldorado. He pulled into the very same parking spot at the edge of the lot. One thing he remembered from that long-ago night was that it had stormed and a large puddle of water had pooled in front of the car, just off the edge of the paved area. Almost as if he could not help himself, Maxwell got out of the rental Cadillac and looked beyond the car. It must have rained. A large pool of dirty black water had formed right in the dirt. At the sight, Maxwell shuddered and stumbled backwards toward the rental car. He fumbled to get inside and lock the doors. The car would not start. Panic seized Maxwell. He tried over and over to start the car. With a final grunt, the engine turned over and he backed up as fast as he could.

As Maxwell exited the airport, he began to calm down. All that came to his mind was that a criminal always returns to the scene of his crime. It had taken Maxwell thirty years to return. He was surprised that his cheeks were wet with tears as he pulled out into the dark New Jersey night. The engine roared as he pressed the accelerator hard and headed back to Atlantic Point Island for the last time.

Chapter Twenty

The sound of the phone ringing was nearly inaudible. Noisy patrons were milling about the store in every direction. Trisha excused herself from her customer and headed for the main sales desk. Taking a deep breath, she picked up the phone, "International Art Gallery, Trisha Marshall speaking."

"Trish, it's Monica. What's all the background noise?"

"It's our annual, Art Aficionado's Sale." The store has been bustling all day. What are you up to?"

"I'm in Atlantic Point."

"You found the park?"

"*We* found the park. Brad's still here with me."

Trisha raised her eyebrows. "Are you and he getting closer again?"

"Trish, don't you ever think about anything else? I haven't had time for romance on this adventure, but I am enjoying spending time with Brad and just maybe…."

"What's the park like?"

"Run down. Today the roller coaster collapsed. There's debris everywhere. The entire place is in a state of horrible decay."

"Do you have any idea why Lydia kept the park a secret for so long?"

"I believe the disappearance of my father is somehow connected to the park."

Trish gasped. "I'm glad Brad's there with you."

"Me too. We found my father's old car parked in a storage garage inside the park today. It was very emotional for me to see it."

"I can only imagine."

"Trish, I want you to spend a few days here with us. If we uncover what I think we will, I'm going to need my best friend around."

Trish detected unexpected dread in Monica's voice. "As a matter of fact, the owner is closing the gallery at the end of the sale to complete an extensive inventory appraisal. I've got several days off."

"Will you come?"

"Of course! It sounds exciting."

"Trish there are no four-star accommodations here. We're staying at Mother's old beach house. There's running water and electric, but the place is very run down."

"I'll come prepared Monica."

"I'm going to put Brad on the phone. He can give you better directions than I can, or you can plug a general address into your GPS. The address to the property is not in any database we have used so far. I'll look forward to seeing you tomorrow afternoon Trish. Have a safe drive and here's Brad!"

"Trish?"

"I'm here Brad, how are you doing?"

"I'm okay. It's been an interesting week. We'll fill you in when you get here." Brad gave Trish the address of the little store near the beach house and confirmed that it registered in Trish's GPS database. Brad estimated the drive from New York would take her about two hours. Brad promised that he or Monica would keep their cell phones nearby in case she got lost and to call when she reached the store. After Trish reiterated the address back to Brad, he confirmed the accuracy and wished her a safe trip before disconnecting the call.

Monica had gone out back and was sitting on an old deck chair looking out past the sand toward roiling waves in an angry sea. It was as though the sea were warning them of the turmoil to come. Monica seemed a million miles away. When Brad put his hand on her shoulder she almost jumped out of her seat. Monica screamed and then started laughing. "You scared me."

"Well, I didn't mean to," Brad replied, as he pulled up a second rickety deck chair and sat down next to her.

"Brad, what do you think happened to my father all those years ago?"

"I don't know Monica. I haven't said much, but I've been thinking about it ever since you first told me about your inheritance. I don't want to upset you, but I feel sure that his disappearance is somehow tied into the park. Lydia's keeping the closed down park for thirty years and Maxwell's having us tailed all the way from Florida seem to confirm that they were both somehow involved."

"The thought of my mother being involved in his disappearance is almost too much for me to bear. How could she have been mixed up in something like this?"

"I don't know Monica, it was a long time ago."

Monica got up to stretch; silent in thought once again. The sound of the waves crashing onto the deserted beach seemed to symbolize the emptiness and dismay that were churning inside her.

"Let's go into town for dinner," Brad suggested.

Monica realized that she was hungry after all. "Sounds good Brad. Belle Brandt's?"

"Where else. There aren't too many choices here unless you want to head out of town."

"Belle Brandt's is fine. Besides, I want to get an early start tomorrow and we need to get a room ready for Trish. Did she say when she would be arriving?"

"No, she didn't confirm when she would be arriving.'

"I'll phone her again after dinner to see what's up."

A quick dinner at Belle Brandt's was much as it had been on their previous visits. Monica gazed around the secluded dining rooms. She and Brad seemed to be the youngest people in the establishment. Apparently no one under retirement age migrated to Atlantic Point anymore. Belle was seated at the end of the bar as usual. Her gaze locked on Monica and for a moment she did nothing but stare, her thoughts were obviously far away. Monica was reminded of Old Joe staring at her during her previous visits. The feeling left her very uncomfortable.

Realizing what she had done, Belle masked her accidental rudeness with a warm smile and a gentle wave in Monica's direction. Ever since Belle had found the 1978 picture of Lydia Scott, her mind had been working overtime.

The resemblance to Monica was startling. Monica had to be related to Lydia in some way. Belle wished she still had the old picture. She questioned everyone working in the restaurant that day, but no one would admit to any knowledge about the mysterious old photo and the wallet.

Belle got down from the barstool with smooth grace. She glided over to Brad and Monica's table, her drink in one hand and two drink menus in the other. "Good evening. My apologies for staring Monica, but you remind me of someone I once knew."

"Good evening to you Belle." Monica was glad that Belle had taken time to speak with her. "They say everyone has a twin somewhere in the world."

"Monica, may I ask you your last name?"

"Why of course."

Before she could answer Brad replied, "It's Roberts."

"I see." Belle didn't seem convinced and her tone indicated she knew they were not telling the truth. "Well I'll let you two enjoy your dinner." There was no invitation this time to join her at the bar later.

After she was gone, Monica asked Brad, "What was that all about? Why did you lie to her?"

"I think we should keep your identity a secret until we're finished here Monica."

"I guess you're right, but I don't like lying."

"Neither do I, but your name could be Roberts someday so it might not be a lie."

Monica was surprised. She reached over to touch Brad's hand. He smiled in return. "It does have a nice ring to it."

After dinner they decided to stop at the bar to smooth things over with Belle. The conversation did not broach the subject of Monica's identity again. Still Monica could not help but feel that Belle had something on her mind every time she looked her way.

Monica's cell phone rang.

"Monica it's Maxwell."

She was shocked to hear his voice. "How are you?" was all she could manage to get out.

"I'm fine. I'm in Atlantic Point. We need to talk."

Monica grabbed the edge of the bar to keep from falling off the barstool. Brad and Belle watched her with alarmed looks.

"We're staying at the beach house. We'll be back there in a half hour. Do you need directions?"

"I know the way Monica." Maxwell's voice had a cold edge to it. Monica was surprised. Despite her suspicions about him, Monica had never heard Maxwell speak to her in that way. A chill ran up her spine. She hung up the phone without another word.

"Who was that?" Brad asked her.

"It was Maxwell Williams, he's going to meet us at the beach house."

Belle could not conceal her own shock. If Brad and Monica had not been so surprised themselves, they would have realized that Belle knew in an instant who Maxwell Williams was. As it was, they were too consumed with their own surprise from his unexpected call.

Monica and Brad paid their tab and made a quick exit.

Belle was now sure of one thing: Monica's maiden name was not Roberts. It was Scott or Williams. Maxwell Williams was the name of the manager that Lydia had been having the long-term affair with all those years ago. He was the man whom she had just about thrown out of the bar after the loud fight with Lydia. Monica had to be the daughter of Lydia Scott and either Ronald Scott or Maxwell Williams was her father. Belle hadn't had this much intrigue in many years. She ordered another drink from the bar and began to sift through the puzzle, the pieces of which had been left shattered in Atlantic Point thirty years earlier.

"Brad, slow down."

"I can't believe he has the nerve to come here after he had us tailed all the way from Palm Beach to Richmond." Brad was angry as he slowed the car.

"Brad, I think we might get some answers to our mystery."

"Do you think we can trust anything Maxwell Williams says, Monica?"

"I guess not, but whatever he has to say, it will be interesting. Do you think we're in any danger Brad?"

"We need to be on our guard Monica. I don't trust Maxwell any longer. I used to have the greatest respect for him."

"He raised me with Mother, Brad. No matter what he's done, it would destroy me if I thought he might harm me. All the times we spent together as a family would be nothing more than lies. It's hard to accept."

"Maybe we'll soon have all the answers."

Maxwell checked into the small motel that he remembered was at the center of the town. What a dump. He hadn't been in Atlantic Point since 1985. Except for increasing dilapidation, nothing had changed. No new buildings, no new restaurants and most of what had been there was closed. The old Brandt place that he and Lydia had spent so many nights in was still open. Maxwell wondered if he would have the courage to go inside.

After checking into the motel Maxwell took a drive through town. Waves of nostalgia and sadness passed over him and he had to choke back tears when he drove into the parking lot of the old Caprice Hotel, the first property that he had ever managed. The hotel was just as dilapidated as the rest of the town.

There had been many good times back then. He was young and the world seemed to be his own. Where had it all gone? Maxwell's last stop was the old general store. The town's only UPS pickup station was inside. Maxwell felt chest pains as he waited for the suspicious old man to review the paperwork that Maxwell provided. What would he do if the packages hadn't arrived?

After an eternity, the man returned from the rear storeroom struggling with the first of the boxes containing the games. Maxwell was relieved as he mumbled something about returning for the rest of the games.

The money had all arrived intact. Tomorrow Maxwell would turn it over to the blackmailer with Monica's help. Then he would sell her on his rehabilitation plan for Atlantic Point Park. It would all be over soon and it could all still come out all right.

As Maxwell lugged his packages the old man stared at him as if he recognized him. Maybe he did. It was of no matter. Maxwell had more important things on his mind. He flipped the old man a $20 tip then headed out the door without so much as a thank you. Maxwell pushed the trunk lid down on the Cadillac and the lock secured the boxes inside.

He started the car and headed out to the beach house. Maxwell hoped Brad and Monica would be civil to him. They already knew they had been tailed. Monica would also know Maxwell had lied to her when she asked for information after first inheriting the park.

With impending dread, the beach house loomed into view. More memories flooded through his mind. How many good times had he, Lydia and Ronald spent in that house before it had all gone wrong? Several lights were visible from the outside, but the house still conveyed a desolate, abandoned appearance. As he walked up to the door, Maxwell wiped the sweat from his brow. It was very humid tonight and the air was very still. Just as still as it had been that fateful night thirty years ago. Maxwell's heart was pounding as he climbed the steps to the front door.

Before he could knock, Brad opened the door. He did not greet Maxwell or return Maxwell's hello. Brad's words were cold, "We're in the living room, I'm sure you know the way."

Maxwell passed through the foyer into the old living room, decorated just as it had been for the past thirty years. Monica was seated on the old sofa. Two lights burned in the background yet did little to lift the gloom that permeated the house.

"Hello Maxwell," Monica said without commitment.

Maxwell could not ascertain her feelings toward him from the neutral tone of her voice. Brad remained standing near the entrance to the living room. Silence hung like a thick veil throughout the gloomy room.

"I spent many happy times here," Maxwell started out. "Your father and mother and I were once the best of friends."

Monica cut him off. "We've been like family for more than thirty years. I don't know what the truth is behind all the deceit, but you owe me an explanation. We know you had our car tailed up the coast. I want the truth and I want it now, all of it, no matter how bad it is."

Caught off guard at her sharp words, Maxwell was reminded of Lydia when she was angry. He could hear Lydia's voice as if she were there in the room with them. "Brad would you please sit down, this is going to take a while."

Brad said nothing, but sat down on the sofa close to Monica, reaching for her hand. Maxwell sat opposite them in an old chair with fabric that matched the decaying sofa.

As Maxwell began, it was almost as if the clock had been turned back thirty years. Monica pictured the events in her mind as though she had actually been there.

"As I've said, your mother and father and I were once the best of friends. We did everything together. We worked in the park together, double dated when I had a girlfriend, had beach parties here at the house and enjoyed every minute of our young lives. The park was doing well in the early days, and then we started the hotel division, which I headed up and grew successfully. Your father and I were like brothers, but in time it all fell apart."

"You had an affair with my mother."

Maxwell ignored Monica's remark and continued with his story. "First Atlantic Point Park started to decline. Then your father and mother began to fight all the time. One night Lydia turned to me. We started an affair that continued until her death. I always loved her, with all my heart.

It's a small town though and a resentful park employee told your father what was going on. Ronald confronted us. It was the ugliest scene of my life. The betrayals by his wife and the man he considered to be his best friend and business partner were too much for him to handle. I always loved Lydia, and deep down, I think I was jealous of Ronald. Maybe not on a conscious level, but somewhere deep inside. Ronald yelled at both of us; he was furious. He stormed through the house knocking over tables and yelling that Lydia was nothing more than a tramp.

Ronald fired me on the spot. I couldn't blame him under the circumstances. Lydia tried to calm him down but the violent tirade continued. The dent in the wall over there was from Ronald hurtling a heavy crystal vase into it all those years ago."

Monica and Brad looked toward the living room's side wall. There was a huge dent just as Maxwell described. The confrontation must have been violent. Monica shuddered. Her head began to swim and she felt as if she were going to pass out. In the background the ongoing sound of crashing waves escalated to a fever pitch in her head. She could not hear a word Maxwell was saying, as black ink edged into her vision. A reassuring squeeze from Brad kept her from passing out.

Maxwell continued, "Ronald threw me out of the house that night and said he never wanted to see me again. I didn't want to leave Lydia alone with him, but she insisted she would be all right. I left. I never saw Ronald again after that night. Lydia told me he packed a few items and left the house without saying another word to her. She never saw him again either. His car was found deserted a week later at the Trenton-Mercer County airport with all his luggage still in the trunk."

Monica just shook her head. She had not been present all those years ago and she didn't want to pass judgment. Her mother was just as guilty as Maxwell for the events that had transpired. Monica recalled the note she had located in the photo albums at the New York Penthouse, *"Ronald, I'm so very sorry..."* Suddenly it all seemed to make sense.

"After Ronald disappeared, Lydia kept me on as the manager of the hotels, but we had to be careful. Whispers and gossip about our affair reached the police. Lydia was investigated for potential involvement in Ronald's disappearance. When I left the beach house that fateful night, I ran into a friend right out front here. He heard your parents continue to fight after he saw me drive away, so he was able to confirm to the police that

Ronald had been alive after I left the house." Lydia had been the last person to see Ronald alive. The investigation focused on her, but there was never any proof that harm had come to Ronald. Lydia had cleaned up all the damage from their fight, long before the police arrived."

Monica pondered all that Maxwell had told them. Brad looked on with a skeptical scowl.

"Atlantic Point Park closed at the end of the 1985 season. Afterward, we moved to Palm Beach. You were born just a few months later. Lydia conducted her own search for Ronald, but we never heard from him again."

"Maxwell, why didn't you tell me this when I asked you for information *after* the staff meeting?"

"Monica, how could I tell you? Lydia and I spent our lives protecting you from this."

"Why are you telling me now?"

"Monica, we're being blackmailed. Someone is threatening to expose your mother for involvement in your father's death. I don't know what information or proof they have. Here are the letters demanding two million dollars."

Monica didn't say a word. Black curtains swept across her entire field of vision. The last thing she remembered was Brad and Maxwell standing over her calling her name.

Chapter Twenty-One

Monica gazed into the mirror. Despite her expectations, there were no dark circles under her eyes. After last night she didn't know what the mirror would reflect. She mentally began to go over all that would be happening during the next ten hours. Drake Donovan had phoned earlier that morning. He would be arriving in Atlantic Point today to estimate renovation costs on the beach house if Monica decided to keep it. That was the most probable scenario since there were no buyers lining up to purchase Atlantic Point real estate. Trisha would arrive later today. The thought of seeing her good friend and confidant brought a smile to Monica's face. Later, when shadows began to fall, she, Brad and Maxwell would turn the money over to the blackmailer at Atlantic Point Park. The thought of being in the dark, deserted park with the person who was threatening her mother's memory made her skin crawl.

The previous night, Maxwell left after Monica had regained consciousness. Before he departed, he agreed to meet Brad and Monica at the beach house prior to traveling out to the park to pay off the blackmailer. Brad even assured Monica he would be civil to Drake Donovan, despite his distaste for his former rival.

Monica was startled from her thoughts when Brad knocked on her bedroom door at the start of the day. Pushing the door open he announced, "I thought you might like some hot coffee this morning." Walking across the room, he placed the tray next to her on the old dressing table. Then he sat down on the bed.

Monica turned to face him. Brad was dressed in khakis and a polo shirt; already showered after his workout.

"How are you feeling today? No more fainting spells?"

"No more fainting spells. I feel much better. Just a little drained."

"I don't want you to go on the blackmail payoff today Monica. Let Maxwell go alone. He has more to do with this than you do. If you want me to, I'll go with him, just as long as you stay here at the house."

"I have to go Brad. I want to know who is doing this and what they know about my mother."

"You may not get the answer to either of those questions Monica. You could be placing yourself in serious danger."

Turning back to the mirror, Monica answered with steeled determination, "Brad, you can't talk me out of this. I have more unanswered questions now than ever. I have to know the truth. I also think we should take Drake along with us tonight. It couldn't hurt to have an extra person on our side."

"For once I think you're right where Drake Donovan is concerned. Come to think of it, this is the first time I'll be glad to see him."

Monica turned around from the dressing table to face Brad, a mischievous grin spreading across his face.

Maxwell emptied a creamer into his coffee and looked around the old diner. It was a relic—one of the few remaining restaurants that were still open in Atlantic Point. He realized how far the town had crumbled in thirty years. In the 1970s there were more restaurants than you could dine at in any given season.

Maxwell pondered the events of the previous evening. Last night had been somewhat of a success. Most of what he had told Monica and Brad was the truth. He just hadn't told them the entire story. Maxwell still didn't feel quite sure Monica and Brad believed him. Monica's passing out had brought the night to an abrupt conclusion. Maxwell hoped with all his heart that there was nothing seriously wrong with her. He was, after all, doing most of this for Monica. Protecting her, just as he had protected Lydia for thirty years.

The thought of going into Atlantic Point Park tonight caused Maxwell to shudder. After thirty years, the park had to be in a horrible state of disrepair. The shadows of his past would not be far away.

Maxwell dumped another creamer into the coffee, examined his spoon for cleanliness and gave the coffee a stir. This couldn't be over soon enough for him. A tightening in his chest reminded him that his health would not sustain too much more stress. Maxwell had to steady his hands to lift the coffee cup to his lips.

"Say goodbye to New York, Drake. It certainly has been fun, but now let the games begin." Janice gave Drake a flirtatious smile as he opened the door to the rental car for her.

"I don't care if we never come back here Janice. I don't like New York. It's your kind of town."

"That it is my love, that it is—but with all our new found wealth, I can learn to love somewhere else just as much. Of course, that's if you're there with me."

"I'll be there Janice, don't worry about that."

Drake went around and started the car. They edged out into the New York traffic stream. Janice had insisted on an early start so they would reach Atlantic Point well in advance of the time scheduled for the payoff. Drake was nervous. The thought of losing his job and going to jail for Janice's illegal endeavors left him with sweating palms. Janice appeared just as cool and assured as she always was.

"Aren't you the least bit nervous?"

"No, why should I be?"

"Because we could spend a lot of time in jail if this thing goes wrong?"

"I don't allow things to go wrong Drake. I've planned for every contingency."

"That doesn't mean that something *couldn't* go wrong."

"The only mistake I made was investing too many years in Caprice Hotels. Now even that will pay off. No more talk about anything going wrong. By this time tomorrow we'll be on the beach at our new address. Nothing's going to stop us now."

Drake felt a single moment of relief. Janice's self-assuredness was comforting to him, but it wasn't long until his anxiety returned. This was one time that Janice had better be right.

Trish departed New York at 10 a.m. She was eager to be away from the city and the mysterious Atlantic Point Park intrigued her. It was still morning when she pulled into a Quick Mart for a cup of hot tea. Trish purchased an extra-large size cup and returned to her car. A short time later she was traveling down route 95 southbound through New Jersey. Trish realized it was the very same route that Monica and Brad had traveled to reach Atlantic Point coming north from Florida. The very same route that they had been tailed on.

A moment of unexpected fear pulsed through Trish. She glanced at the door locks to see that they were in the "locked" position. They were. Even so, she hit the button to make certain they were secured. The electric locks thumped in a positive response. As she proceeded, traffic on 95 south seemed especially light. She traveled closer and closer to Atlantic Point and began picking up very strong vibrations of danger. Trish tried her best to put them out of her mind, but the vague feelings continued unabated.

The knock on the door was so normal and yet so out of place. Brad went to answer the door. It was Drake Donovan. Monica was surprised to the point of shock when Brad said, "Hi Drake, good to see you," and extended his hand to shake Drake's. Drake looked equally surprised but returned the friendly greeting.

Before going to the beach house Drake dropped Janice off at a local restaurant called Belle Brandt's. There weren't many restaurants to choose from in the dilapidated town. Janice had refused to spend even one day in the small motel. Drake glanced up as the sound of footsteps descended the staircase. It was Monica. "Hello Monica. I see we have our work cut out for us here."

"Thanks for coming up here Drake. I know you're still busy with the Virginia project. Has Brad given you the grand tour?"

"No, I just got here. The beach house is larger than I imagined."

Monica had been glancing at her watch all day. She realized that despite the panicky feelings she was having, there was plenty of time to show Drake around the place before they had to go out to the park. "Let's start downstairs. There's no basement, but there are plenty of other rooms." Monica led the way with Drake following and Brad bringing up the rear.

Drake knew he would never be heading up a renovation on the old house, but he couldn't help but take an interest. The place had potential and the tour helped take his mind off the events that would be unfolding later that evening.

The old beach house had an oversized living room, formal dining room, a room for entertaining and a large kitchen. There was a powder room on the first floor and four bedrooms on the second floor, each with its own bathroom, sitting area and balcony. All the rooms were outdated and would need to be completely gutted. Brad and Monica had cleaned up several bedrooms and their adjoining bathrooms. Drake wondered if Monica and Brad were sleeping in separate rooms or if they had cleaned the rooms for potential guests. He forced himself to suppress a laugh.

Drake summed up the renovation costs as they walked along. The tab would easily run over $100,000, but as usual Monica didn't bat an eye when he conveyed the estimate to her. Brad was quiet. Drake wondered if

Brad knew what was going to happen today. Thank goodness Monica and Brad had no idea he was involved in Janice's scheme.

As the tour concluded, a second knock sounded from the front door. The three of them bounded down the steps with Monica in the lead. Monica opened the door. It was Trish. She had gotten directions from the store owner and found the house on her own. Monica greeted her with a big hug. She felt an overwhelming sense of relief that Trish was going to be nearby as she faced the second worst experience of her life, after the death of her mother. Trish already knew Brad and Drake. Brad from his days as Monica's boyfriend; Drake from her past involvement in decorating the hotels.

Trish gave a cheery hello to both of them. The feeling of impending danger stayed with her, but she knew she had to be there for Monica. Monica requested that everyone sit down. In a few moments she shared the story of the blackmail attempt she and Maxwell were facing. Monica did not reveal the nature of the blackmailer's threat. She would do anything to protect Lydia's memory. Monica was glad when no one asked her any further questions. Trish was aghast at the realization of what Monica was facing. Drake said nothing but did offer to accompany Brad, Maxwell and Monica to Atlantic Point Park.

Brad accepted without further comment. Silence descended across the room. Trish glanced outside and realized that shadows were replacing daylight. A cool ocean breeze cast a faint chill over the room.

The rest of the day crept by and tension seemed to build with each passing minute. Late in the day, a third knock at the front door announced

Maxwell's arrival. He was dressed in casual attire, which was unusual for him. Maxwell entered the old living room and was surprised to see Drake and Trish. Monica explained that Drake had agreed to accompany them to the park. Maxwell agreed, but conveyed a stern lecture to Monica that he wished she had not shared the information with anyone else. Monica contained an angry reply and requested that Maxwell sit down with them.

The group decided that Monica and Brad would travel in one car and Maxwell would follow in a second car. Trish would remain at the beach house. Drake would arrive after the blackmailer was in the park using his own vehicle. Drake reflected how perfect the plan was. He would secretly bring Janice to the park after they had all assembled. They would never know he was involved.

Drake left right after their plans had been finalized, explaining that he wanted to get a flashlight from his room at the small motel in town. He got directions to the park from Brad, still amazed that Brad was being so civil to him. Brad needed Drake now or so he thought. Drake figured anyone could be nice when they needed something.

Brad went upstairs to get some gear for the night and Trish and Monica were left alone for the first time. Trish was just as unsuccessful as Brad was at trying to talk Monica out of going on the money exchange. Sighing in frustration, she begged Monica to be careful. Monica promised that she would.

Belle glanced up as a second patron joined the attractive woman that had spent the afternoon in her bar. The man was good looking in a rugged sort of way. Belle was surprised to see him order a soda. He looked more like the whisky or beer type to her.

"Are you about ready to take off Janice?"

"Just a few more minutes Drake. I've been studying this old map of the park I found on Lydia's desk years ago. How convenient that you were able to spend the day with our friends. What were you able to find out?"

"They think I'm going to the park to assist them as a backup. I'm supposed to hide outside the park until the blackmailer leaves so I can gather as much evidence as possible."

"That's wonderful!"

"You can wait for me to walk out with the money, and we'll be on our way. Be sure to slash all the tires on each of their vehicles so they can't follow us."

"I'd already thought of that Janice."

"Just checking, you can't be too sure you know."

The air had grown cooler and the clouds masked what remained of the setting sun. The two cars pulled up to the park at 7 p.m. Brad and Monica were in the lead with Maxwell following. Maxwell was astounded at the condition of the park. He had not returned here since he and Lydia had closed the park at the end of 1985 season. The blackmailer had selected the old haunted house as the place for the money exchange. Maxwell dreaded the thought of even being near the old haunted house or the office building. He stood by in silence as Brad unlocked the massive forged gates. They groaned in protest as Brad pulled them open, and a chill ran up Maxwell's spine.

The paths were littered and barely passable. Several times they had to detour where the old roller coaster had collapsed. Maxwell could still see the cars crashing to the ground when the coaster had derailed all those years ago. One of their best employees had been killed and that was the beginning of the end.

As they proceeded, the old theater came into view. Maxwell had seen more motion pictures there than he could remember. There were no streaming videos back then and no satellite movie channels on demand. If you wanted to see a movie you went to the theater or hoped that one you liked was on TV that night. It was a better age, a time that had now passed him by.

They eventually reached the haunted house and the waiting seemed to go on forever. At 8 p.m. a figure appeared from the deepening shadows. The outline of the figure was that of an attractive woman and she seemed vaguely familiar despite her face being masked by shadows. As she neared, her movements and appearance became identifiable. Monica and Brad's mouths both dropped open as they realized who the blackmailer was. Maxwell just stood there, a knowing smirk on his face. As he had suspected, the blackmailer was Janice Laneer.

"Good evening everyone. How good of you all to attend my "fright night." The cost of admission is two million dollars."

"Janice, are you out of your mind? Maxwell asked her.

"No, I'm in my right mind after spending all those years chasing you for nothing."

"Do you really think you can get away with this Janice?" Monica asked though a distressed and unusually husky voice.

"Of course I'm going to get away with it. You'll do anything to protect Lydia."

Brad had to hold Monica back and she strained against him. "Janice you're crazy," was his single comment to the self-assured blackmailer.

Janice laughed. "Not crazy, just getting what I deserve. Maxwell where is my money?"

"It's right here, in these two bags, just as you specified."

"Open the bags." Janice inspected the two bags. She made Brad, Monica and Maxwell move back far enough so she could react if they tried to rush her. Brad considered doing just that, but he was not sure if Janice was armed.

After a thorough inspection Janice closed the bags and then she said to Maxwell, "Carry the bags out to my car. I had no idea the haunted house was so far from the entrance or that the path would be covered with debris from a collapsed roller coaster. Monica, you and Brad wait here. Don't try to follow me. Your mother was not the person you thought she was, and I'll make sure the world knows everything unless you do exactly as I've instructed you."

"Just what is it that you know Janice?" Monica queried.

"That's not important now that I received your generous payment for my silence. Come along Maxwell, I'm in a hurry."

Struggling with the two moneybags, Maxwell turned and headed back toward the entrance with Janice following behind him. Neither one of them said a word. Maxwell was furious that Janice would betray him in this way, yet he was even more afraid of what she might know and tell. Whatever information Janice had, it had been pieced together from the many times they had shared together. With an unexpected wave of sadness, he realized the depths to which he had hurt her.

When they were near the main gates, Janice told him to stop. "Maxwell, don't say a word. When I'm gone, open this envelope. You'll understand why I did this." Janice leaned over and kissed him on the cheek as she took the two bags from him. Then she disappeared through the gates. A short time later Maxwell heard a car engine start, but he couldn't see any headlights or tail lights. Identification of the car would be impossible. The sound of the car faded as it headed out toward the exit of the overgrown parking lot.

Maxwell stood dumbfounded, clutching the sealed envelope. He was still standing there ten minutes later when Brad and Monica finally reached him. Silently he slid the envelope into his pants pocket.

Chapter Twenty-Two

When they reached the main road, Drake verified there was no traffic and switched on the headlights. Janice leaned across the seat and kissed him so hard he had trouble keeping the car on the road. "We're almost there darling."

Drake grinned, displaying his straight white teeth in the dark of the car. "It did go better than I thought it would. I'll still feel better when we exit the country. How far is it to the airstrip?"

"About 50 miles. Just take your time, we don't want to give the state police any reason to pull us over."

About an hour later Janice pointed out signs for the private airstrip where she had leased a small, luxury jet. Drake would pilot them out of the country and into a new life.

Drake pulled the rental car into the narrow, paved entrance. Dense shrubbery and a starless night concealed the airport's activities from the outside world. Before they could even get out of the car, a slim young man with ruffled brown hair ran toward the car from the office building. Coming around to Drake's side he directed them to pull the car close to the plane so they could unload. Janice's large array of personal luggage was stowed in the trunk. The moneybags she would carry on personally.

There were no other planes landing or taking off. Several small planes were parked in various positions in and around the airport's hanger. The plane's engines roared to life. In just seconds, they were cleared for takeoff. Such a swift clearance authorization was unheard of. Janice must have made a hefty payment to someone to keep the entire airstrip vacant for the evening. Drake didn't care, just so they could get away and the sooner the better.

The plane taxied down the runway. Janice felt a growing thrill as the plane began to gain speed. In a few moments it lifted into the night and relief began to set in. She had done it. When the plane leveled out Janice poured a drink and handed a Coke to Drake. "That's not fair," he complained.

"Very soon you can have all the drinks you want my love. We're just a few hours from a new life."

Complete darkness had settled over Atlantic Point Park. Maxwell continued to stand in a silent, dazed state. He looked ghostly pale. Monica was worried about him. She realized once again that other than Jeanette, Maxwell was all the family she had left. Monica wished Maxwell would just tell her the truth about the past. Then she could help him with whatever had happened.

Brad went outside the park to see if Drake had obtained license plates or any other information about Janice—just in case she decided to continue with the blackmail scheme. A few minutes later Brad returned.

"There's no sign of Drake Donovan and the tires have been slashed on each of our cars."

"Oh my gosh, do you think Janice discovered him out here? He could be lying injured somewhere," Monica asked in a panicked voice.

"I don't know where Drake is Monica. But I do know we're going to need help to get out of here. Those cars aren't going anywhere in their current condition and none of our cell phones are able to pick up a signal in the area surrounding Atlantic Point Park. We'll take the flashlight and look for Drake as we walk." Brad doubted they would find Drake injured in any of the bushes. He felt sure that somehow, some way, Drake was involved in the blackmail scheme.

Brad, Monica and Maxwell started walking over the dark rutted parking lot toward the main road. Their search for Drake yielded nothing. He was nowhere to be found. Brad swept the flashlight across both sides of the overgrown driveway and continued to scan the path in front of them. Maxwell had difficulty walking. Monica was worried and even Brad noticed Maxwell's deteriorating health and labored breathing. Monica held on to Maxwell to keep him steady.

By the time they reached the main road, Brad and Monica both realized Maxwell would never be able to walk back to town. Brad didn't feel comfortable leaving them so he could walk back alone. There appeared to be no other alternative. Just as Brad turned to leave, a New Jersey State trooper appeared.

Monica breathed a sigh of relief. It was obvious Maxwell needed medical attention. The trooper asked them what had happened. Brad explained that they had driven out to see the old amusement park. While they were walking around, someone had slashed the tires on their vehicles.

The trooper admonished them for being on private property then inquired why they had taken two cars. Brad said that they planned to head in different directions after visiting the park. Although the trooper did not appear to be satisfied, he allowed them to pile into the police car. What the trooper told them next was even more of a surprise.

Last year he had been called to the scene of the accident in which the park's owner had been killed. Her speeding car had careened off the bridge going back onto Atlantic Point Island. Monica turned white when the officer commented that they found her dead in the cold water below. When she turned toward Maxwell, she saw a tear running down his face.

After refusing all medical help Maxwell requested the trooper return him to the small motel at the center of town. Monica made him promise to call her if he needed any help. Brad told Maxwell he would take care of repairing the cars the next morning, but that he'd better plan on staying for at least another day.

When Brad and Monica were dropped off at the beach house, they found Trish pacing around inside. She was holding a wine glass and an oversized bottle of cabernet. With both of her hands full she, gave Brad and Monica a light hug.

Monica had to laugh, despite all they had just been through. Leave it to Trish to be drinking wine, looking like a runway model, in an old beach house, in the middle of a deserted town, waiting to entertain friends who had been on a blackmail payoff.

"How do we get some of that wine Trish?" Brad inquired.

"Let me get you each a glass. I've got them right here for you. I noticed that you didn't have time to stock the wine cabinet, so I ventured into town and picked up some rations. We're going to need them if we stay around here for very long!"

Brad rolled his eyes, and at Trish's urging Monica launched into her story of the night's events. Brad would interrupt from time to time to add some details to the story. Monica expressed sincere concern about Drake.

"Monica, I think that Drake was Janice's accomplice," Brad stated for the first time.

"That's ridiculous! He would have never helped her commit a crime."

"Monica, think about it. None of us were hurt. Why would Janice have harmed Drake? She wasn't violent; I don't even think she was armed. It would have been very difficult for her to carry this out by herself. I'll bet if you call the Caprice Hotel in Virginia Beach, you'll find out that Drake hasn't been there for a while."

Trish refilled the glasses with the remainder of the cabernet and went to uncork another bottle. Monica picked up her cell phone. She hit the speed dial menu where she had all her hotel's numbers programmed. When she reached the Virginia hotel, she told the manager-on-duty who she was and explained that it was urgent for her to speak to Drake Donovan.

"Monica, Drake has not been here for over a week."

Shocked, Monica thanked the man and promised she would call the general manager to get a replacement for Drake.

"You were right Brad, he hasn't been there for a week."

The three friends continued to discuss Drake's possible involvement and what to do next. Monica was more determined than ever to find the answers to the mysterious events that had started thirty years ago.

She reflected back to what Horace Goldsmith told her when she met with him to hear the terms of her mother's will. Horace said that the massive office building was constructed during the last season before the park closed for the final time. It was built despite Horace's warnings and objections to Lydia. With a renewed sense of determination Monica announced, "We're going back to the park tomorrow. I think the office building holds the answer to all of our questions."

Monica did not wake up until the noon sun was streaming through the window. Exhaustion had set in so completely, that she had slept for twelve hours. Brad was not far behind her and once again he skipped his work out. Trish awakened at her usual 9 a.m. time and had walked up to the small convenience store to purchase some hot tea and a granola bar. Monica and Brad found her sitting on the old deck reading a paperback under a beach umbrella.

"Good morning sleepy heads. You two have slept late."

"We had a busy day yesterday," Monica chuckled.

"I'll go up to the store and get you both some coffee. What time are we going out to the park?"

"In about an hour if that's all right with you."

"Of course. Now let me get that coffee and you two go and get ready."

Monica was surprised at Trish's eagerness.

Before showering, Brad phoned a local garage and asked the mechanic to meet him in about an hour and a half. The mechanic seemed surprised when Brad gave him the location of the damaged cars.

A short while later Trish returned with the hot coffee and some unexpected sweet rolls, just as Monica was coming down the stairs. As always, Brad was ready before she was.

Monica phoned Maxwell to see how he was doing. He claimed to be fine and was eager to get back to Palm Beach. She explained that they were meeting a local mechanic at the park and they would keep him posted when the repairs were completed. Monica did not want Maxwell to leave just yet. She still had some unanswered questions for him.

When they reached the park the mechanic was already waiting. He was a withered old man with a baseball cap and bib overalls. He spoke in a manner that was not to be hurried. A double rollback truck was parked nearby.

The mechanic was pleasant enough. Brad showed him the damaged tires, explaining that he was to do whatever was necessary to get the two cars on the road. Brad handed him fifteen one hundred-dollar bills.

After the man left, Brad directed Trish to park her car inside the park, realizing he had not closed and locked the gates the night before. No matter what happened today they would have at least one car to take them back to town at the end of their search.

Once inside, they closed and locked the gates. Because of the debris from the roller coaster, they decided to take the other trail back to the far reaches of the park where the office building was located.

Monica had never seen Trish in summer hiking gear before. It was so out of character for her. To all their surprise, she kept right up with them as they progressed through the desolate park. Along the way, Monica told Trish of all that they had discovered during their explorations. The strong vibrations of impending danger returned to Trish once again. She had the strangest feeling they were being watched.

After a long trek, they finally reached the office building. The massive structure stared back blindly. The smoked glass windows revealed nothing of what was inside. "Atlantic Point Corporation" was etched into the concrete apron between the second and third floors. Monica asked Brad why the windows had remained unbroken. His reply surprised her.

"Someone spent a huge amount of money to purchase break-proof glass, solid steel doors and heavy locks. No one was going to get into that building unless they were supposed to."

Brad scouted around the building while Trish and Monica stayed in the front. The windows were unbroken on the sides and rear of the building as well. There were no open or unlocked doors.

Monica had brought the large Atlantic Point master key set as well as the personal key set that had been her mother's. She started trying the locks on the main door with her mother's personal key set and was unsurprised that the ring contained a key to the office building. Calling for Brad, she pushed the heavy iron door open. The door groaned as it swung open on its un-oiled hinges. Monica went in with Trish and Brad following close behind.

The strong smell of dust permeated their senses. Inside was a large reception area. There was no furniture or carpeting. The walls were unfinished plasterboard with hallways leading from both sides of the reception area. A grand staircase swept up to the second floor from the atrium foyer. The office building was so large that they decided to split into three. Trish and Brad would search in separate directions on the first floor and Monica would start on the second floor. As she climbed the stairs, the steps creaked in protest.

Reaching the top, Monica remembered that the building also had a third floor. Behind the grand stairway there was a door concealing another flight of stairs. Deciding to check out the third floor first, Monica climbed the stairs to the very top of the building. The third floor was one large, unfinished room spanning the entire length of the complex. It was empty but revealed the tremendous size of the office building in a single glance.

Returning to the second floor, Monica wound through hallway after hallway. She found dozens of offices. All of them were in the same unfinished condition that the reception area and the attic had been found. It was as if the building had never been used for even one day. There were no calendars, papers or anything else on any of the walls. None of the rooms had any furniture. The tinted windows cast an eerie light over the rooms and made it difficult to see.

There was little of anything in the building except for a thick coating of dust and dirt. Monica found one unusual feature. Nameplates had been attached to the office doors. She wondered what had happened to the people who were supposed to use these offices after the park had closed.

Monica decided to follow one corridor back to the far reaches of the second floor. It was here that she made her first interesting discovery. Monica had stumbled into the office that was to be her mother's. Lydia Scott, President was engraved on a pitted gold nameplate attached to the entrance door.

Monica was intrigued. Before pushing the door open Monica pondered her mother's title, "President." Hadn't Lydia been the Vice President back in 1985 when her father disappeared. Did she already know when the building was built that he would never be returning? The thought was troubling.

With care, Monica pushed the door wide open. It opened against the back wall with a clunk. Inside was the largest office she had seen in the unusual building. It included a reception area, most likely for Lydia's assistants. The reception area was just as barren as the rest of the building. Monica continued back toward the office that had been intended for Lydia. She held her breath as she opened the door.

An even larger office had been built for Lydia. Lydia's office was the only one that had any furnishings. Neutral carpeting had been installed and the walls were painted a light color. Large pieces of expensive furniture had been placed in the office, including a desk. Dust covered all the furniture with a thick white coating. A yellowed calendar desk pad indicated that it was November of 1985. Behind the desk on the wall was a large, framed aerial photo of the park.

One by one Monica opened the drawers to the desk. There was nothing in any of them. The bookshelf on the other side of the room was empty. Two filing cabinets sat with their original keys tethered in the locks. They too were empty, never having been used.

Monica sat down at the desk, as a feeling of confusion settled over her. Why in the world had her mother built this office complex when she knew the park was in such desperate financial condition and her father was missing?

Monica turned around and gazed at the beautiful aerial view of the park that had been captured in the large photo. In the photo the park was filled with well-kept rides, blue skies and summer gardens. Small black dots indicated large crowds of patrons. Squinting to read the small printing in the right-hand corner, Monica noted the photo had been taken, July 4th, 1959.

Discouraged that she still had more questions than answers, Monica headed back to the main floor. She stepped outside to get a breath of air as she waited for Brad and Trish.

A few minutes later they both joined her, stating that they had found nothing but unfinished offices and an unfinished kitchen and employee break area.

"What do we do now? Monica asked.

"I don't know what we should do Monica. I'm all out of ideas. We seem to find more and more questions but no answers," Brad replied as he flecked some dirt off his clothing.

Trish had a different suggestion. "I think we need to head back to town and spend the evening with a nice dinner and a bottle of wine. I've had a strong feeling of danger ever since I neared Atlantic Point. We should evaluate our next move after we review all the information and the events that have transpired. Maybe we're overlooking something important."

An instant later Monica blurted, "You two wait here. There's something I forgot to check upstairs."

"You have ten minutes and we're coming after you," Brad yelled as she disappeared into the darkening building.

Racing up the steps and back the many corridors to her mother's office Monica's heart was pounding in her chest. She passed through the reception area. The door to Lydia's office was still open. Monica went behind the desk and looked again at the aerial photo. She grasped the right side of the photo and yanked. As she suspected, the picture pulled away from the wall on hinges. Behind the picture was a safe. It was locked tight. Lydia had a safe installed behind the large oceanic print in the living room of their Palm Beach home too. Monica had used it many times. She wondered if she already knew the combination.

Whirling the dial, Monica used the same numbers that Lydia had set for the safe at the house. The dark windows and the late afternoon shadows made it difficult to see the numbers on the dial. After a few tries, the old safe creaked opened. Monica spotted a single white envelope inside. She pulled it out of the safe and sank into the desk chair. When she turned the envelope over, she gasped in shock. The envelope was addressed to her.

Chapter Twenty-Three

A heavy gloom settled over Atlantic Point Park as afternoon sunlight gave way to evening shadows. Trish felt as if she would jump out of her skin at the slightest noise. Several times she was sure she heard footsteps through the dense overgrowth. She could still feel someone watching them. Brad insisted that he didn't see or hear anything. Trish punched him on the arm when he began to imitate a ghost and Brad held his hands up to stop her in mock protest.

"Brad I'm being serious."

"I know you are, but there isn't anyone in this park except the three of us."

"I feel sure that someone is in here watching us."

"How could they get in Trish? We locked the gates and we're out in the middle of nowhere."

"There are a lot of puzzling questions Brad. First, we have Lydia's keeping this old amusement park for thirty years after the unsolved disappearance of her husband... A massive office building constructed and never used... Maxwell's having you tailed up the coast... An administrative assistant perpetrating a blackmail scheme... What do you think it all means?"

"Trish, I've thought about it over and over. Either Lydia or Maxwell or both had something to do with Ronald Scott's disappearance and death.

In any case, Atlantic Point Park seems to be where the answer to the questions will be found."

Trish shivered. She still had an overpowering feeling they were being watched.

Monica closed her eyes, then reopened them as if doing so would make her name disappear from the letter she had just pulled from the safe. The letter was addressed to her in handwriting that could only be her mother's distinctive script. Before opening the letter, Monica had a strong feeling the document was going to provide her with a lot of answers.

Monica glanced down at the envelope once more. It was getting darker outside and the tinted windows did not provide much light even when it was bright daylight. Monica took a deep breath and slid her fingernail under the flap of the envelope and clicked on her phone's light. To her surprise, the envelope was not yellowed. The glue held tight and Monica had to rip the edge of the envelope to open it. There were several sheets of paper folded inside. One by one, Monica pulled them out of the envelope. The papers were scented with Lydia's perfume. The presence of her mother was so strong that Monica looked up to see if she were there in the room with her.

The room was empty. The only presence in the room was the deepening shadows that fell across the desk. Monica unfolded the papers and pressed them flat. Taking a deep breath to steady her nerves, she began to read:

November 10, 2014

My Dearest Monica,

How much I have dreaded that this day would come. Knowing that, inevitably it would, has been the hardest part. I never believed it would take more than thirty years. No one should have to carry a burden for so long, but I have no one to blame but myself.

The time has come for you to know the truth. That truth is a difficult truth, with so many veils of deceit that it is difficult for me to know what perspective in time to write this from. I will start at the very beginning. Perhaps in doing so, you will understand the many circumstances that led to the events that have now distorted our lives.

I was very much in love with your father. How much I regret that you never had the opportunity to know him and to love him. You would have been the light of his life. So often he spoke of the day that we would have a child and when that day came, he was gone.

Ronald and I met when I began working in the park's offices in 1974. He caught my eye, but it wasn't until a year later that he finally asked me to go out with him. It was 1975 when we had our first date and we were married by the end of that year. I was just twenty years old at the time. Ronald was so good looking and he was very suave and sophisticated. I was infatuated and I quickly fell in love. It was an easier time back then. I would do anything to turn the clock back to those simple, happy days. It was the one time in my life when being in love meant everything. After the honeymoon, I began to help manage the amusement park. Every year when we opened the iron gates on the first day of the season your father would whisper is my ear, "Lydia, let the show begin."

It was an exciting and happy time that seemed to be without end. We had everything, every happiness. How could it have gone so wrong just ten short years later?

As the 1970s ended, the park began to flounder. Maxwell had left the park years earlier and was running our hotel division. His office was at the first Caprice Hotel on Atlantic Point Island. In retrospect, we should have recognized the park's problems as just a change in the times, but we didn't. For the first time your father and I began to disagree. We argued over what we thought we were doing wrong.

I wanted to continue to expand the hotel business into the south and relocate there. The winters here in Atlantic Point are cold, heartless and lonely. Your father would hear nothing of closing the park or relocating. The park had been in operation for about 100 years. Your grandparents had owned the park since the time of the Great Depression. Nothing I said could convince Ronald to close the failing park and move on with our lives. A horrible roller coaster accident in 1983 sealed the park's fate. Our revenues declined almost to the point of bankruptcy after the tragedy.

As the park's finances continued to falter, so did my relationship with your father. There seemed to be no end to our fights, to our arguing. I couldn't stand it any longer. One night I met Maxwell at Belle Brandt's bar to talk about my problems. After all these years Belle's establishment is still open. That night I turned to Maxwell for friendship, for love, to be comforted. We started an affair.

At one point before the end, your father and I remembered the love we once shared. For a moment, we returned to that magical time when we first met. It was during that loving time that you were conceived.

The magic didn't last. One of the park's employees told your father about the affair that I had with Maxwell. Ronald was furious. He was waiting for me at the beach house when I came home that night. It was the start of the worst night of my life...a night I have been reliving for thirty years.

Your father was violent. I had never seen him so angry. Furniture was overturned. Vases and lamps had been smashed. There was no reasoning with him. Still, he never hit me, despite the tremendous anger that had overtaken him. In desperation and out of fear, I phoned Maxwell. It was a mistake. I just wasn't thinking clearly at the time and it made matters worse.

When Maxwell came over, your father fired him on the spot. I remember Ronald telling Maxwell that he had thrown away all his hard years of work. Your father told Maxwell to just get out; he never wanted to see him again. By this time Ronald had calmed down a bit. Firing Maxwell had given him some control. I told Maxwell to leave, that I would be all right. After Maxwell left, he ran into a friend who spent the remainder of the evening with him at Belle's. This would later prove to be a very beneficial piece of luck, as it provided him with an alibi for most of the evening.

It was very late at night when I packed a suitcase and went out to my car. I wanted to make one last visit to Atlantic Point Park. It was the place where it all began, and I had to see it one more time before I said goodbye. The park was not yet open for the season, so there was no one there when I arrived. I phoned Maxwell from the park's office. As expected, he was still at Belle Brandt's Bar. I asked him to meet me later at the park to say our farewell after I said goodbye to your father. I planned to leave town and never return.

Next, I phoned your father at the beach house and asked him to come out to the park right away. I had one last thing to tell him before I left town. He agreed to meet with me. It was cool that night and I'll never forget how still the spring air seemed to be. When your father arrived, he kissed me. One last kiss...I told him I was pregnant. Ronald begged me not to leave. He said we would work it all out. I knew that having a baby would not solve our problems. I had to start over somewhere else. Ronald tried to stop me and I pushed him away. He lost his balance and fell backwards hitting his head on one of the rocks that lined the gardens along the walkways. I never meant to hurt him. I always loved Ronald. I just couldn't live with him after all that had happened.

I bent down to him, he wasn't breathing. I screamed for Maxwell.

Maxwell appeared from the shadows like an apparition after hiding his car near a service gate that has long since become inaccessible. He bent down and said, "Lydia I think he's dead." I screamed and sobbed that it couldn't be true. Finally, Maxwell took hold and gently shook me.

He said, "Lydia, we've got to think. Do you want to spend the rest of your life in prison?"

I told him I couldn't face that as tears streamed down my face. I was pregnant. Maxwell asked who the father of the baby was. I told him the truth—that it was Ronald's child. The next hours are all a haze. I remember Maxwell dragging your father's body into the haunted house. We locked the door and shuddered at what would come next. The haunted house never opened that last season.

Maxwell and I went back to the beach house and packed a bag of Ronald's clothes to place in the trunk of his car. Ronald had been planning a trip to Europe to buy new rides for the park. We would make it seem as if he had just disappeared. Had Ronald not purchased the airline tickets with his own credit card and signature, the police would have conducted a much more thorough investigation. It seemed we could cover the tragedy so that no one would ever know.

We returned to the park with Ronald's luggage. Maxwell put on an old pair of work gloves and went back into the haunted house to get the Eldorado keys out of Ronald's pocket. What a horrible thing to have to do.

Maxwell drove the Eldorado to the airport with me following in Maxwell's car. We left the Eldorado in a deserted lot at the airport and returned to Atlantic Point Park. Maxwell drove me back to the beach house and then went to his own place. I didn't see him until very late the next day.

I closed all the drapes in the beach house and went about the task of cleaning up the evidence of our earlier fight. Then I had to pretend that *everything was normal until many days later, when I reported Ronald missing to the police. I must have been a better actress that I could have ever imagined. I don't know how I pulled it off, but somehow I did, all while spending every day, every hour in a daze. In time, the police did conduct an investigation, but they believed our story that Ronald had gone on a business trip and had never returned. Maxwell's having an alibi helped.*

Maxwell and I stopped our relationship for a long time after that. Deep down, I knew that your father was the only man that I would ever truly love with my entire heart. I opened the park that year without your father, still heartbroken about what I had done.

The park had its worst year ever. Horace Goldsmith insisted that I permanently close the park at the end of the season. I had no other choice. We were almost out of money and even the hotels were being drained of cash.

For all these years, I have paid the taxes on the park to keep my secret from being discovered. I have spent a small fortune, so that you would be raised without the taint of the scandal that I created. I had to stop by the old hotel for one last look before I came out to the park to write this letter. Atlantic Point Island is so desolate now.

I can't blame the township for forcing me to sell them the park or worse yet to have it confiscated. The town is almost deserted and it would be nice to see it returned to the condition it was in when I was young. But I can't live with the possibility that they will discover the secret that I have kept hidden here for more than thirty years.

Monica, the time has come for me to tell you the awful truth. I can't go on any longer. I know when you receive the news of my death you will be devastated. Know now and always that I love you forever. I pray that you will forgive me for your father's death and for leaving you with my legacy. I cannot face the shame.

I knew that in time you would find this letter in the safe. I needed to tell you so that you can be prepared. When the township removes the park and redevelops the land, they will discover that your father has been buried beneath this office building.

Monica, there are no words that can express to you how very sorry I am.

Love always my dear daughter,
Mother

Trisha gazed around the ruins of the park. She could hear the echoes of the thousands of people that had spent happier times there. Trish could also feel the eyes of whoever was following them through the park. The thought made her shiver as darkness continued to descend over the park. There was just enough daylight to see the glitter from the light bulbs that had once hung in strands overhead but were now smashed into a kaleidoscope of color all over the grounds.

"Trish I'm going up to get Monica," Brad stated. "Do you want to come with me or do you want to wait here?"

"You're not leaving me here alone Brad Roberts. I don't care what you say; I know we're being watched."

Just then a piercing scream sounded from the depths of the office building. Brad started running up the dark steps to the second floor with Trish close behind him. At the top, they were disoriented at the myriad of passageways until they heard an eerie sobbing at the rear of the building.

They followed the sound to an office suite that had once been Lydia's. Passing though the reception area, they entered Lydia's former office. Brad was taken aback when he looked across the room at the desk were Monica was sitting in the shadows. She looked so much like Lydia that he was momentarily frozen in time. Regaining his usual composure, he rushed behind the desk and put his arms around Monica. She continued with heavy sobs. Trish rushed to her side, but Monica seemed unable to speak. Brad noticed there was a wall safe that was still exposed with its door hanging open. He told Monica they were going downstairs and getting out of the building.

In a few moments they were outside. Monica had composed herself somewhat, but still seemed incoherent. Brad locked the heavy steel door to the office building while Trish remained at Monica's side.

Without another word the three of them headed to the main gate. Along the way, Monica mumbled over and over, "It's so awful." Despite repeated attempts to get her to tell them what was wrong, she said nothing else. She seemed completely disoriented.

When they reached the main entrance, Brad opened the gates so they could get out. Trish moved her car out through the gates and Brad moved

Maxwell's repaired rental car inside. Brad then put Monica in the Mustang while he relocked the gates. He ran around to the driver's side and started the engine. Brad drove in silence toward the main road, glancing in the rear-view mirror to be sure that Trish was following. Monica still had not said a single word as they pulled up to the beach house.

Once inside, Trish headed for her wine reserves and uncorked a 1.5-liter bottle. She poured three hearty glasses for the group and handed one to Brad and one to Monica. After a few sips of wine Monica seemed more composed, but she was still teary. She unzipped her handbag and handed the opened envelope to Brad. With his arm around Monica he read Lydia's confession without a word, giving a low whistle as he handed the letter to Trish. Trish became emotional as she read the letter, tears glistening in her eyes. When she was finished, she walked over and gave Monica a hug. Monica had tears in her eyes as Trish gently squeezed her.

The figure looked into the deserted car, wondering why they had left it behind. The three of them had spent all day inside the park and the office building, never realizing they were being watched from afar. Now they were gone, but they would come back to get the car. They had no business being here. The figure headed along well familiar paths, looking for more uninvited guests as he moved deftly toward the hidden exit. He could still hear the calliope music playing from far inside the park as the unused service gate came into view. He knew it was important to stay along the edge of the road in case it became necessary to disappear into the shadows once again. No one could ever know that he was there. Watching, always watching.

Chapter Twenty-Four

After Brad and Trish helped Monica up to bed, they sat together and discussed the recent turn of events. Their conversation was punctuated by extended periods of silence until Trish had finally gone up to her own room. Brad was still wide awake. Under the starlit night, he went down to the beach and walked along the water trying to relax so he could sleep when he returned.

An hour later he returned to the darkened beach house just as a summer storm was starting. Lightening cracked the sky, illuminating and outlining the beach house. It appeared aged and worn before the brief light flickered out.

The night was a restless one. Brad found that he had difficulty going to sleep despite the walk. As the first rays of daylight broke through the window, he gave up and decided to go for an early morning workout on the beach.

Much to his surprise he found Monica standing on the rear deck staring out toward the ocean. He called her name through the breeze. As she turned, the wind caught her hair and swept it across her face. Monica pushed her hair back with her hand in a manner that Brad always found to be very alluring. He wished their lives would return to normal, whatever normal was, so that they could move forward with their relationship. Right now that didn't seem to be a scenario he would be enjoying any time soon.

The police would have to be notified, but Brad knew Monica would want to confront Maxwell first. Brad dreaded that event. Maxwell had turned out to be a liar, even if he had protected Lydia for thirty years. Brad felt sure they would never get the entire truth out of him.

"Good morning Brad." Monica was dressed in a casual blouse that knotted at her waist with a pair of white shorts. She was composed and the effect left Brad with the impression that she was once again in control of her emotions.

"How are you feeling this morning?"

"I think deep down inside I knew my mother and Maxwell were involved. I kept hoping that a different answer would prove me wrong."

"Have you decided what you want to do?"

"I think we need to confront Maxwell before we go to the police."

"You've decided to turn the letter over to them?"

"I think we have to Brad. My mother came to Atlantic Point because she knew the township was intent on demolishing the park. She decided to take her own life when she couldn't talk them out of it." Tears formed in Monica's eyes as she continued. "They will find my father's remains under the office building. It's better if we're up front with the authorities now rather than when they tear down the building."

"There's going to be a lot of publicity Monica. Lydia's name will be ruined. The hotels might even be harmed. Maxwell could spend the rest of his life in jail."

"I know. I just don't want to spend another thirty years concealing my mother's crime. It's too late for that." Monica started to sob uncontrollably.

Brad put his arms around Monica and held her for a long time. He kissed her on the head, and then, after she was composed, he set off running up the beach leaving Monica the privacy she needed to sort out her thoughts.

Monica was still on the deck an hour later when Trish staggered out. She was still hung over from too much wine the night before, but who could blame her under the circumstances.

"Good morning Monica. You look well considering that I look like death warmed over."

"That's not a good choice of words Trish."

"Oops! I guess not." The two old friends shared a moment of spontaneous laughter that provided relief to their oppressive thoughts.

"When Brad gets back were going over to confront Maxwell."

Maxwell was fuming. He had been waiting all day yesterday for some word from Brad or Monica about the repair to his car. He wanted to get out of Atlantic Point as soon as he could. Neither Brad nor Monica had had the courtesy to call him with an update. It was almost noon and still no word from either of them.

The knock at the door was startling. It was too insistent to be one of the housekeepers. Maxwell hit the mute button on the old 19" television set and called out gruffly, "Who is it?"

"It's Brad and Monica."

Maxwell got up and opened the door. "It's about time you two got back to me about my car. Where have you been? I tried the cell phones all day yesterday."

"Maxwell sit down," Brad stated firmly. Maxwell was about to rebuke Brad, but he decided to keep quiet when he saw the grim expressions on Monica face and Brad's clenched fists. He eased down on the bed, wiping his brow at the same time.

"What's this all about?" Maxwell demanded.

"Just read this." Monica pulled the envelope from her handbag as she said it. Maxwell reached for his reading glasses and placed them on his nose. He glanced over them as he read the envelope, "It's from Lydia."

In a letter to Monica, Lydia had confessed to killing Ronald Scott and implicated Maxwell as an accomplice. How could she have done that? After all he had done for her—protecting her for thirty years. Maxwell felt a tremendous tightening across his chest. It was getting hard to breathe. He continued to read the words, but he couldn't believe what he was seeing.

All at once, everything began to swim in the room. Maxwell tried to talk but he couldn't get out the words. He tried to get up but the pain in his chest was crushing. As he fell backwards, his glasses and the letter tumbled to the floor. Maxwell landed on the glasses, crushing them as he fell. The last thing he remembered was Monica's voice calling his name.

Monica started CPR, using the skills she required all her employees to have to potentially save a life. Brad dialed emergency services on his cell phone and then ran to the motel's office to alert them that an ambulance would be arriving. In seconds, he had dashed back to Maxwell's room.

Monica was still working on Maxwell. She had loosened his shirt and paused as he appeared to start breathing on his own. Monica stepped back. It seemed like forever until the paramedics arrived.

The ambulance crew took over, hooking up oxygen and an IV. When Maxwell was stabilized, they moved him to the waiting ambulance. Monica agreed to ride with Maxwell to the local emergency clinic. Brad would follow in the Mustang.

The ride to the emergency clinic was brief. The ambulance heaved from side to side as it traversed Atlantic Point's potholed roads. Monica backed to the rear of the ambulance as the doors swung open and they moved Maxwell to the treatment area. She attempted to follow but was directed to a waiting room in the front of the clinic by a young nurse. Monica paused when she saw Brad speed into the driveway a second later. He jumped out of the car and followed her to the waiting room.

They waited for hours. Several times Monica went to the reception desk only to be told that they were still working on Maxwell. The clinic did not appear to be busy, considering it was the height of the tourist season. Of course, Atlantic Point didn't really have a tourist season anymore.

Brad went outside to use his cell phone to call Trish. The wait could be several more hours and he didn't want her to worry about them. Inside Monica paced nervously. Hours later, the receptionist said they were moving Maxwell to a critical care room, pending air flight to a larger facility. Monica and Brad could see him, but just briefly. Before allowing them to go in the doctor gave them a stern warning, "You are not to say or do anything that would upset Mr. Williams. His condition is precarious."

Monica went into the room first. Maxwell was hooked up to machines from every part of his body. A heart monitor traced what appeared to be an even beat from his heart.

Maxwell pulled at his oxygen mask. "Monica, I loved her. I always loved her."

"I know Maxwell, don't try to speak right now."

"I have to tell you…everything I did, I did for Lydia. She meant everything to me."

"Maxwell, please don't speak."

"I, I …" Suddenly the heart monitor went flat and an alarm sounded. In seconds, a crash team yelling, "code blue" moved into the room. Monica and Brad were rushed outside. Moments later the doctor came through the door. Relief flooded over Monica when he told them that Maxwell was stabilized once again. They were not permitted back inside the room.

It was almost seven in the evening when Brad and Monica returned to the beach house. They gave Trish an update and the three of them decided they would go out for dinner, since there were really no other options for food. Brad and Monica had not eaten all day and Monica didn't feel like going out of town. Trish was eager to see the restaurant where Lydia and Maxwell had started their affair all those years ago, so they agreed on another night at Belle's.

The restaurant was busy as usual. Because of the crowd and without reservations, they were seated at a side table with no view. At this point none of them cared. They ordered a round of drinks and eased back in their chairs.

It had been several days since Monica and Brad visited the restaurant and Belle was glad to see that they had returned. She occupied her usual seat at the end of the bar and had just sent Old Joe to get her handbag from the office.

Word was getting around town that the Scott's beach house was occupied again. Belle knew it hadn't been sold because she knew the only realtor in town. It had to be one of the Scott's occupying it or at least someone they knew. Then a few days ago Officer Grainger had commented that he picked up three stranded people who had been exploring out at Atlantic Point Park. The one who had presented his identification to the officer was named Brad Roberts. Belle had given Brad and Monica directions to the park when they first arrived in town.

The woman with Brad was the spitting image of a young Lydia Scott. Belle surmised that Monica must have inherited Atlantic Point Park after Lydia's death. Why in the world had Lydia Scott's daughter come to the town that her mother deserted thirty years ago?

She wondered what Monica was planning. The township had been after Lydia to do something with the park for years and Lydia had *always* refused. Maybe Monica was going to rehabilitate the park. After all these years, Belle was eager to see Atlantic Point returned to prosperity.

During their last visit, Brad told Belle that Monica's name was "Roberts." Belle decided to try something. She still wanted to know if Monica's real name was "Scott" or "Williams." Belle would tell from Monica's expression if she was telling her the truth.

283

As Belle walked over to Monica's table, she was surprised to see that a third person had joined Monica's group. "Good evening my friends. It's good to see you again. I thought perhaps you'd left town."

"Hello Belle, let me introduce my friend from New York, Trisha Marshall. Trisha, this is our hostess and proprietor Belle Brandt." Belle and Trish shook hands providing each other with a cordial greeting. Monica noticed that Belle's friendly tone had changed to one of suspicion since their last encounter.

"Monica, I must say again, you look so familiar. May I ask you, what was your maiden name?"

Monica paled. She debated what to say, seconds seeming like hours. Ultimately she decided the time had come to be truthful. In the next few days everyone in town would know who she was. "Belle, my real name is Scott, not Roberts. Brad and I are not married, at least not yet anyway."

Brad looked shocked and Belle smiled as her tone became soft and gentle. Monica I knew your mother and father well. I'm so glad that you've decided to come here to Atlantic Point Island."

Monica looked relieved that the truth of her identity was finally out in the open. She asked Belle to join them and Belle told the server to bring them a round of drinks. Belle did not press further for any information. Instead she transported them back in time to the period when Monica's mother and father had been the stellar couple of Atlantic Point. The trio listened with rapt interest.

The next morning, Monica and Brad decided to delay going to the police department until after Maxwell had been airlifted to the larger facility. They didn't want to do anything to jeopardize his life. After a light breakfast with Trish, they headed for the clinic. It had been too late yesterday to transport Maxwell to the nearest full-service hospital. He had spent a long, difficult night in the clinic.

Maxwell was awake when Monica and Brad arrived. Maxwell didn't try to talk, and Monica just squeezed his hand. She recognized that Lydia and Maxwell had both committed serious crimes. She still loved him though, especially after he had protected her mother. A short while later, Brad and Monica were asked to wait outside while the doctor and nurses prepared Maxwell for the helicopter transport.

Monica felt sick in her stomach. If Maxwell died because they had delved into the past, she would never forgive herself. Maxwell was wheeled from the room on a gurney. He looked ghostly pale and his skin had become white and pasty. The sound of a helicopter landing on the roof permeated the building and Maxwell was whisked into the chopper.

"Where is he being transported to?" Monica wanted to know.

"Trenton Medical Center," the nurse replied.

"Will you phone me when he arrives there?"

"Please leave your number at the nurses' station. One of our doctors will travel with him until he reaches the center. It's standard procedure. We'll phone you when he arrives."

After Maxwell was loaded into the helicopter, they watched until it lifted into the sky. Monica jotted down her phone number for the nurses before they left the clinic.

Their next stop was the local police department. The police department of Atlantic Point, New Jersey consisted of five full-time officers and several part-time officers. There was never more than one of them on patrol and one in the office at any given time. The building was old, both outside and inside. A receptionist asked them to have a seat while she went to get the officer on duty. Moments later, a detective was listening intently to their story, occasionally asking for clarification on several points. Monica and Brad explained every detail to the best of their ability.

The disappearance of Ronald Scott more than thirty years ago was still a topic of occasional discussion in the small town of Atlantic Point, although after all these years it was more legend than leads. The officer was familiar with some aspects of the case history. Although the case was still "unsolved" there was no current investigation. The confession that Lydia had written was the first recent lead that the office knew of. He was too young to have worked on the original disappearance.

"We're going to need the assistance of the state police, Ms Scott. We're too small here to handle anything like this. I need to ask you to wait here while they're summoned. I'm going to go into our records room and pull the old files. It might take some time for all of this. I do need to know where Maxwell Williams is at this time."

Monica sighed resolutely. Waiting was all they seemed to be doing over the past two days. "Maxwell is being transported to the Trenton Medical Center as we speak. He had a serious heart attack yesterday and they can't treat him at the Atlantic Point clinic."

"It doesn't sound as if he's going anywhere, but I'm going to alert the state police to hold him at the hospital and arrest him when he is released."

The officer picked up his phone, pressed one of the speed dial buttons and spoke to the state police dispatcher. After finishing the call, he got up and headed through a door at the rear of the office disappearing from sight.

"I feel like running out the door Brad."

"I don't think that would be a good idea."

"I still feel that way just the same."

For the next four hours Monica and Brad told their story over and over again clarifying detail after detail to the state police as well as to the detective from Atlantic Point Island. Lydia's confession was confiscated over Monica's objection. She hadn't thought to make a copy before she went to the police and they refused to provide her with one now.

The police decided that before proceeding, it would be necessary to establish that a murder had even taken place. This would require recovering the remains of Ronald Scott, which meant that the office building would have to be razed. The project would be expensive. Monica agreed to provide the funding necessary to complete the demolition. An hour later, the session concluded. They were free to go but had been asked to notify the police of their future plans before leaving town.

Monica felt drained. So much had happened she couldn't think straight. When they reached the beach house Trish was in the living room curled up on the sofa reading an e-book. She took one look at Brad and Monica and headed for the wine cabinet.

With wine glasses in hand, Monica relayed the day's events to Trisha. Brad just stared out the window. Monica realized she would need to notify Evelyn Smith, Maxwell's housekeeper of his current condition. Evelyn broke into sobs when Monica phoned her. She made Monica promise to keep her posted. Brad and Monica decided not to tell anyone at Caprice Hotels until they had more information on Maxwell's condition. Even if he did recover, he would likely be facing criminal charges as an accomplice to a murder after the fact. Monica wasn't yet ready to explain all that to the hotel's staff.

After Monica finished up her conversation with Evelyn, the phone rang just as she was placing it on the table. It was the doctor from the local medical center. Maxwell had died on the flight to Trenton. The doctor expressed his brief condolences to Monica and then hung up. Monica stared ahead in shock and was unable to speak once again.

Chapter Twenty-Five

The next day was a whirlwind of activity. All of it tainted with the dread of what was ahead. Monica phoned Francine Crowley at Caprice Hotel's headquarters. Francine was shocked to learn that Maxwell had passed away.

"Monica when I think about it, Maxwell did seem to be ill on several recent occasions, but I never expected this."

"Francine, I need you to release a memorandum to all the hotels about Maxwell. Let them know we'll be holding a memorial service when I return to Palm Beach. David Lansing will continue to be in charge until Brad and I return."

"Monica when *are* you returning?"

"I think I'll be back in another week or two. I don't want to explain right now, but events are moving fast up here."

"Take care of yourself my dear. I need you back here."

"I will Francine, I promise."

Next Monica phoned Jeanette at the Palm Beach house. Jeanette became very emotional when Monica broke the news to her about Maxwell. She asked Jeanette if she would go over to be with Evelyn Smith. Monica knew Maxwell's housekeeper would be devastated by the news of his death. At last Monica hung up with Jeanette, shaking her head as she did so.

The last call was the worst. Evelyn Smith began to cry. She became more and more hysterical and Monica was glad Jeanette was on the way over when at last she concluded the call.

"All the troops notified?"

"They're all notified, Brad. Wait until they hear the rest of the news."

"The police did agree to keep wraps on the investigation until the office building is demolished. I'm sure that that your agreeing to pay for the demolition had something to do with that."

"I just want it to be over with Brad."

There was an unexpected knock on the door. Despite the assurances from the police about secrecy, Monica expected the press to come calling at any moment. Gathering her courage, she opened the door. A uniformed state police trooper was standing beside a man dressed in a white shirt and tie. The trooper introduced Detective McAllister from the State Bureau of Criminal Investigations.

Detective McAllister was thin and of average height. He appeared to be about 45 years of age with slick dark hair. He shook Monica's hand. Brad came up behind Monica and introduced himself to the detective, extending his hand as he did so.

"I need to ask you some questions Ms Scott. The case was referred to me after you met with local and state law enforcement officers yesterday."

"I don't know what more we can tell you detective. We spent more than four hours yesterday providing every detail that we have." Monica's voice had become tense and hoarse.

"I'm sure this is difficult, but I need to hear all of it from you firsthand. I've already read the reports taken yesterday.

Monica sighed with resignation. She showed the two men into the living room. The officials gazed around at the ancient furnishings. Monica launched into the story for what seemed like the one-hundredth time. Detective McAllister listened with rapt attention, occasionally interrupting to ask a question or make a clarification. In the end, he did agree to allow Monica to demolish the office building. An officer would be stationed at the sight from the start of the demolition until the corpse was located. At that time, the coroner would be notified.

Monica gave an involuntary shudder at the reference to the corpse. Brad wrapped his arms around her. After two hours the officers left. On their way out Detective McAllister gave Monica his business card so she could notify him if she needed to.

"Brad, we'd better get busy locating a demolition company."

"I'll get started now." Brad grabbed his phone and walked out to the rear deck to collect his thoughts and start a search. A moment later a short list of demolition companies appeared on the screen. He called them sequentially until one agreed to come to the park.

Inside, Trish finally appeared, still in her silk patterned pajamas.

"It's about time you got up," Monica teased her.

"Who were those guys out front?"

"The detectives assigned to the case."

"This is really turning into a big story Monica."

"I know. Do you think you can extend your vacation?"

"Already done. I wouldn't think of leaving you until this is resolved."

Monica hugged her. "Thanks Trish. Now I have a giant big favor to ask of you."

"At your service."

"I need you to drive to Trenton to get Maxwell's remains. No autopsy was necessary since he died of natural causes after more than 24 hours under medical care. When I phoned Maxwell's attorney, he directed me to have the remains cremated and to scatter the ashes over the Atlantic Ocean."

"This gets creepier all the time," Trish commented.

Brad reappeared from the outside deck, cell phone in hand. He had located a demolition company. They would survey the sight tomorrow and begin work the day after that.

The next morning at eight o'clock Brad and Monica met the head of the demolition company in front of the massive iron gates of Atlantic Point Park. Trish had already set off on the drive to Trenton to secure Maxwell's remains from the funeral home. Brad unlocked the gates and began to push them open all the while complaining that he was getting weak from being away from the gym for so long.

Brad explained to the man that there were two main paths to the rear of the park where the demolition would need to take place. The main path was blocked with the remains of the roller coaster, the other path was about the same distance, but it was very narrow.

The man surveyed the crumpled roller coaster and agreed with Brad that they would bring the equipment in through the old service path. It would take several days to clear a path wide enough to bring their demolition equipment through.

Monica seemed to be getting more impatient and agitated with every passing moment. When she snapped at the man that everything needed to be done right now, Brad eased her aside.

"Monica, this is not an overnight job. You have to relax. You already know what happened to your father. Finding the remains is not going to change that."

"I know Brad, but I can't go on like this much longer."

Brad wiped the tears from her eyes. "It won't be much longer."

Later in the day Trish returned from Trenton with an urn that held all that remained of Maxwell. She carefully handed the urn to Monica. Monica gazed at the urn in silence. With measured paces, she walked over to the old entertainment center and placed it on top without another word. They were all completely drained.

The next day Brad, Trish and Monica spent hours watching as a small army of men began removing trees and debris from the path leading to the office building. The path was originally about ten feet wide from the crumbled remains of the pavement. It had narrowed in many places to as little as four feet where trees and overgrowth had displaced the crumbling asphalt. With steady progress the team moved toward the office building, widening the path back to its original ten feet, plus an extra foot on each side.

Near the middle of the second day the path was widened all the way back to the office building. The next step was to remove every piece of glass before demolition started, even though the glass was break-resistant. Before they did so, the police made a complete check of the building. Monica wanted to take a last look as well, but she had to wait until the police were finished. With Brad and Trish in tow, the three made a tour of the entire office building. Monica was still in awe that her mother had spent so much money to conceal her crime. Had Lydia really intended to work in a building that was constructed to conceal her father's grave? The thought was frightening.

When they reached Lydia's office, the aerial picture that concealed the safe was still hanging open on its hinges. Monica asked Brad to remove the picture and take it outside. He had it down from the wall in a few seconds with a pocket screwdriver.

Brad carried the picture to the main floor, being careful not to bang it on any of the walls. Outside the main entrance, the police and the demolition crew waited. The officer in charge gave the picture a cursory examination before allowing Brad to take it.

The demotion crew moved into the building to begin removing the heavy, break-resistant windows. Monica stood by in silence as the building's windows became gaping holes one by one. It seemed ironic that the one building that had remained untouched by time would be the first building demolished.

As the crews finished for the day Monica reached for Brad's hand and began the long walk back to the front gates. From this point on, the police would guard the premises around the clock. Brad left the gates unlocked so the police could change shifts without the key set.

Back at the house Trish had made dinner reservations for Belle Brandt's. Monica and Brad headed upstairs to get showered and cleaned up for dinner. Trish was already showered so she would be ready when they returned home.

Brad updated Trish on the progress of the demolition work, stating that he expected the actual building to start coming down tomorrow.

Monica had been silent until now. "How long do you think it will take Brad?"

"It's pretty big Monica. I'm thinking several days at a minimum. They also have to be very careful since they are looking for evidence."

Monica realized that "evidence" meant the remains of her father.

The three of them headed out to the Mustang. Monica decided she would tell Belle Brandt about the circumstances surrounding her visit to Atlantic Point tonight before the press got wind of it.

For once the restaurant was not busy. Monica was afraid that everyone knew her secret and had left the restaurant to go to the park. She realized such thoughts were ridiculous, but she also knew they would soon be reality.

Belle was nowhere in sight. The three friends ordered appetizers and drinks; sure that their friend would appear at any moment. The restaurant seemed eerily quiet. Monica asked the server where Belle was tonight. It was the first night they had visited the establishment that she had not been there. The server replied that Belle was expected to be in later in the evening.

Near the end of their meal, Belle scurried into the restaurant. She looked harried and her hair had whipped in all directions from the wind. Before Monica could wave her over to the table she disappeared into the back of the restaurant.

Monica desperately wanted to tell Belle what was going on. As a last resort, they ordered another round of drinks, and moments later Belle reappeared. She sat down on her usual barstool without so much as a glance around the room, leaning over to ask the bartender a question in a hushed voice.

As she glanced around the operations, she noticed Monica and her party, providing them a brief wave and a nod. Monica got up and went over to Belle's barstool.

"We enjoyed your stories about my parents so much the other night Belle, I just wanted to thank you."

"I just wish those stories had a happier ending Monica."

Monica paled. She wondered if Belle knew more than she had been letting on about her father's death. Yet for some reason she still trusted her. "I have something to tell you. Would you care to join us?"

Belle had composed herself in the office. Now she just looked perplexed. At last she replied, "I would enjoy that Monica." Belle eased herself down from her barstool, and as she reached Monica's table she gave Brad a hug and patted Trish on the arm.

Monica told Belle her story. Belle's look went from surprise, to astonishment, to shock. At the end she just sat there and with a stunned look and shook her head. For a moment Monica wondered if Belle was all right. She reached over to grasp her hand. "We'll know what happened to my father in a few days." Belle extracted a handkerchief from her pocket and dabbed at the tears forming in her eyes.

Monica asked Belle to please keep their conversation confidential and Belle readily agreed. Making a hasty goodbye to the trio, she headed for the front door of the restaurant. Monica eased back in her chair, unsure what to make of Belle's actions or of her response to Monica's story. As she did so, she glanced to the side hall and gasped as she realized that Old Joe had been standing in the shadows listening. He started to turn away just as Monica looked in his direction. For a moment their eyes locked just before he disappeared down the service corridor toward the kitchen. Monica gave an involuntary shudder: this was not what she needed after all the events of the last few days.

The next morning brought a dark, cloudy sky. All they needed to delay things now was a summer storm. Monica, Brad and Trish reached the demolition site just as the crew was getting ready to start their day. Monica felt as if her nerves were going to break into pieces.

The diesel engines started, each with a clatter and a puff of black smoke. A crane began to pull down the walls and roof, then a bulldozer moved in to push the debris into a pile and finally a scoop lifted it onto a dump truck. Foot by foot, the office building crumbled. Dust bellowed from around the crane with each yank of the building. Sections of the roof began to collapse as the support walls were removed.

Each day the threat of a storm hung overhead, but no storms delayed the progress. A police officer guarded the scene, ready to call the coroner when the time came. Near the end of the third day, all that was left was the cement foundation. It would only be a matter of time from this point forward.

The following morning, the sky remained dark and clouded. Thunder rumbled through the beach house as Monica, Brad and Trish got ready to head out to Atlantic Point Park. A bolt of lightning flashed across the sky. Monica hoped the storm would hold out until the demolition crew completed their grisly task.

It was just after eight in the morning. For the past couple of days, it had been early to bed and early to rise. Each day more tense than the previous. Even Brad and Trish were becoming snappy. At the end of each day they would all head back to the house covered with dust and still waiting for answers.

Monica stayed at the sight all day without leaving. Brad and Trish took turns running out for their lunches, which Monica always refused. The wait was excruciating. Today they would begin removing the foundation. A scoop was used instead of the crane. It began to fleck up pieces of the concrete, starting with the front right corner of the building. The pieces were moved to the dump truck after being examined by the foreman and the police.

By late in the afternoon, the brewing storm still had not turned into rain. Thunder rumbled through the darkened skies, which were broken by occasional flashes of lightening. The scoop continued from one end of the building to the other. After all the concrete was removed, they began removing layers of dirt until a scraping sound revealed the top of a large wooden object. The foreman summoned the commanding police officer. He directed them to continue onward until they were sure of what they had discovered. Monica had been sure she would be ready for this moment. She wasn't. Brad had to support her as more and more of the coffin was exposed. Thunder rumbled ever louder and lightening continued to break through the dark clouds. More and more dirt was removed from around the coffin. The officer on duty summoned the coroner and Detective McAllister.

When enough dirt was removed from around the sides, a forklift was brought in to lift the coffin from the ground. The forklift slid underneath and began to lift upward. Chunks of dirt clung to the sides of the coffin occasionally falling to the ground as it was hoisted. The coffin had unusual coloration from its days as part of the horror display in the haunted house attraction.

Trish began to run toward the front of the park. Monica could not move her eyes and her feet seemed cemented to the ground as Brad continued supporting her. With great care the forklift lowered the box back down onto a tarp. Now they had to wait for the arrival of the coroner and Detective McAllister. Time was at a standstill.

Detective McAllister arrived first. He surveyed the sight and then joined the rest of the crew in their wait for the coroner. It took the coroner all but another hour to arrive. Monica had regained some of her composure, but still clung to Brad.

At last, the coroner arrived driving a dark colored state issued sedan. A hearse followed the sedan. The coroner climbed out of his car and headed for the coffin, oblivious to the people that surrounded the area. He acted with the assuredness of a man who knows his position.

After examining the coffin, he had McAllister take pictures and then directed the foreman to cut the two heavy locks that secured the lid. The first lock broke with ease. The second lock would not break. It took two men grasping the cutters to break the lock. It finally snapped open with a loud crack. With the foreman at one end the coroner at the other end they lifted the lid to the coffin, seeming to take an eternity to do so.

Except for the creaking hinges of the lid, the air was heavy with silence. Everyone held their breath. Monica summoned up all her courage. She was behind the coffin so she couldn't see inside. As she walked around to the open side, her eyes told her what the coroner was saying but she couldn't believe.

The coffin was empty except for two large bags of sand that had become wet and dirty after being in the ground for thirty years. Monica fell backwards into Brad's arms as she passed out. Thunder rumbled one more time and lightening flashed. Rain began to pelt from the sky as the storm let loose in full force.

Chapter Twenty-Six

Monica's reprieve from the horror was short lived. Cold rain pellets and some smelling salts from the coroner's medical bag revived her. She woke up just in time to see the hideous coffin being loaded into the hearse. The caked mud washing off the coffin and the grotesque colors made the scene surreal. For a moment Monica was sure it was a horrible dream from which she would awaken.

The hearse crept out of the clearing, weaving as it hit potholes and followed closely by the coroner. Monica and Brad began the long walk back to the main gate on the now widened path. Before they had gone too far, Detective McAllister stopped to offer them a ride. Monica declined, despite being drenched to the skin from the storm. Mud was caked into her hair from when she passed out and mascara was running down her cheeks. McAllister told them the evidence would be transported to the state crime lab for forensic analysis. He promised he would be in touch with them the next day.

A few seconds later Trish appeared in the Mustang. Despite her questioning frown she was a welcome sight for Brad and Monica. Brad briefed Trish on the unexpected findings as he squeezed into the back seat. Trish was astounded. Monica climbed into the passenger seat.

"I'm sorry I deserted you both. I just couldn't stand to be there any longer."

"It's okay Trish," Monica replied, "You just did what I should have done. Instead, I passed out in front of everyone."

Brad defended Monica. "I don't think anyone is going to judge you for that Monica. We were all shocked by today's events."

The summer storm passed with gray clouds hovering overhead. An unnatural quiet settled over the car as fog rolled into the park and evening shadows began to fall. The main gates to the park materialized through the haze, appearing as they would in a black and white movie, daylight dwindling. Trish shivered as she guided the car out between the open gates. Several police officers remained behind to guard the crime scene, so Brad did not bother to lock up. Fog continued to roll out from the overgrowth making it difficult to keep the car on the old entrance road. Several times Brad gritted his teeth as Trish hit a pothole so hard, he was sure an axle would break. Monica did not seem to notice. She just stared ahead in a silent daze.

It took longer than usual to reach the main highway. The fog was still heavy, so Trish kept the car at low speeds. As they neared the bridge that led out to the main island, Trish almost slammed into the side before righting the car. Monica just stared in horrified silence. Brad wondered if Monica was thinking about Lydia crashing off the bridge last November when all this started.

When the beach house came into sight, it was still shrouded in fog and waves could be heard roiling in the background. They were all surprised that no members of the press were hovering around the front door. The three friends were so tense by the time the car was parked that they could have jumped out of their skins. Brad unlocked the front door and Trish rushed for her liquor reserves. No wine this time, she poured each of them a double scotch.

As the warm liquid burned her throat Monica felt the first touch of relaxation since the day started. Brad seldom consumed hard liquor, but for once he accepted the drink without objection. The three of them plopped down in the living room. Trish turned on a single light. It failed to dispel the gloom. The air seemed damp and cold, tinted with a musty smell that made Monica's stomach feel even worse. Outside, the fog had become so thick that it was impossible to see from the windows. The effect was disquieting and added to the eerie atmosphere hovering around the room.

It was Monica who finally broke the silence. "We now have an empty coffin. Where is my father?"

Brad leaned front as he answered, "I don't know Monica. Someone has gone to elaborate lengths to make it very convincing that your father was buried under the office building. There were only two people who knew about the murder: Lydia and Maxwell. Lydia spent thousands of dollars over thirty years to conceal the grave and then took her own life when she concluded the crime would be discovered. She had to believe that your father was really buried there or why would she have done all of it? That leaves only one other person; Maxwell, and he's dead too."

Trish piped in for the first time, "Do you think Ronald is buried somewhere else in the park?"

"That's a very good question," Brad answered.

"Brad, do you think we'll ever know what happened to my father?"

"I think the recent events and the eventual media frenzy are going to ignite a lot of public interest in solving the case, but after thirty years who knows. The police do have much greater forensic skills than they did thirty years ago."

Trish got up and reached for her cell phone, "I'm going to order some pizza from that place around the corner. We are so close that they can walk them over in this fog. Is anyone else hungry?"

The figure skirted along the darkened buildings of Atlantic Point Park. There were still several police officers in the park. For the past three days construction crews had torn down the office building. The figure watched the recent events from afar, concealed from the crowd of workers and law enforcement agents. He knew all the secret paths that would allow a person passage without detection. For anyone else, negotiating the park with the descending fog would have been impossible, but the figure reached the secret gate without difficulty or detection. He opened the gate slowly so that it did not screech, not wanting anyone to know he was present. In seconds, he had disappeared into the thickening fog.

The first rays of morning slanted through Brad's window. The tattered, old draperies could not keep out the light, but the beach house seemed deathly silent with all the windows closed from last night's weather. Trish and Monica were exhausted and were likely to sleep late if past experience was any prediction. As quietly as he could, Brad descended the steps into the foyer. Glancing into the living room as he headed for the front door, he saw the remnants of their impromptu pizza dinner the night before. He had a slight headache this morning. He wasn't used to drinking hard liquor. Some coffee from Fanny's would cure that.

Brad walked with brisk strides down the front steps of the beach house. In a few moments he was at the store. He could smell the fresh coffee wafting through the screened entrance door. It smelled wonderful. Brad headed for the coffee station and grabbed the largest cup that they had. As he neared the cashier station, he glanced down at the morning newspapers that were stacked on the floor for sale. He gasped when he read the headline:

Thirty-year-old Atlantic Point mystery deepens. Where is Ronald Scott?

The headline sounded eerily like the headline that was written during the original investigation. Brad threw some more coins onto the counter and picked up one of the newspapers. He was surprised that they had been spared personal media attention. The police had kept Monica's whereabouts a secret. The press agencies had contacted Caprice Hotels in an attempt to locate her. At least they were still out of the limelight for the moment. Brad headed back to the house. He dreaded showing the newspaper to Monica, but he knew that he had to.

When he reached the house Brad phoned Francine Crowley at Caprice Hotel's headquarters. When she answered, Brad instructed her to have their acting manager, David Lansing, contact him as soon as he came in. Brad wanted to be sure that the publicity did not harm the hotels, if that was even possible. After Lydia's death just last year, he did not want anything else rocking the corporate boat. Monica was in no condition to deal with business right now. At least Brad could take care of that for her.

After finishing the call, Brad sat down in the living room to read the entire newspaper. Stories, both new and old, covered the front page and most of the first section. From Ronald Scott's disappearance, to Lydia's death last November, to more recent events that included Maxwell's death and the findings at the demolished office building. It was all there, just like something out of a Hollywood horror movie—except that it was real.

When Monica awakened, Brad went to the store to get her some coffee, handing her the newspaper before he left. When he returned, he was surprised that she seemed to be well composed. Monica always amazed him.

"What do you think of the press coverage?"

"It was inevitable. Sooner or later the news was going to get out. While you were gone, Detective McAllister called. He's going to be coming over later to talk to us about the investigation. David Lansing also called on your cell phone. I told him you would call him back. Did you want to alert him about the news?"

"Yes. I'm concerned about the hotels, but I didn't want to bother you with that right now. Maybe with all the press coverage we'll start to get some answers about your father."

"I'm not counting on it Brad."

For the next several hours Brad and Monica waited for Detective McAllister. Trish joined them in the early afternoon when she finally rolled out of bed.

"How *do* you sleep so late?" Monica asked her.

"Just one of my many skills," Trish laughed.

"Honestly! Here's some light reading for you," Monica said as she handed Trish the morning paper."

Trish's eyes widened as she read the front page.

"You better get showered and dressed unless you want the police to see you in your afternoon pajamas Trish."

Trish raised her eyebrows, "That could be interesting."

At two o'clock, a knock on the door signaled Detective McAllister's arrival. Monica and Trish remained seated in the living room while Brad answered the door. Trish had finally dressed after Monica threatened to keep her out of their meeting. When McAllister loomed in the doorway, Monica asked him to have a seat.

"Good afternoon everyone. I wanted to update you and let you know what will be happening from here on out." There was rapt silence as McAllister continued. "You already know the coffin was transported to the state crime lab. It's being treated as a high priority case since this is the first real lead we've had in thirty years."

"How can an empty coffin be called a lead?" Monica wanted to know.

"We may be able to tell if it has ever had a body in it. It will be tested for any human remains including hair, blood and bone. If we find any

DNA, we'll need a sample from you Ms Scott to confirm if it is from your father. Preliminary testing earlier today did not reveal the presence of any of those items." Monica just shuddered.

"That coffin was part of the Dracula display in the old haunted house." The paint colors match those that were used in the display," Brad offered.

"We've already taken samples of the remaining paint in the haunted house to verify that, but I would say that your conclusion is likely accurate. We have also tested the area in the haunted house for evidence of human blood, but there is so much water damage, there's no guarantee."

Monica gave a cynical reply, "Imagine testing an amusement park haunted house for real blood."

McAllister did not acknowledge the parody and instead continued talking. "We did locate two sets of keys hidden in the lining of the coffin. One large ring was tagged, AP Master One and there was a set of General Motors car keys with a Cadillac crest on them. Someone went to great lengths to make sure that it would look like your father disappeared with all his keys. However, if we don't find any other evidence, we're just about back where we started from. Ronald Scott disappeared without a trace in May of 1985."

"Do you think he's buried somewhere else in the park?" Monica wanted to know.

"It's a distinct possibility, but the park covers 800 acres, with multiple structures. A search could take years and still turn up nothing."

"Do you think my father could still be alive?"

"No. If he were still alive, why didn't he ever come forward? He didn't commit any crime that we know of, and he owned several successful businesses. Why would he leave all of that in the hands of the woman who had betrayed him? It would be my last belief that he would still be alive. I would like to know more about Maxwell Williams though," the detective queried.

"He was my mother's business partner for all the years of my life. Maxwell moved to Florida, as did my mother at the end of 1985 after they closed Atlantic Point Park. Maxwell was like a father to me and he was my mother's companion for many years. He was also a company employee when my father ran the business here in Atlantic Point."

"Why did he come to Atlantic Point now?"

"When I inherited the park I was determined to find out why my mother had kept it a secret from me for all these years. The township wants to confiscate it for redevelopment. Monica glanced at Brad wondering whether to continue. The glance was not lost on McAllister.

"If you are concealing any information in this matter, you could be charged as an accessory after the fact Ms Scott. You need to tell me everything."

"Maxwell came to town to pay off a blackmailer. He told us that someone was going to ruin my mother's name unless a payment of $2 million was made."

"Do you know who the blackmailer is? McAllister demanded.

"It's two people," Monica answered. "Maxwell's former executive assistant, Janice Laneer, and our former corporate director of engineering, Drake Donovan."

"And you chose not to involve the police?" McAllister sounded angry.

"Maxwell chose not to involve the police." Monica answered in defense.

"Do you have any idea how these persons came to have this information? Could either of them be involved in the original crime?"

"I have to presume Maxwell gave the information to Janice piece by piece through many years of after dinner drinks. Janice is a very sharp woman. I believe she compiled the information together over time and Maxwell had an affair with her at one point. I knew about it because my mother confided to me that she was very hurt. I always wondered why she didn't fire Janice after that, but now I think she realized that Janice knew too much. Eventually, Maxwell and my mother resumed their relationship. To the best of my knowledge, Janice did not know my family before we moved to Florida. Drake is too young to have been involved in the original crime."

"Did you participate in the blackmail payoff Ms Scott?"

"Maxwell funded all the money. Brad and I did go along to see who the blackmailer was."

"Do you realize that you could have been injured or killed?"

"I guess it wasn't the best thing to do. You need to understand Detective; all of this has happened to me over a very short period. I'm not thinking as clearly as I do under normal circumstances."

"Do you want to file a criminal complaint against Janice Laneer and Drake Donovan?"

"I need to think about that. Can I give you an answer later?"

"You need to give me an answer soon. In the meantime I'm going to place an all-points bulletin for the two of them. They have some explaining to do. They may know even more than they've let on to you. I also need any evidence you may have against them."

Monica walked over to the old entertainment center. She lifted the urn containing Maxwell's remains. Under the urn were the four gray letters, still in their original envelopes. Replacing the urn, she handed the envelopes to McAllister. He in turn placed them inside a clear plastic bag, careful to touch only the edges.

McAllister turned to leave. As he did so his curt words echoed through Monica's ears, "I'll be in touch."

Belle sat down at her desk. It was still early in the afternoon. The bartender had brought her a cup of hot tea and some scones on a tray along with the morning newspaper. Belle had a lot on her mind. Old Joe had disappeared yet again. For the past week he had seemed edgy and distracted. More and more he had not been showing up for work and on more than one occasion, Belle had gone looking for him. The disappearances were getting to be more frequent and longer. When Belle asked him where he had been, he just mumbled some incoherent words and went to work as if nothing had happened.

Belle worried about Old Joe. He had lived on the second floor of the bar for the last ten years. He didn't seem to have any family, or at least none that Belle knew of. If he continued to keep disappearing, she would have to find someone else to do his work. Belle was fond of Old Joe and she had in essence become his guardian, but she had worked too long and too hard to let the restaurant go downhill because he would not show up for his shifts. Perhaps he would reappear tonight.

Belle eased back and opened the daily newspaper. She was so shocked at the headlines that she knocked over the tray with the tea and scones on it. They went clattering to the floor.

The press had caught up with Monica. They had been outside the beach house since the day after the gruesome discovery in the park, with Monica, Brad and Trish held up inside most of the time since. After some consideration, Monica decided to hold a press conference. Monica had Trish inform the press that she would make a statement and answer questions at one o'clock in the afternoon. Monica finally made a decision that she had been thinking about ever since she was in New York for the reading of the will. It seemed like a lifetime ago. Even Brad and Trish would be surprised.

"Will the two of you stand beside me?" Monica asked them.

"Of course," they both replied in unexpected unison.

Right at one o'clock Monica opened the front door to the beach house. She had dressed in a black business suit, the only one she had packed for the trip. Her hair hung seductively around her shoulders. Brad thought she looked spectacular in light of their present circumstances.

Right away, microphones and cameras and cell phones were pressed into Monica's face. News trucks from all the major and local news channels crowded the street outside the beach house, satellite dishes pointing skyward.

Monica smiled conveying a sense of warmth and professionalism. It was a smile that Brad knew well from his years of working with her. Monica would charm the crowd, even under dire circumstances. Brad beamed with pride as he turned his gaze toward her.

For the next few minutes, Monica answered question after question. She remained poised and in control as the questions became more difficult. To the best of her ability, Monica attempted to protect her mother. She portrayed the events that happened thirty years ago as a tragic accident. As the questions began to slow, Monica told the reporters that she had one request. The crowd became hushed.

"First of all, I want to request that anyone with information about my father, Ronald Scott, to please contact the local police department or the New Jersey Bureau of Criminal Investigation." Murmurs went through the crowd. "I also have an announcement to make." Again, the crowd became silent hanging on Monica's every word. Brad and Trish studied Monica with puzzled looks. "Atlantic Point Park will be reopened."

Chapter Twenty-Seven

Dr. Richard Stamford had been a plastic surgeon for the better part of the past twenty years. In the early days of his career, he had faced felony charges for providing criminals with new faces for exorbitant prices. Just as he was about to be brought into the justice system the Special Projects Division recruited him. Stamford was so good at what he did that the government preferred to have him work for them, rather than to rot away in a prison somewhere uselessly. A full pardon for his crimes had been the agreement in return for his services. Later when he was no longer needed, Stamford returned to private practice with a clean record. This time though, he made sure he didn't know any more information about his patients than their medical history and a fictitious name. He was no more ethical today than he had been twenty years ago—just more careful.

Today's case was just past seventy years old. Stamford's expertise would remove twenty to thirty years from the face of the patient and give him a new look. The final result was dependent on factors outside Stamford's control. As usual, Stamford did not know the patient's real name, nor did he care to.

The man was not in the best of health. Stamford had to monitor his vital signs with the most careful attention to detail. The anesthesiologist had been alerted to the special needs of the patient and payment for the operation had been received twenty-four hours before the patient arrived at the clinic. A certified check totaling $100,000 had arrived via overnight

314

courier. $50,000 for the procedure and another $50,000 for Stamford's confidentiality. A tidy sum for a day's work.

"Everyone ready?" Stamford inquired. He was gowned head to toe. All that could be seen was the intensity in the surgeon's watery gray eyes. After receiving confirmation that he could proceed, Stamford made the first slice into the patient's skin with the ultra-sharp scalpel.

The surgery was uneventful and several hours later Stamford placed the final sutures. He wrapped the patient's face in heavy gauze bandages and secured the bandages with white plastic tape. When Stamford was finished with the procedure he went out and disrobed.

Belle was upset. Old Joe had not returned last night. She began thinking about when she had last seen him and realized that two full days had passed. Late last night after the bar closed Belle had driven around town for hours. She checked every place he might have gone. Nothing. For all Belle knew Old Joe might be dead or injured somewhere. By the time someone found him it could be too late.

Belle tried to stop her mind from reaching unwarranted conclusions. Maybe Joe would show up today. Belle sipped her tea and unfolded the morning newspaper, eager to read the latest events regarding Randall Scott's disappearance and the Atlantic Point Park saga. She wasn't disappointed. The newspaper was filled with numerous articles, a history on the park, and a press conference by Monica Scott. That Monica was one gutsy woman, Belle reflected.

When she reached the end of Monica's press statements, she did a double take. Monica was going to reopen Atlantic Point Park. What an enormous undertaking. Belle hoped Monica knew what she was in for.

Janice was enjoying every day of her new Caribbean life. Continuous sun, surf and sand were the ingredients that her dreams were made of. Each day she and Drake enjoyed drinks and fresh tropical cooking on the large deck overlooking the ocean just outside the condominium that Janice had purchased. Sometimes they went out for a romantic dinner or to a local club. For a while it seemed Drake was enjoying his new life too, except that more and more he seemed to be growing bored. Drake had not reached the point in his life where he could enjoy doing nothing forever. In the past he had always led a busy life renovating the hotels, but now a feeling of discontent was settling over him.

Wearing a scant, two-piece bathing suit, Janice sat down on a rock pier that jutted out into the ocean. The waves rolled slowly onto the shore. It was relaxing after the tense days that had preceded their arrival on the islands. Janice thought back to the night she and Drake made their final escape. When their plane reached cruising altitude Drake set the autopilot until they neared their destination in the Cayman Islands. The landing had been uneventful. Janice had leased the entire private airstrip, just as she had done in New Jersey. There were only a couple of employees at the airport to help them land safely and all been well paid for their services and their silence.

Janice had a new car waiting for them when the plane landed. It was a white, convertible Mercedes SL. Perfect for a sunny climate. Janice and Drake loaded their luggage and their cash into the small trunk. Janice took the wheel.

Later that night they divided the blackmail money and set up separate bank accounts in the days that followed. With Janice's other investments and her Caprice Hotels retirement money she could live well with or without Drake Donovan. Drake though had only the money he obtained in the blackmail scheme, which was considerable. It would keep him for a while, but not forever. Janice had already decided to cut him loose before he ran out of cash. She would not support him. That would free her to move on to someone who was her financial equal or better. Still, Drake was great in bed and Janice did enjoy his company. She might as well take pleasure in him while it lasted. Janice knew things were going to go in a whole new direction in the near future.

Preliminary plans to reopen Atlantic Point Park started as soon as Monica had concluded the press conference. Horace Goldsmith, her New York attorney drove to Atlantic Point with his assistant Marie Morris. They arrived at the beach house one afternoon at lunchtime. Monica gave each of them a hug. Trish excused herself and set out for a day of shopping and sightseeing in the more prominent resort towns of southern New Jersey. Her vacation time was running out. Brad stayed to attend the meeting with Monica.

"A lot has happened since we met in New York, Horace."

"I have to admit the letter Lydia left you in the old safe threw me off my game."

"You can imagine the shock that I felt!"

"I guess it has been very hard on you my dear. In all the years before and after your father's disappearance I never considered for a single moment that Lydia could be involved in any way."

"Horace, what are the criminal charges for what Mother did?"

"There could have been a number of potential charges: involuntary manslaughter, conspiracy, filing false police reports and insurance claims, potentially others. It doesn't matter now. Lydia is at rest. She carried a heavy burden for most of her life. I think she paid many times over for whatever crimes she was guilty of."

"Can any of her crimes harm the hotel company now?"

"I don't believe so Monica. Your father had no relatives left that could claim any civil damages. Except for bad publicity, I think the worst is behind you as far as the businesses are concerned. In reference to that, I recently received a call from Maxwell William's attorney."

Monica raised her eyebrows and Brad sat up. Marie continued taking notes for Horace, assuming the posture of silence she always maintained at such times. She had worked for him for so many years that she almost became an invisible person during his meetings.

"Maxwell's house in Palm Springs and a sizeable inheritance has been left to his longtime housekeeper Evelyn Smith. She'll be able to live there for as long as she chooses. Maxwell's minority stock holdings in

Caprice Hotels Corporation are to be liquidated at a point in time selected by his attorney over the next 24 months."

"Perhaps I should purchase Maxwell's shares in the company Horace? We could make his attorney an offer now."

"You already have controlling interest in the hotel company Monica, but it wouldn't hurt to enhance your position if the price for the stock is reasonable. All of Maxwell's other remaining assets are to be liquidated and placed in an estate account. The attorney requested written confirmation from you that Maxwell's remains were disposed of as directed."

Monica glanced at the entertainment center. The urn still sat there untouched. "I still need to take care of that," she replied.

"Monica, Maxwell did not leave anything to you. Frankly, I was quite surprised. His attorney would not disclose to me what was to happen to his assets once they were placed in the estate account."

"At one time I would have been hurt by Maxwell's decision to exclude me from his will, but not anymore. I don't want anything from him. He wasn't the person I thought he was, and he destroyed my mother. Mother was convinced that Maxwell had buried my father beneath the office building to protect her. Who knows what he really did with the body or why."

"Do the police have any hope of solving the crime?"

"Detective McAllister didn't give us much encouragement the last time he was here. He stated that they would be right back where they started if they couldn't get forensic evidence from the coffin."

"I hope they can soon offer you some closure Monica."

"I hope so too. I asked you here today for a special reason Horace."

It was Horace's turn to raise his eyebrows.

"I want Brad to take over Maxwell's position as President of Caprice Hotels. David Lansing can take over as Regional Manager of the hotel properties. I also want to reopen the Park. We need to set up a separate company and I want Brad to be a partner in the project."

Horace looked quite surprised. "Monica, that park was causing huge financial losses by the time it closed. You already know that. It will take a massive investment to get it started again with no assurance of a return."

"It was a different era in 1985. I spoke to the town council after I held the press conference. They have several groups of investors that are willing to help redevelop the town and the park. I know it will take a lot of money, but I already own the land. I would never do anything to jeopardize the hotel company, but we wouldn't even have the hotels if it hadn't been for the success of Atlantic Point Park."

"Are you sure I can't change your mind Monica?"

"No, I am insistent this time."

"Then I'll get busy."

As the meeting concluded Marie piped in at last. With a twinkle in her eye she said, "Monica you were always a stubborn little girl." Horace, Brad and Monica all laughed.

Both Horace and Marie gave Monica a hug as they left for the drive back to New York City. Marie told Brad he'd better take care of Monica or he'd answer to her. Brad assured her that he would.

When Trish returned late that day from her shopping trip, Monica asked her to sit down in the living room.

"I want you to help run the new park Trish. We need your creative skills to make the business successful. It's going to take a lot of marketing savvy and you've got that and more."

"Monica, you know I don't want to leave New York City."

"You'll be just two hours away. You can go back every weekend and even keep your condominium there. The park will only be open for three or four months in the summer. The rest of the winter you can spend in New York at the gallery or even in Palm Beach with me."

"I have to admit I've been getting bored at the art gallery. I'll agree to at least think about it, but no promises."

Monica went out on the rear deck to enjoy what was left of the waning summer day. Since she hadn't brought her tablet on this trip, she began to sketch her ideas for the park on a white lined notebook. It was already July and there wasn't much time left. Monica wanted to have a small portion of the park opened by Labor Day. A celebration would be held for the unveiling of her future plans for redeveloping the park as a modern attraction.

Monica would need to fill in the potholes and ruts to make the entrance road drivable and the main parking lot safe for the guests. The front gates would need to be sanded and repainted back to their glossy black appearance. A couple of the concession stands would be rehabilitated so that she could serve complimentary champagne and refreshments. Protective barriers would need to be put up to keep people from getting into the many areas that were unsafe. As a final part of the project, she wanted to have at least one prominent ride in working order to complete the grand opening.

Monica was so deep in her thoughts that she didn't hear the person walking up behind her. She jumped when Detective McAllister called her name.

"I didn't mean to scare you Ms Scott."

"It's okay. I hope you have some news about the investigation for me Detective."

"I do. It's not what you want to hear though."

Monica tensed up.

"We haven't been able to find any DNA in the coffin. No hair, no blood, no bodily fluids; nothing to indicate that it ever held a body."

Monica gave a heavy sigh. "Where does that leave the investigation?"

"We're not going to give up, but there aren't a lot of leads. The only thing we have is the letter from your mother. Lydia obviously believed your father was buried under the office. The one suspect who could give us the answers is dead."

"Why would Maxwell have gone to the trouble of making it look like my father was buried in that grave when he wasn't? It just doesn't make any sense."

"It doesn't to us either."

"Have you located Drake or Janice?"

"Again, negative. They too have disappeared without a trace."

"I'm not surprised that you haven't found them."

"Why is that?"

"Because Janice Laneer is someone that you can never really get to know or understand. She's very aloof and she's very cunning. I will be surprised beyond words if you ever catch her."

Detective McAllister gave her a questioning look and then turned to leave stating yet again that he would be in touch.

The patient groaned in pain and began pawing at his face. The attending nurse pulled his arms back down to his sides, but the patient was too strong. Unable to hold him back, she pressed the alarm button and an orderly rushed into the room. He placed restraints on the patient so no harm would come to the new face that Dr. Stamford had created. The nurse also gave the patient a shot of morphine and in a few moments deep sleep returned.

Even after twenty years of nursing, it was still unnerving to see patients with their entire heads wrapped in heavy white bandages. The bandages were so thick that the person was mummified, yet you could still see their moving eyes and mouth. It was frightening when the clinic closed for the day leaving the small skeleton night crew. With the lights dimmed throughout the clinic and the parking lot darkened, every sound took on a frightening new meaning.

If it weren't for the exceptional pay that Dr. Stamford provided, the nurse would have quit a long time ago, but she needed the money and could not accept another position with lower pay.

At six in the morning, the lights in the clinic came back on. Familiar and comforting sounds were made by the kitchen crew getting breakfast ready to serve the patients who were well enough to eat. This patient was not one of them. It also meant that in just one hour the nurse's shift would be over.

Near eleven o'clock at night on the same day, the nurse returned for duty once again. Minutes after her arrival the lights dimmed, and the guard secured the building while the skeleton crew and patients prepared for another long night. The special patient was quiet and still bandaged. The nurse settled back in her chair to use her electronic reader that she had recently purchased to help pass the long nights. Except for recording the patient's vital signs for the next eight hours she had nothing else to do.

At about three o'clock, the nurse was startled by a noise. She had dozed off and she jumped as the door's unexpected opening awakened her. It was Dr. Stamford. The nurse had always thought the doctor was very creepy. He was even more so in the dim night lighting of the clinic.

Surprised beyond words, the nurse just uttered, "Dr. Stamford."

"Yes nurse, just relax. We're going to be moving this patient."

The nurse was so startled by the events that she was again unable to speak. They had never before moved a patient in the dark of night.

The lights in the patient's room remained dim. Two ambulance attendants appeared with a gurney. The patient was eased to the gurney by the attendants and strapped down tight. They wheeled the gurney into the darkened hallway and Dr. Stamford followed. The door swung closed leaving the nurse alone in the empty room. She was afraid to look out into the hallway.

Slowly she walked over to the window. The blinds were closed tight against whatever was going on outside. She edged them apart, just enough so that she could see what was going on.

The rear doors of an ambulance were open. The ambulance was lighted inside, starkly framed against the pitch-black night. The nurse watched them load the patient into the back. The rear doors closed, and the attendants went up to the cab. The ambulance drove away into the night; its emergency lights unused. As the ambulance pulled away, Dr. Stamford glanced in the direction of the patient's former room. The nurse was able to get the blinds closed in the nick of time. A second later she watched as the doctor climbed into a black Lexus sedan and drove off into the night.

The nurse slumped back into her chair, her heart pounding. If she made it until the morning, she would never come back to this place.

Chapter Twenty-Eight

The delicious scent of Jeanette's cooking wafted through the Palm Beach house. It provided such a feeling of normalcy that the past few weeks were almost reduced to the status of a bad dream. Yet nothing could turn the clock back to the innocent time before. The document that Monica was holding bore witness to that fact.

Monica had returned to Palm Beach to look after her hotel concerns. She would be flying back to New Jersey soon to address the multitude of details that Atlantic Point Park's reopening would require of her.

Before leaving Atlantic Point, Monica and Brad scattered Maxwell's ashes into the Atlantic Ocean outside the beach house. Monica was teary when she opened the urn and poured the ashes into the rough waves. She still had mixed feelings about Maxwell. Francine prepared a note of confirmation as requested by Maxwell's attorney. It was the first thing Monica signed when she went into her office upon her return. Now there was closure in one part of her life.

Monica gazed up at the oceanic print that Lydia had purchased on their first visit to Trisha's art gallery. How long ago that shopping excursion now seemed. Midnight nuzzled into Monica's hand staying as a constant companion since her return home. Even Star and Swirl stayed close by and Jeanette rarely left the estate, cooking hearty meals every night and talking endlessly about what had happened.

Midnight's cold nose brought Monica back to the present. She stared again at the document. How many times had she read it and yet it still didn't seem to be reality. Before exiting Atlantic Point, Horace Goldsmith made a final stop at the local police precinct. His reputation preceded him, and he was able to coerce a copy of Lydia's confession from the police for Monica. It was that copy she held in her hand now. There was one line that Monica read over and over again. It seemed to sum up the happiness that her parents and Atlantic Point Park had once shared, *"Lydia, let the show begin."*

It was the secret line that her father whispered to her mother every year at the park's grand opening. Monica could not stop pondering how events in her parent's lives had spiraled out of control, just like the roller coaster, with an ultimate crash to the ground.

Brad was swamped with work. First, he had gone to New York City to meet with Horace Goldsmith for the purpose of setting up the new company that would run the amusement park. Then he had assumed his new duties as President of Caprice Hotels upon his return to Palm Beach. Monica did not get to see him often and she felt very alone.

Jeanette came into the living room and Monica poured her a glass of wine.

"Dinner will soon be ready Miss Monica. I am so glad you are home with all of us."

"I can't tell you how glad I am to be home Jeanette. I missed all of you!"

"We missed you too. Now you come to the dining room. I have a great treat for you."

As always, Jeanette had outdone herself. Garden fresh vegetables kabobs had been grilled and served with sautéed rice, fresh rolls and a Greek salad. For the first time in ages, Monica ate well. All too soon she would be on a plane bound for Atlantic Point. As always, Midnight did her best to attract handouts, despite Jeanette's half-hearted attempts to shoo her out of the dining room. The cats remained perched on two chairs that stood guard beside the china cabinet.

At ten o'clock each evening Brad called to update Monica on company business and just to chat. Monica waited eagerly for his calls. Everything was proceeding smoothly with their transition to new management. Brad was well liked before his promotion to president and it helped him get cooperation from the staff as he settled into his new role.

Horace had forwarded final legal documents to Brad incepting the new corporation that would operate Atlantic Point Park. As decided, Brad would be a fifty percent partner with Monica in the operation just as Monica's mother and father had been. The land would remain under Monica's sole ownership.

The final documents were just what Monica had been waiting for. Now she would book a flight to Trenton and return to Atlantic Point Island to make the arrangements for the Labor Day grand opening event. With just three weeks left, time was running out.

After hanging up with Brad, Monica purchased a ticket to Trenton. She quickly booked a first-class seat. The airline search reminded Monica she would need to hire someone to set up a website capable of e-ticket sales along with all the other social media accounts that would be necessary to market the park.

Trish was in the gallery's small office talking with the owner, Mr. Vaughn. He had always been a very fair boss and mentor to Trish. She dreaded telling him about the decision she had made to leave, but she wanted to give him as much notice as possible.

Ever since Monica extended her the offer to become involved in the new Atlantic Point Park, she had thought of nothing else. Trish still loved the art gallery and she loved New York City. Until now it had been her whole life. But the thought of something as new and exciting as reopening the ancient amusement park intrigued her.

It was a fantastic opportunity and held the additional benefit of allowing her to remain involved in the gallery for a significant part of the year. She would still be close to New York, which was what brought her to a decision.

"Trisha dear, just tell me what's on your mind. We've been together for too many years to be anything less that forthright with each other."

"I know, and that's what makes this so very hard. I've been offered a position by my dear friend Monica Scott."

"Why I know Monica well, she's one of our best customers…and her dear mother, how much I miss her."

"I miss her too. Monica wants me to become involved in the reopening of her new project, Atlantic Point Park, and I've decided to accept. It will mean that I have to curtail my involvement in the gallery and work for just part of the year if you will allow me."

"Why my dear, that's perfectly acceptable. You've done a fabulous job of turning your protégés into fine art critics and this will give them an opportunity to advance. But Trisha you must promise me that you won't leave me for good. I want this gallery to be yours one day."

"I will stay involved Mr. Vaughn, I promise you that. Thank you so much for supporting me!" Trish stated as she gave him a gentle hug.

Janice looked across the al fresco dinner table at Drake Donovan. They were dining at Seascape tonight. She had decided to send him on his way. Coming right to the point she said, "I want you to leave Drake." If Janice expected surprise on the part of her lover and accomplice, it was not evident in his face.

"It's been a great adventure Janice and I've already cleaned out my belongings. I'll be on the next plane out of here tonight."

Janice did her best to hide her surprise behind her cool demeanor, but for once she could not conceal her surprise.

"Can't hide your surprise can you gorgeous? I can take just so much of this island lifestyle. I need to get my hands dirty once in a while and I'm not talking about another blackmail scheme."

A knowing smirk spread across Janice's face. She pushed back her dark red hair with the alluring flair she was known for. Drake got up from the table, still looking as handsome and as elegant as she would always remember him to be. He leaned down and kissed Janice on the lips. It was a hard, rough kiss. The kind she had enjoyed from Drake too many times. In a second, he disappeared into the star lit night. Janice signaled the server. "Bring me a bottle of your best champagne. I want to celebrate."

In seconds the server reappeared with the champagne. The bottle opened with a loud pop and the golden bubbles tricked into Janice's champagne flute. As the server turned to leave, she gently touched his arm. "Perhaps you'd join me in a glass. I'm all alone this evening."

The bandaged patient was becoming restless. He was eager to be on his way despite the doctor's orders that he remain secluded in the rehabilitation center until more healing had been accomplished. Every day the doctor would make his rounds to examine his work, then the nurse would change the gauze bandages. The patient was forbidden to see his own new face and he was not permitted into the other areas of the rehabilitation center. A private nurse stood guard at his door. They would not risk using any of the center's staff.

The patient was not used to being told what to do. It was with reluctance that he had learned to let others take charge. With a patience he was not known for, he obeyed the doctor's orders. It would be just a few more days until he was transported to his new life. Who would have thought that after all these years he would have a chance to start over? A new life with a new face…a young face.

Belle could not believe that after all these days Old Joe had not reappeared. In desperation, she notified the police. They listed him as a missing person, but their attitude seemed to be that if he drifted into town ten years ago, perhaps he had just drifted back out again. Belle didn't think that was a likely event.

Belle knew that Old Joe would never leave on his own without telling her he was leaving. In the last days before he disappeared, he was as agitated as she had ever seen him. Belle wondered if all the events stirring the town had been too much for him. Old Joe drifted in and out of coherency, sometimes speaking with complete clarity and other times stuck in a past that Belle could not understand.

In any case he had generally been a dependable worker until the days right before he disappeared. Belle was sitting on her stool at the end of the bar as she always was when she was not circulating through the restaurant. She almost fell off the stool when Monica Scott came in and gave her a hug. "My dear, you've come back to us."

"I have to get the park ready for the grand opening event. I wish I had more time, but I've got less than three weeks."

"Monica, what an exciting time for this old lady. I told you when I grew up that I had spent many happy times in that park. It's more years ago than I can count, but now it seems like yesterday."

"Belle you're *not* an old lady. I just want to do my part to rejuvenate the town and the park. My family's success all started here in Atlantic Point. I didn't even know the park existed until the reading of my mother's will."

"All of this must be very hard on you Monica."

"It has been Belle, especially the part about my mother." Tears welled in Monica's eyes.

"We're tough girls Monica, and a lot alike," Belle told her in her gravelly voice. "Everything's going to work out just fine. I just know it."

Somehow Monica knew that Belle was right.

"I need to ask you a favor. Old Joe has disappeared. If you see him will you call me right away?"

Monica couldn't help but feel relief that the strange old man who stared at her relentlessly was not around anymore. Still, she could not help but feel compassion for him and she hoped that no harm had come to him. "Of course I will be on the lookout for him, Belle."

Belle took a sip of her Coke and paused before finally commenting, "I am going to help you with your new venture Monica. I want to be transported back to the time when I first came to Atlantic Point. I guess I'll need to be around to make that happen, so you've put some renewed hope in this old gal."

Monica put her hand on Belle's then gently gave her a hug.

Brad arrived at the Trenton-Mercer County Airport on the Friday before Labor Day. The weeks since he and Monica had been in Atlantic Point went by so fast that the days were a blur. Brad looked around for Monica. He was reminded of Ronald Scott's abandoned car as he scanned the airport parking lot for the Mustang. Brad was relieved when he spotted Monica waiting for him at the end of the sidewalk. For all the answers he and Monica now had, there were still so many questions that were not answered.

Monica got out of the car and gave him a hug and a kiss.

"Wow, with that greeting I think I'll get back on the plane and do it again."

"Oh Brad."

"Are you going to tell me what you've been up to?

"I'm going to show you. I'll drive, you just watch."

Brad raised his eyebrows as he got into the car.

Monica would not tell him anything she had done as they drove from the airport toward Atlantic Point Island. Instead, she insisted that Brad update her on the hotels' operations.

The car finally neared the entrance to Atlantic Point Park. A large amount of overgrowth had been removed beside the entranceway. A prominent new billboard proclaimed, *"A New Adventure Coming Soon... Atlantic Point Park's Grand Reopening."*

A swath had been removed from both sides of the main driveway and although there had not been time to repave the lane, the potholes and ruts had been filled in. The parking lot had been improved in much the same way. The massive entrance gates, the scripted Atlantic Point Park lettering, and one hundred feet of fencing on both sides of the gates had been repainted to their original glossy black.

Brad got out to open the gates. As he did so, Monica pressed a button on the visor and the gates swung open in silent grandeur. Brad looked on in awe.

Inside the park, barriers had been erected about one thousand feet into a giant square. All the debris had been cleaned up inside the barriers and potted flowers and palm trees had been trucked in to make a quick appearance change. Two of the concession stands had been nailed back together and repainted in bright colors. Multiple displays with artist renderings done by Trish told the story of the park's planned return to viability. Monica had done so much in such a short time that Brad was amazed.

"Were you able to get any of the rides in working order Monica?"

"Unfortunately not. They're all too far gone, but the carved animals on the carousel have been garaged and are being restored for next spring."

On the way back to the beach house Monica handed Brad a gold, engraved envelope. The scripted letters stated, "Brad Roberts, Partner." Brad grinned as he opened his personal invitation to the Grand Opening of Atlantic Point Park.

When they reached the beach house Brad was amazed again. There was obvious renovation going on at the beach house too. Walls were being patched, new bathroom fixtures sat in unopened cartons and they now had a working stove. Brad was sorry to see he was still being housed in the guest bedroom, but he had a feeling that things were going to change for him and for Monica. They both dressed in casual clothes and headed to Belle Brandt's for dinner.

Saturday and Sunday whirled by. Monica was on the phone with the event coordinator every free minute. An upscale event with food, champagne and music had been planned. The caterer would bring portable food heating equipment and Monica had rented a generator to power the temporary lights. Now all they needed was a sunny day.

At last Labor Day weekend arrived. It was beautiful. White clouds fronted a blue sky. Humid summer air mixed with the first breath of autumn announced the changing of the seasons. After coffee, Monica and Brad headed out to the park to oversee the final preparations. The caterer had already arrived with his team and was setting up. For the next four hours Monica and Brad worked to check and recheck every detail for the evening's events. Then they rushed back to the beach house, showered, changed, and returned to the park in gown and tuxedo. It would be just a short time until the guests arrived. Monica breathed a sigh of relief when their first arrival turned out to be Trisha, elegantly attired in a black evening gown. Her sleek black hair cascaded over her shoulders.

Belle drove over the bridge on her way to the much anticipated evening celebration. She felt giddy, as if she were a kid again. Belle chuckled to herself, "If not a kid then at least a young spirit." Belle slammed on the brakes. She wondered if she were seeing a ghost. It was Old Joe walking on the road in the direction of Atlantic Point Park. Belle's Buick squealed to a stop and the engine stalled.

Belle popped the locks open and Old Joe climbed into the car. He looked pretty grimy and his face appeared to be black and blue. He just grunted, "Fell, fell," in answer to her questions about what had happened to him. A wave of relief swept over Belle. Old Joe was too disheveled to attend a formal party, but she would be late if she turned back now. He would just have to stay in the background. Monica would understand. Belle restarted the stalled car and headed toward the park.

The "invitation only" crowd was huge and valet staff scurried to park the expensive cars that were quickly filling the lot. Belle pulled in and Old Joe rushed out of the car and disappeared into the crowd. Belle would tell Monica to be on the lookout for him. She hoped he was not going to disappear again.

Servers circulated about pouring champagne and Belle reached for a sparking glass at her first opportunity. She spotted Monica chatting with some state representatives, then overheard Monica make a comment about redevelopment money. Belle could help with that too. Monica gave Belle a quick wave, but they didn't have time to talk.

The 1959 aerial print of the park, the one that Monica had found in the old office building, was protectively displayed near the gold scissors that would cut the ribbon for the grand reopening. Trish's staff had done a wonderful job of restoring the photo to its original appearance. Monica had taken her place beside Brad, just outside the gates. She and Brad would ceremoniously cut the red ribbon, then the gates would swing open to the crowd for the first time in three decades.

Right at seven o'clock the contemporary music that the band had been playing stopped, bringing a pause to the cacophony of chatter. Calliope music started to play, and the crowd awed as hundreds of LED lights in a multitude of colors flicked on overhead. White spotlights illuminated the iron gates. Monica beamed as she and Brad used the giant scissors to cut the thick red ribbon and applause and cheers erupted when the ribbon finally split. The gates slowly opened to the crowd for the first time since they had closed on Labor Day thirty-one years ago. As Belle watched, she thought again how much Monica looked like Lydia. Belle could still see Lydia opening the park all those years in the past.

The live band switched back to a more contemporary beat, merging old with new and the crowd cheered. Cameras flashed. The air crackled with electric excitement. Brad watched Monica beaming as she reopened her family's legacy. Suddenly, out of nowhere, Old Joe came up behind her, emerging from the crowd. Monica saw him out of the corner of her eye. She had to smile at the old man's determination to get through the throngs of people and be part of the event. Belle would be glad he was back.

Old Joe was now beside Monica, and for once he didn't unnerve her. With such a large crowd present she had no reason to feel afraid. Old Joe pushed toward her and suddenly whispered something into her ear. It took a moment for the words to register. But they did, just before Monica passed out in front of the crowd: *"Lydia, let the show begin."*

Chapter Twenty-Nine

As Monica fell backwards, Old Joe caught her. He repeated over and over again, "Lydia, Lydia, what's wrong?" Brad rushed toward Monica, too shocked to realize what the old man was saying. Belle had been standing front and center. Old Joe's words were not lost on her.

Old Joe actually believed that Monica was Lydia. But how could that be? Old Joe was not around in 1985 when Lydia Scott had been the socialite of Atlantic Point. There was no way he could know that Monica looked like a young version of her mother.

Suddenly the pieces of the puzzle assembled themselves like a ton of bricks. Belle's mouth dropped open and she clutched reflexively at her necklace. It couldn't be. The wallet Belle had found with the picture of Lydia Scott and the inscription, "All my love, Lydia…the empty coffin…Old Joe thinking Monica was Lydia. Belle said the words she was thinking aloud, "Old Joe was really Ronald Scott."

Belle's mind continued working oblivious to the actions of the crowd around her. When Old Joe first appeared in town, Ronald Scott had already been missing for twenty years. During that time his body and his mind had changed so much that no one, not even Belle, had suspected his true identity. Belle wondered if Old Joe really knew who he was.

Old Joe lowered Monica to the ground and a confused look overcame him as Brad rushed to her side. Belle couldn't get any closer because of the mass of people. She watched as Old Joe moved farther and farther away, fading back into the shadows. Belle had to get to him before he disappeared yet again. She watched helplessly as Old Joe disappeared into the night.

Brad tried to disperse the crowd so that a man claiming to be a doctor could approach Monica. After flashing credentials, the doctor revived Monica with yet another dose of smelling salts. Brad wondered what had caused her to pass out again. He was really starting to worry that something was very wrong. Monica's vital signs seemed to be okay. The doctor urged Brad to take Monica for a thorough medical evaluation.

Trish stepped up to the microphone. Expressing assurance to the crowd that Monica was all right, she resumed the festivities. Brad eased a very shaky Monica out toward the parking lot. He had to provide a lot of support to keep her upright. The sound of the crowd faded into the background as the convertible rolled out toward the main road.

Monica was still silent as the beach house came into view. She had regained some strength and was able to walk up the steps without support, refusing to go to the medical clinic for the prescribed evaluation. Brad poured her a glass of wine and she sipped it in the living room where she settled onto the old sofa.

After a period of silence, she was able to tell Brad the truth she had unwittingly uncovered.

"Brad, do you remember reading in Mother's final letter the part where she said my father always whispered in her ear just as the park was opening each season?"

"Yes, of course I do."

"Do you remember what it was that he whispered to her?"

"Yes. He always whispered, *Lydia, let the show begin.*"

"Exactly."

"But what does this have to do with your passing out?"

"There were only two people on this earth who knew that my father whispered that line to my mother every year at the park's annual opening."

"Your mother knew and your father knew."

"Yes! And tonight, as I was opening the park, Old Joe came up behind me."

"Monica you have me very confused."

"Be patient Brad. You'll understand in a minute. When Old Joe came up behind me, he whispered in my ear, *Lydia, let the show begin.*"

"How could he know that line, and why did he call you Lydia?"

Monica answered as a knowing look paled Brad's face. "Brad, there's only one way he could know that line. Old Joe is my father and he thinks that I am his wife."

Belle watched as the crowd dwindled away. Old Joe was nowhere to be found. She even waited until the catering people had packed up all their gear. Monica's friend Trisha Marshall was the last one to leave. Trisha had one of the guys from the catering staff help her lock the gate. As she turned to leave, she saw Belle standing with tears in her eyes.

"It was a very emotional evening Belle."

"Yes, yes I know."

"Why are you crying?"

"I found Old Joe by the roadside tonight on my way out here. I was so relieved. Now he's disappeared again."

Trish remembered the man from the night he was staring at Monica from the shadows of Belle's restaurant. She wondered how Belle could feel safe out here alone looking for him. "Is there anything I can do to help you locate him?"

"I don't think so. I'm going to go back to town. Please call me if you see any signs of Old Joe."

Trish loaded the aerial photo, the gold scissors and the ribbon into her car before setting off. The thought of being in Atlantic Point Park with Old Joe lurking around in the shadows was not appealing. Trish locked the car doors and then watched as Belle drove off toward the main road, following suit. She would be glad to get back to New York for a while.

The following morning, Belle drove out to Monica Scott's beach house. She had Monica's cell phone number, but she decided against calling first. When Belle knocked at the door, Monica answered. She had large dark circles under her eyes. Belle knew in an instant that Monica knew the truth.

Belle reached out and took Monica into her arms as Monica broke into tears. Brad appeared from somewhere inside the house and hustled the two crying women into the living room.

"You know the truth, don't you Monica?"

"Yes I do, and you know too."

"I figured it out at the grand opening when he called you Lydia. During the summer I found a wallet without any identification. The only thing inside was an old inscribed picture of your mother. It disappeared from my office before I could figure out who it belonged to."

"Where is my father now?"

"He disappeared again after you passed out. I couldn't get to him through the surging crowd."

A worried look appeared on Monica's face. "We have to make sure he's all right."

"I know dear."

"Has he always been in such a confused state?"

"Ever since he appeared in the bar all those years ago, he's been like that. Sometimes he makes more sense than others, but he's changed so much I would never have suspected Old Joe was your father."

"We need to contact the police. Brad would you do that?" Monica asked in a feeble voice.

"On my way," Brad answered as he headed for his cell phone.

A short while later Detective McAllister appeared. He was incredulous that Old Joe and Ronald Scott were one and the same, even after hearing the evidence that Belle and Monica presented. After some haranguing, he placed an all-points bulletin for Old Joe.

The whine of jet engines indicated that the plane was about to take off. The private, twin-engine jet had a pilot, co-pilot and one attendant. If you were going to fly, then you might as well fly first class. The sole passenger settled back into his seat as the plane lifted off the ground. White cloud puffs raced by the windows as the jet climbed higher and higher.

As soon as the pilot leveled the plane, the "remain seated" sign blinked out. The man headed for the opulent bathroom. He wanted to observe the remarkable new face he had been given by Dr. Stamford. He stepped in front of the lighted mirror.

Most of the bruising was fading away. He had not seen skin so smooth on his face for more than forty years. In their place was a tight forehead and all the wrinkles and sags below his eyes were only a memory. A new aquiline nose replaced the slightly too large nose that he had looked at for his entire life and a new chin added character and a youthful appearance. Colored contact lenses and a dose of hair color finished the transformation.

After a long period of staring, the man returned to his seat. He declined the alcoholic beverage the attendant offered and accepted a club soda with lime instead. The man did not want to regain the fifty pounds he had lost. His health was continuing to improve, and he wanted to keep it that way.

After several hours the pilot announced that the plane would be landing in a short time. Not long after the announcement the plane began its descent. Typical airport scenery appeared and a few seconds later the wheels touched down. When the "remain seated" sign blinked off for the final time, the man unbuckled his seatbelt and stretched while the pilot opened the door and the attendant obtained the man's luggage.

Warm air enveloped the man as he exited the plane and palm trees swayed gently in the breeze as the clean smell of the ocean permeated his new consciousness. The man began to look for his companion after presenting his passport to the authorities, a passport that had a new name with a new photo. The man continued to survey the lush surroundings. In time he spotted her with a tropical flower accenting her flowing hair. She was looking just as beautiful as he had always remembered.

He walked in her direction, wondering if she would recognize him. In a second a smile broke out on her face as she swept back her red hair. Even with all the changes, she was the one person who would always know.

"You look very handsome for a dead man Maxwell."

"I would have to agree with you Janice, but I'm a long way from dead."

"Do you know how much I've always wanted to spend my life with you?"

"I know that now. It just took me a lifetime to realize that I wanted the same thing." Maxwell embraced Janice tightly, ending with a long kiss that spoke of the feelings that he had hidden from himself.

Maxwell relaxed on Janice's deck, looking out through the swaying palm trees and gardens toward the quiet ocean. He flashed back to that horrible night, more than thirty years ago now, that had brought him to this time and place.

When Lydia shoved Ronald Scott backwards, Ronald had indeed stumbled, hitting his head on the rocks that lined the paths of Atlantic Point Park. After Lydia screamed, Maxwell calmed her down, then dragged Ronald's lifeless body into the haunted house attraction. Maxwell and Lydia went back to the beach house to pack Ronald's luggage. There was so much to do after you had just killed somebody.

Later in the night, they returned to the park in Maxwell's car. He had the unpleasant task of getting the Cadillac's keys from the body, never realizing that Ronald was still alive. Then, Maxwell drove Ronald's Cadillac to the Trenton-Mercer County Airport and Lydia followed. After abandoning Ronald's car in a deserted lot, they returned to the park so Maxwell could secure access to the body before the morning crews arrived. To his great surprise, Maxwell found that Ronald was still breathing. He never told Lydia the truth.

When he drove Lydia back to the beach house, she believed that Ronald was truly dead, and that she had killed him. Maxwell returned to the park alone and exhausted one final time that endless night. He lugged Ronald into his car and drove him to a distant hospital, narrowly missing the arrival of the park's morning employees. Ronald regained consciousness but was incoherent. Maxwell had removed all of Ronald's identification from his wallet before he left him in the hospital. He had to create a false name for Ronald on the spur of the moment, and the first name that came to his mind was "Joe."

In time, the doctors informed Maxwell that the severe internal bleeding Joe had sustained would render permanent brain damage. With Ronald out of the picture, Lydia would now be Maxwell's, but not if Ronald were still alive in some institution, existing indefinitely as a vegetable. Lydia would have stayed with Ronald out of guilt or perhaps because she really did love him, more than she loved Maxwell, a fact that he could not admit, even to himself.

Maxwell had to make Ronald Scott disappear forever. Late the following night, he and Lydia returned to the deserted park. Earlier in the day, Maxwell had placed two sand bags into the empty coffin and hid Ronald's key sets in the lining of the coffin, while Lydia went about her normal duties at the park. He did not believe Lydia would ever check inside the coffin, but just to be sure, he put two sturdy locks on it. Using the park's construction equipment, Maxwell and Lydia excavated a grave and buried the coffin in an undeveloped area at the far reaches of the property. Despite Maxwell's objections, Lydia had insisted on constructing the enormous office building to conceal a crime that only Maxwell knew had never occurred.

Maxwell paid for all of Ronald Scott's care for the next twenty years. It was a hefty tab, and one he didn't relish paying, but it was worth it. Lydia had turned to Maxwell over and over again through the years, but she never loved him in the way she had loved Ronald. Nor would she ever marry him.

When Ronald was released from the care facility after two decades, Maxwell lost track of him. He was all too glad the payments had stopped draining his cash. The doctors assured Maxwell that Ronald's memory was gone forever. He had been rehabilitated to the point that he could hold a basic job but nothing more. That was all Maxwell needed to hear. He could go on with Lydia, but he could never tell her the truth. She would have hated him forever.

Janice appeared on the deck. Maxwell realized just how much he owed her. When Janice left Atlantic Point Park the night she collected the two million dollars, she handed Maxwell an envelope with instructions how to reach her if he ever changed his mind about things.

After the heart attack, Maxwell had used one of the attendant's cell phones to reach Janice, so that if the police were watching they would never be able trace the call through the clinic's switchboard or through Maxwell's personal cell phone. She had taken care of all the details, from faking his death, to arranging for the plastic surgery and even forging a new name and identity. All Maxwell had to do was recover and climb on the private jet when the time came.

Maxwell realized that while his criminal charges were in actuality very small, his moral crimes were great. Maxwell had convinced Lydia that she killed her husband and allowed her to live a life of guilt. Maxwell would forever carry the burden for what he had done to Lydia, Ronald and Monica. Despite a new face, he was still the same self-centered man underneath the smooth skin.

A knock came at the door. Brad answered. Outside Belle was standing on the steps with Old Joe. Brad smiled as he called back inside the house, "Monica we have guests."

Monica caught her breath as Belle and her father came into the house. It was probably the first time he had been in the house since the night of the terrible fight with her mother. Monica wondered if he remembered anything about that night.

Old Joe walked into the living room grasping Belle's hand. In many ways he almost seemed like a child.

"When did he come back?"

"He reported to work this morning."

"I'm so relieved. Belle do you know if he's had any recent medical care?"

"I made sure he got to the doctor from time to time, but it wasn't easy."

"Do you think he would be willing to undergo a thorough exam to be sure he's all right? Perhaps something can be done to improve his quality of life."

"I think that's a good idea Monica."

Old Joe continued to stay in the apartment he had lived in for the past ten years above Belle's bar. Monica hired a guardian to keep him from wandering off alone when she and Belle could not keep an eye on him. The next few weeks were difficult. Monica and Belle drove a reluctant Old Joe back and forth to a large neurological facility in Trenton. With modern technology, they would have a better understanding of what damage Ronald had sustained when he fell and what, if anything, could be done about it.

After an MRI, dozens of tests and much waiting, they would have their answer. Old Joe was outside with a nurse while Monica, Brad and Belle waited for the doctor. Everyone was on pins and needles when the doctor came into the conference room.

The neurologist explained with pictures how Ronald's fall had damaged his brain, especially his long-term memory and communication areas. He was also able to tell by the extent of the damage that Ronald had either received poor or delayed medical attention when the original injury caused internal bleeding.

"If he had received prompt treatment it would have increased the chances of a complete recovery and a normal life may have been achieved." The doctor continued, "Although there is no way to know for sure."

As it was, they could still help him with a therapy program that would allow him to better develop the areas of his brain that were undamaged. Of course, at his age, it was anyone's guess how much improvement would occur.

Monica felt sick to her stomach as the doctor continued. She realized how Maxwell had ruined their lives. His selfishness in wanting Lydia all for himself had caused her father to become incapacitated when medical treatment was delayed. Maxwell had allowed her mother to spend a lifetime thinking she had committed a murder that never happened. He was even responsible for Lydia's suicide following thirty years of guilt. Monica despised Maxwell Williams. She left the doctor's offices angry and determined to erase every trace of him from the hotels and from their lives.

When they reached the beach house, Monica invited Belle and her father for dinner. She was eager to try out the new kitchen that the contractors had just finished. Monica hoped that in time her father would move into the beach house, but she would not push him in any way.

Monica was surprised when her father answered with a pleasant and coherent "yes." During the meal he even participated in the conversation on several occasions. Monica held tight to any hope that she would have the opportunity to know him as her father and for him to know her as his daughter.

After dark, Belle and her father prepared to leave for the restaurant. Monica kissed her gently on the cheek and hugged her father tightly before he left with Belle. Brad and Monica were finally alone in the house. Monica placed the dishes in the new dishwasher and she and Brad settled onto the plush new sofa.

"You want to get to know him as your father, don't you?" Brad's comment was more of an observation than a real question.

"He's not the only man I want to get to know."

A knowing smile crept across Brad's face at Monica's announcement. He was suddenly glad he had resumed his workout routine when he was back in Palm Beach.

"I think it's time to move your stuff into my bedroom starting with yourself."

Without another word, Brad took Monica's hand and led her up the steps into the master bedroom. A warm and gentle breeze jangled the wind chimes Monica had hung in the bedroom window. Brad began to undress Monica as she reached for his belt. He fumbled for the light switch just before they fell back on the bed together. It was the night they were both hoping for. It was worth the wait.

About the Author

John has always enjoyed reading novels of mystery and suspense. *The Hardy Boys* and *The Three Investigators* were early favorites that became the foundation of his growing book collection. It was those simple, early literary collections that prefaced his becoming an author.

For many years, John's education and long hours at work took priority over his writing career. The interesting places that were figuratively traveled to in hundreds of novels translated into a career in hotel management that spanned several decades. John's caring manner toward guests that arrived from all corners of the earth was central to who he is as a person and is reflected in his writing style.

With changing times came new careers and new directions. John returned to scholarly pursuits in the fields of finance and accounting, complementing his skills as a business manager and entrepreneur. When he's not working, which isn't often, John enjoys spending time with family and entertaining friends at home. John is passionate about earth and animal causes and the beaches of the Atlantic seaboard are his choice for vacations.

John holds an undergraduate business degree from Millersville University and graduate degrees in finance and accounting from Wilmington University in Delaware, where he is an adjunct instructor.

johnrhertzler.com